Highland Echoes

Fated Hearts Book 2

By
Ceci Giltenan

This is a work of fiction. The characters, incidents and dialogues in this book are of the author's imagination and are not to be construed as real. Any resemblance to actual events or persons, living or dead, is completely coincidental.

No part of this book may be reproduced or transmitted in any form or by any means, electronic or mechanical, including photocopying, recording, or by any information storage and retrieval system, without permission in writing from the author.

Duncurra LLC
www.duncurra.com
Copyright 2015 by Ceci Giltenan
ISBN-10:1942623062
ISBN-13:978-1-942623-06-9

May 2015
Cover Art by Earthly Charms

Produced in the USA

Praise for Ceci Giltenan

"Few authors touch hearts so deeply."
- *Sue-Ellen Welfonder, USA Today Bestselling Author*

"Fine historical romance writing at its best."
- *Suzan Tisdale, Bestselling Author of Scottish Romance*

"Ceci Giltenan continues to leave me spellbound weaving her trail of exceptional books that are absolutely magnificent the ones that stay with you long after you have read it. Yes, Highland Intrigue is definitely one of those kind of books."
- *Barbara, Tartan Book Reviews*

"Ceci Giltenan tells beautiful stories with strong characters and an intriguing storylines"
- *Lily Baldwin, Bestselling Author of Scottish Romance*

"Ceci's books get better and better"
- *Tarah Scott, Bestselling Author of Scottish Romance*

Other Books by Ceci Giltenan

The Fated Heart Series

Highland Revenge, Book 1
(a Scrolls of Cridhe novella)

Highland Angels, Book 3
(Coming Summer 2015)

The Duncurra Series

(Available as digital, paperback and audio books)

Highland Solution, Book 1

Highland Courage, Book 2

Highland Intrigue Book 3

Dedications

This book is dedicated to mothers and daughters.

To my mother who is my biggest fan and more of a rock than anyone will ever know.

To my daughter who fills me with joy and whom I adore. Her tiny hand held a piece of my heart from the moment she entered this world on the Feast of St. John the Baptist and it always will.

To Lily Baldwin and her sweet wee lass, my inspiration for Grace and Kristen. What matters most? Kindness. What never helps? Panicking.

To my cousin Charlene who was blessed by the love of two mothers. One who gave her life and in love, let her go. And the other, who in love, embraced the tiny life entrusted to her and raised her to be a truly lovely woman.

And finally to all my readers whose lives have been touched by the unique love of a mother, a daughter, or any woman in one of those roles.

.

Pronunciation Guide

Bhaltair	VAHLtare
Catriona	kuh TREE nah
Eanraig	ANE ray
Eoin	OHwen
Fiona	feeOHna
Innes	in NEZ
Naomh-dùn	NAYV DOON

Glossary

bairn   (BAIRn) A baby

burn   A small stream

canonical hours   The medieval day was ordered by these times, rather than clock times
Vigil, Matins, Lauds, Prime, Terce, Sext, None, Vespers, Compline.

compline   (COMP lin) Night prayer, after sunset, before bedtime.

costrel   A vessel for carrying water, like a canteen.

eejit   A slang term meaning idiot.

ell   A medieval unit of measure that varied widely. In some places it was the distance from the elbow to the tip of the middle finger. In Scotland it was twice that amount or approximately a yard.

gob   A rude slang term meaning mouth.

kertch   Also called a *brèid* (BREEdt): a square of pure white linen folded in half and worn by married women to cover their hair. It is a symbol of the Holy Trinity, under whose guidance the married woman walks.

lauds	(LAWDS) Sunrise.
league	A unit of measure equal to 3 miles or 5.6 kilometers. In the middle ages it was considered the distance a typical person could walk in an hour.
matins	Just before sunrise
neep	Turnip.
none	(rhymes with bone) Literally the ninth hour, about 3 in the afternoon.
peevers	Hopscotch. This game dates back to Roman times. Peevers with a burden, is playing hopscotch carrying something heavy.
prime	After the first hour of daylight, about 6 in the morning.
quoits	An ancient game similar to horseshoes except a quoit is a closed ring.
sext	Literally the sixth hour, noon.
shinty	A game played with sticks and a ball, related to an Irish game called hurling (similar in some ways to field hockey). This game dates back to the pre-Christian Celtic people and is still played today.
skelp	Hit, beat.
sweetling	An endearment.
terce	Literally the third hour of daylight, about 9 in the morning.
wheesht	Shh, hush.
vespers	Evening prayer, sunset.
vigil	The night office, the period from compline to matins (just before dawn).

"The sound of a kiss is not so loud as that of a cannon, but its echo lasts a great deal longer."

– Oliver Wendell Holmes, Sr.

Prologue

May 1317, the Isle of Lewis

The cold May rain had been unrelenting but finally through the misty gloom Catriona could see the small fishing village that was their destination. The journey from the northern tip of Scotland to the Isle of Lewis with her new husband had taken hours through the rainy, rough seas. She had prayed to all the saints, fearful she would never see land again. Now she whispered her prayer of thanks that they had arrived.

Catriona had defied her parents by marrying Tristan Murray. Her father would be utterly furious when he found out. She believed, without a doubt, that if he had the opportunity, her father would make her a widow in the blink of an eye. She and Tristan could not risk staying anywhere near her clan's land. Tristan, who had trained to be a warrior, wouldn't even risk joining the ranks of another clan for fear they would be discovered. Together, they fled to the northern coast where Tristan had found work on a fishing vessel.

The captain never questioned why they wanted to leave the mainland. Rather, he assured them they would be welcome on the isle. One look at Tristan's well-muscled body told the captain all he needed to know—Tristan would be an asset. "Laird Morrison earns a great deal off of the clan fishermen. As long as ye are willing to work, ye'll have a home with us," the old captain had assured Tristan.

Home.

The fishing village was certainly not remotely like the home she was leaving. Still, she loved Tristan with all her heart and he loved her in return. Her home, where ever she found herself, was with this man who held her heart so firmly.

Tristan wrapped his big, strong arms around her from behind. "My beautiful bride, we're almost there. Are ye excited?"

She turned in his arms to look at him. The wind whipped his dark hair. His storm gray eyes twinkled and his face was alight with unrestrained joy. His excitement chased away any lingering doubt she might have had. She smiled up at him. "Aye, I am. I can barely believe we are married and away. I'm a little scared though."

"What scares ye, love?"

"What if Da finds us?"

He tightened his grip on her. "He won't. He'll search, but only amongst the ranks of soldiers. He would expect me to sell my sword-arm but never to do this, to become a fisherman."

"This is such a huge change for both of us."

"Aye it is, my sweet love. But it's the only way we can be together. Ye know it's true."

"Aye, I know. I'm sorry. If my father cared a whit about me, I wouldn't have had to force ye from the life ye planned for yerself."

"Enough of that Catriona. This was as much my decision as yers. The life I had planned would have meant nothing without ye in it. Nothing." He kissed the top of her head. "Once ye captured my heart, I couldn't have lived without ye. Nay, we both set this course and we will follow it together. I'm sure it will be hard at first, but I know we can build a life here."

Build a life. Aye, that is what they were doing. They had chosen not to accept what lay in store for each of them—a life directed by others, over which they had no control. They would never have been allowed to follow their hearts and marry. If they hadn't taken steps to change their fate, she was certain their lives would have been filled with heartache and regret. Tristan was right. This was the only way. "Aye, we'll build a life together. I like the sound of that."

And build a life they did.

Chapter 1

Late April 1340, the Isle of Lewis

Grace Breive bounced her three year old daughter Kristen on her hip nervously as she waited with the rest of the villagers to pay the spring rents to Laird Morrison. The previous September her father and Callum, her husband, had made the accounting to the laird. That seemed like a different lifetime now, as if it had been a dream. A dream which had crumbled she lost her husband and both parents. At one and twenty, she was alone but for her wee daughter.

A table and chair had been placed near the village well at which the laird sat. His son, Fearchar, stood beside him. She noticed Fearchar staring intently at her several times. His open appraisal disturbed her.

Behind them was a wagon into which goods, provided in lieu of coin, were being loaded under the watchful eye of a number of the laird's guardsmen.

When her turn came, she stepped forward, stood Kristen on the ground beside her, and curtsied. "Good day Laird."

"Good day, Mistress Breive. My condolences on the loss of yer mother."

"Thank ye, Laird."

"I'm sure it was a terrible blow, coming so soon after the accident."

She swallowed hard against the knot forming in her throat at the reminder of all she had lost. *Don't show them any weakness.* She steeled herself. "Aye, Laird, it was but I'm managing." She stepped closer to the table and handed him a small pouch containing the coins for her rents."

He spilled the coins into his hand as a slow smile

spread across his face. "Aye, ye seem to be managing nicely. Well done."

"Thank ye, Laird." Relief flooded her. She curtsied, intending to take her leave when Fearchar stepped forward.

"Wait," he growled. "Ye haven't been dismissed."

The laird frowned. "She has paid her rents in full, son. There is no reason to keep her."

"Father, ye can't mean to leave a young widow living on her own."

"I don't see the harm." The laird smiled at her again. "This is her home. She is a skilled weaver and appears to be able to care for herself and her daughter. Unless something changes, I'm inclined to let her continue doing so."

"Father, I think ye are overlooking the obvious. She hasn't been alone that long."

Laird Morrison's brow furrowed. "Tristan and Callum died in October. She made it through the winter quite well."

Grace grew increasingly uncomfortable. They talked about her as if she were a head of livestock. Yet, she knew better than to say anything. She stood still, holding Kristen's hand tightly, looking down and waiting to be addressed, or excused.

Fearchar persisted, "Her mother was still alive to help her. I understand she only passed away two months ago. Nay, I think it's a mistake to risk leaving her on her own."

Lachie, an old friend of Grace's father spoke up. "Laird, her mother had been gravely ill since before Tristan and Callum died. Grace has managed quite well."

"Aye she has," agreed Hamish, another of her father's friends.

"And with no help from any of ye?" Fearchar said, his voice dripping with scorn.

Kristen began to fret and tug at her hand. Grace picked her up again. "Wheesht, Kristen," she whispered, bouncing the child, trying to keep her quiet.

"She's no bother to anyone," assured Lachie's wife,

Sheila.

Fearchar ignored the words of support from her friends. "Father, clearly they all feel sorry for a lass who has lost her parents and husband in the space of a few months. But come next winter when she is unable to feed her sniveling bairn, none of them will thank ye for leaving her here in their midst."

Grace was stunned. She couldn't imagine why Fearchar was pushing this issue.

The laird considered Grace for a moment. "What say ye lass? Ye would be more than welcome to work with the weavers at the castle. I might even be able to find a new husband for ye from amongst my guardsmen. The sooner ye remarry the better."

Grace didn't want another husband and she certainly didn't want to go live at the castle. She didn't understand Fearchar's motives so she chose her words carefully. "Laird, yer offer is most kind, but this is my home. I believe I can provide for myself and my child *here*. I would prefer not to leave."

Fearchar glared at her, but the laird seemed convinced. "Then ye shall stay, at least through Michaelmas. If ye are managing well enough at that time and there is no risk of ye becoming a burden to yer neighbors, I will allow ye to continue to live here."

She wasn't sure what she had done to draw Fearchar's ire but she thought it best to leave before he could raise any further objection. She curtsied again, somewhat awkwardly with Kristen still in her arms. "Thank ye laird." Clutching Kristen close, she wove her way through the villagers. No sooner had she made it to the edge of the village than Fearchar appeared at her side. He grabbed her elbow roughly, sneering at her. "Allow me to see ye home, mistress Breive."

Grace tried to extricate herself from his grip. "That isn't necessary. I'm sure yer father needs yer assistance."

Fearchar only tightened his grip, his fingers digging

cruelly into her arm. "Nonsense," he said, giving her arm a jerk. "Clearly, he doesn't need my assistance. He certainly doesn't listen to my advice."

He strode angrily away from the center of the village, pulling her along beside him, causing her to stumble. She was afraid. No one had ever handled her so roughly. "Please stop, ye're hurting me."

He ignored her, yanking her beside him until they reached her little cottage, well out of sight of the people gathered in the square. He shoved her against the front wall. Kristen whimpered.

Fearchar grabbed Grace's face with one hand and painfully squeezed a breast with the other. He leaned in, planting a brutal kiss on her lips.

Holding her daughter with one arm, Grace tried without success to push him away with the other. When Kristen started wailing, he let Grace go, raising his hand as if ready to backhand the child. "Nay, don't hurt her!" She turned her back to Fearchar, sheltering Kristen with her body.

Fearchar yanked Grace back to face him. His hand still raised, she covered Kristen's head with her free hand, preparing to fend off the blow. But he didn't strike either of them, he simply glared at her. Slowly he lowered his hand. "Ye will be living at the keep before the end of the summer and then ye will be mine to use when I want ye. That is my promise. It will be better for ye if ye decide to come of yer own accord, sooner rather than later. If ye resist me on this, I will make ye sorry." He turned and strode back to the village square, leaving her terrified and trembling with a screaming child in her arms.

"Wheesht, Kristen." Grace patted her back, trying to soothe her even as she rushed inside their little cottage and barred the door. "Wheesht, little one," she crooned. "He's gone now. We are home. Everything will be fine." Kristen stopped wailing, but her little body still jerked with sobs.

Everything will be fine. Even as she said it, Grace knew it was an empty promise. Everything would have been fine if she had just been allowed to live her simple life and raise her daughter quietly, unnoticed. Even that pale dream now laid shattered amongst all of her others. Fearchar had a reputation of being both cruel and self-indulgent. Grace was certain that he would make good on his promise.

She swayed back and forth, humming a lullaby, lulling Kristen to sleep.

There was work to do, but Grace needed to feel the comfort of her sleeping daughter in her arms for just a few more minutes. Instead of tucking Kristen into bed for a nap, Grace sank into a chair simply holding her precious babe and remembering the sweet perfection their lives had been just months ago.

She thought of her parents. Of the many gifts they gave her, by far the most wonderful had been their capacity to love. They showed their love to her and to each other without reserve. Perhaps then it came as no surprise when, at seventeen, she too gave her heart without reservation to Callum Breive.

A tear slipped down Grace's cheek as she remembered her husband. When she caught his eye, he had been a tall, shy, slender lad of nineteen with sandy brown hair and gray eyes who was alone in the world. He worked on the fishing boats with her father and as much as her father had hated to admit it, he liked and respected the young man. After about a year her parents had finally consented for them to be wed. She delivered their wee perfect lass, Kristen, nine months later, on the day after Grace turned eighteen.

Had it only been six months since her world began to unravel? It seemed a lifetime ago.

Shortly after Michaelmas, her mother became ill and never completely recovered. Then, late in October, a terrible gale blew up suddenly, early one afternoon. Wind, rain, and ice pellets pounded the little cottage. Grace's anxiety had risen as darkness fell and her father and husband hadn't returned.

"What never helps, Grace?" Her mother had asked

the question that she had asked for as long as Grace could remember. It was intended to teach her to stay calm.

"Panicking. Panicking never helps, Mama."

Still, it had been all Grace could do to keep from panicking when Sheila came to tell them the small fishing boat Tristan and Callum worked had gone down in the storm. Lachie and his men on a nearby vessel had witnessed it, but were barely able to stay afloat themselves and could do nothing help.

Maybe her mother would have been able to recover from her illness if the heart of her heart hadn't been ripped from her and dragged to a watery grave. However, the loss of her husband took a toll on Catriona's already fragile health. She finally succumbed to her illness in February.

Sheer determination had kept Grace rising to face each new day but she kept them fed and earned enough to pay the rents. She had convinced herself she could build a life for her daughter. Perhaps not the one she had always imagined, but at least they had a roof over their heads, food in their bellies, and some measure of security.

Security. How could she have been foolish enough to believe they were secure in any way? She gave a mirthless laugh, which caused Kristen to stir, drawing Grace from her memories to the present where there was work to do. After soothing her back to sleep, Grace tucked her in. She had barely left the bedroom when a soft knock sounded at the cottage door. She called through the door, "Who's there?"

Sheila answered, "Friends, love. Ye can let us in."

Grace unbarred the door and opened it. She expected to see Sheila and Lachie but there were also several other men from the village. They all wore grim expressions. Sheila rung her hands and looked to be on the edge of tears. Lachie said gently, "Grace, lass, we need to talk with ye."

"Aye, Lachie. Come in, but we'll need to keep our voices down, Kristen is napping."

They filed in, some taking seats, others standing, all clearly worried. "Ye all look so somber, surely it isn't that bad." But she knew that was wishful thinking.

"Sit, lass," Lachie said and guided her to the chair by the hearth. "What happened after ye left the square? I saw Fearchar leave as I spoke to the laird about me own rents. I worried that he was after ye so I excused myself as soon as I could, only to see Fearchar, clearly angry, striding back to the square alone. Were ye able to get back here and bar the door?"

"Nay, he caught up to me and insisted on *seeing me home*."

Several of the men groaned. "Did he hurt ye, lass?" asked Hamish?

"Nay, not really. He tried to kiss me. It scared Kristen." Grace didn't admit to how much it had scared her too.

"What did he say to ye?"

A hot blush rose on Grace's cheeks and she looked at her hands, clenched in her lap. "He said that I will be living at the keep before the end of the summer and then...then..."

"Then what, lass?" prodded Lachie.

"He said...I will be his to use when he wants." Grace's voice was barely audible but by the men's reactions, she knew they had heard her.

Several men swore under their breaths.

A pained look crossed Lachie's face. "Aye, that's what I feared. He threatened some of us before he left."

Grace was shocked. What could he do to her friends? "Threatened ye? How?"

"He told me that he will not take any further public support of you kindly," said Hamish.

"Aye," said another villager, "and he's done worse. He told me he would be greatly pleased by anyone who tells the laird that ye have become a burden."

Grace bowed her head. "It is worse than I thought."

"Ye know we won't lie about ye Grace," said Lachie. "But when Fearchar wants something, he usually gets it. He will not rest until he has ye, regardless of what we do. The only thing to do is get ye off the island."

Sheila knelt beside Grace, and took her hands. "Yer mama and da weren't born here on the island. Do ye know anything about their families?"

Grace sighed. "I don't know much. My Da was a Sutherland."

"I can get ye to Sutherland territory," Lachie assured her. "We'll sail to Durness. I have friends there who will be able to see ye safely south to the Sutherlands' holding."

"Does yer mother not have people there too?" Hamish had asked. "If ye can't find yer da's kin, perhaps yer mother's family would take ye in."

"Nay, I don't think she has anyone," Grace said. She didn't want to admit that she didn't even know her mother's surname.

"Then it's settled," said Lachie. "Gather what ye can carry. We will leave on the high tide tomorrow morning."

Grace was horrified. "Must I go right away? After all, the laird agreed to let me live on here, at least through the summer."

Hamish shook his head. "Nay, Grace, Lachie is right. There is no telling what Fearchar is likely to do to get what he wants. In fact, I don't think ye and Kristen should remain in this cottage one more night. When ye are packed, ye'll come and stay with me and my wife."

The assembled men all nodded or murmured their agreement.

"Aye, that's a good plan, Hamish," said Lachie. "If he comes looking for ye tonight, lass, he won't find ye, and ye'll be gone before daylight."

Tears welled in Grace's eyes and her throat constricted. She knew they were right. Leaving was the only answer, but that didn't lessen the pain. This was her home. The memories of her parents and her husband were steeped into the very walls. Still, unless she wished to be Fearchar's leman, she had no other choice. She bit her lips and blinked to keep from crying. Finally, she nodded saying, "Aye, well, if we are leaving at first light, I must get ready."

The men took her cue and rose to leave. Sheila hugged her. "I'll send one of the lads up later to help ye carry yer things."

~ * ~

It didn't take Grace long to pack. Her most valuable possession, the loom which had been her mother's, was too large and would have to stay. She did have a small ribbon loom that she could take along with a fair amount of linen thread that she had already spun and dyed. She also packed her wool combs, cards, distaff, and drop spindle. If she couldn't weave, she could certainly spin and perhaps sell the yarn. Thankfully, she hadn't purchased her new wool yet. She also packed her father's knives and several small hand tools. Other than their clothes and some household linens, she and Kristen had few belongings.

Of course there was the box.

She walked to the hearth and removed a stone, behind which was a small cavity containing the box. Without bothering to replace the stone, she sat with the small finely carved wooden box which held their few valuable belongings on her lap. She traced her fingers reverently over the gorse flowers and rooster carved into the lid while she gave in to her tears for a moment.

Finally she opened it and looked at each precious item within. There was her father's silver filigree brooch, a gold pendant set with a pearl, and gold brooch resembling a ring of bog myrtle, both of which were her mother's. She had never seen them wear these bits of finery. There was also a single gold coin bearing the image of a fleur-de-lis on one side and a man on the other, who, based on his halo and animal hair cloak, she assumed to be St. John the Baptist. The only other coins she had ever seen were the pennies, half-pennies, and farthings used in every-day commerce. Grace had no idea what the gold coin was worth, but she knew it was valuable.

Ah, and the letter was in the box too. She turned it

over in her hand, remembering the afternoon her mother had told her about it. The letter was to Tristan's mother. It looked as if Grace would be able to deliver it now.

The sound of the bedroom door opening drew Grace from her memories. She swiped the tears from her eyes, replaced the box's contents, and tucked it in with the rest of their belongings.

Kristen padded across the room to her, rubbing her eyes sleepily. She crawled up in Grace's lap for a cuddle. "Is the bad man gone?"

"Aye, sweetling, he is."

"I don't wike him."

"We don't have to worry about him anymore."

"What if he comes back?"

"Well, my precious, if he comes back he won't find us here."

"Why? Wiww we hide?"

"We are going on an adventure, pet. Tonight we will stay with Hamish's family and then tomorrow we are going on a boat."

"A boat? Wike Da's boat?"

"A bigger boat. We will go across the water to Scotland on Lachie's boat."

"I wike Wachie."

Grace laughed. "I like him too."

~ * ~

When Lachie's youngest son arrived, he frowned at Grace's bundle of belongings. "Is that all?"

Grace smiled. "Aye, lad, that's all."

He cocked his head. "It's hard to believe someone's whole life can fit into such a small bundle."

Grace laughed. "That's not my whole life, lad. That's just things. This is my whole life." With that she scooped Kristen up and tickled her until her daughter giggled and squirmed.

Eyeing her with doubt, he simply nodded. "If ye say so. Still, I thought ye'd have more. I'll carry this down and

I'll take Kristen with me if ye want me to. Mam said ye might want to visit the grave one last time."

Grace sobered. "Aye, I would like to say goodbye, but I'll take Kristen with me."

He nodded, picked up the bundle, and left the cottage. Grace watched him for a moment before saying to Kristen, "Do ye want to climb the hill?"

Kristen's eyes lit up. "Aye, Mama."

"Then we will." She twirled around with her once, making Kristen squeal with glee before putting her down. "I just need to put out the fire first." Grace went to the hearth and smothered the fire with cold ashes. She took Kristen's hand and walked out without looking back. She didn't want the last memory of her home to be cold and empty. They walked to the little church at the edge of the village where Grace stopped and looked over the low wall into the church yard where her mother was buried. She made the sign of the cross and said a silent prayer for the souls of those she'd lost.

Kristen looked up at her. "I want to cwime the hiww mama. Ye said we could."

"Aye, sweetling, we are going too." She didn't enter the graveyard or stay any longer, her loved ones weren't here. Instead she walked past the church to the path leading to the top of the promontory, which looked out over the village and harbor. She picked Kristen up, putting her on her shoulders to carry her up the hill.

When they reached the top, she set Kristen on her feet in the tall grass, warning her as she always did, "Don't go near the edge."

"I won't, Mama. I dust wanna pick fwowers." She immediately busied herself picking the meadow flowers that were just beginning to open to the rare spring sunshine.

Grace looked around, trying to absorb it all one last time. This was one of her favorite places. She came here as a child with her parents, her da carrying her up on his strong, broad shoulders just as she had Kristen. She also walked here with Callum when they were courting.

Here, alone, there were no memories of sickness or loss; she had only spent happy hours in this spot so it is where she would say goodbye. She basked in the glow of those sweet memories until Kristen stood at her feet, her arms outstretched with a fist full of flowers, and demanded, "Up."

Grace swung her into the air, making her squeal and giggle before hugging her close. "Are ye ready to go on an adventure, sweetling?"

"Can I see over fust?"

"Aye, one last time." Grace walked with her as close to the edge of the cliff as she felt comfortable and looked down at the sleepy little village by the edge of the sea that had been their only home.

"Goodbye," whispered Grace, "we'll miss ye."

"Goodbye, we'ww miss ye," echoed Kristen somberly.

Chapter 2

Late May, 1340 Sutherland Castle

When Grace and Kristen arrived, Lachie's friends, Dugald, a merchant, and his wife, Mary, had been extremely kind. Grace and Kristen had stayed with them in Durness for nearly a month until Dugald was ready to make his twice yearly trip to Inverness. He had two wagon loads of goods to sell there but they were delivering Grace and Kristen to Castle Sutherland on the way.

They were near enough now to see the castle in the distance. Grace began to worry. She hadn't known anything about her parents' families until just before her mother died. After her father and Callum had died, Grace's life became a blur of work punctuated by too little sleep but the day she learned she might have a grandmother was etched in her memory.

She had been working her loom as quickly as she could, making the most of the waning light while Kristen napped, snuggled next to Catriona.

Her mother had called to her, "Grace, my sweet, come sit with me. I wish to speak with ye for a moment."

"Mama, I won't have the light long and it is much easier to work while Kristen is napping."

"I know, sweetling, but this is important."

Grace sighed but stopped what she was doing and went to sit by her mother. Once so strong and beautiful, her mother had wasted away to practically nothing. Her dark auburn hair, which had been so much like Grace's own, was dull and streaked with gray. Her green eyes no longer sparkled. Grace took her mother's frail hand in her own.

"What do ye wish to tell me?"

"My beautiful lass, I love ye so very much. I am so sorry."

"Wheesht, there is nothing for ye to be sorry for."

"There is more than ye know and I need to tell ye, my sweet." Her mother closed her eyes.

"Ye are tired, Mama. It will wait until ye are stronger."

"Grace," her mother said, her voice surprisingly firm, "ye know full well, I am never going to be stronger. This will not wait."

Grace blinked back tears. Her mother had just given voice to the fear in Grace's heart. After having lost her father and her husband, in spite of all her efforts, her mother was indeed slipping away too. "Aye, Mama. I'm listening."

"Ye know yer father and I came here from the mainland right after we were married." Grace nodded and her mother continued. "We told ye we had no families but that wasn't true."

Her mother's words shocked Grace but she tried not to let it show. "It wasn't?"

"Nay. Yer da and I fell in love but my father wouldn't let us marry. He vowed to kill yer da if he ever saw him again. We ran away together and came here." Her mother panted; the effort required to talk had nearly been too much for her.

Grace kissed the back of her mother's hand. "None of that matters now, Mama."

"Aye, Grace, it does. I don't ever want ye to seek my family out. I won't even tell ye who they are. Yer grandfather, if he still lives, will see ye and Kristen as commodities or worse, kill ye out of anger and revenge. Promise me ye will never seek them out."

Grace wasn't sure what her mother meant by *commodities* but she had never seen such abject fear in her mother's eyes. "I promise, Mama."

Her mother closed her eyes for a moment, trying to

catch her breath. When she was calmer, she said, "But yer father may have family left. He was from Clan Sutherland. His mother, Innes, worked at the castle there, in the kitchens. We never told anyone where we went." She paused again, struggling to breathe. "My father was ruthless. If he ever found out what clan yer da was from, they would be in danger and so would we. Yer da and I are beyond my family's reach now. I think he would want his mother to know...what happened...why we couldn't tell her...how much we loved each other. I wrote a letter...for yer da...years ago." Her mother gasped for air between words. "He feared sending it. My father..." A tear slipped down her mother's cheeks. "It's in the box. I'm sorry we caused so much pain...but God help me...I would do it again. I loved him so."

"Mother, please, rest. We can talk again later."

Her mother shook her head, tears flowing freely. "Be happy, Grace." With that her mother had closed her eyes. The effort to tell Grace all of this had exhausted her and she drifted off to sleep. She never awoke again, dying a few days later.

The memory now caused Grace's heart to ache. She missed her mother so very much.

If her grandmother, Innes, still lived, she had heard nothing from Grace's father in twenty-three years. If Innes had passed away, it was possible the Sutherlands would not remember Tristan from so many years ago. Grace prayed that they would let her stay in any case. Maybe they would welcome her skills as a weaver.

When they reached the castle gates, Grace told the guard she was looking for Innes Murray.

"She'll be in the kitchens. I'll find someone to show ye there."

Relief washed over Grace. At least her grandmother was alive.

"Well, lass, it seems we have reached the right place," Dugald said.

"Aye it does. Thank ye for everything." Grace gave him a quick hug.

The older man blushed crimson. "It was nothing. I wish ye God's blessings, lass."

"Dugald," his wife called from the wagon seat where she held a sleeping Kristen on her lap, "we can't just leave her here until we know she'll be welcomed."

"Mary, that's kind of ye, but I have delayed ye enough. I'm sure Kristen and I will be fine." Grace climbed up on the wagon to lift her daughter down as one of their sons handed down the bundle of her belongings. Kristen woke, but not fully. She popped her thumb in her mouth and rested her head on Grace's shoulder.

Mary smiled at her. "Well, just in case, we will stop back by here on our way home. If things aren't working well, ye'll always have a welcome with us.

Tears welled in Grace's eyes. She prayed that her grandmother would accept her, but fear of the unknown prevented her from refusing the offer. "Thank ye, Mary. I truly appreciate that."

After saying her goodbyes, Grace followed one of the guards through the gates, across the outer bailey, into the inner bailey, then around to the kitchens. Before returning to his post, the guard opened the door for her, calling in, "Innes, there's someone here to see ye."

The kitchen he showed her to was empty save for a white haired woman who stirred a pot hanging over the fire. The midday meal had been served and cleared. This was the quiet pause in the afternoon, before work began again for the evening meal.

The older woman smiled. "Do I know ye lass?"

Grace hesitated a moment, trying to figure out what to say. The forthright approach seemed best. "Nay, ye don't. My name is Grace Breive and this sleepy lass is my daughter, Kristen. I am Tristan Murray's daughter."

The news stunned Innes. She dropped the long spoon she held. "Ye can't be. Nay. Tristan—Tristan disappeared years ago. I never heard a word. I thought him dead."

Disappeared? Her mother hadn't made that detail clear. "I'm so very sorry for yer pain but I am his daughter." Grace slipped a hand in her pocket and pulled out her da's brooch. "This was his. Do ye recognize it?"

The old woman burst into tears. "Aye, I do. That was my husband's and then Tristan's." She rushed across the room and wrapped her arms around both Grace and Kristen. "By all the saints, lass, I can't believe it—after all these years. He left. He was young and so angry. I thought he would forgive me eventually and come home. That was the last I saw him."

Grace returned her hug. She didn't know what to say. "Please, sit down," she said, gently guiding her weeping grandmother into a chair. "I know this has been a shock. I don't understand it all myself, but perhaps we can sort it out together."

When her grandmother had regained some control, she asked, "Where is Tristan now?"

The anticipation in her grandmother's voice caused a lump to form in Grace's throat and tears prickled the back of her eyes. She took a deep breath. She hated having to break the old woman's heart again. "I'm so very sorry to have to tell ye this, my father died last October."

As Grace expected, this brought on a fresh wave of tears but the old woman recovered a bit quicker this time. "Tell me, child. Tell me everything."

"I'm sorry but I don't know everything. We lived on the Isle of Lewis. I knew my parents hadn't been raised there, but I thought neither of them had any living family. My father and husband were fishermen. They both died when a gale struck and their boat went down."

"Oh, my poor sweet lass, ye are a widow. I was widowed young too. I'm so sorry for ye. I thought it would kill me at the time, but I had Tristan, I had to go on."

"Aye, that is just how it was. I had to for Mama and Kristen. Mama had been very ill, ye see. I needed to take care of her. Finally, a few months ago she told me why she and Da had come to the isles in the first place. Apparently her father didn't want her to marry my father so they ran away together."

"But why didn't he tell me? I would have understood why he couldn't come home. Why didn't he just send me a message telling me he lived?"

Her plaintive tone tore at Grace. She understood her parents' reasons; still, her heart ached for her grandmother. "My mother said her father vowed to kill Da so they ran away. She feared her father. She wouldn't even tell me her family name. She didn't want me to ever seek them out. She made me promise I wouldn't. Do ye know anything about her?"

Her grandmother shook her head sadly. "Nay, I don't. Ye see, as I said, Tristan left as a very young man. He had trained here as a soldier but I didn't want that for him. I told ye I was widowed, Tristan's father died at the battle of Falkirk when Tristan wasn't much bigger than yer wee lass. I couldn't bear the thought of losing him in the same way. I asked Laird Sutherland to release him, to have him work in the stables or on a croft, anything but wield a sword. He was my only child." She bowed her head for a moment. Clearly these were painful memories.

"Did the laird refuse?" asked Grace gently.

Innes shook her head. "Not outright. Laird Sutherland said he wouldn't force Tristan out, because he was a skilled warrior, but he would talk to Tristan, giving him the option to work elsewhere if he so desired."

"I don't understand. Why would he leave if the choice was his?"

"It was my fault. I shouldn't have interfered. When Tristan found out what I had done, he was furious. He said if I couldn't stay out of his life, he would stay out of mine. He left the next day. He was only twenty. He never contacted me to tell me where he went. Laird Sutherland might have tried to find out for me, but as it had been my interference that caused Tristan to leave in the first place, I didn't want to risk pushing him farther away.

"For the first few months I was certain he would return home. Then after a couple years, I simply prayed to hear from him. I just wanted to know that he lived and was happy. Finally, after so many years had passed, I believed he must have died. And, now I learn that he has and I was never able to tell him how sorry I was. How I regretted interfering." Her grandmother began weeping again.

Grace was stunned by her father's thoughtlessness. She offered the only explanation she could think of. "It sounds as if he married my mother just months after leaving home. If my mother's father was as ruthless as she believed, I can only think my da's silence was meant to protect ye. Still, I am so very sorry." They sat in silence for a few moments before Grace said, "I have a letter to ye from my da that my mother wrote for him. Maybe it will explain things."

"I can't read. We'll go to Father Francis. He'll read it to us. I could ask the laird but he is away."

"I can read it to ye if ye wish. Apparently Da composed it years ago but feared sending it."

A look of excitement crossed her grandmother's face. "Ye can read? Aye, please read it to me. But if ye have had it for months why haven't ye read it before now?"

"The letter was written to ye, not me. I didn't want to read it without yer leave. Would ye hold this sprite for me while I fetch it from my bag?"

Her grandmother gave Kristen a warm smile that reminded Grace poignantly of Da. "Hold my great-granddaughter? Aye, I'd love to."

Kristen was beginning to wake more fully now but she happily snuggled into the old woman's lap.

Grace found the small, carved wooden box, producing the letter from it. "Here it is." She broke the wax seal and the sight of her mother's beautiful handwriting caused her heart to ache, but she took a deep breath and started reading.

Dear Mother,

I have tried to compose this letter so many times. Each time, I have started by explaining why I left so suddenly without ever revealing where I went. I have finally realized the "whys" are of the least importance. So first I want ye to know I love ye. No mother deserves to be treated as I did ye. From the depths of my heart, I am sorry. I said terrible things. I shouldn't have left angry. But even having left, I should have at least told ye where I went. There are no excuses.

Why then am I not coming to ye in person, falling on my knees, and begging yer forgiveness? Sadly, I cannot without endangering everyone I love, including ye, my dear mother. I can only tell ye the story and hope ye understand.

When I left, I worked as a soldier with another clan. There, I fell in love with the laird's daughter and she with me.

Shocked, Grace stopped reading for a moment. The laird's daughter? Her mother hadn't mentioned that detail either but it explained why she could read and write. Grace read on.

We knew there was little hope her father would allow the marriage. He had plans for strategic alliances that included betrothals for all of his children. Following our hearts meant escaping together, marrying in secret, and living in hiding. I was unwilling to subject my love to this without at least trying to approach her father. Still as unlikely as he was to agree, I could not risk losing her forever. She slipped from the castle and I escorted her to an abbey to wait for me while I met with her father.

I returned to the castle before anyone knew she had left. I begged her father for her hand. Not surprisingly, he refused. He saw my request as an insult, believing that ambition and greed rather than love motivated me. He banished me, vowing to kill me if he ever saw me again. If he had realized his daughter was already gone I have no doubt he would have cleaved me in two at that moment.

I suppose defying ye wasn't bad enough, I also defied the laird I chose to serve. I left the keep, returned to the abbey, and married the woman I loved, promising to devote my life to her.

Perhaps it will ease yer heart to know that due to the risk of discovery, working as a soldier with any clan would never have been possible. Nor could I ever lend my sword-arm to an enemy of Scotland.

We chose another life but in so doing had to sever all ties. I want more than anything for ye to meet my precious wife. I love her more than life itself. I cannot imagine living without her. However, she fears her father. She fears the power he wields and believes his need for vengeance against us could endanger anyone who has knowledge of our whereabouts.

I realize now that not only have I robbed ye of a son, but of a beautiful, loving daughter by marriage, and of grandchildren. We have a lovely newborn daughter. We also had a fine son who we tragically lost to illness a few days ago. Sadly, I now fully understand how devastating it is to lose a child. If you feel a fraction of the loss I feel for my son, I will never be able to apologize for causing you such pain.

Perhaps someday, when my wife's family no longer poses a threat, ye will be able to meet the woman who captured and holds my heart as well as the children born from our love. This is my fervent prayer. Until then, please accept this meager apology for my shameful behavior and believe that I love and respect ye more than ye can ever know.

With love,
Tristan

This was certainly not what Grace expected. She looked up from the letter, her grandmother dashed at the tears coursing down her cheeks. Grace loved her father dearly. She believed him to be generous, strong, and noble. It was hard to read about these things her parents had done, which seemed so very selfish and yet were born of deep abiding love for each other. Clearly that love had pushed aside everything else and thus had caused great pain to others. Duty to one's family, clan honor, loyalty to a liege lord, none of these things had been more important than the love they felt for each other. It was beautiful and heartbreaking at the same time. She couldn't help but wonder what choice she would have made. She thought of her beloved Callum. Would she have married him if she had faced the same circumstances her parents did? She didn't know the answer.

"I'm so sorry, Grandmother. After these many years, this seems so little."

"Child, I thought Tristan long dead. I had given up all hope. Now I know what happened to take him from me all those years ago. I know he didn't hold a grudge against me, and that he regretted his actions. I wish things could have been different, but to live a life filled with love is a blessing. I would have wanted nothing more for him. These are not small things." In a brighter tone she added, "also, I now have a beautiful granddaughter and great-granddaughter to dote on. And perhaps someday I can meet the lass who won Tristan's heart."

Grace's eyes filled with tears. "Nay, grandmother, I'm sorry to say she passed away from her illness in February, shortly after she told me all of this. I have no one left in the world now but Kristen and ye."

"Well, my sweet lass, ye've found me now and ye'll have a home here forever. I'll speak with Laird Sutherland about it when he returns but have no fears, he'll welcome ye."

"I won't be a burden, Grandmother. I am a skilled weaver, but I will work at anything."

"Ye could never be a burden, lass, don't worry about that. I'm sure the laird won't object to ye and Kristen living with me. My cottage is inside the castle walls, in the outer bailey. Come with me. I'll take ye there."

Chapter 3

Soaked by the late spring rain and chilled to the bone, Bram Sutherland thought the gates of home had never looked so inviting. It had been a long, wet ride from Castle MacKay. The skies had only cleared in the last hour. They would have been welcome to stay another night waiting out the storm at Naomh-dùn, the MacKay stronghold, but thankfully his father had declined. Bram couldn't stand the thought of spending another minute there. His betrothed had married Eoin MacKay. Bram hadn't wanted to linger and be reminded of his loss.

Letting Fiona MacNicol go had been the right thing to do but that didn't make it less disappointing. Until yesterday he hadn't even met her. But once he had, he found her not only beautiful, but strong, loyal, and possessed of a loving heart—a heart that was, unfortunately, deeply in love with Eoin MacKay. Even though Bram had been tempted to force the terms of their betrothal contract, her heart would never belong to him and he couldn't bear to see her unhappy.

They slogged into the courtyard. His father gave his mount to the care of a stable hand. "Son, I expect supper is nigh on the table. Leave yer beast to one of the lads. We'll fill our bellies with good food and ale and try to put this mess behind us."

Bram generally preferred to care for his own horse and while he had been looking forward to the warmth of hearth and home for hours, arriving at the start of the evening meal had disadvantages. He was less than anxious to face the onslaught of questions about what had happened and why they didn't have Fiona MacNicol with them. "I'll see to Goliath myself but I won't be long."

"Bram, ye could have had her. The law was on our side."

"Nay, Da, we have been through this. It would have been

wrong. Fiona and Eoin love each other."

"Bah. Love. Kentigern MacKay would never have stood for this." His father's tone of voice clearly conveyed how unimportant that detail was.

"Perhaps not, but he is dead. Eoin is laird and in spite of being solid allies for years, if we had forced the issue, he would have become a mortal enemy to the Sutherlands until either I lay dead or he did. Not to mention the fact that I would be married to a woman who would have hated me forever. This was the right course."

"Whether it was or wasn't, it's done now and we'll need to find another way to ally with the MacNicols. I think I must consider Bhaltair's daughter for Boyd, and the sooner the better. We need to get that sorted while they are young—before either of them gets any foolish notions about love in their heads."

Bram just shook his head at his father's utter dismissal of the emotion. Bram had understood from an early age that he would marry a woman of his father's choosing, a woman who strengthened clan ties. He hadn't thought much about love and perhaps had discounted its importance as thoroughly as his father had. That was until he saw Fiona and Eoin together. He didn't want to admit it, but he envied them.

His father must have taken his silence for agreement, because he continued, "Aye, the more I think about it, the more I'm convinced. I will take care of it as soon as Laird MacNicol has recovered. And we will find a bonny bride for ye too, Bram. That young Anna MacKay is quite a pretty thing, even if she is a bit too bold for her own good."

"A bit too bold? That is an understatement. Whoever marries her will have his hands full. I'm not sure I'm up to the task. Besides, she is very young."

"Seventeen is not that young. But there is also Annice..."

"Nay, Da, please, can't this wait? I don't wish to discuss another betrothal at the moment and I need to see to Goliath."

"Fine, we won't discuss it now. It can wait...a few days. Don't dwell on this, Bram."

"Aye, Da."

His father turned toward the keep, calling as he went, "Don't be all night. Yer mother will want to hear every detail of what happened and I don't have the patience."

By all the saints, Bram loved his mother but he didn't have

the patience for an inquisition tonight either. Bram led Goliath into the stable, removed his tack, rubbed him down, and fed him an extra portion of oats. When he had finished, he was still not anxious to face the crowd certain to have formed in the great hall. He could avoid it by going straight to the kitchen. Innes would give him food and ale and he could slip up the backstairs, avoiding the great hall altogether tonight. He actually might be able to get through this day without having to rehash everything yet again.

Bram walked from the stables through the outer bailey heading to the rear entrance to the inner bailey, near the kitchens. As he passed one of the small dwellings located within the outer bailey, a woman's voice, perhaps the most beautiful voice he had ever heard, drifted toward him on the breeze. He stopped to listen. The tune was unfamiliar and he couldn't quite catch the words, but it was delightful.

He followed the enchanting melody, drawing close enough to the source to understand the lyrics.

Hush my sweetling, hushaby,
The sun sets slowly in the sky,
Tis time to sleep for evening's nigh,
Hush my sweetling, hushaby.

Hush my sweetling, little dove,
Mama's heart is filled with love,
Papa watches from above,
Hush my sweetling, little dove.

They were the nonsense words mothers crooned to bairns, but he was entranced by the soft, sweet voice of what could only be an angel. He stopped in front of the tiny cottage to listen.

Hush my sweetling, little sprite,
Too soon ye'll wake to morning bright,
So sleep now through the still dark night,
Hush my sweetling, little sprite.

The woman stopped singing words but continued to hum her lullaby until finally her voice faded away altogether. Bram was so captivated by the music it took him a moment to realize it had emanated from Innes' cottage. However, it certainly was not Innes singing. She would be in the kitchen or the keep now, overseeing the evening meal. Who was it then?

As if in answer to his unspoken question, a young woman he had never seen before stepped out of the cottage. She was perfectly lovely. Her face was delicately beautiful; as angelic as her voice. Rich auburn hair spilled from under a white kertch in soft curls that reached well past the middle of her back. Tall for a woman, she had full breasts and her belt cinched a narrow waist. She stretched and rolled her shoulders, her movements graceful and oddly enticing. Bram felt a twinge of disappointment when his brain registered the kertch. She was married. Of course she was—she had been crooning a lullaby to a child.

When she cast a glance his direction, she gasped and stumbled backwards, feeling blindly for the door latch. "I didn't see ye there. Ye startled me."

"I'm sorry, I didn't intend to." Why was he apologizing to her? He had committed no offense. He took a step toward her.

She went from frightened to ferocious in a matter of seconds. "Stay back. What are ye doin' here anyway? Who are ye?" she demanded.

Who did she think she was? She was certainly in no position to demand anything from him. "I think, lass, it is ye who needs to start explaining. Who are ye and why were ye in Innes' cottage?"

"Innes is my grandmother, she asked us to stay with her."

"Yer grandmother? Innes has no children. I won't tolerate liars, no matter how lovely they are. Who are ye? I want the truth and I won't ask again."

She scowled, affronted. "I am not a liar. I told ye, Innes is my grandmother and she did have a child, a son named Tristan. I am his daughter, Grace Breive."

Tristan, aye, he had a vague memory of that. "I stand corrected. She had a son. But Tristan died years ago."

"Nay, Tristan disappeared years ago. He didn't die."

"And ye are his daughter, Innes' long-lost granddaughter. How sweet. And unlikely. What game is this? Innes is important to Clan Sutherland. I don't want anyone taking advantage of her, playing on her feelings."

"I am not playing on her feelings. I am her granddaughter and have proven that to her. But it's a long story and I don't see how any of this concerns ye."

"It concerns me, Grace, because everything at Sutherland concerns me. I am Bram Sutherland, Laird Sutherland's heir."

Grace became immediately contrite. "I'm sorry, sir. I meant no offense. But, I have told ye the truth."

"The babe ye were singing to is yers?"

"Aye, I have a young daughter. I should go back inside. I just stepped out for a bit of air. The rain kept us indoors all day." Again, her hand groped behind her, searching for the door latch.

"This isn't over, Grace Breive. If ye and yer husband want to live at Sutherland, ye will need permission from the laird, whether ye are Innes' granddaughter or no. And I hope ye do have proof of who ye are. I won't allow ye to hurt Innes in any way and giving her false hope about a long lost son would kill her." He took a step towards her, reaching past to lift the latch, which so far had eluded her hand. "Goodnight, Mistress Breive."

He was surprised by the expression on her face. It wasn't anger or fear of discovery. The green depths of her eyes were guileless and she appeared...was it grateful?

"Goodnight laird—I mean Bram—I mean sir. Goodnight." She backed through the door and closed it.

He stood there for a moment, trying to sort out his thoughts about this newest addition to the clan. It all seemed odd. He would speak with Da about this...but not tonight. He resumed his walk, entering into the inner bailey. He had almost reached the kitchens when his brother Ian called to him. "Bram, there ye are. Da sent someone to fetch ye from the stables, but I figured ye were avoiding dinner in the hall and I'd find ye in the kitchens."

Ian was two years younger than Bram. For brothers, they looked nothing alike. Both were tall, but Bram had fair hair and blue eyes like their mother and Ian had dark hair and brown eyes like their father. Their temperaments were vastly different as well. Although Bram smiled easily, he tended to be quiet and often serious. Like Laird Sutherland, he revealed very little of what he was thinking, sometimes appearing aloof. Even so, most of their clansmen considered him level-headed and fair. They believed he would make a good leader when his time came. Ian, too, was quick with a smile but that was where the similarities ended. He enjoyed a good time, and seemingly took very little seriously. However, Ian was acutely observant and absolutely forthright. Most people knew exactly where he stood on any issue. As different as they were, Ian was truly his best friend. "Aye Ian, ye know me well. Do me a kindness and tell Da ye didn't find me."

"Ah, well now brother, I could tell Da ye weren't in the kitchens, because ye weren't. But Mother is anxious to see ye too and ye and she can see right through any guile."

Bram sighed heavily. "I suppose it was vain hope to think I could avoid this." Bran fell in step by his brother as they walked to the keep.

"Aye, it was. Ye know how excited mother was to finally have a daughter, or at least a daughter-to-be. Da would only say that ye were the one who chose to release the MacNicol lass from the betrothal. When Mam kept asking questions he roared for someone to fetch ye from the stable and then he stomped off to his solar with a jug of whiskey under one arm."

"Damn, I wanted to talk to him about Innes."

"Ye heard about her long-lost granddaughter?"

"I just met her. Ye knew about her?"

"Aye, she arrived the day ye and Da left for Naomh-dùn. She seems nice enough. Innes adores her."

"I wish we knew more about her. It is hard to believe their story and yet I don't see what they have to gain by lying."

"Innes is certain the lass is her granddaughter. She had a brooch that belonged to Tristan."

"What about her husband? Have ye met him? What is he like?"

"She has no husband. She's a widow. She arrived with just her daughter, a few days ago. It was the day ye and Da left."

"A widow? She is an awfully young widow."

"Bram, let this go for now. Innes is thrilled. Tomorrow will be soon enough to sort out Innes' granddaughter. Besides, it will likely take ye all evening to answer to mother's questions."

"I suppose ye are right. Well then, let the interrogation begin," said Bram as they entered the keep.

~ * ~

Grace leaned against the door, listening for Bram Sutherland's retreating footsteps. For much too long a moment, she heard nothing. Then, finally, the crunch of the gravel told her he was leaving.

So that was Bram Sutherland. How could ye have been so rude and stupid, Grace? Her initial shock at finding a man standing outside the cottage had quickly shifted to fear. She supposed that feeling threatened, her protective instincts had kicked in and she had gone on the offensive to keep Kristen safe. Perhaps that is also why she didn't correct him when he assumed her husband was with her. Still, he would find out soon enough.

She had to admire how he wished to protect her grandmother though. But the idea that he thought he would have to protect Innes from Grace was worrisome. Now Grace feared she had only made it worse. She sat down and put her head in her hands as she realized she had just stirred the ire of another laird's son.

Chapter 4

When Innes had returned to the cottage the previous evening, Grace told her about her confrontation with Bram.

"Don't worry so, Grace," her grandmother chided. "Laird Sutherland is reasonable, as is Bram. When they see the letter, and yer father's brooch, there will be no question as to who ye are."

Still Grace worried and hadn't slept well.

The next morning, she was helping in the kitchen, cleaning up after breakfast. Innes kneaded bread dough as Kristen stood on a chair beside her, playing with a small ball of dough, imitating her great-grandmother's actions. "Mama, I'm making bwead."

"I see, sweetling. Grandmother, let me know if she is too much underfoot."

Maisie, a large woman in her fifties who was her grandmother's second in command, laughed heartily. "Grace, love, that wee one could be swinging from Innes' hair and yer granny wouldn't complain."

"Aye, that's true," said Innes as she planted a kiss on the top of Kristen's head. "'Tis glad I am to have ye both here."

Grace furrowed her brow. "I just don't want her to be a burden."

Maisie put her hands on her hips. "What's the matter with ye today? Ye've been brooding all morning."

"She is worried about meeting Laird Sutherland," said Innes.

"Well, put that worry out of yer head, lass, Laird Sutherland isn't all that fearsome. Sure, he can be a bit crusty, but what man can't? I can't imagine what he would object to."

"She ran into Bram last night, and it sounds like he was, what did ye call it? Crusty?" said Innes. "I figure he was on his way to the kitchens."

Maisie grinned. "Avoiding the hall, was he?"

"After hearing about all that happened, I can well understand why," said Innes.

"What happened?" asked Grace.

"It seems another man married his betrothed before he could claim her," said Maisie.

Dear God, if that had happened to Fearchar Morrison, Grace firmly believed a clan war would ensue. "Will there be repercussions?"

Her grandmother smiled. "Nay, I don't think so. It isn't as if it was a love match. The marriage was arranged by the laird and her uncle. It seems they all came to an agreement that it was for the best."

Just then a maid servant stepped into the kitchen. "Innes, Laird Sutherland wishes to speak with ye and yer granddaughter now."

"Aye, thank ye Ellie. Grace, go fetch the letter and brooch. The Laird will want to see them."

"Aye, grandmother." Grace hurried out of the kitchen and to her grandmother's cottage. Her memories from the last day she stood before a clan laird were not pleasant. She was so nervous now, it felt as if her heart was in her throat. What would she do if the laird turned her away? She hadn't even considered that eventuality. She was suddenly profoundly glad that Dugald and Mary had offered her a home with them in Durness. When she reached the little cottage, she had allowed fear to overtake her.

What never helps, Grace? She heard her mother's sweet voice say the words that she had repeated so often when Grace was small.

Panicking. Panicking never helps, Mama. She took a deep breath to calm herself, but her hands still shook as she located the box and removed the articles she needed. She slipped them in her pocket before tucking the box away again and rushing back.

When she returned to the kitchen, Innes had brushed the flour from Kristen's clothes and was just wiping the last of it from her face. She looked up at Grace. "Grace." Her grandmother's voice was stern. "Ye must wipe that terrified look off yer face before we meet the laird."

Grace nodded and took a deep breath. "Aye, Grandmother." The only experience she had in dealing with a laird was a few short weeks ago when she had paid her rents. Grace's grandfather was a laird and her own mother feared his power and vengeance. Fearchar's threats echoed in her brain. Ye will be living at the keep before the end of the summer and then ye will be mine to use when I want ye. That is my promise. It will be better for ye if ye decide to come of yer own accord, and the sooner the better. If ye resist me on this, I will make ye sorry. But, she hadn't told her Grandmother about Fearchar's threats so Innes surely wouldn't understand Grace's fear now.

She picked Kristen up and they walked to the large square tower keep. Grace hadn't been inside it yet. For that matter she had never been inside any keep. When they entered the hall she was awestruck. The ceilings were vaulted stone. She had never seen anything but timber or thatch. Three men sat at what was obviously the laird's table. One was Bram and she assumed the older man was Laird Eanraig Sutherland. The other man looked so much like a younger version of the laird that he too must be a son.

When they reached the table, they both curtsied, Grace a bit awkwardly because she held Kristen.

The older man said, "Good day to ye, Innes."

"Good day, Laird," her grandmother responded pleasantly.

"Is this the young woman who claims to be yer granddaughter?"

Grace cringed inwardly. Claims to be?

But Innes seemed unbothered by his choice of words. "Aye, Laird, this is Tristan's daughter, Grace, and her bairn."

Grace's said, "Good day, Laird."

Kristen echoed, "Good day, Waird."

The laird's lips twitched. "Good day, lass. Ye have very nice manners for such a wee one."

Kristen grinned and nodded. "I know."

The laird laughed outright.

Grace whispered, "Kristen the nice thing to say is 'thank ye, Laird'."

"Fank ye, Waird."

"Ye are welcome, lass. What is yer name?"

"Kwithten."

"Kristen. That's a bonny name."

Kristen smiled shyly before burying her face in Grace's neck.

"Grace, yer daughter is lovely."

"Thank ye, Laird."

He turned his attention to her grandmother. "Innes, thank ye for introducing us to yer guests. Now, I would like to speak with Grace alone. I'm sure ye won't mind taking this lovely wee lass back to the kitchens with ye for a bit?"

For the first time, a look of concern crossed Innes' face. "Laird, Grace is my granddaughter."

"And I'm yer laird. I've asked ye to leave us for a bit." His voice lost some of the warmth it had when he had been speaking to Kristen.

Innes cast a worried look at Grace. "Aye, laird. Come with grannie, poppet."

Grace put Kristen down. The little girl happily took Innes' hand and walked towards the door with her. Kristen asked, "Wiww we make more bwead?" as the pair left the hall.

Grace stood stiffly, waiting for the laird to address her, acutely aware of the three men scrutinizing her.

Laird Sutherland considered her in silence for a long moment before speaking to her. "Grace, these are two of my sons. I believe ye've met Bram." He inclined his head to the tall, blond man on his right.

She had only seen him in the evening light and hadn't noticed his crystal blue eyes or what a fine looking man he was.

The laird gestured to the man with dark hair and brown eyes who sat on his left. "And this is Ian."

She curtsied, lowering her eyes for a moment. Perhaps she should have said, pleased to meet you, but she wasn't sure she could force the untrue words across her lips.

"And ye, lass, purport to be Tristan Murray's daughter."

"I am Tristan Murray's daughter."

Now the laird's voice lost all hint of warmth. "Are ye now? We believed he died ages ago. And here, ye show up with a bairn, no husband, and a farfetched story about him living for years as a fisherman on the Isle of Lewis. Have ye any proof?"

Grace became increasingly more uncomfortable as she stood there. Aye, she had proof. The letter was her strongest evidence, but now she wondered about the wisdom of showing it to them. As her father couldn't read or write, they might not believe the letter was actually from him anyway. Furthermore, given that they were none too welcoming, she worried about how they would react to the information about her mother. If somehow they learned Catriona's identity, they might contact her clan. Her mother had warned her never to do this. Nay, she wouldn't show them the letter unless she had to.

"Aye, I have proof." She reached into her pocket and

pulled out the brooch, leaving the letter safely tucked away. She handed the old silver fastener to the laird to examine. "This belonged to my father. My grandmother says it was originally my grandfather's."

The Laird turned it over in his hand before handing it to Bram to examine. "I accept that this is Tristan's pin, but that doesn't necessarily make ye his daughter. Perhaps someone gave it to ye with a story about a dead man. Ye decided to be his long lost daughter and show up with a bairn at his mother's door. I do not believe a warrior the likes of Tristan Murray suddenly left everything he knew to live the humble life of a fisherman. Who are ye, lass? I want the truth!"

His raised voice and the angry tone scared Grace. "I have told ye the truth. I am Grace Breive. My parents were Tristan and Cat Murray." At the last second she decided only to reveal the familiar name people used for her mother. She repeated her parents' story and the details of their deaths.

"So Innes told me, but ye have no proof of that. Ye have nothing but a dead man's brooch. And, while it's been a long time since I've laid eyes on him, ye don't look anything like him, or like Innes for that matter."

"I looked like my mother. Everyone said so."

He harrumphed.

"Why is that so hard to believe? Only one of yer sons resembles ye."

He frowned at her. "Well aren't ye a bold, lass? Actually, my son Boyd looks like me as well. Still, that's a fair enough point. But why was it Tristan never told his mother where he was, that he had a family, or even that he lived? Innes was broken hearted. I know he was angry when he left but I wouldn't believe him to be so callous."

Facing the disapproving stares of the men, Grace wasn't sure what to say. The fact was, she too had thought it callous but she had seen the fear in her mother's eyes and therefore understood her reasons. She sighed. "I don't know all of the details. I know they feared my mother's father. She told me that before she died."

"As I have already told ye, Tristan was a good warrior. When I knew him, with the hubris of youth, he feared no one. Who was the formidable man that could make Tristan Murray tuck tail and run?"

She shook her head. "I don't know. My mother feared him

even on her deathbed. She wouldn't tell me and made me promise never to try and find her clan."

The Laird frowned. "I just don't believe it. I don't believe he would cower before anyone. I would sooner believe him dead."

"Laird, I can't explain what I don't understand myself. I'm certain he must have been a good warrior. He taught me…things…about weapons."

"What things?" asked Bram.

"How to care for them and how to use some of them. I can shoot a bow, but not as far or as accurately as he could. He said the best skill a woman could learn was how to handle knives because it took less strength. He was particularly skilled at throwing knives. He could pierce an apple thrown into the air."

The laird gave her an odd look. "Aye, he could. I've never seen anyone else do that."

"I can." She couldn't keep a note of pride out of her voice. "He taught me. I can hunt small prey with only a knife."

All three men looked as if they didn't believe her.

"Really?" asked Bram, sarcasm dripping from his voice. "I believe ye, thousands wouldn't so I fear ye'll have to prove it." He walked around the table and handed her his small dirk, a look of challenge in his eyes.

"If I do, will ye believe me?"

The laird looked at her appraisingly for a moment before answering. "Aye. If ye can pierce a thrown object with a knife, I will believe that Tristan Murray taught ye how and that he is yer da. Mind ye, there're no stores of apples left from the fall harvest, so ye'll have to take aim at a neep. Ian, send someone to fetch us one and meet us outside. Yer mother would frown on throwing knives in the hall."

"Aye, Da." Ian nodded and left the hall.

Grace weighed the knife in her hand to get a feel for the balance. She ran her thumb along the blade, feeling the point. She frowned. "Laird, neeps are much harder than apples."

"Aye, but it is fairly safe to claim ye can pierce a thrown apple, when there aren't likely to be any around to throw."

"Nay laird, that's not what I meant. I can hit a neep, but the blade needs to be very sharp. This one isn't. May I have a sharpening stone?"

Grace took the tiniest bit of pleasure at the look of surprise on his face.

"Aye, of course ye can. Bram, fetch her a stone."

Bram too nodded and left the hall on his errand.

Laird Sutherland motioned toward the door. "Shall we go outside?"

"Aye, laird."

She walked with him to the outer bailey. Once there, the laird frowned at the activity. "There are too many people here. I don't want to risk anyone being hurt by a lass hurtling knives." He ordered some of his men to clear the bailey.

While she waited, Grace tried to get a better feel for the knife. She flipped it in the air, catching it deftly each time. She walked over to a wooden building that appeared to be a barracks. She threw the knife repeatedly, testing the balance and perfecting her aim with it. She had only one chance at this. She had to prove her boast.

Chapter 5

Bram had spent the previous evening wondering about the lass who claimed to be Tristan Murray's daughter. When she entered the hall with Innes, he was struck again by how beautiful she was. Seeing her stand with her arms encircling the babe on her hip stirred a deep yearning within him. He did want a wife and children and had expected to marry Fiona MacNicol before the end of the summer. That was water under the bridge now.

He had reined in his wandering thoughts and watched as his father interrogated the lass. Bram was even beginning to believe she might be telling the truth until she made the outrageous statement about her skill with a knife.

Now he had returned with the sharpening stone and stood with his father and Ian watching her handle his dirk with skill, throwing it repeatedly into the same spot.

Ian broke the silence between them. "What do ye think, Da? Could she be telling the truth?"

Their father shook his head. "It's not an easy story to believe."

Bram nodded in agreement. "But she didn't back down or make excuses. She gave forthright responses and admitted when she didn't know the answer."

"Aye, but both of ye are too young to remember Tristan. He was a strong, skilled warrior. The idea of him hiding from his wife's father, like a scared rabbit, is ludicrous."

"But Da, what does she stand to gain by the lie?" asked Ian.

"A home with an old woman who desperately wants the story to be true," answered their father.

"Aye, but where is the harm in it? Her appearance has brought Innes only joy."

"Ye have a point," Bram agreed. "After all, Innes has nothing for her to inherit and by all accounts the lass seems willing to work and earn her keep."

"The harm is that we know nothing about her. What if she is a whore who grasped onto a story she heard in an effort to improve her station? What if she has run away from a husband? Would I want her marrying one of my clansmen if these possibilities were true? Worse, what if she is a spy for one of our enemies? I don't know if she can be trusted. Besides, if this is all a lie, a temporary convenience, and she leaves as suddenly as she appeared, Innes will be devastated."

Bram nodded. "And if she doesn't leave, her past could surface at any time, creating a terrible problem for us." He didn't want to believe that the lass was a whore, or a spy, or even a runaway wife but he understood his father's caution.

Grace seemed to have become comfortable with his knife because she walked across the bailey towards them. Before she could say anything, Bram gave a little bow, presenting her with the stone as if it were a thing of great value. "The stone ye requested, Mistress Breive."

She accepted the stone, ignoring his mocking tone. "Thank ye."

She spied the water trough outside of the stables and walked to it. Wetting the stone and blade, she carefully honed it. Periodically she laid the stone down, and balanced the knife by its point on the middle finger of her left hand.

"By all the saints, what is she doing?" asked Ian.

Their father smiled for the first time since Innes left with the babe. "She is testing the sharpness of the point of the blade. She will try to balance the blade on her finger until the point is so sharp the weight of the dirk will be enough to puncture the skin."

They watched her work the blade for a few more minutes, until she tried to balance it and pulled her hand back. She caught the knife with her other hand even as she sucked the blood from her finger.

"I've never seen anyone do that," said Ian.

"Nor I," agreed Bram.

"Well I have. Be careful when she gives it back to ye, Son. I'll warrant it has never been that sharp before. Tristan Murray sharpened blades like that and I guess I have my answer. Whether she can pierce the neep or not, she is Tristan's daughter."

Bram was surprised by the relief he felt that she hadn't been lying to them. "Then we are done here, Da?"

His father grinned at him. "Nay, I want to see if she is as

good as her Da."

She cleaned the stone and blade before walking toward them resolutely. "I'm ready, Laird." Her tone was serious but she appeared focused, not fearful.

His father looked at her for a moment before saying anything. Bram scowled. It was a way his da had of intimidating people but they hardly needed to intimidate her more.

His da's manner was gruff and his tone disapproving when he finally said, "Well, it's about time. Yer only throwing at a neep, lass. Ye could split a fly's hair at twenty paces with that knife now." Anyone who knew Laird Sutherland would have recognized that as a complement.

Grace Breive simply straightened her back, looked him directly in the eye, and said, "My Da always said, there is no such thing as good enough."

His father frowned, clearly trying to suppress a grin, but Bram and Ian chuckled. At Grace's confused look, Ian explained, "Oddly enough, our da says the same thing."

Their father dismissed the comment with a wave of his hand. "Enough of this. The dirk is good and sharp now, so let's get on with it. Ian, on my count throw the neep in a high arc."

"Aye, Da."

"Three, two, one, throw."

Grace instantly focused on the vegetable hurtling skyward, letting the knife fly seconds later.

Thud. The knife hit the neep, causing it to veer off its trajectory and drop to the ground.

Ian whooped, "Ye did it!"

Grace walked calmly to pick up the knife and neep before returning to face his father. Bram expected to see triumph or pride written there or even the determined look she wore as she prepared the knife, but he didn't. She appeared just as tense and anxious as she had when she first stood before them in the hall.

Again, his father kept his serious demeanor for moment, staring her down. Finally, he gave her an approving smile. "Well done, Grace. I was convinced ye were Tristan's daughter when I saw how ye prepared that knife. He is the only man I have ever known to do that balancing trick to test the sharpness. Ye are welcome to live here with yer grandmother. Ye are one of us."

Clearly relieved, her shoulders sagged. "Thank ye, Laird," she said softly. Was that a tremor in her voice? "Am I excused then?"

"Aye, lass, ye can go."

She curtsied, saying, "Good day, Laird," before taking her leave of them.

They watched her go for a moment. "She is rather pretty," observed Ian.

For some reason, that annoyed Bram.

"Aye, she is," agreed their father. "There will be any number of men who will happily marry that young widow. Cam would make her a fine husband."

This annoyed Bram too. "Da, it hasn't been that long since she lost her husband and parents. Give her time to adjust before ye have her married off."

"Aye, of course I will. Besides, we need to find a bride for ye. Come with me to my solar and we can discuss our options."

That was the last thing Bram wanted to do. He scrambled to find an excuse to postpone another bride discussion, "Ah…Da, I'll be along in a while. I just realized Grace kept my dirk. Anyway, ye haven't picked a wife for Ian yet, discuss it with him." Before his father could argue, Bram followed in the direction Grace had gone.

He had barely rounded the corner, heading toward the kitchen, when he saw her. She had stopped, head down, one hand covering her face, the other clutching his dirk, still stuck in the neep. She was trembling. Was she crying? He approached her, touching her shoulder. "Grace, lass, what's wrong?"

Startled, she spun around to face him. "Nothing. I'm fine."

By the angels, she had just performed a feat that no man he knew could do and instead of feeling elation, she was crying. She dashed at the tears on her cheeks even as she denied being upset. Something compelled him to touch her. He reached out and cupped her cheek in one hand, lifting gently so he could see into her lovely green eyes. "Please don't cry. Is there something I can do?" He brushed a tear away before letting his hand drop.

She shook her head. "Nay. Really, I'm fine. It's just—just—I was afraid. I love my grandmother. She is all Kristen and I have left."

"Yer grandmother is important to us as well. We didn't want to see her hurt again."

She nodded. "Last night, I admired how protective ye were of her. It's just that I never imagined anyone would think I was trying take advantage of her. My parents' choice has caused her so much pain."

"Aye, it has. My father knew yer da and respected him. I think that is why it was so hard for him to believe the story."

"Please understand, sir—"

"Call me Bram."

"Bram. Please understand…they believed they were doing the right thing. I loved my husband. We were very happy. But my parents, their love was beyond description. My father adored my mother and she was devoted to him. They lived for each other. My mother lost her will to live when Da died."

"Yer husband died too. Ye went on."

"I had to, for Kristen's sake. I couldn't lose myself in grief. That life is over. If I try to dwell there…well I just can't. I try not to think about how much I miss them. But just now, when I had to prove to ye that I was their daughter by doing something I spent much of my life learning from my da…feeling the balance of the knife, honing the point and edge, taking aim…the memories were so strong. I was just overwhelmed for a moment."

What an eejit he was. He had seen it as only a test of skill, one any man might play at and wager on. Grace wasn't a man, and it hadn't been a few pennies at stake. Her future had rested on the contest. Furthermore, he hadn't even remotely considered the memories it might conjure, reminding her of all she had lost. "I'm sorry, Grace." It was very little, but he didn't know what else to say.

~ * ~

The man standing in front of her confused her. He had been determined to ensure that Innes wasn't hurt but he had hurt Grace with his mocking attitude. Her encounter with Laird Sutherland and his sons had done nothing to improve her opinion of powerful men. However, Bram had followed her and showed her concern.

He had wiped a tear from her cheek.

How long had it been since anyone had done that? When Da and Callum died, it was all she could do to handle her mother's grief. There had been no one to comfort Grace.

Now he offered her an apology. But instead of leaving well enough alone, she couldn't stop herself from asking, "What are ye sorry for?"

Bram cocked his head, clearly surprised by her question.

"What?"

"Ye said ye were sorry. What are ye sorry for? Are ye sorry for thinking I was a liar? Are ye sorry for doubting me when I said I could do this?" She waved the somewhat ridiculous looking knife with the neep stuck on the end. "Or are ye sorry I'm crying because I miss my da?"

He appeared to be at a loss for a few moments. Finally, he answered. "I'm sorry for all of those things. I can see we hurt ye today. I swear it was for the right reason, but still, I'm sorry. I wish we had shown ye a bit more consideration."

"I'm sorry too."

"What are ye sorry for?"

"I'm sorry my parents' choice hurt the people they left behind. I swear it was for the right reason, but still, I'm sorry." She echoed his words.

"Grace Breive, like Da said, ye are a bold one, but ye make a fair point."

Grace was frankly stunned that she had said those things. She felt heat rising in her face and looked down for a moment. "I'm usually rather nice. I think ye bring out the worst in me."

"I wouldn't say that."

She gave him a rueful look. "Well, I have never stolen anything before and I walked off with yer dirk. I'm sorry." She pulled the neep off and held the knife out to him.

His eyes twinkled. "I'm not."

She wasn't sure what that meant, but she decided she had already been far too forthright. She looked down at the vegetable in her hand. "I think my grandmother needs to serve roasted neeps at dinner."

Bram laughed appreciatively. "I think so too. In fact, I'm going to walk ye to the kitchen and ask her myself."

Grace was appalled. "I didn't mean that. It was only a jest."

"And a good one. Da will see the humor in it…but if he doesn't, it was my idea. Maybe I'll ask her to stick a knife in one."

Grace shook her head. "Oh, please, for the love of all that's holy, don't do that."

He took her elbow and started pulling her with him as he walked toward the kitchens. "I can just imagine the look on his face now."

"Nay, Bram. Ye can't do that."

He laughed again. "Has anyone ever told ye ye're bossy?"

"I said ye bring out the worst in me, but please don't do this."

"Fine, no knife. But we will have roasted neeps."

Just as he promised, when they reached the kitchen, Bram asked Innes to serve roasted neeps at dinner. When he explained why, Innes, Maisie, and the other women working in the kitchens laughed heartily and complemented Grace on her skill.

Before he had taken his leave, Lady Sutherland arrived. Clearly she was surprised to find her eldest son there. "Bram, what on earth are ye doing here?"

"I escorted Mistress Breive back after her meeting with Da because I wanted to make a special request for dinner."

Lady Sutherland arched an eyebrow at him. "Since when have ye cared what was served for dinner, as long as there was enough of it?" The women all chuckled.

"I just had a sudden desire for roasted neeps."

Lady Sutherland's musical laughter filled the kitchen. "Yer father told me what happened. It serves him right. In fact, I think I'll serve him one on the end of my knife."

Grinning at Grace, Bram said, "I think that is an excellent idea, Mother."

Grace buried her face in her hands.

Lady Sutherland laughed again. "Come with me now, Son, and leave Innes and her staff to their work."

The day before Pentecost was a day of fasting, so only the evening meal would be served. Still, there was a flurry of activity as the women prepared for the feast of Pentecost. Hours later, when the kitchen had been put to rights during the afternoon lull, Innes sat dozing by the hearth in her cottage, as Kristen napped on a pallet in the tiny bedroom.

Grace had obtained some new wool and had skirted and washed it in Durness while staying with Dugald. She had prepared it to the point it could be carded and wound on her distaff for spinning. She would take this opportunity to further work the wool. She opened the chest her grandmother had given her for storing her belongings in order to return the brooch and letter back into the box for safe keeping and to get her cards and distaff.

The creak of the lid caused Innes to stir from her sleep. "Ah, Grace, lass, I'm sorry. I didn't intend to nap."

"Ye have earned a wee rest grandmother, I didn't intend to

wake ye. I was just putting the letter and brooch away. I thought I'd spin this afternoon."

"That reminds me. I was surprised that the laird wasn't convinced of who ye were by the letter."

"Grandmother, I didn't show him the letter."

"By the saints, lass, why not? Ye wouldn't have had to prove anything more if he had read that."

Grace sighed. "I was afraid."

"Why, pet? He would have believed ye fully then. I told ye, Laird Sutherland is fair."

"I know ye did, but that letter reveals that my mother was a noblewoman, the daughter of a clan chief."

"What harm would there be in that?"

"What if he insisted on trying to find out who she was?"

Her grandmother shook her head. "I think he would have respected yer wishes."

"Do ye? Are ye absolutely sure? When my mother told me about her da—well I have never seen that kind of fear in her eyes. I can only believe that her fears were well grounded. She was terrified that her father might visit his revenge on me or use me as a commodity. I wasn't sure what she meant, but now that I know she was the daughter of a Laird, I can only assume she feared he would force me into a political marriage." Grace looked down for a moment before continuing. "Grandmother, I know what men with power can do. On Lewis…Laird Morrison's son…well, he is ruthless and has a reputation for cruelty. So while ye trust Laird Sutherland, I still worry about powerful men. Perhaps it is best if the past remains in the past where my parents left it. What if I am discovered and my mother's father forces me into a marriage? I was not raised as a noblewoman. My child is the daughter of a fisherman. What if my husband wouldn't allow Kristen in his home?"

The color drained from her grandmother's face. "I hadn't thought of that."

"Grandmother, I wish I were braver. I wish I could find mother's father and tell him how many lives were ruined by his actions. But I can't risk it and I promised mama I wouldn't."

"Aye, lass, I understand now. We will keep the contents of the letter secret."

~*~

At the evening meal, Bram's father took the roasted neeps

with good humor. When his mother waved one on her knife under Eanraig's nose, his father laughed, saying, "Rodina, I would be the tiniest bit more impressed by yer skill with a knife if that neep hadn't been lying perfectly still on yer trencher when ye pierced it."

Bram found himself glancing around the hall, wishing to see Grace among the serving maids. He knew she wouldn't be, she had a bairn to mind, but that didn't stop him from hoping.

Perhaps no one else noticed, but his sharp-eyed mother missed very little. "Bram, lad, what has ye so preoccupied?"

Bram flashed her a smile. "Nothing, Mother."

"Ye don't lie well, lad."

He laughed. "Fair point. I guess I was just thinking back over the events of the last few days."

She touched his hand. "I am sorry about yer betrothed."

It was Innes' auburn-haired granddaughter who occupied his thoughts, not Fiona, but he didn't correct her. "There is nothing to be sorry for. We weren't meant for each other. It's not as if I had had the chance to grow fond of her. I didn't know her."

"Nay, ye didn't know her but I know ye. For certain ye wouldn't admit this, but while ye might not have grown fond of her yet, ye had begun to grow fond of the idea of marriage."

Bram laughed but he didn't deny her words. He couldn't.

"Well, my braw young lad, ye said it yerself, ye evidently weren't meant for each other. Fate has something else in store. So the lass who is meant for ye is still out there. Ye just have to get busy and find her."

"Ye sound like Da now."

It was her turn to laugh. "I suppose I do, but it's true and ye'll get no closer to finding her if ye keep evading yer da when he wants to discuss the matter."

His mother was right. Considering his desire to marry, he wasn't sure what he was avoiding. The image of Grace, focused and determined just before she let his knife fly, flashed in his mind. He smiled.

"So ye agree, lad?"

"With what?"

"Bram, where is yer mind tonight? Do ye agree that ye need to discuss potential betrothals with yer da?"

"Oh. Aye, Mother. Perhaps I'll discuss it with him tomorrow."

Chapter 6

Bram didn't discuss the issue of his betrothal with his father the next day. It was Pentecost, one of the three most important holy days of the year, celebrating God's gift of the Holy Spirit to the Apostles.

That morning, the church had been decorated with pink and red flowers, as symbols of the Holy Spirit. A carved wooden dove was attached to a thin cord, looped over a rafter. Before mass, the cord was pulled until the wooden dove rested just under the rafters. During Mass, when the sequence hymn, Veni Creator Spiritus was sung before the gospel, a boy was given the task of lowering the dove.

This was usually a beautifully symbolic representation of the descent of the Holy Spirit, but occasionally the boy chosen would make a wee mistake. The dove might descend at the wrong time, or much too quickly. Bram looked up at it before Mass began and grinned. "I remember the year ye were chosen to lower the dove," he whispered to Ian.

"I'm not sure anyone will ever forget that," Ian said. "It wasn't my fault. The cord was stuck and the dove wouldn't move."

"Aye, so ye gave it an almighty yank, and it flew…right over the top of the rafter. It came crashing down on the altar, barely missing the priest's head. Da took a switch to ye for that."

"And he took a switch to ye for laughing so hard that ye fell off yer seat."

"It was worth it. To this day it is one of the funniest things I've ever seen in Mass."

Ian grinned conspiratorially. "I tried to talk Boyd into making it fly when it was his turn. I told him to pull it up and down a few times to really get it swinging."

"That must have been after I had left to train."

"Aye, but it didn't work. Boyd asked Da how hard he needed to pull the dove to get it to fly."

"And Da took a switch to ye again, when he found out

who gave Boyd the idea."

"Aye. No sense of fun, our brother."

"Wheesht," their mother hissed.

The dove came down during this Pentecost Mass, without a hitch. As with other great feasts of the Church, the solemn Mass was only the start. There would be games in the village square, as well as a huge feast later in the day followed by music and dancing lasting into the night. In fact, Pentecost was celebrated with games and other festivities for an entire week.

As he left Mass, Grace Breive's auburn curls caught his eye. Kristen walked beside her, holding her hand. He quickened his pace until he reached her side. "Good morning, Grace, Kristen."

"Good morning, sir," Grace answered.

"I've asked ye to call me Bram."

"I have a wed wibbon," declared Kristen, waving the red ribbon she held.

"Aye, and that red ribbon was supposed to be for yer hair, miss," Grace chided good naturedly.

"I can't see it when it's in my haiw," said Kristen.

"Well, she has a point," said Bram, winking at Grace. "What good is a ribbon if ye can't see it?"

Grace smiled. "Don't encourage her."

He believed this was the first smile she had given him. It lit her face, making him want to see much more of it. "Will I see ye later at the feast?"

"I doubt it. I'll be helping Grandmother in the kitchen. There's so much to do."

"Grace, ye really must take some time to enjoy the festivities. If ye can't get away for the feast, at least come for the music and dancing later."

"Thank ye, but nay. I suspect it might be a bit overwhelming for my wee lass."

"Nonsense. There will be lots of children there. Surely ye have memories of great feasts from when ye were small?"

"Nay. Our village was a fair distance from the keep—too far really to attend feasts and the like."

"Ye've never been to a proper feast?"

"I wouldn't say that. We had village celebrations."

"'Tisn't the same thing at all. Ye must come." Bram wasn't precisely sure why this had become so important to him, but he wanted her there. He wanted to see her laughing and smiling. He wanted to dance with her. "It's a holiday, don't say me nay," he cajoled.

"I fear I must. We may go down to the village to watch some of the games for a while later. Now, I really must get to the kitchen to help Grandmother. Good day, Sir Bram." She curtsied, picked Kristen up, and hurried off.

Kristen waved her ribbon over her mother's shoulder, calling, "Good day, Sir Bwam."

As he watched her retreat, he felt a keen sense of disappointment.

~ * ~

Grace's stomach had fluttered when Bram approached her after Mass. She was beginning to like his warmth and friendliness. And while his idea of serving the laird roasted neeps the previous evening had embarrassed her at the time, she had to admit that it was very funny. His ability to make her laugh was as attractive to her as his golden good looks.

The thought of attending a feast with music and dancing had tempted her, but her better judgement intervened. It wasn't that she shouldn't attend. Her friends and even the priest who served their clan had advised her to remarry as soon as possible. Ye are very young and ye have a bairn to consider. Ye need to marry again, ye need the protection of a husband. They had been right. If she had married a young man from their village, Fearchar Morrison would not have been a threat.

Avoiding that kind of celebration had been more an act of self-preservation. Her losses in the last year had nearly overwhelmed her. If she never gave her heart to anyone, she would never again feel that kind of agony. She had built a fortress, walling out everyone but Kristen, and now Innes, to avoid that kind of pain.

Developing an attraction for the laird's son was even more foolish. Absolutely nothing could come of it but heartache. Better to stay well out of his path.

As she hurried through the inner bailey to the kitchen, two of the young women, Peggy and Moyra, who worked in the kitchen and served in the great hall, caught up with her.

Peggy was short, well curved, and had a riot of light brown curls, which regularly escaped the braid that tried to tame them. Moyra was taller, reed thin, and had straight blond hair. Both were vivacious and talkative. When they teamed up, it could set Grace's head spinning.

"Did I hear ye correctly just now?" demanded Peggy.

"I didn't say anything," said Grace.

Kristen waved her ribbon at them. "I have a wed wibbon."

"Aye, pet, I see," said Peggy.

"She doesn't mean just now, she meant just now a few minutes ago when ye were talking to the laird's son," said Moyra.

"Oh," said Grace.

"Well?" asked Peggy.

"Well, what?" asked Grace.

Moyra harrumphed. "Well, did we hear ye right? Did ye just say nay to the young laird when he asked ye to come to the feast?"

Grace nodded. "Aye."

"Are ye daft?" both women said in unison.

Grace feared they might make her daft, but she wasn't quite there yet. "Nay. There is too much to do and I have Kristen."

"Ye are daft," said Moyra.

"Aye. If Bram Sutherland made a point of asking me to anything, I'd be there," said Peggy.

"Aren't ye afraid ye'll make him angry?" asked Moyra.

Grace stopped, suddenly concerned. "Does he have a bad temper?"

Peggy shook her head. "Nay. But if ye didn't know that before ye said 'nay', maybe ye shouldn't have said it."

Grace started walking again. "The two of ye are the daft ones. I wasn't ordered to go to the feast, he just asked if he would see me there and he won't so I said nay."

Moyra said, "There will be lots of single men there. Ye will never find another husband this way."

"I'm not looking for another husband."

"That makes it very hard to find one then," said Peggy. "Ye really should start looking."

Grace just laughed. They were hopeless.

~ * ~

By midday, when things were well underway in the kitchen, Innes chivvied Grace out for a while. "Take Kristen down to the village and join in the fun."

Men were playing shinty just beyond the village. She didn't know much about the game but generally it wasn't a good game unless there were a few black eyes and bloody noses. From a distance she saw some of both so she figured it must be going well. She decided to avoid the mayhem, so she walked with Kristen to the village green.

They stopped to watch some people playing quoits, tossing flat metal rings at iron spikes in the ground. A young man with hair so black it was nearly blue was tossing the quoits, ringing the iron spike with every throw. When his turn was finished he handed off the quoits and walked toward Grace. "Ye must be Innes' granddaughter. Grace, isn't it?"

"Aye, and this is my daughter, Kristen."

"I'm Michael MacBain. I'm a guardsman."

"I'm pleased to meet ye, Michael."

"Ye can't possibly be as pleased as I am," he said, taking her hand and bowing low over it. "Tell me, are the rumors true?"

Grace's brow furrowed. "What rumors?"

"That ye plucked a flying neep from the sky with a wee flick of yer knife."

Grace felt the heat rise in her cheeks. "Oh, that. Aye, I did that."

"A lass with that kind of aim must surely be good at quoits. Care to try yer hand?"

Grace had played quoits before and she was quite good at it. "I won't today, but thank ye."

"Are ye sure? Ye might have a bit of fun."

"I'm sure."

"Michael, leave the lass be and come finish the game," one of his friends called.

"Well, if yer sure then. But save a dance for me tonight." Michael went back to his friends before she could tell him she wouldn't be at the feast.

"Mama, I want to pway peevers," Kristen squealed when she saw a group of children playing the hopping game on a course scratched into the dirt.

Grace played this game with Kristen, but with very lax rules. "We'll go watch."

As they drew nearer, Grace noticed several women chatting to one side as the children played. They were perhaps a little older than Grace and she assumed they were the mothers of some of the children.

"Can I pway wif them?" Kristen asked.

"They look very good at this. Maybe today we should just watch."

"She can play," said a slender lass with dark hair who looked to be about eight. "We let my baby sister play." The lass leaned in and whispered loudly, "We don't count their mistakes. It's just for fun."

"Thank ye, lass, that's kind of ye. Her name is Kristen."

"Mine's Teasag," the lass said, taking Kristen's hand and walking her to one of the courses.

"And my name's Una," said one of the women with a grin. "Teasag is my daughter and it's a good thing they don't count mistakes because they practically have to redraw the course when my little one is through."

"I'm Grace. Very nice to meet ye."

"Yer Innes' Grace? I'm Senga and this is my sister, Nell. My older sister Nell."

"Aye, I'm Inne's granddaughter. It's a pleasure to meet ye."

The third woman smiled warmly. "Aye, I'm her older sister—by a few minutes. We're twins. She loves telling folks that."

Grace enjoyed chatting with the women. Not surprisingly, the story about Grace's arrival and why her parents had fled to Lewis had apparently made the rounds but the knife throwing incident seemed to capture even more attention. She enjoyed the light banter and they made her feel very welcome.

After a while, Teasag came over and tugged at her mother's hand. "Mama, ye said ye would play with us."

Una grinned at Grace. "Have ye ever played peevers with a burden?"

Grace laughed. "Aye, I have."

"Then ladies, choose yer burdens," said Una as she scooped up a giggling lass of about two. Nell and Senga also picked up small children who squealed with glee.

To the absolute delight of the older children, the women took turns hopping the course for roughly half an hour, each with a child on her back. Nearly through with one turn, Grace stood balanced on one foot with Kristen clinging to her back. She had leaned forward to pick up her stone when she lost her balance. She toppled forward, catching herself with her hands, but having failed that round, rolled to one side, landing on her arse to the vast amusement of everyone present.

Kristen chortled with an abandon Grace hadn't heard in months. She pulled the child into her lap, planting kisses on her face, causing Kristen to laugh harder.

The laughter from the onlookers quieted rather suddenly when Una said, "Good afternoon, sir."

"Don't let me interrupt ye ladies," a smooth masculine voice said.

Grace looked up into the mirth-filled eyes of Bram Sutherland. "Mistress Breive, allow me to help ye up."

Mother of God. Grace felt the color rise in her face. What a sight she must be sitting in the dirt with her skirt twisted around her legs. She looked more like a ragamuffin than a responsible, grown woman with a child. Sighing, she accepted the hand he offered, letting him pull her to her feet.

"Are ye enjoying yerself?" Bram asked, his impossibly blue eyes twinkling with delight.

She brushed the dirt from her clothes to focus her attention on anything but his eyes. "Aye, thank ye, sir."

"Mama, can we go again?"

"Nay, Kristen, I think it's Nell's turn now and we should be going. I promised Grandmother we wouldn't be too long." Turning to the women, Grace said, "good day. It was lovely to meet ye all."

"We will see ye later at the feast then?" asked Nell?

Bram arched an eyebrow at her.

"Uh…nay, I'll be helping my grandmother in the kitchen."

"But it is yer first feast day here," said Una. "Ye can't spend the whole night in the kitchen."

"That is exactly what I told her," said Bram.

"Aye—well Kristen…" Grace shrugged. "Thank ye again for letting us join in." She curtsied to Bram. "Good afternoon, Sir Bram."

Kristen mimicked her curtsy. "Good affernoon, Sir Bwam."

"I was walking back to the keep anyway. I'll go with ye."

The other women all grinned.

"Thank ye, but it isn't necessary."

"It's no trouble at all."

If anything, Grace's blush grew deeper and the grins on the other women's faces grew wider.

Chapter 7

Bram told himself that he hadn't been strolling through the village merriment in search of Grace, but when he found her, he knew it was a lie. Seeing her laughing and enjoying herself in the midst of a group of woman and children playing peevers took his breath away. When she fell and just sat in the dirt laughing and kissing her daughter, he couldn't imagine a more beautiful sight. A woman who knew deep sorrow and yet could still relish the joy of life was surely a treasure.

Now she walked beside him, silently. While he missed the liveliness she displayed moments ago, her sudden shyness and warm pink blush was equally as appealing.

"So, ye met a few of the village women?" he asked.

She nodded. "Aye."

"We pwayed peevers," said Kristen.

"I saw ye playing. It looked like ye were enjoying it."

"Aye." Kristen nodded exuberantly then giggled. "It was funny when mama feww down."

Bram chuckled. "Did yer mama think it was funny?"

Kristen nodded again. "Aye. She waffed a wot. Didn't ye mama?"

Although still blushing hotly, a smile flirted on Grace's lips. "Aye, sweetling, I did."

"Do ye like it when yer mama laughs, Kristen?"

The wee lass grinned. "I wike it a wot."

He leaned down conspiratorially, "I do too."

Grace gave a little laugh, glancing sideways at him. "Are ye trying to make me perish with embarrassment?"

"Nay. I'm just trying to coax that smile back."

She looked down shyly, but couldn't suppress a wee smile.

With her guard down a little, perhaps he could talk her into at least coming to the hall for the music and dancing after the feast. "The women were right, ye know."

"About what?" she asked.

"It is yer first feast day here and I don't want ye to spend the whole night in the kitchen."

She shook her head and opened her mouth, poised to speak, but he put up his hand to stop her. "Don't say me nay again. At least say ye'll consider it."

After a few moments she said, "I'll consider it."

"Thank ye."

~ * ~

The feast was sumptuous and while Bram ate his fill, he wasn't happy that Grace had helped prepare it but didn't take part in it. He anxiously waited for the food and trestle tables to be cleared away so the dancing could start. He kept watching the doors to the great hall, not wanting to miss Grace when she arrived.

Ian, who had been dancing with one partner after another all evening, approached with two tankards of ale. He sat beside Bram, shoving one tankard into his hand. "Who are ye waiting for?"

"I'm not waiting for anyone," said Bram irritably. He took a long pull of ale, avoiding his brother's eyes.

"Nay? It sure looks like ye are waiting for someone. Ye've kept yer eyes on the doors all evening."

"Well, I'm not waiting for anyone."

Ian shrugged. "Suit yerself."

Bram took another drink, trying to ignore his over-observant brother.

After a few moments, Ian said, "I know ye aren't waiting for anyone, but ye do know that there are musicians and dancers outside? Maybe the person ye aren't waiting for is there."

Damn. Ian was right. Bram hadn't even thought about that. When they had great feasts, there wasn't enough room in the hall for all of the clan members who attended. There was always food and drink set up on tables outside and after the meal there was music and dancing there as well. Maybe Grace was there. Bram drained his tankard, stood, and began winding his way through the revelers in the hall.

"Ye're welcome," called Ian.

Once outside, Bram stood on the top of the steps, looking over the crowd. Every flash of coppery hair caught his eye, but none of it belonged to the woman he sought. He wandered through the crowd, nodding as people called greetings to him, but avoiding being pulled into conversations. After searching for what felt like ages, he resigned himself to the fact that Grace had stayed in the kitchen all evening, despite his request.

That was it. If she wasn't at the party, maybe she was in the kitchen. Again, he worked his way out of the throng of people and around to the back of the castle. He stopped in the open doorway. She had her back to him, sweeping the last bit of dirt into the hearth.

"Are ye still considering whether to join in the festivities?" he asked.

She spun around. "Oh. I—I—ye startled me."

"I'm sorry. I was hoping I could convince ye to come enjoy what's left of the celebration."

She met his gaze. The vulnerability he saw there for a moment shook him to his core.

She sucked in a quick breath and looked away. "I told my grandmother I would finish tidying the kitchen for her."

He glanced around. "It looks like ye have." He crossed the room, took the broom from her, and stood it in the corner where Innes kept it. He turned back to her and held out his hand. "Come with me."

Her hand flew nervously to her throat. "But Kristen—"

"Is evidently tucked in bed and safe with Innes."

At her continued hesitation, he said, "Grace, please. Are ye always this stubborn?"

Her brow furrowed and she gave a small shrug. "I've already told ye, ye bring out the worst in me."

There it was again, that glimpse of vulnerability that he didn't understand. It stirred a distinct desire to protect her from whatever caused her distress. "If ye don't want to join the revelers, I will walk ye home. But I would very much like for ye to return to the party with me."

~ * ~

Grace stared at the beautiful man who held his hand out to her, enticing her to go with him. Why was she resisting this so diligently anyway? He was just being kind to her, perhaps to make amends for the way they had doubted her the day before. What harm was there in accepting his kindness and enjoying the festivities?

"I'll go for a little while."

The smile that spread across his face was heart-stopping. "Good."

She turned away for a moment to snuff the candles before walking past him to the door. He followed, taking her elbow and guiding her to the front of the keep.

Grace had never seen anything like it. It looked as if everyone in the village had attended from the very young to the very old. The front courtyard was filled with people, the very center of it left a bit more open to give the dancers room. Una was dancing with a fierce looking warrior who must be her husband. Senga and Nell were there too, families in tow. The doors to the great hall were open and it too was teeming. Peggy waved merrily at her from across the courtyard.

The atmosphere was more festive than anything she had ever experienced in her little village but perhaps the best part was the music. Melodies from flute, lute, and recorder all intertwined and were carried forward on the driving beat of a hand-held drum, stirring the feet of the people dancing. She was simply enthralled.

She felt Bram tug at her elbow. "Shall we go into the hall?"

"Oh, but this is wonderful," she said. "Can we just stay here?"

He grinned. "Anything ye wish, Grace." As one song ended, he asked, "would ye like to dance the next one?"

"Aye, I would," she answered.

He took her hand and together they joined the dancers. The music started again, and Grace lost herself in it. She loved dancing but it had been ages. The familiar patterns and steps came back to her as easily as breathing. Callum hadn't enjoy dancing as much as Grace. He had humored her and tried a couple of times but she knew he didn't like it, so she never pushed.

Bram, on the other hand, performed the dances with skill, just as her father had and seemed to enjoy it as much as she did. After they had danced five or six dances and she was quite out of breath, he led her off the dance floor. "Ye should rest a bit. Wait for me here and I'll get us some ale."

"I can get our drinks," said Grace, feeling slightly embarrassed at the thought of the laird's son fetching her a drink.

"Nay, lass, ye've worked all evening, allow me."

"But ye shouldn't—"

He put a finger on her lips and grinned. "Grace, don't

argue."

She smiled at him. "Fine. I'll wait here for ye."

She turned back to watch the dancers as Bram walked away. In a few minutes she felt a hand at her elbow. She turned, expecting to see Bram, but it wasn't him. It was the dark-haired man named Michael she had met earlier on the village green. "Oh…hello."

"Good evening, Grace." His smile was warm and friendly but it didn't have quite the same effect on her as Bram's. "I've looked for ye all evening. I had finally despaired of ever finding ye."

"I—I—was working in the kitchen most of the evening."

"Ye seem to be enjoying the music."

"Oh, aye, I am."

"Would ye care to dance with me?"

"Well, I've just—"

"Good evening, Michael," said Bram from behind him. There was a definite chill in his voice.

Michael either didn't recognize it, or chose to ignore it. "Bram, aye, 'tis a good evening. Better now that I have finally found this beautiful lass." Turning his attention back to Grace he said, "so, Grace, will ye dance with me?"

"Nay, she won't," said Bram. At Michael's questioning look, Bram added. "She's been dancing and needs some refreshment." He handed her a tankard. "Here's yer ale, Grace."

"Ah, well, perhaps later." Michael gave her a small bow and moved away.

Bram frowned. "Do ye know him?"

"Not really. He was playing quoits on the village green today and introduced himself." At his continued scowl Grace asked, "is there something wrong?"

"Nay."

"Are ye angry with him for some reason?"

"Nay. Michael MacBain is a good warrior—a good man."

"Oh."

Grace wasn't sure where that spark of surliness came from but it disappeared just as quickly. They drank their ale and chatted about nothing in particular. When she finished her tankard he pulled her into the center of the courtyard for several more dances. Finally, exhausted she said, "I really should be going now. It's late, I'm tired, and Grandmother will be worried."

"Well, if ye must go, I'll walk with ye."

"Thank ye, but it isn't necessary."

"Have I already mentioned tonight how stubborn ye are, Grace Breive?"

She laughed. "Fine, walk me home."

When they had left the inner bailey, leaving much of the noise of the crowd behind them, Bram asked, "Did ye enjoy yerself?"

"Aye, I did. Thank ye."

"I don't think I have ever enjoyed dancing quite so much."

They had reached Innes' cottage. She stopped in front of the door and smiled up at him. "I'm sure I haven't."

He looked at her intently. "Well then, we will have to do it again."

"I'd like that." It had truly been a wonderful evening.

"Good. Then ye'll give me no argument about attending the feast on St. John's Eve in three weeks."

"What?"

"Ye heard me." He grinned. "No argument." He reached behind her, and lifted the latch as he had the night she met him. "Good night, Grace."

Chapter 8

Bram continued to avoid his father and all talks of betrothals for the next few days. The week after Pentecost was a holiday week and the weather for the first few days was particularly fine. That made it easy enough to stay out of his way.

However, Bram was equally as intent on seeing more of Grace. He found reasons to walk past the kitchens and Innes' small cottage, hoping to see the lass who captivated him. He saw her occasionally but didn't have the opportunity to exchange more than a few words each time. And while he was certain she had enjoyed the time they spent together on Pentecost, once again, she was polite and guarded when he saw her in passing. Perhaps it was because other people were around. One evening he did hear her singing lullabies to Kristen. He waited outside, hoping she would come out for a bit of air. Sadly, she didn't.

Then by midweek the weather changed and they were lashed with cold rain for several days. He didn't see her at all then. On Friday afternoon the rain slowed to a drizzle. Intending to exercise Goliath, Bram walked to the stables. As he entered, a woman's voice and child's laughter floated from the hayloft. He knew instantly whose voices he heard.

He climbed the ladder, following the enchanting sound. Grace and Kristen sat in the hay with their backs to him. Close to them was a mother cat with a litter of kittens squirming and playing next to her.

"I wanna hold one," said Kristen.

"Sweetling, they are very little and fragile. We don't want to hurt or scare them. What matters most, Kristen?"

"Kindness," the wee lass answered.

"That's right. And being very careful is the way to be kind to a kitten. So, come here and sit in my lap. We'll hold one together until I'm sure ye know how."

Kristen squealed and scooted into Grace's lap. "Wheesht, Kristen. Ye don't want to make so much noise ye scare them either."

When Kristen was settled in her lap, Grace said, "Now, make a bowl of yer hands, like this." The lass cupped her hands as her mother had shown her. Grace stroked the mother cat's head. "Ye don't mind if we give one of yer babes a cuddle, do ye?" Gently she lifted a tiny grey kitten in one hand. Putting her other hand under Kristen's little ones, she placed the kitten in her daughter's cupped hand, keeping her own hand in position next to the kitten protectively. The little tableau was beautiful.

"What's her name?" Kristen asked.

"I don't suppose she has a name yet."

Kristen leaned her head down, rubbing her cheek against the kitten. "She's soft."

"Aye, pet, she is."

"Can we take her to show gwanny?"

"Not today. She is too little to leave her mama."

"What's her mama's name?"

"I don't know. Robert told me where to find her, but he didn't mention her name."

Robert was the stable master and it explained how Grace came to be there. Bram cleared his throat, causing her to start and look over her shoulder for the source of the sound. "Whisky."

"What?" asked Grace. Kristen too twisted to look at him. "Careful, Kristen, ye're still holding the kitten."

Bram smiled. "The mother cat, Robert calls her Whisky." He climbed the rest of the way into the loft and crouched down beside them. With one finger he rubbed the tiny kitten's head. "If ye could name a kitten, Kristen, what name would ye give it?"

Kristen's brow furrowed, causing him to smile. She clearly was giving it serious thought. After a few moments she said, "Spwite."

"Spwite?" he asked.

Grace laughed. "She means 'Sprite'. She can't quite pronounce it yet."

"That's what I said. Spwite."

He grinned. "Why Sprite?" he asked.

"My mama calls me her wee spwite sometimes."

"Well, I suppose that's a fine name for a cat then."

Kristen beamed at him. "Do ye wanna hold one? Mama will show ye how."

"Kristen, I'm sure Sir Bram knows how to hold a kitten

and we should go see if granny needs any help."

"She aweady said she didn't when Wobert told us about the kittens."

Grace smiled apologetically at him. "The rain has kept us indoors. Long days stuck indoors make wee lassies restless. Robert thought this might be a nice distraction."

Bram smiled at her. "I expect so." He didn't want them to leave just yet. "In truth, Kristen, it has been a long time since I've held a kitten. Perhaps ye could show me how."

Kristen nodded vigorously. "Ye make a boww wif yer hands wike this. Then mama needs to put her hand under yers to keep the kitten safe."

Bram cupped his hands and winked at Grace. "I'm ready."

Grace laughed. "Kristen, I think Sir Bram's hands are big and strong enough to hold a kitten without my help."

He gave a mock sigh. "I suppose I can manage alone if I must." Sitting in the hay, he reached for a tiny black and white kitten, cradling it in one hand, while rubbing its head with the other.

"Yer s'posed to use boff hands," Kristen chastised.

"Kristen, it's all right. See, one of his hands alone is bigger than both of yers."

"Wike Da's hands were."

"Aye, pet. Like yer da's were."

The grief that appeared in Grace's eyes caused Bram's heart to ache.

Kristen's chin began to tremble. She looked up at Bram. "There was a storm. Da and Gwandda didn't come home fwom the boat. Gwamma was sick. She died too. Me and Mama were awone. I miss my Da. And Gwamma and Gwandda too."

Grace bent her head down, resting her cheek on the top of Kristen's head. "I miss them too, sprite, but we aren't going to cry for them anymore are we?"

"Nay," said the wee lass, but her chin still trembled.

"And why won't we cry?"

"Because, they are in heaven wiff God and the anjoes."

"Aye, they are with God and the angels and heaven is a lovely place."

Kristen nodded. She brushed her cheek against the kitten's fur again. She smiled. "The kitty is soft."

Just like that, Kristen had bounced back from her moment

of sorrow. Her beautiful mother didn't recover quite as quickly. The haunted, troubled look in her eyes lingered. Bram felt he needed to say something. "I'm sorry for yer loss, Grace."

She blinked and looked away for a moment. After taking a deep breath she looked at him again, her eyes bright with unshed tears. "Thank ye," was all she said.

He wished with everything in him that he could pull her into his arms and erase the shadows from her eyes. The intense feeling caught him by surprise. He reached out and brushed away a tear that had escaped from the corner of her eye.

~ * ~

He had done it again. He had touched her face, tenderly wiping away a tear. And for just a moment she didn't feel quite so alone. She thought back to the evening of the feast. She hadn't felt alone then either. As she looked into his clear blue eyes she wondered what it would be like... Nay get that out of yer head, Grace. He is the laird's son and heir and ye are the cook's granddaughter.

She looked away. She kissed the top of Kristen's head before saying, "We really do need to get back to granny, poppet."

Chapter 9

Although the rain had continued through the day on Saturday, by Sunday morning a fresh breeze had swept all the clouds away, leaving clear blue skies. Grace attended Mass with Innes and Kristen. For months, Mass had left her cold. The beautiful liturgy that she had once loved was just one more reminder that she was alone. She went through the motions, but that was all. Her mind wandered. Grace found her eyes drawn repeatedly to Bram, who sat with his family in the front of the church.

He puzzled her. After he had walked her home on Pentecost, she lay on her pallet thinking about the evening. It had been wonderful but it was one evening. That was all. She couldn't let it become anything more. Since then, their paths had crossed on several other occasions. Each time he stopped to chat for a few moments. She tried to remain guarded and maintain distance, while he acted as if they were old friends. His banter was light and pleasant and truthfully, she began to look forward to seeing him. It was nice to have a friend—as long as that was where it stayed.

Then Friday afternoon he joined them in the loft. Kristen had reminded her of the loved ones they had lost and for the first time, she felt solace. Her grief had lessened ever so slightly. Still, she didn't know exactly what to make of this and it scared her.

Please God, I don't think I can take any more. I can't love someone again. Especially someone who can't love me in return. Please protect me from this.

When Mass was over, she walked home with Innes and Kristen. Home. It was beginning to feel like home.

Kristen interrupted her thoughts. "Can we cwimb the hiww?"

The hill. The promontory overlooking her home. She sighed. Maybe this wasn't quite home yet. "Nay, Kristen."

"But I want to cwimb the hiww."

"We can't, Kristen."

"But I want to."

Grace wanted to as well, but the memories hurt. She took a deep breath. "I do too, but I told ye, we can't. Besides, we have work to do."

Kristen pouted. "But we used to cwimb the hiww after Mass."

"What is it she wants, Grace?" asked Innes.

Grace sighed. "She wants to climb the hill. On Lewis, there was a promontory that rose above the village. From the top of it ye could see the whole village and out to sea. On fine days, especially Sundays, we would climb the promontory."

"Ye and Kristen?"

Grace swallowed hard. "Aye, and Callum. Just like I did with Mama and Da when I was a little girl." Innes took her hand and squeezed it lightly.

"I picked fwowers and sometimes we ate on the gwass," Kristen added.

"Hmm," Innes said, tapping her forefinger on her lips. "Well, my dears, it isn't the 'hill' that ye climbed before, but the hill there, rising behind the castle, leads to the cliffs overlooking the firth. It's just a short walk."

Grace stopped and looked at her grandmother. "But there is work to be done."

"And many other hands to do it."

"Can we eat on the gwass?"

Innes captured Grace's gaze. "It is up to Mama, sweetling. What do ye say, Grace? I'll give ye a packet of food so ye can 'eat on the gwass'." Her grandmother's eyes twinkled as she imitated Kristen.

Grace considered it for a moment. The peace of a quiet afternoon with her daughter, like they used to have, was enticing.

"Pwease, Mama."

"All right, Kristen. We will climb a new hill today."

In no time at all Grace was ready to go with a small sack of food, a costrel of water, and her wee daughter skipping at her side. She hadn't left the castle walls since she had arrived over a week ago. As she approached the gates, one of the guardsmen called to her. "Good morning, Mistress Breive. Where are ye and that wee lass going on this fine day?"

She recognized him as Maisie's son, Donal.

"We are going to cwimb a hiww and eat on the gwass,"

said Kristen with glee.

Grace laughed at Donal's confused expression and explained, "We are going to climb a hill and eat on the grass."

Donal grinned. "Is this something ye do often? Eat on the grass?"

"We used to. Kristen decided that it was a fine day to do it again."

Donal nodded. "Aye, I expect it is. Enjoy yerselves then. But to be safe, stay within sight of the castle."

"Aye, we will. Thank ye, Donal."

As they walked, Kristen kept a steady chatter going. When the slope became a bit steeper Grace swung Kristen up onto her shoulders. Finally, they reached the top and Grace stopped in awe. The view was spectacular.

Even Kristen stopped her prattle, eventually breaking the silence with, "It's pwetty."

"Aye it is, pet."

"Can I pick fwowers?"

"Aye, but ye must stay away from the edge."

"I know mama."

She wandered with her daughter, looking under rocks, picking flowers, and playing games. When Kristen grew tired, Grace sat leaning her back against a rock with Kristen in her lap. They nibbled at the bread and cheese Innes had packed for them while they played a guessing game.

"I see something blue and white," said Grace.

"The sky," squealed Kristen.

"Aye, the sky. Now, I see something big and gray."

"The wock."

"Aye, the rock."

"I want to do one, Mama."

"All right, sweetling."

Kristen looked around searching for something to describe. Her eyes clearly lit on something behind Grace. "I see something, gween and bwoo and white."

"Hmm. Is it another rock?"

Kristen shook her head and giggled. "Wocks aren't bwoo."

"Is it the sky?" teased Grace.

"Mama, the sky isn't gween."

"Nay, I don't suppose it is. Is it flowers?"

Kristen grinned, shaking her head again. "It isn't fwowers.

Do ye give up?"

"I suppose I must. I can't imagine what it is."

Kristen pointed down the hill. "It's Sir Bwam's pwaid."

"What?" Grace scrambled to her feet and looked down the hill in the direction that Kristen had been looking. Sure enough, Bram climbed the hill towards them, looking angry.

~ * ~

It had been a damned frustrating day so far.

Bram had caught a glimpse of Grace as he left Mass. He wanted to weave his way through the worshippers to her side but he couldn't. He escorted his mother. When they had returned to the keep, he intended to go to the kitchen. He couldn't get his mind off of Grace. She was a beautiful woman, any man would think so. Aye, that was the reason…only, he knew it wasn't. There was something about her beyond her beauty that stirred something deep within him. He had glimpsed it several times on Pentecost and then again in the hayloft, but he couldn't define it. Yes, he would go to the kitchen.

Unfortunately, his father had stopped him. "Ye have avoided me all week, Bram. If ye want any say in who yer bride will be, ye will join me in my solar."

"But, Da, I won't be long—"

"Nay. My solar. Now."

The discussion hadn't gone well. Well, in fairness it wasn't much of a discussion. It was somewhat one-sided. His father had a list. Each woman on the list represented an alliance with a strong clan. Eanraig had taken care to describe exactly the political advantages each one brought. Frankly, any one of them would be an excellent strategic match and would certainly be good for the clan, but Bram found reasons why he shouldn't marry any of them.

His father had finally reached his limit. "What is the matter with ye, son?"

Bram didn't have an answer he could give his father. He couldn't say he was enchanted with the beautiful Widow Breive, the cook's granddaughter. He had finally said, "I don't know any of these women."

His father had pounded his fist on his desk. "Ye don't need to know them! Ye just need to pick one to marry."

"Then why does it matter what I think? Pick the alliance ye want."

"Fine. If that is the way ye want it, I will send a message to Ranulf Sinclair asking for a betrothal to his daughter Annice."

Bram gritted his teeth. "So are we done here?"

"Aye. We're done."

"Then please excuse me."

Bram rose to leave. He had his hand on the door when his father said, "Son, if this is about Fiona, ye need to let it go."

Bram sighed. "It isn't about Fiona. Send the message to Laird Sinclair." He had left the solar without waiting for a response from his father, striding down the hall to the solace of his own chamber. The day so far had been maddening. He'd crossed the room to the window which looked out on the headland rising behind the keep.

Movement caught his eye—someone was on the cliff. It only took one glimpse of auburn hair spilling from under a white kertch to tell him who it was. What is Grace doing out there? It was dangerous. By the saints, she had Kristen with her. He swore and left his chamber, heading downstairs and out of the keep.

As he crossed the inner bailey, Ian had fallen in step beside him. "By the look of ye, I'd say the discussion with father went extremely well."

He scowled at his brother, "Leave it, Ian."

"Where are ye going? Ye look ready to kill someone. God pity the soul."

"God will need to have pity on yer soul if ye don't drop it."

Ian grabbed his shoulder. "What in the hell is the matter with ye?"

"Nothing. Grace is on the cliff. I saw her from my chamber."

Ian looked at him as if he had lost his mind. "What's wrong with that?"

"She's on the cliff. With the wee lass. Alone." At the blank expression on Ian's face he roared, "it's dangerous!"

"Maybe in a storm, but it is a fine day. Bram, people walk on the headlands all the time."

"Well, women with children shouldn't walk it alone." Bram shook his head and continued on his mission.

"I'll go with ye," said Ian cheerily. "In the mood ye are in, maybe ye shouldn't walk it alone." Bram had given him a quelling look. "Or maybe I'll just stay out of yer way."

"Good choice."

He had continued on his path, charging through the gates without speaking to the guards posted there. Now, starting up the hill, he saw Grace sitting with her back against a boulder. When Kristen pointed towards him, she scrambled to her feet, scooped Kristen into her arms, and put the large rock she had been leaning against between them. Damn. She was afraid of him. He managed to calm his temper before he reached them. "Good afternoon, Grace, Kristen."

"Good afternoon, sir," she said in a tight voice.

"Grace, I have asked ye to call me Bram." He couldn't keep the irritation from his voice.

"Have I done something wrong?"

"It is dangerous up here."

She was incredulous. "Dangerous?"

"Aye Grace, dangerous. The cliff is a sheer drop."

"It is wike the hiww we cwimbed at home. We don't go neaw the edge," Kristen said solemnly.

"Aye. Bram, I grew up in a fishing village on Lewis. I am well familiar with sea cliffs."

"There are rocks protruding from the ground everywhere. Kristen could get hurt."

"We are careful. If I needed to avoid rocky ground to keep her safe, I fear I would have to leave the Highlands."

"But ye are a woman alone. It isn't safe."

"I have been a woman alone for quite some time now. I can take care of myself. I promised Donal I would stay within sight of the keep and I have a knife with me. Ye haven't forgotten my particular skill with knives have ye?"

"It's still dangerous. Come, I'll walk ye back to the keep."

"But we haven't finished our bwead and cheese. We awways ate wif Da on the gwass."

"Wheesht, Kristen. Bram, I appreciate yer concern but it isn't necessary. I'm not yer responsibility."

"Of course ye are. Ye're a clanswoman, a Sutherland. That makes ye my responsibility. Come now." He held out a hand to her.

She smiled at him. "But we haven't finished our bread and cheese."

"Ye can sit on the gwass wif us and have some too," Kristen offered.

Dear God, had he ever been given an offer he wanted to accept more? "Well, I suppose I could stay with ye for yer midday meal. But then ye must come back to the keep with me."

Bram had attended many a fine feast but he was fairly sure he had never enjoyed a meal more than the one spent sitting in the "gwass" with the woman who captivated him and her wee daughter.

They didn't return to the keep as soon as they were done eating. Thankfully, Kristen had immediately curled up in Grace's lap and fallen asleep. Bram wasn't as anxious to return to the keep as he had led them to believe. He and Grace talked while Kristen napped. He told her about his family and the clan. She told him about her family and her husband and about losing them. He marveled at her strength. She had shouldered a burden that would have crushed many. Bram found himself feeling jealous of a dead man—the man who had called this wonderful woman his own.

Kristen had probably napped for close to two hours, but when she woke, he was sorry it hadn't been longer. "Well, now that this wee poppet is awake, I should escort ye back to the keep."

"Ye needn't do that, Bram. Kristen isn't fully awake yet, so I will carry her down. Ye go on ahead. We'll be slow."

"Ye can't carry her down the hill. It's dangerous. Ye might stumble with her."

"Ye worry too much. I carried her up the hill. I think I can manage to carry her down."

"And ye argue too much. I will carry her down." Without waiting for an answer from Grace he scooped the wee lass up. Kristen wrapped her little arms around his neck, snuggling close, and his heart melted. He started down the hill before looking over his shoulder and saying, "Are ye coming?"

She shook her head in exasperation. "Aye, I'm coming."

Chapter 10

Eanraig Sutherland had been baffled by his son's behavior. If Fiona wasn't the problem, what was? Whatever it was, this was unlike him and he would have to get over it. Frankly, Eanraig was glad Bram had left the choice up to him. The alliance he most sought was with the Sinclairs. The Sinclairs had feuded with many clans over the years. While they had never been at odds with the Sutherlands, neither had they been close allies either.

Still, his son worried him. Bram had complained that he didn't know any of the women on the list. Know them? Ridiculous. He would get to know the one he chose. It was the way of things.

With resolve, Eanraig had composed the letter to Laird Sinclair, sealed it, and had it ready for a messenger to carry the next day.

With that task finished, he rose from his desk and walked to the window. It was too fine a day to stay in. Perhaps he would take his wife for a ride. Rodina loved surprises like that. Before he turned away from the window, something on the headland caught his eye. He stopped to look, smiling when he realized it was a young couple with a child. The bairn slept in her mother's lap. He looked more closely and saw coppery auburn curls emerging from under a white kertch. It was Grace Breive. Well, that was good. She seemed like a fine lass and needed another husband eventually. However, Eanraig's good humor fled when he realized it wasn't a villager or a member of his garrison who sat beside her, but his son, Bram.

Damnation, she was what had him so distracted. Frankly he couldn't blame his son. Grace was a striking young woman but if Bram had some notion of love in his head, it would have to be nipped in the bud.

That evening, during supper, Eanraig launched his campaign.

"Bram, the messenger will deliver my betrothal request to

Laird Sinclair tomorrow. I feel certain Sinclair will agree. We could have the entire thing resolved within the next fortnight."

Bram nodded but said nothing.

Rodina's face lit with a smile. "Oh, Eanraig, ye're seeking a betrothal with Annice Sinclair? That will be wonderful. Don't ye think so, Bram?"

"Aye, Mother. It will be a valuable alliance."

"I expect she has grown into a lovely young woman. I believe we saw her last at her oldest sister's wedding to Andrew MacLeod. Do ye remember Annice? She was quite a bonny lass."

"Mother, that was six years ago. I was one and twenty and took no notice of a lass of twelve."

His mother pursed her lips. "Well, she was a bonny lass of twelve. Her sister Joan, God rest her soul, was an extraordinary beauty."

"Now her, I remember," said Ian. "At the time, I thought Andrew MacLeod was the luckiest damn man in the Highlands."

"Mind yer language, Ian," his mother scolded. "Their mother is a very attractive woman too. I expect Annice is every bit as lovely as Joan was."

"It is an alliance, Mother. I don't see how her appearance matters," said Bram irritably.

His father shook his head. "It doesn't. She could have the face of a pig and it would still be worth pursuing the betrothal. The fact that she is attractive is an added boon which I thought ye might appreciate." Eanraig took a long pull of ale from his tankard. "If everything goes well, we might still be able to hold the wedding at the end of the summer."

"Oh, how wonderful," gushed Rodina.

"I don't see a reason to rush things," said Bram.

"Rush things?" Eanraig was incredulous. "August isn't rushing things. Political climates change, Bram, and potential brides grow older. If we want this alliance we must move quickly. If Sinclair wants ye married immediately, ye will be married as soon as the banns are announced, make no mistake." Although Eanraig didn't say it, he prayed Sinclair did want the wedding soon. Perhaps it would put to rest whatever daft notion Bram had of love.

~ * ~

Eanraig sent the messenger the next morning, as planned. The more he thought about it, the more confident he became that an alliance with the Sinclairs through Bram's betrothal was an even better choice that Fiona MacNicol had been. After all, there still was a MacNicol lass who Boyd could marry. Sinclair only had one daughter left.

He was still chuffed about this fortunate turn of events later that day when he entered the stable in search of the stable master. Several men in his garrison were tending their horses, evidently preparing to go out on patrol. He overheard one of them say, "Aye, she is quite a bonny lass." He smiled and stopped to listen.

"God's bones, bonny doesn't begin to describe her. I was on the gate the day she arrived. Breathtaking she was and that was travel worn."

"That hair," said another one. "I wish she'd leave off wearing the kertch. She's a widow anyway. By the Rood I'd like to see her cloaked in nothing but that hair."

"As if ye'd be looking at her hair if she had nothing covering her other assets," said another man, who laughed heartily at his own jest.

Eanraig grinned. If he wasn't much mistaken, they were talking about Grace Breive. His son wasn't the only one whose head she turned. Maybe this little problem would work itself out.

"Don't waste yer time imagining her assets." Eanraig recognized the voice as belonging to Michael MacBain, one of his guardsmen. "I have my sights set on winning that lass and I don't want to have to kill any of ye for having impure thoughts about her."

"Don't waste our time? The way I hear it, ye might be wasting yer time, unless ye don't mind taking Bram's leavings," said the first man.

"And what is it ye hear?" asked Michael.

"Moyra told me Bram demanded that Grace attend the feast at Pentecost."

"I doubt Bram demanded anything of her. It isn't like him," said Michael.

Calder, another guardsman with a deep rumbling voice, said, "I don't know, Michael. Una said Bram seemed rather taken with the lass."

"And how would yer wife know that?" asked Michael.

"She saw them together in the afternoon on Pentecost and she assures me women know these things." Calder's tone suggested he didn't take Una's comments too seriously.

Another man said, "Well, Peggy told me when the lass finally did make an appearance during the dancing, Bram never let her go and was seen leaving with her."

Michael snorted. "Well, lads, this is what I know. Bram will never be allowed to pursue the widow Breive beyond a casual dalliance.

"And ye won't have the same problem?" asked Calder.

"Calder, I am the youngest of ten and the seventh son. My father is dead and frankly, when I decided to stay here after completing training, I think my oldest brother, who is laird now, completely forgot about me. I have sworn fealty to Laird Sutherland, not my brother. And while I don't particularly like the idea of taking Bram's leavings, as ye suggested, I would consider it where that beautiful woman is concerned. If he breaks her heart, I am more than happy to be the one to pick up the pieces."

Eanraig left the stable having forgotten why he went in the first place. The conversation concerned him. Clearly, Bram's infatuation with Innes' granddaughter hadn't gone unnoticed by the clan. Kitchen staff, members of his garrison, and villagers had all evidently seen enough to convince them of something. Considering what Eanraig himself had seen and the way Bram was currently behaving concerning his betrothal, it was likely that at least some of the speculation was true.

On the other hand, Michael was absolutely right. Bram had responsibilities to the clan that did not involve Grace Breive. Eanraig needed to do everything in his power to encourage Michael. Michael was a strong, reliable man and he would be an excellent husband for Grace. Aye, this could solve the problem. Of course, it wouldn't hurt to discourage Bram too.

After the midday meal, Eanraig said, "Bram, I'd like to speak with ye privately about a few matters. Join me in my solar."

"Aye, Da," Bram agreed, but he looked less than happy.

When they were seated, Eanraig didn't mince words. "I'm worried about ye, Bram."

"What worries ye, Da?"

"I saw ye on the headlands yesterday with Innes' granddaughter."

"And that worries ye? I saw her walking with her wee daughter and was concerned for their safety. They are new here and could have been hurt."

"When I saw ye, ye didn't appear to be warning her of dangers, ye seemed to be sitting having a cozy conversation."

"By all that's holy, father, I was just being friendly. She is alone here. She needs friends."

"And that's it. Ye are just friends."

"That's it."

"And it was just because ye are friends that ye danced all evening with her on Pentecost?"

"I certainly did not dance with her all evening. I was in the hall most of the evening, ye saw me there."

"Perhaps it wasn't all evening, but ye were seen dancing with her."

"Aye, I danced with her. I went out for some fresh air very late in the evening. She was alone and I danced with her. I've danced with a lot of clanswomen over the years, Da, and it has never bothered ye before."

"Nay, and if that's all it is, it doesn't bother me now. But ye have responsibilities to this clan."

"I understand my responsibilities perfectly, Da."

"Good. As long as ye do."

"I do. Is that all ye wished to discuss?"

"Aye, ye can go."

Bram stood and bowed slightly, saying, "Then I'll bid ye good afternoon."

~ * ~

It took every bit of Bram's control to keep from slamming the solar door. He was angry and frustrated. Had he not just had a conversation with his father the day before about his responsibilities to the clan? Bram knew what was expected of him.

He also knew that he had just lied to his father. Grace was more than a friend to him, or at least he wanted her to be. Damn.

He strode down the hall, intending to go out to the lists and vent some of his frustration, but as he passed his mother's solar, she called to him. "Bram, lad, could ye come here for a moment? I need ye to get some things down for me."

He sighed. "Aye, mother, what can I do?"

She pointed to the top shelf inside a wooden cupboard. "Could ye pass me down those lengths of fabric? I can't reach them."

He was easily able to reach the shelf and handed her the fabric. "Do ye need anything else?"

She cocked her head and looked at him. "Nay, but ye seem irritable. What's bothering ye?"

"Nothing."

"Nothing? Yer da asked to speak with ye alone and I see ye striding down the hall afterwards, looking murderous. Do ye expect me to believe nothing is wrong?"

He smiled at her. "Well nothing important. Da just wanted to remind me of my responsibilities to this clan."

"Regarding what?"

"Regarding my betrothal."

"I thought that was all but set? Last night yer father said he was sending a message to Laird Sinclair."

"Aye he did. I suppose that is why I was frustrated. I know what my responsibilities are."

She smiled warmly at her son and caressed his cheek. "I know ye do, Son." She turned back to the fabric, shaking out one of the lengths to examine it. "But something seems amiss."

"Nothing is amiss, Mother. I guess…well, did ye ever wish ye could have chosen yer own husband?"

She harrumphed. "That could never have happened. It isn't the way things are done. Ye know that, Bram."

"I know, but have ye ever wished it were different?"

She looked pensive for a few moments. "Nay. I've never found any value in imagining 'what might have beens'. My fate was determined by my birth, just as yers was. As yer da reminded ye, we have obligations to our clans."

"Ye never imagined what it would have been like to marry for love?"

"I grew to love yer father, and he me. What more could I want?"

Bram knew his parent had a congenial marriage, better than many noble marriages. But he had never witnessed the kind of love he had seen between Fiona and Eoin, or which Grace described between her parents.

At his silence, Rodina canted her head and said, "That isn't the answer ye were seeking, |Son?"

He smiled. "I guess it was. After seeing the love Fiona held for another man—well, I don't think I could bear being married to someone who pined for someone else."

"Ah, ye are concerned about whether Annice will be happy or might have fallen for someone else as Fiona did? Ye have a kind heart, but ye worry too much, Bram. Ye are a good man. The two of ye will find happiness together. I haven't seen Annice in years, but she was a lovely child, raised to do her duty. She would have to have been. Old Laird Sinclair would have tolerated nothing less. He was not a man to cross. As I recall, he approached father seeking a betrothal to me for Ranulf. Yer grandfather Urquhart politely refused him but I remember him telling mother that he would never send a child of his to live with that devil."

Bram frowned and his mother smiled indulgently at him. "Ye see? Ye are a good man. Ye are already worried about her welfare and happiness."

He wasn't as good a man as his mother believed. He hadn't been thinking about Annice's happiness as much as he had been his own.

Chapter 11

Grace had been living at Sutherland castle for two weeks and she had fallen into a comfortable pattern. She helped her grandmother some in the kitchen in the mornings, through the midday meal. In the afternoons, Grace worked her wool or wove linen ribbon.

Today she stood spinning in the main room of the little cottage while Kristen napped in the bedroom. The door was open to let in the breeze. She was left to her thoughts as she spun. It occurred to her that she hadn't seen Bram since Sunday afternoon on the headland, four days earlier. She had enjoyed his company more than she cared to admit, and now she missed it. She remembered her prayer asking God to protect her from loving a man who was out of her reach. Perhaps God had finally started hearing her again.

A knock at the door shook her from her musings. She looked up; Michael stood on the threshold. "Good afternoon, Grace."

"Good afternoon, Michael. Innes isn't here."

He laughed. "'Tis ye I was looking for. Ye have visitors." He stepped aside so Mary and Dugald could enter.

Grace beamed and opened her arms to her friends. "Thank ye for seeing them here, Michael."

"'Twas my pleasure," he assured her before leaving.

"Grace, ye are looking well," said Mary.

"Aye, ye are, lass. Have the Sutherland's welcomed ye?" asked Dugald, going straight to the point.

"They have. I had to prove that I was Innes' granddaughter, but once I did, I had no more trouble."

Mary gave her a sad smile. "I know I shouldn't have wished it, but a bit of me hoped ye wouldn't want to stay here."

Grace hugged her. "Oh, Mary, ye were so kind to me. But my grandmother is extremely happy we are here. She spent so much of her life alone, I couldn't leave her now for anything."

"And it's right that ye should stay here with her," said Dugald, "but if anything should change, ye know ye always have a home with us.

"Aye, ye do. We'll be back this way near Michaelmas, just in case."

"Thank ye, Mary, Dugald. I believe my life is here now, but I would love to see ye anytime."

They chatted with her for a little while. When Kristen toddled sleepily from the bed room, Grace said, "I would love to take ye around to the kitchen to meet my grandmother."

"Oh, nay," said Dugald. "I fear we have stayed too long already. We left the lads with the wagon, in the village."

"By the tavern," added Mary, giving Grace a knowing look. "If we don't go soon, we'll never get them away and we need to get a bit further along today."

"We'll walk with ye to the gates then," said Grace.

When she had seen them off, with repeated hugs and a few tears from Mary, Grace started to go back to the cottage, but Michael stopped her. "Are they relatives from yer mother's family?"

"Nay. They are friends. Actually, close friends of my father's dearest friend. We stayed with them in Durness briefly just after we left Lewis. Dugald is a merchant. He and his family escorted me here on their way to Inverness."

"And they stopped on the return trip to make sure ye were happy, or to talk ye into leaving with them?"

Grace laughed. "They wanted to be assured that I was well. But, aye, they would have been happy enough for me to go with them."

"Well, I'm glad ye decided to stay."

Grace smiled at him. "Thank ye, Michael. Having been separated from Innes my whole life, I don't think I could ever leave her."

~ * ~

Bram had taken Goliath out for exercise. He needed time alone to think. After the discussion with his father, and then his mother, Bram had tried to stay away from Grace. He had obligations that didn't include her. It was better if he set all thoughts of her aside. He spent hours convincing himself that this was the right path.

But in the end, despite it being the right path, he just

couldn't follow it.

When he was with her he felt…complete. It was as if he had found something that he didn't realize he had lost, but once found he couldn't live without. How could he let that go? He simply could not imagine a future without Grace in it—or worse, with her there, but out of his reach.

As he rode to the gates, there she was, the woman who had consumed his thoughts for days. She stood at the gate chatting with Michael. Although she was likely just passing the time of day with him, seeing them there together made Bram realize that there was something even worse than her being out of his reach. He didn't think he could bear seeing her in the arms of another man.

"Good afternoon, Michael, Grace."

"Good afternoon, Sir Bwam," chirped Kristen.

"Good afternoon, my lady," he said, grinning at Kristen.

She giggled. "I'm not a wady."

"Are ye not?"

"Nay. I'm just a wee wassie."

"Well, my wee lassie, where are ye and yer mama going?"

Kristen looked up at Grace. "Where are we going, mama?"

Grace smiled. "Well, we came to the gate to say goodbye to some friends and now we are going back home."

Bram dismounted. "I'll walk as far as the stables with ye."

Grace shrugged. "If ye wish." She turned to Michael. "Good day, Michael."

"Good day, Grace. Good day, sir," Michael answered.

Bram frowned for a moment. He was rarely addressed so formally by the guardsmen and wondered for a moment why Michael had done it.

Grace took Kristen's hand and walked toward Innes' cottage. Bram walked beside her, leading Goliath. "Ye had visitors?" he asked.

"Aye. Friends." At his questioning look she added, "the merchant who brought me here and his wife. They stopped by on their return from Inverness."

Before he could find out more, Kristen asked, "What's his name?"

"Who, pet?" asked Grace?

"Sir Bwam's horse?"

Bram smiled at her. "His name is Goliath."

"Gowiaff," echoed Kristen. "He's vewy big."

"Maybe he just looks big to ye because ye are so very small," said Bram.

Kristen shook her head. "Nay, he's vewy big."

Bram laughed. "I guess he is. Would ye like to see what it is like to sit on his back?"

Kristen's eyes grew big. "Nay. He's too big. I might faww off."

"Ye won't. I promise I'll keep ye safe. Do ye want to try?"

Kristen nodded, her eyes still wide.

Bram swung her up onto Goliath's saddle. She held onto the edge of the saddle for dear life. "Don't wet go."

"I won't." He kept his right hand at her waist. When he sensed her relax a little he asked, "would ye like to ride?"

Kristen shook her head.

"Not even one step?"

Her little brow furrowed as if she considered a very weighty issue. Finally, she gave him a slow nod. "One step."

He smiled at her and urged Goliath forward one step.

Kristen still looked scared and gripped the edge of the saddle, but she said, "One more step."

Bram smiled at her and urged Goliath forward another step.

"One more," said Kristen.

Bram chuckled. "It's only a few more steps to the stable. Would ye like to ride until we get there?"

She looked at him wide-eyed, but gave him another slow nod. Keeping his hand on her waist, Bram walked Goliath the ten paces to the stable door. By the time he stopped, Kristen had a broad grin on her face. He lifted her down to the ground.

"I wode Gowiaff, Mama," she exclaimed, throwing her little arms around her mother's legs.

"I saw. Ye were very brave. What do ye say to Sir Bram?"

Kristen turned to look at him. "Fank ye."

Bram gave her a small bow. "Ye are very welcome, my sweet, wee lassie."

He looked at Grace. Her eyes were filled with warmth. "Thank ye. That was very kind."

Without thinking, he reached out to her, caressing her cheek. "Ye are very welcome too."

She swallowed hard. "We—we should be going."

He dropped his hand. "Then I wish ye a good afternoon."

~ * ~

As Grace walked on she realized that earlier she had been seriously mistaken. God hadn't heard her prayer. She was very much in danger of losing her heart to Bram Sutherland. She should avoid him at all costs. If God wouldn't protect her, she would have to do it herself. Even so, she couldn't get him out of her mind.

Unfortunately, that became even harder to do than she thought it would be. Bram walked by the little cottage for the next several afternoons as she worked wool or spun outside while Kristen napped. They chatted about nothing in particular but she began looking forward to the few minutes he spent with her every day.

On Saturday evening, as soon as she had put Kristen in bed, she stepped outside to enjoy the cool evening breeze. To her surprise, he was there, leaning against a nearby building.

"Wh—what are ye doing here?"

"Listening to ye sing."

"What?"

"I love to hear ye sing to Kristen. I have since the first night I met ye. Somehow, I'm drawn here more evenings than not."

"Just to listen to me sing?"

"Well, I also hope to see ye."

She sucked in a breath. "I don't understand."

"Don't ye? I thought it was rather obvious. Grace, ye have enchanted me. I enjoy being with ye."

Everything in her screamed at her to push him away. Now. Before it hurt even more. But she couldn't. After all, he wasn't declaring his love for her. He had only said he enjoyed being with her and she felt that way too. Could she just let him in a little? Just enjoy time spent with him for what it was? Finally she said, "I like yer company too."

His smile was as bright as the midday sun. Oh, it was so easy to look at him. He walked to her, taking her hands in his. "Oh my beautiful lass, for a moment I feared ye would send me away."

She smiled. "I fear I should, but I cannot."

"Will ye let me walk the headlands with ye and Kristen tomorrow afternoon?

"Ye must be willing to eat on the 'gwass'," she said with a cheeky grin.

Bram grinned back. "I'd like nothing more."

"Then I will see ye tomorrow."

She could do this. She could take what he was able to give her and still firmly hold onto her heart.

The next afternoon, their walk on the headlands was wonderful. It felt as if he had been a friend forever. They talked and laughed and simply enjoyed the time together. Yes, this was possible.

Chapter 12

During the evening meal, six days after Eanraig sent the betrothal request to Laird Sinclair, the messenger returned. Eanraig's brow furrowed as he read it.

"He didn't refuse, did he?" asked Rodina.

"Nay he didn't, but he didn't agree either. He says he has promised his children he will consider their wishes when arranging betrothals. Therefore, he would like Annice to have the opportunity to meet Bram before we discuss anything."

"Well then, it is just a matter of time. Send Bram to the Sinclairs for a visit. What lass wouldn't be impressed with Bram?"

Eanraig kept his voice low, so as to prevent Bram, who sat at the other end of the table, from hearing. "I mean no offense, Rodina, but ye are his mother and ye only see the good. Since we returned from the MacKays he is surly and bad-tempered."

Rodina laughed. "With ye perhaps but he knows how to charm the lassies when he wants to."

Again, Eanraig kept is voice low. "I fear that is the problem. Of late he doesn't want to charm any lass but Innes' granddaughter. This is the second Sunday in a row that he has spent the afternoon walking the headlands with her."

Rodina frowned. "Surely not."

"I'm afraid so," Eanraig assured her. "She is the only lass he danced with on Pentecost, and in addition to walking with her on the headlands, he has been seen chatting with her at Innes' cottage. If I send him to the Sinclairs, he could sabotage the whole thing just to avoid marriage. Perhaps I should seek a betrothal for him elsewhere."

"That would be a shame," said Rodina. "I can't help but think he will like Annice once he meets her."

"I suppose we could invite the Sinclairs to come here."

Rodina nodded. "Perhaps that is better anyway. Since she will be living here, it will give her the opportunity to see her new home. And it will give a little time for this infatuation to run its course, for I'm sure that's all it is."

Eanraig wasn't sure, but he did need some time to find a solution to the problem. "Aye, ye are probably right. I will send a message back inviting them for a visit."

Eanraig cleared his throat. "Bram," he said in a voice intended to carry to all assembled. "We have received good news from the Sinclairs." The grim expression on his son's face told him that he had been right. "They would like the opportunity to meet ye before finalizing the betrothal so I am inviting them for a visit."

Bram nodded but said nothing.

A frown flitted briefly across Rodina's face. "Son, aren't ye excited by the news? Ye said yerself ye didn't want to marry a lass who pined for another. Ye can make sure that isn't the case."

"Aye, Mother, it's fine."

~ * ~

Damnation. Bram had hoped Sinclair would turn down the proposal. He had hoped for more time. With time he might have had the opportunity to get to know Grace better. He might have been able to talk his father into letting him chose his own bride. Still, he had some time. He would do what he could.

The next day, his father asked him to ride with several guardsmen to some of the outlying farming communities to check on the status of crops. It would take three days to do the full circuit. Bram wanted to speak with Grace alone before he left, but she usually worked with Innes in the kitchen in the mornings. Still, he would stop by the kitchen to pick up their provisions and at least see her before he left.

When he reached the kitchen, the usual morning flurry of work was underway. Kristen knelt on a bench, eating a bowl of porridge but Grace wasn't there.

"Good morning, Sir Bram," called several of the women.

"Good morning, Sir Bram," said Innes cheerily.

"Good morning, Sir Bwam," chirped Kristen.

"Good morning, ladies. Innes, where is Grace this fine morning?"

"Yer lady mother sent for her. Is there something I can help ye with?"

"What did my mother want to see Grace about?"

"Now, lad, ye'd have to ask her that. Yer mother doesn't seek my approval on her plans for the day." The other women laughed. "Is there something I can help ye with?" she asked again.

"Nay. Well, aye, I'm riding out to check on the crops for my father. I need provisions for six men for three days."

"Aye, I know," said Innes. "Donal has already collected them."

"Ah, well, good then. I guess I'll just be going. Kristen, lass, tell yer mama I'm sorry I missed her." That raised a few eyebrows, but Bram didn't care.

~ * ~

This was only the second time Grace had been inside Sutherland keep. The first time had been exceedingly uncomfortable. Ellie, one of the lasses who served in the keep, had come to the kitchen immediately after breakfast to tell Grace that Lady Sutherland had sent for her. Now Grace stood before her. "Ye wished to see me, my lady?"

"Aye, Grace. I hear you are a weaver."

"I know the craft well, but I don't have a loom."

"I understand ye have a ribbon loom on which ye are particularly talented."

Grace knew her ribbons were beautiful but humility wouldn't allow her to acknowledge this. "I do have a ribbon loom, my lady, and I can weave ribbon."

Lady Sutherland looked at her closely, as if examining her dress. "Ye can weave ribbon and yet ye've nothing adorning yer own clothes."

Grace smiled. "I can't earn a living if I use the ribbon I weave on my own clothing."

Lady Sutherland laughed. "I suppose not. What do ye weave with?"

"For ribbon, I mostly use linen thread. I can spin it and dye it myself. I sometimes buy linen thread in colors that I can't make myself. I can make more varied designs that way."

"Have ye ever woven with silk thread?"

"Aye, my lady."

Lady Sutherland held out a strip of deep green ribbon that had a quatrefoil worked down the center in cream and yellow colored thread. "My husband bought this from a ribbon merchant several years ago but I only had enough to trim the neck and sleeves of one garment. I think this pattern would be even more beautiful worked on blue ribbon with cream and using gold thread instead of yellow. Is that something ye could do?"

"Aye, my lady, but I don't have any silk."

Lady Sutherland smiled. "Well, I have silk thread but no Sutherland weaver who knows how to work with it. If I give ye some thread, can ye weave a small piece for me so I can see yer skill? Then if I am happy with it, I will have ye weave more for me."

"Certainly, my lady."

"If I do have ye weave more for me, could ye have several ells completed soon? In a week or so?"

"Aye, my lady. I might not be able to help in the kitchen as much, but if that is acceptable, depending on how much ye want, I could have it ready for ye."

"I suspect yer skills are put to better use weaving than washing pots. My oldest son's betrothed will be visiting us soon and I want it as a gift for her."

"That would be a lovely gift, my lady. I can work a small piece for ye today and ye can decide." Betrothed? Grace didn't realize that Bram had been betrothed again. That bit of knowledge hurt more than she had expected it would.

"Excellent. Bring it to me after the evening meal and I will decide." She gave Grace a spool of each color thread she wanted used and the small piece of ribbon to use as a pattern.

"As ye wish, my lady." Grace curtsied and left, heading for the kitchens. Even just with linen thread she truly enjoyed creating the beautiful designs she could work on ribbon. The chance to make them using the silk thread Lady Sutherland had given her was something that would normally have thrilled her. However, the fact that her creation was to be a gift for the lass Bram would marry dampened her joy.

When she reached the kitchen, Innes was anxious to hear what Lady Sutherland had wanted. As Grace started to tell them about the ribbon, Kristen tugged at her skirt. "Mama, Mama, Mama."

"Kristen, ye are being impolite. Please wait." Kristen frowned but waited until Grace had finished telling the women about the Lady Sutherland's request. At the mention of who the ribbon was being made for, several women looked surprised but no one commented.

"Thank ye for minding yer manners, Kristen. Now what did ye want to tell me?"

"Sir Bwam is going away for free days and said to teww ye he was sowwy he missed ye."

Grace felt a blush rise in her cheeks. Perhaps that is what prompted the surprised looks. "Thank ye, Kristen." She decided it was best to ignore the awkwardness so she said, "Grandmother, I'll have to work on the ribbon all day if I am to have a sample done for Lady Sutherland tonight."

"Of course ye will, lass. Go on now and get started."

Grace took Kristen back to the cottage. Kristen entertained herself just outside the front door, while Grace set up her loom and began the process of weaving. She could see Kristen through the open door.

Sometime after midday, Moyra knocked at the door. "Innes said when ye didn't come up to the kitchen, she reckons ye were too focused on yer work to realize it's time to eat. She sent me with a basket for ye."

Grace looked up. "Thank ye, Moyra. My grandmother was right, I had lost track of time. I love weaving ribbon and the silk thread Lady Sutherland gave me is beautiful."

Moyra looked at ribbon. "Grace, I don't think I have ever seen prettier. I think yers is nicer than the bit she gave ye as a pattern."

"Thank ye."

"Do ye mind that it's for Bram's betrothed."

"Why would I mind?"

"I thought ye and Bram...well he seems to take a special interest in ye...I thought maybe..."

Grace rolled her eyes. "Bram doesn't take a special interest in me and he is the laird's son. I know better."

"Well, he was asking for ye before he left this morning."

"He probably just noticed that I wasn't in the kitchen."

"Peggy wasn't there. He didn't ask about her."

"Moyra, really, I'm sure he just saw Kristen there and wondered where I was."

"So ye don't mind that he's betrothed?"

"Nay Moyra, I don't mind that he's betrothed." Even as she said the words her insides twisted a bit. "It really doesn't matter who the ribbon is for, I like making it."

"Well, it is lovely. I'd best be getting back to the kitchen now."

"And I'd best be feeding my wee lass."

When Moyra had left, Kristen said, "Gwanny made us a basket, can we cwimb the hiww and eat on the gwass?"

"Not today, sweetling. Mama has work to do."

"Making wibbon?"

"Aye, making ribbon."

"Can we go tomowwow?"

"Maybe for a little while. We will see."

Kristen gave an exaggerated sigh. "Aww wight."

Grace laughed. "I love ye my wee sprite."

When they had finished eating, Kristen laid down on her pallet to rest. The morning sun came through the front window of the cottage, but there was less natural light in the afternoon. Grace wanted to work outside in the light, but she didn't have a small table. There was nothing for it, she dragged a stool outside, put her loom on it, and knelt next to it to work.

She didn't know how long she had been working like this, when a shadow fell across her work. "What on earth are ye doing, Grace?"

She looked up into Michael's warm smile. "I'm weaving ribbon for Lady Sutherland."

"But why are ye kneeling on the ground to do it?"

She smiled. "I need good light and in the afternoon it's better outside. But I don't have a table small enough to carry outside, so I had to improvise."

"Lass, ye can't work for hours on yer knees."

Grace shrugged. "It's the only way I can have the light. Well, that is as long as no one stands in it." She looked pointedly at him.

He laughed. "I'll move, but I am going to find ye a table."

"Ye needn't bother, Michael. I don't want to take ye away from yer own work. I'll manage."

He shook his head. "I said I'll find ye a table, Grace."

"But—"

He waved off her objection as he walked away.

In no time he was back with two trestles and a much smaller board than was normally used for a table. He set it up for her. "Here, now for the love of God get off yer knees. This will work for now. I'll see about getting ye a proper table that is small enough for ye to move wherever ye need it."

"Thank ye, but this is fine. Ye needn't bother—"

"Don't tell me what I needn't bother doing. I am in the habit of doing what pleases me and it pleases me for ye to have a table."

"But—"

"Don't argue, Grace. Just say 'thank ye, Michael.'"

She smiled. "Thank ye, Michael."

She had to admit, it was much easier to work sitting at a table. When it was time for the evening meal, Grace had produced a little less than an arm's length, roughly half an ell, of fine ribbon.

"It's pwetty, Mama," said Kristen.

"I hope Lady Sutherland thinks so," Grace said as she tucked the loom with the ribbon attached, as well as the spools of thread, into a basket.

Grace walked with Kristen to the kitchen, where they always ate with Innes. While they were eating, the serving maids cleared the tables after the meal. On seeing Grace, one of them said, "Grace, Lady Sutherland says ye're to come to the hall now."

Grace nodded. "Thank ye. Grandmother, will ye mind Kristen for me until I come back?"

"Of course I will, lass. Ye don't think she'd like any honey cake, do ye?" Innes said, winking at her.

"I would," said Kristen.

"Aye, well, save me some," said Grace, kissing her daughter's head before she left.

Grace took the basket to the great hall. Although the meal had been cleared away, the trestle tables were still set up and people, mostly men-at-arms, still sat at them. She walked to the refectory table where Lord and Lady Sutherland sat. Ian sat with them, as did a number of guardsmen, including Michael who smiled broadly at her.

She curtsied. "Good evening, my lady, Laird."

"Good evening, Grace. Do ye have some ribbon to show me?" asked Lady Sutherland.

"Aye, my lady. It is still attached to the loom. If ye like it, it is better to weave it in one long piece. If ye don't like it, I'll take it off the loom now." Grace sat the basket on the table, removing the loom and unfurling the finished ribbon for Lady Sutherland to inspect.

Her eyes grew wide. "Grace, this is beautiful. It is finer than the sample I gave ye."

"Thank ye, my lady. I'm glad ye like it."

"What is this?" Asked Laird Sutherland.

"I heard Grace could weave ribbon so I gave her silk thread and a sample of ribbon that I liked," explained Lady

Sutherland.

Laird Sutherland reached for the ribbon. "Let me see it."

Lady Sutherland rolled her eyes. "Because ye are an expert in such finery?"

He snorted. "Nay, I just want to see it." He fingered the ribbon and moved it into the candlelight. "This is very nice and worth ten times the cost of the thread at least."

"It probably is," said Lady Sutherland, "but this isn't meant to be sold."

"Ye plan to use it on a new garment?" he asked.

"Nay, I plan to give it to Bram's betrothed."

"That is an excellent idea, Rodina."

She frowned at her husband, and to the amusement of the other men at the table, said, "Ye always sound so shocked when ye say those words."

"Mother, ye should know by now that Da is surprised when anyone other than him has a worthy idea.

"Where's yer loyalty, Ian?" Laird Sutherland asked?

"I have two parents, Da."

"Thank ye, Son," said Lady Sutherland. "Grace, this is beautiful work. I would like at least ten ells of it. Can ye have that for me in a week?"

"My lady, it is difficult to weave much more than an arm's length in a day. That much would take close to two weeks."

"I would really like it finished in ten days. I'll send more thread to ye tomorrow."

Ten days? Grace would have to work at least ten to twelve hours a day to complete ten ells in ten days. She wasn't sure that was possible, but she would have to try. Arguing with Lady Sutherland in front of so many people would be disrespectful. "Aye, my lady. I'll do my best." She put the loom back into her basket, curtsied, and started to leave.

"Ye haven't been dismissed," said Laird Sutherland.

Grace froze. "I'm sorry, Laird."

"Do ye think ten ells will be sufficient, Rodina?"

She nodded. "It should be enough to fully trim one garment."

"I think another ten ells of a different design would be nice."

"Aye, husband. That would be a very generous gift indeed. A very generous gift." To Grace she said, "then when ye have finished this one, Grace, I'll decide on another design for ten more."

Twenty ells? "M-my lady. Using the silk thread and working an intricate design, I-It takes about an hour to make a finger's length."

"Well, you will certainly be busy for the next three weeks then, because that is when the work needs to be completed," said Laird Sutherland.

"A-aye, Laird."

"Now ye are dismissed, Grace," he said.

"Thank ye, Laird. Good evening, my lady, laird." Grace curtsied again and left the hall. Twenty ells of ribbon in three weeks. How was she going to do this? She wasn't sure it was possible. It would certainly mean she needed to work as long as there was good daylight on fine days. On rainy days she would have to work by candlelight. What would Laird Sutherland do if she didn't finish in time? She was working herself into a panic. What never helps, Grace? Panicking. Panicking never helps, Mama. She stood outside the keep alone trying to gain control before she returned to the kitchen.

The rear door opened. Michael stepped out and walked towards her. "Are ye all right, Grace?"

She nodded, fearing her voice would reveal how close to tears she was.

He put his hands on her shoulders and dipped his head to look into her face. "Nay, ye aren't. Ye look terrified."

"I'm not sure I can make as much as they want me to in just three weeks. Today was a fine day. It is harder to work when I don't have sun. And I have Kristen to care for."

"Then ye won't make as much or it will take longer. Lass, ye can only do what ye can do."

"But what will the Laird do if I can't make the twenty ells he wants?"

"My guess is tell ye to finish it or settle for less. Grace, don't let this scare ye so. He isn't unreasonable."

She nodded but expecting her to do intricate weaving for ten to twelve hours a day, on top of other responsibilities, seemed unreasonable to her.

"Ye still aren't convinced, are ye?"

"Nay," she whispered.

"What worries ye most?"

"I have a wee daughter to care for. She entertains herself well, but she is only three. I have always worked around what she needed and it has been enough."

"Then we will get ye some help. What if Calder's lass, Teasag, came to help mind her for a while, at least in the morning?"

"Teasag isn't much more than a wee lass herself."

"She's eight, she has younger siblings, and it isn't as if ye are leaving them alone. Ye'll be close by but ye'll have an extra pair of hands and eyes."

"Aye, ye're right. That would help."

"Then, I'll see to it."

She nodded. "That's very kind of ye."

He peered into her eyes again. "Better now?"

"Aye. Perhaps, with a few hours' help from the lass, I can to do this."

"Good. Get some rest. Ye'll have Teasag and a proper table tomorrow."

"Really, the trestles and board ye brought me today are fine."

"Ye are a fierce one for arguing, Grace. What did I tell ye earlier?"

She smiled. "Thank ye, Michael."

"Ye're welcome, lass."

Chapter 13

The next morning, Grace rose just after daybreak and took care of the household chores as she usually did, while Innes went to the kitchen to begin her day. Thankfully, because Innes ran the kitchen, Grace didn't have to worry about preparing or cleaning up after meals at home. However, there was still plenty of other work required to keep the cottage tidy and the people in it clean. The sun was up for eighteen hours on these midsummer days but it was the twelve hours in the middle of the day that provided the best light. If she could finish her other work and have Kristen dressed and fed by terce, the third hour of daylight, she would be able to get a good start on her weaving.

A few minutes before the church bells rang terce, Michael arrived with Teasag. He carried the small wooden table he had promised. Grace had only just returned from the kitchens with Kristen after breaking their fast.

"Good morning, Grace. Will I leave this table outside?"

"Aye, thank ye, Michael. I can work by the window inside in the morning, but I like working in full light." To Teasag she said, "good morning, Teasag, I am so happy that ye are able to help with Kristen for a bit."

Teasag beamed. "I don't mind. I can stay until Kristen takes her nap."

That would give Grace seven hours of uninterrupted work. If she could squeeze a few more in during the late afternoon while minding Grace herself, she could accomplish quite a bit. "I truly appreciate yer help," said Grace.

Michael smiled. "Well, I'll be going. I have the watch on the gate from terce to none. If ye need anything, send word."

"Ye needn't—" At his raised eyebrow Grace smiled. "I mean thank ye, Michael."

The morning flew by. It was so much easier to work and concentrate with Teasag there to distract Kristen. Grace was able to block out everything, even the usual activity of the outer bailey, as long as she didn't have to worry about Kristen.

She had to smile though. Teasag seemed quite enthralled by the process of weaving ribbon and stopped playing occasionally to watch Grace for a minute and see her progress.

When it was time for the noon meal, Grace sent Teasag and Kristen to the kitchen to eat. "But what about ye?" asked Teasag.

"I'll eat something later. Perhaps after Kristen wakes from her nap."

When Teasag returned after they had eaten, she carried a small basket. "Innes said ye were to eat this. She said stopping for a few minutes won't hurt."

Grace smiled at her. "I will stop a bit later, don't worry." Teasag frowned, but didn't argue. Grace kissed Kristen's forehead. "Kristen, pet, it's time for a rest."

Kristen yawned. "But I'm not tired."

Teasag rolled her eyes and Grace winked at her. "Well don't go to sleep then. Just lay down and close yer eyes for a few minutes."

"Awight, Mama. I won't, cuz I'm not tired." She yawned again but went inside the cottage to her pallet.

When Kristen was out of earshot, Teasag said, "My younger sister puts up a much bigger fight."

"Sometimes Kristen does too. It's always worse the more tired she is."

"Aye, it's the same for my wee sister." Teasag paused a moment. "Um...would ye mind...well, I mean I told Mama, I would come home when Kristen was napping, but could I watch ye weave for a bit?"

"If ye told yer mother, ye'd be home, ye should go, but if ye want to stay and watch tomorrow and it is all right with her, ye can. I'll even teach ye how to weave with yarn."

"Would ye?" Teasag clasped her hands in front of her and bounced on the balls of her feet. "I'd like that."

"Good. As long as it's fine with yer mother, it is the least I can do for all the help ye are giving me."

"I'm sure it will be all right." She darted away, stopped, and ran back. "I'm sorry. Have a good afternoon. I'll see ye tomorrow at terce."

Grace grinned. "I'll see ye in the morning."

Grace's mother had first taught her to weave with wool on

linen warp threads. She would need a flat piece of wood. Michael's watch was over at none, perhaps he could get that for her. Grace could set it up for Teasag this evening so as not to waste daylight.

Happy about the idea of teaching Teasag how to weave, Grace worked the afternoon away. It seemed it had been no time at all before Kristen walked out of the cottage, rubbing her eyes. "I told ye I wasn't tired."

Grace smiled at her, holding out her arms. "Aye, ye told me."

Kristen snuggled into her mother's arms for a few moments.

"Can we cwimb the hiww?"

"We can take a little walk. I need a break but I don't think we can go to the top today."

"Can I pick fwowers?"

"Aye, ye can."

Grace moved the table, stool, and loom inside. She and Kristen walked to the gate in the outer wall as the church bell rang none. The watch had changed as they approached.

Michael grinned at her. "Things are going well?"

"Aye, they are. Thank ye for yer help."

"My pleasure."

"Can I trouble ye for another small thing?"

"Anything that is in my power."

"I need a thin piece of wood a little wider than the length of yer hand and about as long as yer arm from the elbow to the finger tips. The smoother it is the better."

"That should be no problem. What do ye need it for?"

"Teasag. She wanted to stay and watch me weave while Kristen napped. I told her she could tomorrow if her mother agrees and that I would show her how to weave yarn. I need it for that."

"Grace, will that take too much of yer time?" asked Calder who was also coming off duty too.

"Nay, it is rather simple really. It is how my mother first taught me to weave. If ye think it will be all right with Una, I will set it up for Teasag tonight."

"I'm sure it will be. I suspect Teasag is thrilled," said Calder.

Grace nodded. "Aye, I think she is."

"Michael, since it is for my wee lass anyway, I can find the wood."

Michael clasped his chest in mock affront. "And deny me the opportunity to serve? I think not."

Calder laughed. "Suit yerself."

"I usually do, Calder," Michael said with a bold grin. "Grace, lass, I'll bring it to ye a bit later."

"Thank ye. That will be good. Kristen and I are taking a short walk. I need a bit of a break."

"Where are ye going?" asked Calder.

"I wike to cwimb the hiww," chirped Kristen.

Calder frowned. "The headlands?"

Grace nodded. "Aye, but not far today."

"Grace, I'm sorry, ye can't," said Calder.

"Why not?"

Micheal was frowning too. "Bram left orders. Ye weren't to walk the headlands with Kristen alone."

"Are ye jesting?"

"He's concerned for yer safety, Grace," said Calder.

"So are all Sutherland women forbidden to walk the headlands?" Grace had trouble keeping the irritation out of her voice.

"Nay. Just ye," said Michael.

Grace was bewildered. She had lived most of her life well away from the Morrison clan leaders. She answered only to her parents, then her husband, then...no one. Well that wasn't quite true. She left Lewis because of Fearchar. Still, she left rather than submitting to him. "Can he do that?"

"Aye, he can," said Calder. "In fairness, Grace, I prefer that my wife and children stay off the headlands if I'm not with them.

"Well, I'm not his wife." This was exasperating. "What if I just walked through the gates and up to the headlands?"

"Please don't. One of us would have to stop ye," said Calder.

"Or go with ye. He said ye weren't to walk them alone," said Michael.

"But that isn't what he meant, is it?" she asked.

Calder shook his head. "I don't think so."

"Still, if ye are determined to go, Grace, I'll go with ye," said Michael, "and deal with Bram when he returns."

Grace sighed. "I can't ask ye to do that. If we can't go on our walk, I'll say good afternoon. Come Kristen, let's go home."

"But ye said we could cwimb the hiww and I could pick fwowers."

"I'm sorry, pet, we can't go for the next few days."

"Why?"

"Ask Sir Bram when he returns," said Grace bitterly. "Come, sweetling, if we can't go walking, I have to get back to work."

"But ye said I could pick fwowers."

"How about ye play peevers instead?"

Kristen nodded eagerly.

When they reached the cottage, Grace scratched a peevers court into the dirt. She played with Kristen for a few minutes before bringing the table, stool, and loom back outside and resuming her work. When Kristen became bored with peevers, Grace told stories and sang songs with her as she worked.

She accomplished much less while distracted but still as the shadows began to grow long, Grace had completed about half again as much as she had the previous day.

Michael arrived with the wood she requested as she was putting away her supplies. He carried the table and stool inside for her. "It looks like ye accomplished quite a bit today."

"Aye, I did. Having Teasag to help with Kristen made a huge difference." Grace frowned. "That and not taking a walk, I suppose."

"I'm sorry about that, Grace."

"It isn't yer fault."

Kristen climbed up on a stool by the table and opened the basket sitting there. "Ye didn't eat yer basket of food."

"Nay, I guess I didn't."

Michael frowned. "Ye haven't eaten since morning?" He looked in the basket, took out a hardboiled egg, peeled it and handed it to her. "Eat."

She rolled her eyes but took a bite out of it, grumbling, "I don't need to be told when to eat. I am a woman grown."

"God's teeth, do ye do anything without arguing?"

"Of course I do."

"And, ye are going to prove that to me by arguing?"

She frowned at him, but finished the egg.

"Now that I know ye aren't going to perish of hunger, what did ye need this board for?"

"Ooh, I'll show ye." She opened the chest containing her

belongings, removed an iron bradawl, a small carving knife, two colors of linen thread, and a small, flat piece of wood. "May I have the wood?"

He looked at her curiously, but handed her the wood. It was the perfect size, exactly what she had asked for. She sat at the table and using the bradawl, bored eight holes in a line, equally spaced across the top of the board, about a knuckle's width from the edge.

"What are ye doing?"

"I'm making Teasag a simple tape loom." She used the carving knife to make the holes a little bigger and smooth the edges.

He continued to watch her work. "Ye do handle a knife well."

She smiled. "People who try to stop me from taking a wee walk with my daughter would do well to remember that."

He laughed. "I should probably warn Bram about that, but I'm not sure I will."

When she was finished she held it up for him to see. "Done."

"That's it? It doesn't look remotely like yer loom."

"It isn't, but it is easy enough to learn with this. I'll show ye." She cut lengths of linen thread and put one strand through each hole. She tied each strand of linen in slip knot over the small flat piece of wood. When she had finished, she took the loose ends on the other side of the loom, looped them into a knot about a foot from the end, braided the threads to the end, and looped the end into another knot.

"These are the warp threads," she explained. She looped the braided end around a table leg and tied it. Sitting on a stool, she placed the wood between her knees, wedging it against the edge of the stool and pulling down on the strip of wood holding the end of the warp threads. This pulled them taut. "She'll weave yarn using a tapestry needle over and under the warp threads. I'll show her how to make it into a belt."

She looked up at him and was pleased to see he looked sufficiently impressed. "If she likes it, I can show a woodworker how to make one that will open the sheds alternately like my ribbon loom does."

"Grace, this is brilliant."

"I bet ye're sorry ye became a warrior now." She teased.

"Alas, it is too late for me. But Teasag will love it."

Kristen had been watching raptly. "Can I do it, Mama?"

"Very soon Kristen, when ye are just a bit bigger."

She smiled. "Gwanny says I get bigger evwy day."

"Aye ye do, pet."

Michael said, "Speaking of yer granny, I expect it's time for the evening meal and ye need to eat. Come with me to the hall?"

Grace shook her head. "Oh, nay, we eat in the kitchen."

Michael frowned at her. "But everyone working in the castle dines in the hall."

"My grandmother doesn't." Grace decided not to point out that she didn't work in the castle.

"Well, I'll walk with ye to the kitchens then."

Ye, needn't bother was on the tip of her tongue. Michael's eyebrows shot up in challenge. Grace laughed. "Thank ye, Michael."

Chapter 14

By Wednesday evening, Grace had completed almost five ells of the intricate ribbon. She couldn't have done it without fine weather and Teasag who stayed at the cottage now every day until none. The lass worked her own weaving while Kristen napped. But Thursday dawned gray and rainy. The gloomy day meant Grace had to use candlelight in order to see well enough to do the intricate work. Even then it was a strain. By the time Kristen had awoken from her nap, Grace had barely finished half an ell.

"Teasag, sweetling, I have to stop for a while. Working in the poor light is causing my head to ache. How about if Kristen and I walk ye home?"

"But it's raining. Ye needn't go with me."

"I want to. I need the break and it looks as if the rain has slowed to a heavy mist."

"All right. If ye want to."

They covered their heads and headed out into the mist. When they reached the castle gates, Donal was on the watch. "And where are the three of ye braw lassies headed on such a damp day?"

Grace knew what Donal was really asking and it annoyed her. "Just walking Teasag home, Donal." Grace snapped.

He smiled knowingly. "Ah, ye found out. I didn't figure ye'd take it very well."

She looked down and pressed two fingers into the bridge of her nose. "I'm sorry, Donal. It's not yer fault. There's no rule about me going to the village is there?"

"Nay, lass." He grinned at her. "Enjoy the fine weather."

When they reached Teasag's home, the rain had picked up again. Una fussed, ushered them inside, and gave them a warm tisane. "Grace, ye needn't have come with her. Now ye and Kristen have to walk back in the rain."

"Aye, but it isn't a terribly cold rain."

"She needed the walk, Mama, she has a headache," said

Teasag.

"Ah, well, it doesn't surprise me. Ye have been working yerself too hard. An afternoon with a bit of leisure is just what ye need."

After a warm drink and a nice chat, Grace did feel better. Kristen too enjoyed playing with Una's children. "Thank ye, Una. It has been a lovely break but it's growing late and I still have to do some more weaving. Kristen and I should be heading back now."

The rain hadn't let up. If anything it had become heavier. Grace carried Kristen so she could cover both of them with her plaid and move as quickly as possible. They hadn't gone far when men on horseback rode through the village, approaching from behind her. As they drew near, she heard Bram's voice. "Grace? What in the name of all that's holy are ye doing out in this weather?" He was off Goliath and at her side in an instant.

This was the absolute last thing she needed. "I don't see how it is any concern of yers."

"It concerns me, Grace, because I care about ye. Let me help ye up on Goliath and ye can ride with me the rest of the way."

"I've had just about enough of yer concern." Grace walked faster.

"Mama, I wanna wide Gowiaff."

"Not now, Kristen."

"But I wanna ask him."

"What to ye want to ask me, pet?" Bram said, taking Kristen from Grace and covering the child with his own plaid.

"Why we couldn't cwimb the hiww."

His eyebrow shot up. "That's what this is about, Grace?" She glared at him. "We'll discuss it later." He handed Kristen to a guardsman who, like Bram had done, covered Kristen with his plaid."

"But I wanted to wide Gowiaff."

"And ye shall, but let's get Mama up there first." Turning back to Grace, he lifted her onto Goliath's back before she could protest. Then he put Kristen on her lap and swung up behind them both.

It was pointless to argue with him, but nevertheless it fueled her ire. He pulled her close and wrapped his plaid around them before urging Goliath into a trot.

Even as irritated as she was, it had been a long time since a man had held her so close. She liked his touch. He felt so warm and strong.

They hadn't gone far when a rider approached from the castle. Because Bram's plaid partially covered her head and face, she couldn't immediately see who it was.

"Good afternoon, Michael, where are ye headed in this foul weather?"

"Back to the castle now. I just learned that Grace had walked Teasag home earlier when the rain had all but stopped. I didn't want her to have to walk home in this."

"It's just a summer rain," said Grace in exasperation.

"That doesn't mean it won't chill ye to the bone if ye are out in it long enough," said Bram. "It was good of ye to come for her, Michael. Ye have my thanks."

"Ye know me. I live to serve," said Michael, drawing chuckles from the men around them. He turned his horse and cantered back to the castle ahead of them.

With the mix of irritation and attraction that flooded her already aching head, Grace decided silence was her best option. The less she said, the better.

They were riding through the outer curtain wall in no time. The men riding with them stopped when they reached the stables, but Bram kept going until he reached Innes' cottage. He dismounted, lifted Kristen out of Grace's lap, and set her down in the doorway, under the eaves and out of the rain. Then he lifted Grace down.

"Thank ye," muttered Grace, opening the door for Kristen.

"I'll return when I've seen to Goliath."

"There's no need. We're safe within the castle walls now."

"Ye're obviously angry so we have things to discuss. I'll be back." He mounted Goliath and rode back towards the stables.

She stepped inside, shaking her head. Somehow this was all a little beyond belief. She shut the door. Damp and bedraggled, Kristen stood in the middle of the room. "I'm a widdle cold."

"Me too," said Grace. She stoked the fire to life then redressed Kristen in warm dry clothes before putting on dry things herself. At the midday meal, Innes had sent someone with a fresh loaf and a small iron pot filled with soup. Grace hung the half-full pot over the fire to rewarm it. Perhaps after an early supper, she could put Kristen to bed a little early too and try to work a bit more on the ribbon by candlelight.

More than enough time had elapsed for Bram to tend Goliath and he hadn't returned. Grace accepted that as a blessing from the God who of late, seemed to have abandoned her. Kristen sat at the table eating her bread and soup and Grace had just set her own on the table beside Kristen's when someone knocked on the door.

She looked towards heaven. "Aye, I suppose it was too much to hope ye'd started listening."

She opened the door to Bram, who appeared to have washed and changed clothes himself. Handsome didn't begin to describe him.

"Sir Bwam," exclaimed Kristen.

"Good evening, Kristen. Grace, may I come in?"

Still piqued from earlier she answered, "Would it do any good to say nay?"

He chuckled. "Probably not."

"Then of course, come in. Make yerself comfortable. Would ye care for a bowl of soup?"

He ignored her mocking tone. "Thank ye. Aye, I'd love a bowl of soup." He sat at the table across from Kristen.

Grace dished up another bowlful, cut a slice of bread, and placed both in front of Bram.

He made the sign of the cross and bowed his head. "Bless us, O Lord, and these thy gifts which we are about to receive from thy bounty through Christ our Lord. Amen." He made the sign of the cross again before breaking off a bite of bread, dipping it in the soup, and eating it.

She stared at him. Her father, and then her husband, had always asked a blessing. When she lost them, she couldn't bring herself to say the words, doing so reminded her poignantly of her loss. But listening to him pray the familiar words didn't reinforce her grief—just the opposite. She felt...connected.

"Eat, Grace."

At a complete loss, Grace didn't understand the effect he had on her. She frowned and took a spoonful of her own soup.

Kristen didn't seem to be similarly bothered. "Sir Bwam, why couldn't I pick fwowers on the hiww? Mama said to ask ye."

"Ah, that's right, ye mentioned that in the village."

Grace could feel his eyes on her, but she felt off-balance and refused to look at him.

"Well, Kristen, I worry about ye and yer mama. I like to

know that ye're safe and I think it might be dangerous for just ye and yer mama to climb the hill alone. I want to be with ye when ye climb it so I can make sure ye are safe."

Grace thought that was ridiculous.

Kristen said, "Oh," as if it made perfect sense to her.

"Do ye remember I was looking for yer mama the morning I left?"

"Aye. Ye said I was to teww her, ye were sowwy ye missed her, and I did."

"That's right. I wanted to see her before I left so I could ask her not to walk up the hill with ye until I got back.

"Ye didn't teww me that."

"Nay, I didn't. It was so important that I worried, being such a wee lass, ye might forget. So, I told the guardsmen to tell yer mama.

"I wanted to pick fwowers and mama needed a bwake fwom the wibbon."

Bram looked bewildered. "A break from the ribbon? Grace, what does she mean?"

"I mean a bwake fwom the wibbon. The wibbon mama's making for Wady Suverwand." At his continued confusion, Kristen said, "I'ww show ye." She started to climb down from the table.

Grace stopped her. "Nay, Kristen. Ye mustn't touch the loom. Even when ye are a big girl and are allowed to touch the loom, ye must never put it on a table with food—ye never want to risk spilling something on the ribbon. Besides, ye need to finish eating yer supper."

"Did I understand her correctly? Ye are making ribbon? For my mother?"

"For Wady Suverwand," said Kristen as if Bram had misunderstood her.

"Lady Sutherland is Sir Bram's mother, Kristen. Please eat yer supper."

"Is that what she wanted to speak to ye about the morning I left? Can ye make ribbon?"

If the prayer moments ago had made her feel connected, talking about the ribbon she was making for his betrothed had quite the opposite effect. "Aye, it is why she summoned me and yes I can make ribbon. It's just another kind of weaving. My ribbon loom was small enough to bring with me from Lewis."

"How did my mother know ye could weave ribbon?"

Grace did not want to talk about this. "I don't know. I expect someone told her. A few women have bought ribbon from me."

"And ye are weaving ribbon for her."

"She had silk thread that she wanted woven into ribbon."

"Teasag hewps."

Bram gave Grace another questioning look. "Teasag helps? How does Teasag help ye weave ribbon?"

"She pways wiff me while mama weaves."

"Kristen, sweetling, I want yer mama to answer me."

"Teasag plays with Kristen while I weave." Grace repeated exactly what Kristen had said.

Bram was beginning to look frustrated. "I understood that much. What I want to understand is why? Teasag is awfully young herself. Why do ye need her to mind Kristen?"

"Because mama has a wot of wibbon to weave for yur twoved."

Grace really didn't want to explain this. "Kristen, Sir Bram asked me to answer. Finish eating yer supper, please." To Bram she said, "yer mother asked me to make ten ells of blue ribbon and she wanted it fairly quickly. For the last couple of days, Teasag has come to play with Kristen, while I weave. And, aye, Teasag is young, but she isn't left alone with Kristen. She is just here to help occupy Kristen so I can focus. We walked her home today. We were on our way back when ye came upon us."

"Ye walked her home in the rain? A guardsman would have done that."

Maybe it was her aching head, or how befuddled she felt around Bram. Maybe it was spending hours every day constantly reminded that the man she felt attracted to, whose company she usually enjoyed, was marrying someone else. And maybe it had been building up for days, but Grace was overcome by a wave of anger. She banged both fists on the table. "Honestly, Bram, ye are behaving as if ye think I am a witless child. I'm a grown woman. I have been alone," her voice broke. She swallowed hard. "I have been alone for a long time and managed quite well without someone telling me where I can and cannot walk, or what I must or must not do. The rain had practically stopped—when we left the castle, it was just a mist. Aye, it started up again, but it's a summer rain and it was just a walk from the village. There was no fear of us freezing." Grace stood and walked from the table. She was so upset her whole body trembled. She spun around to face him again. "And, for that matter, I am nothing to ye. I am the cook's granddaughter! By everything that's holy, can ye please tell me why ye feel the need to interfere in my life?"

Her eyes fell on Kristen who looked at her with a very concerned expression. She simply said, "Mama, what matters most?"

Grace's shoulder's sagged. It was the question her mother had asked her when she was little and she in turn asked Kristen. It was a simple tradition to help remind a child of what was truly important, especially in a stressful situation when remembering was hard. If Kristen had been cross and angry, Grace would have asked it of her. "Kindness matters most, Kristen. Thank ye for reminding me of that."

"And what never hewps?"

Grace smiled at the second question that often followed. "Panicking never helps."

Kristen smiled and stretched her arms towards Grace. Grace picked her up and held her close. Kristen whispered loudly, "Ye aren't awone, Mama. Ye have me."

"Aye, I do, sweetling."

Finally, she looked at Bram, who still sat at the table, his fingers steepled under his chin, wearing a concerned expression not unlike Kristen's had been. She apologized. "I'm sorry for losing my temper. Ye simply meant to keep us safe. I understand now. Thank ye for coming by and helping me see that."

"Nay, Grace, I don't think ye do understand."

"But, I do. Ye needn't worry about it. I won't keep ye any longer this evening." She added, "thank ye for coming by," again hoping he would take the hint. She needed time to regroup, to reinforce the walls that protected her.

"Grace, I'm not leaving yet. The fact that ye believe ye are nothing to me clearly tells me ye do not understand. I said we had things to discuss, and we still do."

"We can discuss them tomorrow. I need to put Kristen to bed. I'm tired and I still have work to do."

"Put Kristen to bed and we'll discuss it tonight. Any work ye have will wait."

Chapter 15

Normally Bram enjoyed riding over their holdings, meeting with the crofters, and ensuring that all was well in the clan. This time he hadn't. He had wanted to be at home—to be with Grace. He hadn't even had the chance to speak with her before he left. He worried about her and Kristen. In the little time he had known Grace, he had been struck by her strength, confidence, and sheer will to survive. But as much as he admired these traits, they were what concerned him as well. He feared she wasn't aware of her own limitations and was fairly certain she wouldn't seek help when she needed it. Those flaws could be dangerous.

When he had ridden into the village with his men and he saw her trudging through the rain he couldn't help but believe his fears were well founded. To top things off, she fairly bristled with anger—at him.

How could he explain the deep need he felt to take care of her and keep her safe when he didn't completely understand it? He told himself she was his clanswoman and because she was a widow he had certain responsibilities to her. But when he stepped in the little cottage that evening and his heart nearly exploded, he knew what he felt went way beyond that.

The scene that met him when he arrived had been a glimpse of everything he wanted in life, everything he had ever prayed for. No longer just marriage and a family, he wanted to marry this strong, beautiful woman who stirred his deepest needs and desires and be a father to her child who he also adored. He wanted to love and protect them both. Nothing would have stood in his way if he had been born anyone except a laird's son. But even considering that, he knew he could accept no other bride. There had to be a way to marry Grace and as he asked the blessing, he prayed silently for God's help in finding it.

His goal had changed from simply making her understand it was his obligation to protect her, to convincing her that he loved her. But first, he had to convince her that she didn't hate him. He wasn't sure what had gone on in the three days he was gone, but he suspected there was more to it than he currently understood. When Grace's temper snapped he was even more certain of it. She was completely unaware of how important she was to him or she would never have shouted, I am nothing to ye, I am the cook's granddaughter, and that caused his heart to ache. He wasn't going to let her push him away. Aye, they had things to discuss.

She shook her head in resignation. "Fine. Kristen, are ye finished eating?"

"Aye, Mama."

"Then help me clean up the dishes before bed."

Bram could only wonder how much help a three year old could be.

Grace poured warm water into a wash basin from a kettle that sat on the hearth. She gave Kristen a small towel. As Grace washed each item, she handed it to Kristen who dried it carefully—if not perfectly—and laid it on the table. When she was done, Grace whispered something in Kristen's ear. Kristen nodded and went into the bedroom.

Bram arched a brow at Grace.

Grace said, "Chamber pot," by way of explanation, causing him to grin.

While Kristen was out of the room, Grace put the clean dishes away, drying anything the lass had missed. When Kristen returned, Grace wet one end of the towel and washed Kristen's face and hands. "Now, little miss, it is time for bed. Can ye say good night to Sir Bram?"

Perhaps "saying" good night was what Grace intended, but Kristen launched herself at him, hugging him. "Good night, Sir Bwam."

Without thinking about it, Bram returned her hug and kissed her forehead. "Good night my sweet, wee lassie."

When Kristen released him, Grace took her by the hand. "Pardon me for a few minutes."

"Certainly," he answered and just as he hoped, when she disappeared into the bedroom, she began singing to Kristen. He couldn't imagine ever tiring of this.

Far too soon she stopped singing, softening to a hum as she always did. He glanced around the room. There was only one chair in the little cottage and it sat by the hearth. There were four stools at the small table where he sat, but he didn't want to have this conversation with a table between them. Placing one of the stools opposite the chair, he sat on it and leaned his back against the stone face of the hearth, leaving the chair for Grace.

She had said she was tired and when she emerged from the little bedroom she looked it. Perhaps he should have let this go until tomorrow but he didn't think it could or should wait. She came no farther into the room than the door. With a sigh she said, "So, ye believe we have things to discuss."

"Aye, I do. Please, come sit down." She headed towards the table and started to sit in the stool farthest from him. "In the chair, Grace." He would have laughed if she didn't look as if she were facing an executioner. She moved to the chair but would not meet his eyes.

"First, ye must know I don't think ye are a witless child. Far from it. Ye may be the strongest, brightest, most confident woman I have ever met. I wouldn't want ye ever to think otherwise."

She finally looked at him, but said nothing, so he continued. "I know the terrible losses ye have suffered in the last year have played a huge part in making ye as strong and independent as ye are. But I fear ye've learned to rely so much on yerself, ye fail to see that ye aren't alone anymore. Ye are right, there is nothing wrong with taking a walk in a summer rain if ye wish to. But there is if ye were doing it because ye didn't feel ye could ask for help."

"I didn't need help. I wanted to walk her home. I…" Grace looked away for a moment. "Are we through now?"

"Nay, we aren't. Ye were upset that I left an order forbidding ye to walk the headlands alone."

Anger flashed in her eyes for a moment. "Aye, I was, and ye have explained that ye think it is dangerous."

"But ye don't think so."

She looked at him again. "Nay, I don't. I told ye once that I have lived my whole life near sea cliffs."

"But ye haven't lived yer whole life here."

"I don't see the difference."

"Clearly. But I do. The village ye lived in, was it very large or near other villages?"

"Nay."

"Did ye know everyone who lived in it?"

"Aye, I did, but I don't see—"

"Did they know ye? Did they know yer Da would have killed anyone who harmed ye?"

"Aye, I expect they did."

"Would they have protected ye in his absence?"

"Aye, of course they would. But I—"

"Can ye say the same things now?"

It was the first time he had ever seen her look unsure. She swallowed hard. "Nay."

"So the village here is much larger, ye don't know everyone, they don't know ye and as far as most people believe, ye are under no man's protection."

She blinked as if staving off tears. "Aye. I suppose so."

"Grace, I'm not saying this to hurt ye and I didn't leave orders about walking the headlands because I don't think ye know the dangers of the terrain. I know ye have skills with a knife and I hope there isn't a Sutherland who would try to do ye or Kristen harm in any way, but when ye are alone with her, ye are more vulnerable. So the main reason I left the order was to make it absolutely clear to everyone that ye are under my protection."

"I'm a clanswoman. I thought that was a given."

"Sweetling, my responsibilities to ye, my desire to keep ye safe, go much deeper than that."

"But why? I'm noth—"

"Stop. If ye ever say ye are nothing to me again, ye will sorely try my patience. Grace, ye are everything to me." He sat forward on the stool taking her hands in his. "I care about ye, I want to guard and protect ye because I adore ye." He looked into her beautiful green eyes and was lost. "Grace, I love ye."

~ * ~

Grace hadn't wanted to listen to him. She just wanted him to leave. It was too hard to be around him. As angry as she had been over his high-handed tactics, when she was with him she couldn't think straight. She had steeled herself before leaving the bedroom. She would show no emotion. Just listen and nod Grace, then he will leave and yer heart will be intact.

But in spite of her resolve, she couldn't just listen and nod. He stirred her emotions. As he explained why he had left orders about walking alone on the headlands her anger faded. It was not her skills he doubted. She hadn't considered the things he had. When he told her he wanted everyone to know she was under his protection, she felt valued. She had taken the security of her father's, and then her husband's, protection for granted until it was gone.

But when he told her he loved her, her heart fell.

"Ye can't love me. Ye can't. I can't let ye." Grace felt panic rising. "I can't do this again. I can't ever do this again. I will not survive it."

"Grace, stop."

"Nay. Ye don't understand, Bram. I promised myself I would never risk that kind of pain again. I knew I was in serious danger here. But I thought I could just feel a little. I thought I could just experience a whisper, an echo of love. But I can't. I want it too much and my heart is too fragile. It is better to feel nothing than to love someone who I can never have—someone who is destined to break my heart."

"Grace, please stop. Listen to me. Why would ye say ye can never have me? I love ye. I'm offering myself to ye and want ye by my side forever."

She pulled her hands from his. "Nay, Bram. I will be no man's leman, no matter how much I love him."

Her words shocked and clearly angered Bram. "I would never ask that of ye, Grace. What have I done that would ever give ye such an idea? How could ye possibly believe I value ye so little?"

Grace stared at him in disbelief. "How could I ever be anything but yer mistress? Ye are betrothed, Bram. Under the law, ye are essentially already married."

"I am not betrothed."

Grace was shocked and angered by the blatant lie. "Nay?" She flew out of the chair and across the room to get her loom. "Then why have I been working practically every moment of usable daylight to weave ten ells of intricate ribbon as a gift from yer mother to yer betrothed?"

He looked as if someone had knocked the wind out of him. "Grace, I swear to ye, I am not betrothed. I don't know why my mother said I was."

"Why are ye lying to me? Yer father said the same. He— never mind, it doesn't matter." She turned her back to him, placing the loom on the small table to keep from dropping it.

"Grace, I am not lying to ye. I am not betrothed and I have no idea why my parents suggested otherwise or why they asked ye to do this."

She ignored him. "God, why have ye abandoned me? I have never asked for much. I haven't. A healthy child. Aye, Ye granted me that. Keep my husband and father safe on the water and bring them home each night. But Ye let them perish. Restore my mother to good health so I wouldn't be left alone. Ye denied me. Let me raise my daughter in peace in our little home. Again the answer was nay."

Bram touched her shoulder. "Grace, stop, listen to me."

She continued her angry rant against God. "Fine, Lord, I understand, these were things I suppose I didn't deserve so I asked one more thing. Something small. Please just help me protect my heart. Don't let me fall in love. I swear I won't ask for anything else. Just spare me the pain of more loss by not giving me anyone else to love. I can live without love. I can. But even that Ye would not grant me. What have I done? Why do Ye refuse to hear the simplest of my prayers?" she started to sob.

Bram turned her to him and gathered her in his arms. "Wheesht, Grace, please don't cry."

~ * ~

Bram held her while she sobbed. He had been right earlier, more had happened in the last three days than he knew. How could his parents have done this? They lied to her and set her what seemed to be an impossible task. No wonder she looked tired and needed Teasag's help with Kristen. He was beyond angry with their interference but he knew he had to set that aside for a while. He needed to help the woman in his arms. The woman who had railed against God for allowing her to fall in love. She loved him.

He scooped her up and walked to the chair, where he sat holding her in his arms. She didn't fight him. Quite the opposite, she nestled against him, accepting the comfort he offered. When her tears stopped, he said, "My sweet lass, I am so sorry for what ye have been through over the last few days. I'm sorry if the orders I gave made things worse and I am extremely sorry that my parents led ye to believe that I am betrothed. It is true that they seek a betrothal for me to Annice Sinclair but I will not consent to it. I love ye with all my heart. I will have no other wife but ye."

"That isn't possible, Bram. Ye know it isn't."

"I don't know that. I will tell him tonight what I think of his interference."

"Please don't. Ye don't know what he might do, who else

might be hurt."

Before he could answer there was a knock at the door. Without thinking he called, "In."

Ian entered the cottage and on seeing Bram holding Grace on his lap swore, "Damnation, Bram. What are ye thinking?"

Before he could stop her, Grace was out of his lap and across the room. Keeping her back turned from both him and Ian, she appeared to be swiping tears from her face.

Bram followed her, placing himself between Ian and Grace. "Ian, keep yer voice down. Kristen is sleeping and for that matter what the hell are ye doing here?"

Ian shut the door and in a quieter voice said, "What am I doing here? I'm searching for ye, and I prayed I wouldn't find ye here. Da has been told that ye returned this evening and is furious that ye haven't bothered to show up for supper yet to give him a report."

"There is nothing to report. All is well and I had something more important to attend to."

Ian shook his head. "Bram, this"—he motion towards Grace—"is pure folly."

"That's what I have tried to tell him," said Grace. The plaintive note in her voice tore at Bram's heart.

Bram turned towards her, taking her in his arms again. "Grace, please don't lose hope. Let me speak with my father. I love ye and I will see this through." He lifted her chin and kissed her. It was their first kiss, and far too brief to satisfy him, but her response thrilled him. When he broke the kiss, he rested his forehead on hers. "I swear to ye, I will do what I must to see we are together. But I understand yer fears. Give me a little time to deal with my father." She nodded but the look of doubt and fear in her eyes spoke volumes. "Good night, my love. Tomorrow is St. John's Eve. There will be bonfires and dancing. Ye'll go with me." He kissed her again, before leaving with Ian.

They were barely out of earshot of the cottage when Ian confronted him. "Have ye completely lost yer mind? What in heaven's name possessed ye to promise Grace that the two of ye can be together? Ye know that isn't possible—not unless ye mean to have her as a mistress."

"I mean to have her as a wife," snapped Bram.

Ian gave a mirthless laugh. "A wife? Da will never stand for that. How could ye even suggest it? Please tell me ye didn't say that to her." Ian cast a glance at him. "By the Almighty, Bram, ye did. Have ye no regard for her or Innes at all? Ye can't marry her and I saw the way she looked at ye just now. She thinks she loves ye and it will break her heart."

"I will marry her Ian. I will convince Da."

Ian shook his head. "This is heading straight for disaster."

"Thank ye for yer support, Ian," Bram said bitterly. "If the situation were reversed—"

"Ye would be lecturing me about my responsibilities to the clan. At least one of us is worried about what this will do to the lass."

Bram stopped and faced his brother. "Don't ever suggest that I am not concerned about Grace. I told her and I'm telling ye, I will do whatever it takes. I am going to tell Da now."

"Bram, ye can't do that." Ian put his hand up to stop Bram's argument. "Nay, listen to me. If ye march into that hall and declare in front of the clan members present that ye are going to defy yer laird and marry Grace Breive, what will happen? Da won't stand for it. He can't accept that from anyone and maintain the clan's respect. He could banish ye, and before ye say ye'll go happily with Grace, think about it. He could refuse to let her go. He is her laird, not ye. Perhaps worse than banishing ye, he could force Grace to marry a man of his choosing immediately. He could drag her up here tonight."

"He wouldn't."

"Keep thinking that way and she could be wedded and bedded before ye can get yer head out of ye arse. Ye might have a hope of swaying him privately but if ye push him in public, he'll push back. Harder."

Ian had a point. Bram would willingly face any punishment from their father, but he couldn't risk Da's wrath falling on Grace. He had to ensure she was safe before he did anything. "Ye're right. I will discuss it with him privately, after I am sure he can't harm Grace."

"So, what are ye going to tell him now when he asks why ye're so late for supper?"

"I'll tell him the truth. Grace and Kristen had been caught out in the rain this afternoon and I brought her home. I just stopped by to make sure the child was well."

Ian snorted. "That would explain why the child was tucked up in bed and the mother was curled up on yer lap.

"Fine. I stopped by to check on them both."

Ian nodded. "That'll raise a few eyebrows but at least it is believable and superficially true."

Chapter 16

Although it had rained all night, by terce on Friday morning the sun began to break through the clouds. Even though Bram had assured Grace the previous evening he was not betrothed, she thought it best to finish making the ribbon Lady Sutherland had requested.

Just as she had for the last three days, Teasag arrived to help with Kristen but she was more excited than usual. "Tomorrow is the Feast of Saint John the Baptist so tonight there will be bonfires and dancing. I love bonfires and dancing."

Her enthusiasm was contagious, setting the tone for the day. Grace too began to feel the anticipation. The previous evening, Bram had declared his love for her and even though it scared her, she wanted him in her life. Tonight she would be able to dance with him again and knowing that caused a flutter of excitement in her belly that she hadn't felt in ages.

When time came for the midday meal, Grace decided to take a break so she walked to the kitchens with Teasag and Kristen. The atmosphere in the kitchen seemed tense. Innes said very little and seemed anxious and hurried. Initially Grace thought it might simply be because of the extra work that always led up to a holiday. There would be a feast tomorrow and the preparation would have been underway for days. However, then Grace noticed that several of the women stared boldly at her, disapproval written on their faces.

Something was amiss and now, while she was accompanied by the two lassies, was the wrong time to address it. "Grandmother, I thought we'd just take a wee bite with us and stay out from underfoot today."

The relief on her grandmother's face surprised her. Innes' standard answer to comments like that was that they were always welcome underfoot. Today she said, "Aye, that's the best idea today." Then she quickly wrapped bread, cheese, and some smoked fish in a cloth and handed it to Grace. "Oh, and Grace, will ye be able to help me this evening?"

"Aye, of course, Grandmother."

Something was definitely wrong. Even before Grace had started working on the ribbon, Innes had never asked for her help. Grace had just offered it. For the last few days, when Grace offered to help when daylight waned, Innes refused. Whatever it was, Grace felt sure Innes would tell her later that afternoon. There was no reason to worry about it.

Later, while Kristen napped, Innes came from the kitchens. Teasag had finished weaving her belt and Grace was showing her how to finish it.

Innes smiled at the lass. "That is lovely, Teasag."

"I'm going to wear it to the festival tonight," said Teasag proudly.

"Aye, ye should. Are ye excited?" Innes seemed distracted.

Teasag nodded. "Oh, aye. I can't wait."

"Well, then, why don't ye hie yerself home a bit early today. I'm sure Grace can do without ye for the rest of the afternoon."

Teasag looked to Grace for approval. It was clear to Grace that Innes wanted to speak with her alone. "Aye, Teasag, that is a wonderful idea. Ye can finish knotting this off at home."

"Will I come tomorrow?"

"Nay, sweetling, 'tis a holiday. When ye come on Monday, bring yer empty loom and I will teach ye how to thread the warp."

"All right, I will. Maybe I'll see ye tonight when I'm wearing my new belt?"

"Maybe," answered Grace.

When Teasag had left, Grace looked at her Grandmother. "What is wrong?"

"Am I so obvious?"

"Grandmother, I love ye and I can tell when ye are upset."

"Aye, I am upset, Grace. There are whispers passing through the clan today."

"Whispers?"

"Whispers about ye. They are saying that Bram came here yesterday before even speaking to his father. They say he had been back for hours and he didn't even show up when supper was served. He didn't come to the great hall until Ian went looking for him."

"And what did Bram say?"

"That he had come across ye and Kristen walking back from the village in the rain and he had only stopped in to check on ye both."

"That is true. We walked Teasag home when the rain stopped yesterday afternoon, but it started raining again. He saw us home."

"Aye, lass, but then he came back. Why?"

Grace looked down. She hadn't considered that Bram's presence in the cottage yesterday might start whispers. Grace firmly believed the truth was always best. "I had been angry with him. When he left, he gave an order that Kristen and I couldn't walk on the headlands alone."

"Why would he do that?"

"He thinks it's dangerous. I only found out about the order when Kristen and I started to take a walk one afternoon."

A smile flirted at Innes' mouth. "I expect ye were a bit angry over that."

Grace smiled. "Aye, and I made it clear to him."

"That poor man."

"Anyway, he brought us home, but after he had taken care of Goliath and changed out of his wet clothes he came back. He wanted to talk to me, to explain why he did it."

Innes looked serious again. "But surely that didn't take hours."

"It didn't. At least it didn't feel like hours. But I did lose my temper, and well…"

"Ye didn't listen to him right away."

"Something like that."

"Well, he has done ye no favors. The whispers will die soon enough if ye stay away from him. That's why I asked ye to help me in the kitchen tonight. I will let most of the women go early because of the celebration. They'll know then that ye'll be here. Folks are already speculating about what might happen between ye this eve. They say he danced with no one but ye the night of Pentecost. Ye mustn't be seen with him tonight."

Grace's heart fell. As much as she had looked forward to spending the evening with him, Innes was right. Bram might be planning to declare his love for her to his father, but he clearly hadn't yet and until he did, Grace would suffer the sting of wagging tongues. "Aye, Grandmother. I will help ye in the kitchen."

~ * ~

Bram had found this day to be nothing but frustrating.

After holding his tongue about Grace the previous evening, he hoped to find a chance to speak to his father privately today, but his father managed to avoid him. Bram knew Da was avoiding him because he had spent so much time recently trying to avoid Da, he recognized the signs.

By early evening, he gave up, instead seeking out Grace. He needed to tell her of Ian's concerns and why he hadn't spoken to his father yet. He intended to take Grace and Kristen to the bonfire on the village green. However, there was no answer when he knocked on the door.

He wondered if perhaps she had already left and asked the guardsmen on watch but she hadn't left the castle walls. He thought she might be in the kitchens but he knew the admission he made the previous evening had probably started threads of gossip that would only be fed if he sought her out in front of the women working in the kitchens. He would try again after the evening meal.

Even that didn't work. Just as the meal ended, his father, who had managed to disappear for the whole day, decided that the family should go to the village celebration together. There was nothing for it; he had to try to bring Grace with them. "Da, Grace doesn't know many people yet. I thought I would accompany her to the festivities."

His mother laughed. "Ye are so very thoughtful, Bram. Someday ye will make a truly great leader for this clan, but ye needn't worry about Grace. I understand Innes gave many of the women an early evening so they could join in the celebration with their families. Grace will be helping her finish up in the kitchen tonight. After all, they have been apart for so long I'm sure they want to spend as much time together as possible."

"Mother, if ye were so worried about their time together, it surprises me that ye gave Grace a colossal task to complete that would keep her out of the kitchens." Ian kicked him under the table.

"Ye heard about the ribbon? Oh I wanted that to be a surprise. But, Bram, she likes weaving ribbon and she is very skilled at it. Just imagine what Annice will think of such a lovely gift. Twenty ells of silk ribbon. It would turn any lass's head."

Bram struggled not to lose his temper. "Twenty ells? That is quite a gift." Grace had only mentioned ten.

"Aye. I thought so. At first I asked her for ten ells of blue ribbon with a quatrefoil pattern woven in cream and gold. When yer father saw it, he was so impressed, he thought ten more in another color and pattern would be simply perfect."

"Twenty ells. Ye don't think that is asking a bit much, Da?"

"Nay, I do not. She arrived at our door with nothing but two extra mouths to feed. She can earn her keep like every other member of this clan does."

There was a difference between expecting someone to earn their keep and requesting something completely unreasonable. He was on the verge of telling his parents this when Ian kicked him again and said, "Da, I've been meaning to ask ye, have ye had any news from Boyd recently. Is his training going well?"

Ian had effectively changed the subject and prevented a public confrontation but Bram had difficulty reining in his temper. His parents' callousness, particularly his mother's, had frankly shocked him. She was normally a warm, generous, kind woman. Bram remained quiet and irritable for the rest of the evening, refusing to be pulled into the festivities. He hoped vainly that Grace would come to the village on her own.

As the night wore on and the celebration became more raucous, his parents returned to the keep. Not long after that he found Ian. "I'm leaving. Ye'll have to represent the family for the rest of the night.

"Bram, I'm sorry the evening didn't go as ye had hoped."

"This can't go on, Ian. If Da keeps avoiding me, I will see Grace safely off Sutherland land and once she is safe, tell him my intentions. He can banish me if he wishes."

"Bram, don't do anything rash. Please. Ye may be able to talk him around. I don't want to lose ye and Da won't either. Besides, I don't want to be Laird Sutherland. That is yer cross to bear."

"Good night, Ian." At this point Bram refused to promise anything.

When he returned to the castle he walked around the outer bailey, past the little cottage. It was dark and quiet. He knew it would be—they were long asleep. He walked to the rear entrance of the inner bailey, heading to the keep. To his surprise there was a light in one of the kitchens. He went to the door. There she was, illuminated by the soft light of the dying fire, sitting in a chair by the hearth. For a moment he thought she had fallen asleep, but she turned her head to look at him.

"Grace." He crossed the room and knelt in front of her.

She caressed his cheek. "I'm sorry. I couldn't leave. I so wanted to dance with ye tonight."

"Oh my precious lass, I'm the one who should apologize. I left yer cottage yesterday prepared to tell my father I intend to marry ye. But Ian—he thought I might be putting ye into jeopardy if I defied Da publically. He pointed out that even if Da was inclined to let us marry, he couldn't give in if I showed that level of disrespect. I don't care for myself, but Grace, Da could force ye to marry someone else. That would kill me. I have to speak with him privately to have any hope of a life with ye."

"I'm glad Ian stopped ye. I don't think I could have—how could I have..." She leaned forward and to his heart-stopping delight, kissed him.

He stood, pulling her from the chair and into his arms, returning her kiss, deepening it.

She responded in full measure. She put her arms around his neck, entwining her fingers in his hair.

When he finally broke the kiss, he drew a ragged breath. He had never desired a woman so intensely.

She laid her head on his chest and he rested his cheek against her hair. "Grace, there is another way."

"I don't understand."

"There is another way we can be together and my da would not be able to interfere."

"How?"

"Marry me. Tonight."

"Father Damien wouldn't risk yer father's wrath by marrying us without permission."

"Then we won't ask him. We can go to the Dominican abbey a few hours ride away."

~ * ~

Grace wanted to marry Bram more than anything. They could do this. They could be married before morning and nothing could part them. Aye was on the tip of her tongue. "But Bram, won't that be the same as defying him publically? There will be no chance for ye to prevent a rift if we do that."

"I don't care. Grace, we will return for Kristen and Innes and make a home elsewhere if we must."

Grace's heart fell. That was exactly what her parents had done, which had caused so much pain. "How can we do that? Ye will be banished from yer clan, yer family."

"It is a sacrifice I am willing to make."

"Ye aren't the only one who will suffer, ye must realize that. It's what my parents did. I know the pain it caused Innes, the pain it will cause yer mother. I'm not sure I can inflict that on anyone. Maybe it is best to at least try another way first."

He stepped back from her, cupping her face with both hands. "I don't want to risk losing ye."

"If yer da cannot be swayed, I will marry ye at the abbey. But ye owe it to the ones ye love to try to convince him."

He kissed her again and she nearly lost her resolve. She wanted nothing more than to be his forever. Had she actually asked God to keep love away? When the kiss ended, she was left with a burning need but it was a temptation she could not give in to. "I should go."

Chapter 17

On Sunday, the day after the feast of Saint John the Baptist, during the midday meal, the messenger finally arrived from the Sinclairs. Eanraig frowned as he read the message he brought.

"Do they not wish to come?" Rodina asked.

"Nay, they'll come. But Laird Sinclair says clan business will keep them from traveling immediately. They will arrive in about three weeks."

"Well that's not so long. There is a lot to do to prepare for guests anyway."

Eanraig lowered his voice. "Aye, but Bram is spending increasingly more time with Innes' granddaughter."

"Ye've never been concerned by yer sons' dalliances before?"

"Because that's all they were. A bit of fun. If she were just warming his bed I wouldn't worry, but I fear this is different. He continually seeks her out. Ye notice he's not at the table? Do ye know where he is?"

"Nay, but—"

"He's on the headlands with her and the wee lass. This is the third Sunday in a row he's done that."

"Well, if they are out in the open and chaperoned by a bairn, what could happen?"

"I've already told ye, if she is willing I don't care if he's tupping her. But being seen to court her is entirely different. People will begin to speculate about where his affections lie. Then they will begin to talk about it and that talk might reach Sinclair ears, ruining any chances we have of a betrothal."

"I know ye've been hoping for this alliance with Sinclair, but can't ye achieve that some other way? Could ye let this affection Bram feels run its course? Perhaps if we ignore it, he will lose interest."

"And what if he doesn't? What if he wants to marry her?"

"Would that be so bad if it made him happy? I know it isn't the usual way of things but she seems like a good lass."

"She is a good lass, any parent would be proud of her, but that doesn't matter. Even if she were the finest lass in the Highlands, it doesn't change the fact she is a fisherman's daughter. This alliance is important and there is no better way to achieve it."

"Why is it important? Until a few weeks ago Bram was betrothed to Fiona MacNicol. The Sinclairs weren't important then."

"But they were. Rodina, sometimes ye seek an alliance because the clan would be a powerful friend, like MacLeod and Ross. Other times ye make an alliance because the clan would make a dangerous enemy. MacNicol and Sinclair fall into this category. Now that Alex has taken over from Bhaltair, the MacNicols may pose less of a threat but since that alliance fell through it is vital to form a bond with Sinclair."

"Is there another way?"

"Nay, he has two sons and only one unmarried daughter. A few years ago, before the old Laird died, I tried to get him to let his youngest grandson train here but he had other plans. For the good of the clan Bram has to marry Annice Sinclair."

"I suppose ye're right. I just hate to see him get his heart broken."

"I do too. Still, maybe ye are right and he will lose interest in a few days."

Lose interest. Even as he said the words he thought it unlikely. Still, maybe there was a way to help things along. They had accepted Grace at her word that she was a widow. Just because she proved herself to be Tristan Murray's daughter, that didn't mean that she was all she said she was. Perhaps she wasn't married and the child was a bastard, or she might still be married. She could be hiding any number of sins, which if brought to light would change his son's mind. As soon as the meal was over, Eanraig dispatched a messenger to the Isle of Lewis with orders to visit each of the three clan chiefs on the island and see what could be learned about the woman calling herself Grace Breive.

~ * ~

By the next morning, the talk Eanraig feared had already started. He began hearing rumors about how fond Bram seemed of Innes' granddaughter. Bram apparently stopped by Innes' cottage regularly and had been seen lingering outside like a lovesick swain hoping to catch a glimpse of his beloved. Bram had even issued an order that Grace was not to walk on the headlands without him.

Eanraig worried that he would not learn anything about Grace's past until it was too late. He needed to take steps immediately to separate them. First, Innes' cottage was within the outer curtain wall, making Grace far too easily accessible. This was simple enough to fix.

Second, gossip seemed to be more rampant in his clan than fleas on a beggar. A few tales told within earshot of the right people might be all that was necessary to make Bram rethink his relationship with Grace. Eanraig had a momentary twinge of guilt at the thought of this. Ruining a lass's reputation was a bit underhanded. But he assuaged his conscience with the fact that she wasn't a maiden, she was a widow. Eventually the rumors would blow over after Bram was securely married to Annice.

With righteous resolve, he left his solar ready to set his plans in motion. He was barely out of the great hall, when he saw Bram striding toward him. "Good morning, Father. I tried to speak with ye yesterday but ye were occupied."

"Ye were occupied yerself yesterday, Son."

"Ah, well, that's what I want to talk to ye about."

"I'm sorry, it will have to wait. I have business to attend to this morning."

Bram followed him. "This is important."

"Not so important that ye couldn't meander over the headlands with Mistress Breive instead of waiting for me yesterday. Therefore, ye can wait until I am finished today."

Eanraig strode off. Bram had as much as said he wanted to discuss his relationship with Grace and Eanraig needed to put that off as long as possible.

Chapter 18

It had been four days since Grace had agreed to marry him and Bram still hadn't been able to get his father alone. Bram would speak with him today, or simply elope with Grace. The midday meal was drawing to a close when Bram tried yet again.

"Father, I still need to speak with ye privately."

"I've been terribly busy. I really don't have time today. It will have to wait."

Bram's temper was sorely tested. "This will not wait another moment. Please, can we speak in yer solar?"

His father huffed. "I suppose I can take a few moments."

Finally. Bram followed his father from the hall.

When they reached the solar his father glared at him. "What was it that simply could not wait another moment?"

"Da, I wish to get married."

"And I wish for ye to get married. Problem solved."

"Da, please. I know ye want me to marry Annice Sinclair, but I can't."

"Then we will find another worthy bride for ye."

"I have already found a worthy bride. I love her with all my heart. I cannot, I will not live without her. I am begging ye to please allow this."

His father snorted. In a mocking tone he asked, "And who is the lass for whom ye have this infatuation?"

"Yer condescension is not appreciated."

"Fine, who is it ye love so madly ye would fail to consider the good of the clan first?"

Bram sighed. This was not going to end well. "Da, I love Grace Breive."

"Grace? Ye can't be serious."

"I am serious."

"She is nobody. The daughter of a warrior turned fisherman and coward, the granddaughter of a cook. Son, I know ye think ye love her. Ye are young, she is beautiful and readily available. She is the proverbial bird in the hand. Lad, she isn't an acceptable bride but that doesn't mean ye can't enjoy her. She is a widow, keep her as a mistress for as long as ye wish, but ye can't marry her."

"Da, I could never marry one woman while in love with another."

"Well aren't ye very high-minded? Many men in our position keep mistresses they adore. I don't care if ye fill her belly with a bastard every year until she grows too old to bear children. She does not have the skills or breeding to become the wife of a laird. Annice Sinclair does. What's more, an alliance with the Sinclairs is vital to the clan. I've heard enough of this ridiculousness now. Ye will marry Annice if she agrees. If not, ye will marry some other suitable woman whose family will be an asset to this clan. Ye will produce an heir and ye will have a wife capable of taking her place beside ye in leading this clan. What ye do with Grace is not for me to judge."

Bram's anger and disappointment rivaled for control. He had done what he promised so he stood to leave. "I'm sorry ye consider this ridiculous. I will bid ye farewell and ask that ye give me the opportunity to say goodbye to Mother too. Grace and I will leave immediately. If Innes wishes to join us, I will allow it. I'm certain Ian will make a fine clan leader someday."

"Bram, sit back down. This is utter nonsense. Ye are not throwing away yer birthright for a woman. If yer love for each other is so profound, she would love ye enough not to ask ye to do that. And for that matter, if ye love her too much to keep her as a mistress, ye would let her go so she might find happiness elsewhere."

"Father, ye haven't taken me seriously since the moment I stepped in the solar. I didn't expect that ye would like what I had to say. I didn't even expect ye to understand. Out of my love and respect for ye, I wanted to address this privately, hoping to avoid causing ye embarrassment. Rather than simply eloping I thought it important to try to explain it to ye. For that I expected at least a modicum of respect. However, ye have treated me with disdain, insinuating that I am no more than a green lad, smitten for the first time. Ye have offended me by suggesting that I would treat the woman I love like a whore, and ye have insulted her by assuming she would accept that. There is no reason to sit back down. There is nothing left to say."

His father clenched his teeth. "Ye expected respect, when ye so easily set aside the needs of the clan for yer own personal desires?"

"There has been nothing easy about this and it goes way beyond desire. I am willing to sacrifice anything for the clan. Anything but the woman I love." Bram looked down for a moment. "I see no other choice. Farewell."

"Nay. Stop. Ye'd sacrifice anything for the good of the clan, would ye? Anything except the woman ye love?"

"Aye."

"Would ye sacrifice one month?"

"What do ye mean?"

"Give me one month. Agree not to marry Grace for one month. Agree to at least meet Annice Sinclair and give her a chance to win yer heart. If ye will do these two things, at the end of one month if ye still wish to, ye shall marry Grace with my blessing."

One month. Bram didn't want to wait one day longer, much less a month. However, his father had offered him a choice. If it meant he and Grace could marry with his father's blessing, surely they could wait one month. "Aye. Thank ye, Father. I'll give ye a month."

"And ye'll keep an open mind about Annice?"

There was no sense in arguing. His father would learn soon enough that Grace held his heart and always would. "Aye, I'll keep an open mind about Annice."

"And ye'll stop seeing Grace until then?"

"Nay. That wasn't part of the bargain."

"But, Son—"

"Nay, Da. I said I wouldn't give up the woman I love and I won't. Not even for a day."

~ * ~

Bram went immediately to tell Grace. The day was gray, so Grace was likely inside. He knocked at the door and was surprised when Teasag opened it.

"Good afternoon, lass. What are ye doing here?"

"I help mind Kristen while Grace weaves, except Kristen is napping now. Grace is teaching me to weave."

Bram glanced over Teasag's head to where Grace sat working. She looked up and smiled. She was always beautiful, but when her face was lit with a happy smile she took his breath away.

"Good afternoon, Bram. Would ye like to come in?"

"Aye." He nodded subtly toward Teasag. He didn't want to discuss this in front of her.

Grace clearly took his meaning. "Teasag, I probably won't work anymore today after Kristen wakes. Ye can go home if ye wish and I'll see ye tomorrow."

"All right. Can I take the loom with me to show Mama?"

"Sweetling, it is yer loom. Of course ye can take it. I've told ye that before."

Teasag blushed. "I know ye said that, but…"

Grace smiled again. "There is no but. It's yer loom."

Teasag grinned and untied the bundle of warp threads from the table leg. "Thank ye, Grace. I'll see ye tomorrow."

"Aye, lass, I'll see ye tomorrow."

When Teasag left, Bram asked, "Was that an old loom of yers?"

"Nay, it's a new loom of Teasag's—I made it for her."

"Ye made it?"

"Aye, while ye were gone. I asked her father if it was alright and Michael found the wood for me."

"I'll have to take a closer look at it next time. And while I didn't come here to discuss looms and weaving, why are ye still working on that ribbon?"

"Bram, I was given a task by Lady Sutherland. I can't just not do it. Besides, it is almost finished. A little bit more this afternoon and I will have ten ells."

He drew closer. He had never actually looked at what she was weaving. "Grace, this is beautiful."

She beamed. "Thank ye. I actually do love this. I have never had this much beautiful silk to work with. I'll be able to give it to yer mother by tomorrow afternoon."

"Well, if it is truly for my wife, she will be giving it back to ye in a month's time."

"What?"

"I spoke with my father this afternoon. After a rather heated discussion I told him I would do anything for the clan except give up the woman I loved."

"And he accepted that?"

"Not completely. Since I said I would give up anything but ye, he asked me for one month and I agreed."

"I don't understand."

"He asked me to wait to marry ye for one month. He wants me to meet Annice but after that, I can marry ye with his blessing."

Grace's brow furrowed. "I suppose that's not unreasonable. One month."

"Grace, please don't worry. I love ye. Meeting Annice is simply a formality."

She smiled. "I'm not worried. I didn't dare hope that he would give us his blessing. This is almost too good to believe."

"Well believe it. We will be married and living here at Castle Sutherland in a month."

Chapter 19

Grace wanted to be thrilled at the thought of marrying Bram in a month's time without angering his father. But she couldn't help but worry. Laird Sutherland was a powerful man and that power scared her. Still, Bram was so happy it was hard not to get caught up in his enthusiasm.

She didn't doubt that his parents were not remotely pleased and she soon learned they had no intention of shielding her from their displeasure. When she went to the keep the next afternoon with the completed ribbon, Lady Sutherland scolded Grace in front of everyone at work in the hall.

"I am extraordinarily disappointed in ye, Grace."

"I'm sorry, my lady, is the ribbon not as you wanted it?"

"The ribbon is fine, it's lovely, that's not what I'm talking about. How dare ye seduce my son? Who do ye think ye are? Ye have no business setting yer sights on him."

"My lady, I—"

"I did not give ye leave to speak," she snapped, "and it is high time ye remembered yer place. Ye are a weaver, the daughter of a fisherman, the granddaughter of a cook—a servant in my household. Ye will start behaving as befits someone in yer station instead of playing the wanton for my son. Have I made myself clear?"

A wanton? "But I haven't—"

"Don't dare argue with me. I want an answer. Have I made myself clear?"

"Aye, my lady." There would be no changing her mind anyway.

"Now ye will come with me to my solar. I will give ye the thread and a sample for the next ten ells of ribbon."

Grace followed quietly in her wake.

Lady Sutherland gave her a sample of ribbon that had extremely intricate vines and flowers worked in shades of gray on black ribbon. "I want something like this, only I want the background to be cream, the vines worked in silver and green, and the flowers worked in shades of rose. Can ye do it?"

"My lady, this is a very difficult pattern."

"That's not what I asked. I asked if ye can do it."

"Aye, my lady, but—"

"Ye will learn to hold yer tongue. The answer is aye or nay. Nothing more."

"Aye, my lady."

"Good." Lady Sutherland handed her a basket containing the silk thread. "I want it in ten days."

While it had taken her ten days to weave the first ten ells, what Lady Sutherland was asking now was much more difficult. "Pardon me, my lady, but I don't think I can do that."

"Ye completed the first design in ten days."

"Aye, but the weather was mostly fine, so I had good light. Also, this design is more intricate and ye want more colors. It takes more time."

"I will see that ye have plenty of candles if necessary. Ye will complete this in ten days. I'm sure ye can do it if ye focus on yer work instead of my son."

Ah, this was punishment. Grace simply nodded. "Aye, my lady."

Lady Sutherland's attitude softened a bit. "Grace, this can only end in heartache for both of ye. Surely ye realize that."

"I pray it doesn't, my lady."

Lady Sutherland shook her head in frustration. "Go. Ye need to get to work. I want to see a hand's width tonight. I will come by Innes' cottage after the evening meal."

"Aye, my lady." Grace curtsied and left the solar. As she walked through the hall, she was not surprised by the critical stares and whispered comments.

At the cottage, Teasag still worked her little loom while Kristen slept. "Did she like it?"

"I think she did. She asked me to make more." Grace showed her the sample of ribbon and the beautiful silk thread.

"This will be even prettier than the last," gushed Teasag.

"Aye, and a lot more work. I was hoping to take a break this afternoon, but I need to get started. Would ye like to see how I warp the loom?"

Teasag nodded enthusiastically.

So Grace spent the rest of Kristen's nap time warping the

loom with cream colored thread while she described the steps to Teasag. By the time Teasag left for her home, Grace had the pattern started but to complete the "hand's width" that Lady Sutherland asked for, she had to keep working. Kristen played nearby, carrying on a long conversation with herself. Teasag had helped her build a tiny village from rocks, twigs, and leaves.

Grace wasn't sure how long she had been working like this when a shadow fell across her loom. "Grace, have ye fed the child her supper yet?" asked Michael.

"Michael, ye have an awful habit of standing in my light."

"Aye, well someone should or the two of ye will starve. New colors? Ye've started the next ten?"

"I have and she wants to see a hand's width tonight. I need to work, as long as the light is decent."

"Ye have to eat. Both of ye do."

"We'll be fine for a bit longer."

"Would it help at all if I took Kristen to the kitchen? Innes can see she gets her supper and send her back when she's done— preferably with a wee morsel for Kristen's mama."

"I couldn't ask ye to do that."

He gave a mock sigh. "Grace, will ye never learn?"

She laughed. "All right. It would be very helpful if ye took Kristen to the kitchen. Thank ye, Michael."

"Ye're welcome, Grace. Kristen, my fine wee lassie, would ye mind terribly showing me the way to the kitchens?"

Kristen giggled. "Mama, Michael doesn't know where the kitchens are."

"Well then, ye'd best show him so he doesn't starve."

Kristen took his hand. "Ye go this way."

A few minutes to focus her undivided attention on her work was just what Grace needed. She had almost finished with the sample Lady Sutherland requested when another shadow fell across her work. "Why are ye still working, Grace, and where is Kristen?" asked Bram.

"I'm working because yer mother wants to see a short length of the new pattern she requested, by the time the evening meal is over. Kristen is with Grandmother, eating her supper."

"Then ye should be eating yer supper too. Grace, I'll talk to mother. This can wait until tomorrow."

"Nay, Bram, it can't. She wants another ten ells in ten days. I need to work as long as I can to finish it."

"That is ridiculous. Ye don't need to do this, Grace."

"Aye, I do. I don't want to make her angry and I don't want ye to argue with yer mother over something as silly as ribbon."

Bram frowned. "I don't like this at all."

"Just let it go. When I finish this, if she asks for ten more in ten days, I may need yer help, but let me try to appease her."

"If that is what ye wish. Is there anything I can do to help?"

"Ye can carry the table inside for me." She picked up her loom and the basket of thread.

"Gladly, if it means ye are stopping for the day." Bram carried the table into the cottage.

"Well, I'm not stopping. I will work by candlelight until yer mother comes."

"My mother is coming here?"

"I told ye, she wanted to see a sample after the evening meal."

"I didn't know she was coming here. I will at least ask her to set more reasonable expectations."

"Please don't, and please leave before she gets here."

"Grace, my parents know I intend to marry ye. They shouldn't be surprised to find me here."

"But she's upset. She…" Grace couldn't tell him that his mother accused her of shameful behavior. "Please, let's just try to do what they wish for the next month. Perhaps I can earn their respect."

"Even if ye don't immediately, ye have mine, love, and they will come around." He pulled her into his arms and gave her a kiss that caused her toes to curl. She didn't think she would ever get enough of his strong arms and tender kisses. Before Grace was ready to let him go, Kristen pushed the door open, and Moyra followed her into the room. Kristen grinned and threw her arms around Bram's legs. "Sir Bwam!"

"Oh, my. Sir Bram. I thought Grace was working and couldn't come to the kitchen."

"She was, Moyra. I just helped carry her work table inside."

"Oh. Well, here, Grace. Innes sent ye a bowl of stew and said ye were to stop and eat it while it's warm."

"I heartily agree," said Bram. "I'll stay with ye while ye

eat yer dinner. Moyra, I'm sure ye're needed back in the kitchen."

"Aye, sir. Goodnight, sir."

When Moyra left, Grace sat down wearily at the table. "That will start quite the story."

"I love ye, Grace. That's not a secret so I don't see this as a problem."

Grace nodded but she knew better. He was the laird's son and she was the cook's granddaughter. Any unkind words wouldn't be attached to him. One month, Grace. One month.

She ate her stew quickly while Kristen sat in his lap listening raptly to a story he told her. When he reached the end, Grace had finished and washed the bowl. "Say goodnight to Sir Bram now. It's bedtime."

"Goodnight, Sir Bwam," she said, giving his neck a hug and kissing his cheek.

"Goodnight, my sweet wee lassie." He stood, still holding Kristen. "Good night to ye too, love." He kissed Grace's cheek and put Kristen in her arms. "I'll see ye tomorrow."

Once Grace had Kristen in bed, she lit candles and continued working on the new ribbon. She had a hand's width completed—enough to show the full pattern—by the time Lady Sutherland knocked on the door.

Grace opened it and was surprised to see Lady Sutherland hadn't come alone.

"G-good evening my lady, Laird."

"Good evening, Grace," said Laird Sutherland. "Lady Sutherland said she was coming here to see a sample of the new ribbon and I decided to come with her."

"Please come in. Can I offer ye a seat?"

He stepped inside, looking around appraisingly. "I haven't been in this cottage for years. I had forgotten how small it is. Hmm."

"We won't be staying long, dear. May I see the ribbon, Grace?" Lady Sutherland's icy aloofness was the complete antithesis of the woman Grace first met, the woman who laughed about serving roasted neeps to her husband.

"Certainly, my lady, the loom is here." Grace motioned to the table. "It will be easier to see the pattern in the candlelight."

Lady Sutherland moved past her husband, taking the loom in her hands to get a closer look at the ribbon. A fleeting look of delight crossed her countenance before her stern mask returned.

"This will be fine. Ten ells, Grace. I will not be happy if I hear ye've been slacking."

"Aye, my lady."

"Grace, ye can weave on a cloth loom too?"

"Aye, Laird."

"Hmm. I suppose there really isn't room for one here though, is there?" he said.

"I suppose not, Laird."

"Well, goodnight, Grace. The ribbon ye wove is beautiful. There is a large market for finery such as that. We will have to consider the best way forward."

The best way forward? What did he mean by that?

Chapter 20

Grace barely had time to think over the next few days. She had to complete an ell of ribbon a day to meet Lady Sutherland's request and as she had tried to explain, this pattern was quite a bit more difficult. Every evening Bram stopped by to see her. It was the brightest spot of her day, but it was also the most difficult. Bram became increasingly worried about how Grace pushed herself, urging her to let him speak to his mother. Grace became increasingly committed to completing the ribbon without interference.

Still, she looked forward to the knock on the door that signaled at least a temporary stop to work. Kristen too became excited every evening, wondering when "Sir Bwam" would get there. After putting Kristen to bed, Grace had a few quiet moments alone with Bram. They kissed and talked of the future, and kissed and argued about ribbon, and kissed a little more. For four evenings, she had a glimpse of heaven and she cherished each moment. When they argued about ribbon on Saturday evening he had managed to extract a promise from her that she would take a break and go for a walk on the headlands after Mass.

So as usual on Sunday, Grace walked to the church in the village with Innes and Kristen. However, this morning something was amiss. Villagers gave her hostile stares and whispered behind their hands. Innes seemed confused, but Grace heard the epithets uttered by several less discreet Sutherlands. Words like wanton, harlot, and whore were being bandied about and clearly they were referring to Grace.

Innes seemed unaware so Grace held her head up and ignored the insults. Apparently Bram's visits, as brief and chaste as they were, had not gone unnoticed. She would have to tell him to stop, and then maybe it would blow over. When Mass was nearly over, she whispered, "Grandmother, I need to get started on the ribbon, would ye mind if I went ahead?" She had ignored all the spitefulness she was capable of.

"Nay, of course not, pet," Innes whispered back.

So as soon as the final blessing was spoken, she picked Kristen up and hurried out of the church, avoiding as many people as she could.

Bram caught up to her before she reached the outer curtain wall. "Grace, love, what's yer hurry?"

"I have work to do."

"Sir Bwam," squealed Kristen, reaching her arms to him.

He took Kristen from Grace and walked beside her. "Hello my sweet wee lassie." He greeted Kristen with a kiss on the cheek. "Grace, ye promised to take a break today."

"Are we going to cwimb the hiww?"

"Aye, we are," answered Bram.

"But not until later, Kristen. I need to work for a while first."

"Grace, this has to stop. Ye just need a few more days. My mother will understand."

"Nay Bram, she won't. She made herself very clear. Please, I don't want to talk about this. I just need to get to work."

He stopped, grabbed her shoulder, and turned her to face him. "Ye're upset. What's happened?"

"Nothing. Come, Kristen, come with Mama." Grace reached for her.

Kristen frowned. "I wike Sir Bwam."

"I'll carry her to yer cottage." His statement brooked no argument. "And Grace, clearly something is wrong."

"I can't talk about it now. Little ears."

Kristen tugged on her ears. "I have wittle eaws."

"Yes ye do, sweetling," said Grace.

"Then we will talk about it later, while Kristen naps."

"Fine." Grace worried that she shouldn't be seen walking the headlands with Bram, but at least that was out in the open where no one could speculate about what they were doing.

When they reached the cottage, Bram put Kristen down. He reached out and caressed Grace's cheek. "I'm worried about ye, love."

She leaned into his caress. "I know. It will be all right. We'll talk later. I'll get a packet of food from the kitchen and meet ye at the gate after the bells ring sext."

~ * ~

Grace was able to get several hours of work in before

midday. Just as she was putting her loom away, Peggy appeared at the open door. "Laird Sutherland asked me to fetch ye. He has an announcement to make before the midday meal and he wants ye and Innes both there."

This worried Grace but there was nothing she could do. "Aye. I'll just get Kristen and go to the kitchens."

When Grace and Kristen arrived at the kitchens, Innes was in the midst of the usual flurry of activity, which occurred just before a meal. Grace was not warmly welcomed as she had been until a few days ago, although several of the women called greetings to Kristen.

When Innes saw her she said, "Ah, there ye are, lass. The laird has something important that he wishes us to hear."

"That's what Peggy said. Do ye know what it concerns?"

Innes laughed. "Nay lass, I've never claimed to know his mind except where his preference in food is concerned. But we shouldn't keep him waiting. Come now."

Grace followed Innes and the other women from the kitchen into the hall. Kristen walked beside her, holding her hand. When they reached the hall Laird Sutherland stood and called for quiet. Bram was at one end of the long refectory table but his expression revealed nothing.

"Innes, before we begin our meal, I have an announcement that I would like everyone to hear. But first, remind me, how old were ye when ye started working in the kitchens here?"

Innes smiled broadly. "I was ten and four, Laird, but then ye knew that."

"Fifty years. Ye've been serving this clan, keeping bellies full, and creating wonderful feasts for fifty years. I was just a bairn the age of yer lovely wee Kristen when ye started."

"Now, Laird, did ye call me in here to remind me of how old I am?"

Laird Sutherland gave a warm and genuine laugh. Clearly Grace's grandmother had enjoyed a long and friendly relationship with him.

"Nay Innes, never that. I just want to recognize yer long and faithful service to my household. And I would like to reward ye. Ye have recently discovered yer granddaughter and great-granddaughter and after so many years of separation from yer family, I realize that time with them is precious and ye spend much too much of yer time working. I think after fifty years, ye deserve an opportunity to rest and spend time with yer family."

"Oh, Laird, I'd like that."

Grace did worry that her grandmother worked long strenuous hours. It was time for her to let others carry the load. She glanced again at Bram, who now wore a slight frown.

The laird winked at Innes. "I thought ye would. So, it is with deepest gratitude that I announce this will be the last meal ye preside over here at Castle Sutherland. Maisie will take over the running of the kitchens. Furthermore, it has come to my attention that yer cottage, while perfect for one, is a tad small for three. I want ye to have space to be comfortable so I have had a cottage in the village prepared for ye and will see ye moved in there tomorrow."

Grace glanced at Bram again. His face now wore a scowl.

"Laird, I have lived in my wee cottage for so long, I can't imagine living anywhere else."

"I know it will be a change for ye, but I'm thinking of yer lassies too. Grace has demonstrated excellent skills as a weaver. I would like for her to be able to practice her craft and there simply isn't room for a cloth loom in yer cottage. However, a new loom and an abundant supply of wool and flax has already been delivered to yer new home."

Grace was floored. This was extraordinarily generous and she was thrilled at the idea of weaving more than just ribbon again. "Thank ye, Laird. That's very kind."

"Ye're welcome, Grace. Yer skills are truly extraordinary."

"Thank ye, Laird."

"Now, ye may return to yer duties and serve the meal."

Grace followed Innes back to the kitchen. Innes was thrilled. "Grace, pet, this is wonderful. Now ye can weave to yer heart's content and I can help mind the little sprite."

Grace wasn't sure she could fit another minute of weaving into her day, but it would be nice to spend more time with Innes and have help minding Kristen. "Aye, Grandmother, it will be perfect and I must admit I am thrilled at the idea of having a cloth loom again."

"The laird has seen all the hard work ye've done, lass."

Grace couldn't help but think the Laird had other motives, but she wouldn't dim Innes' joy by mentioning them. "Aye, I suppose that's it." She hugged Innes. "I am so happy this pleases ye."

~ * ~

Bram wasn't waiting for them when she and Kristen reached the gate in the curtain wall. Of course he wasn't there. What had she been thinking? He had been in the great hall. Calder was one of the men on duty. "Where are ye heading, Grace?"

"We're going on our Sunday walk."

"We're going to cwimb the hiww," said Kristen.

"Grace, I can't let ye go alone. Ye know that."

"I didn't intend to go alone. Bram asked us to meet him here. I guess he was delayed. We won't go far."

"Ye won't go at all. And Grace, spending so much time with Bram is a mistake. Go on home now and leave him alone. I understand ye have a lot of work to do anyway."

"But—"

"Ye heard me, Grace."

Taken aback, all she could say was, "Aye. Good day, Calder."

It occurred to her that once they lived outside the castle walls, there wouldn't be guardsmen to stop her taking a walk with her daughter. If it hadn't been for the hostility she had encountered that morning, she would walk to the village just to give Kristen some sort of outing but she couldn't face that again. Instead, she turned back toward the cottage but Kristen pulled hard on her hand. "Mama, we were going to cwimb the hiww."

"I know, sweetling, but we can't right now."

"But Sir Bwam said we could."

"We misunderstood him, Kristen. We'll do it another time."

"But I wanted to eat on the gwass and Sir Bwam said we could."

"I'm sorry, sweetling, but Teasag's papa says we can't right now."

Kristen was spiraling downward as only a tired, frustrated three year old can. "Nay! I want to cwimb the hiww and Sir Bwam said we could," she yelled, sitting down on the ground and crying for all she was worth.

Grace understood her disappointment but there was no point in trying to reason with a screaming child. She picked Kristen up and carried her back to the house, garnering plenty of stares.

Eventually Kristen calmed down. They ate the meal that they had been taking with them, and Grace put her to bed for a nap. She had barely taken out her loom when Bram appeared in the doorway. "Grace, love, I'm sorry. I was leaving the keep to meet ye at the gate when Da told me my presence was required at the midday meal. I had no idea what he had planned."

After having dealt with a petulant child for the last hour, Grace was feeling a little petulant herself. "It wouldn't have mattered if ye had lifted that ridiculous order about me walking on the headlands alone."

"It's not ridiculous. We've been through this. It's in yer best interest."

"I can promise ye, dealing with a disappointed child who's screaming 'Sir Bwam said we could' loud enough that everyone in the village could hear, is not in anyone's best interest, least of all mine."

"It's no reflection on ye. It was my fault."

"Why she was screaming doesn't matter. All small children breakdown now and again. The problem was what she was screaming."

"Why was that a problem?" He came inside the cottage and sat on a stool at the table by her.

"For the same reason that ye being here with me alone is a problem. Apparently I am the subject of clan gossip at the moment. That is what upset me this morning."

"What's being said?" he demanded.

"I don't know exactly, but after hearing words like 'whore' and 'harlot' I can guess."

"What? This will stop immediately."

"Bram, ye may be the laird's heir and ye can control a lot of things, but ye can't control what people think. Trying to quash rumors with defensiveness is likely to make things worse. The only way to quiet the gossip is to stop the behavior causing it."

"But ye haven't done anything."

Grace rolled her eyes. Men could be incredibly dense sometimes. "I danced with ye at Pentecost, I've walked the headlands with ye on Sundays, and ye've spent time with me here, every evening for the last few days."

"There's nothing wrong with any of that."

"I guess that depends on yer point of view."

"Dancing, walking, a few minutes spent together of an

evening? I enjoy yer company—I love ye and intend to marry ye, what point of view am I missing?"

Grace actually laughed. "I love ye too but I expect that is the crux of the problem. I am the daughter of a fisherman and the granddaughter of a cook—or a former cook now." She echoed his mother's sentiments from a few days ago. "I have no business falling in love the laird's son or seducing him into fall in love with me."

"Seducing me?"

Grace frowned and nodded toward the bedroom. "Wheest."

Bram lowered his voice. "If anything, I did the seducing. Ye dragged yer feet the whole way."

"I'm sure that's not the way they see it. I suspect yer da relieved Grandmother of her duties and is moving us outside the castle walls to put some distance between you and me."

"Aye, well I'm certain of that but it won't do any good. I won't give ye up, Grace. He knows this. He agreed to it."

"But he doesn't have to make it easy. Honestly, Grandmother seems very happy anyway. Perhaps if ye stop visiting me until this month is over the gossip will die."

"This gossip will die, whether I visit ye or not. I am going now to see if I can set a few things straight. I will be back in a bit and we will 'climb the hill' after Kristen wakes."

"Really, Bram, I—"

"Nay, Grace, I don't want ye hurt by this." He gave her a quick kiss and left.

Ah, my love, I'm afraid that is inevitable.

~ * ~

By the time Bram returned to Grace, his anger had cooled, but barely. When he started asking questions, people were more than willing to share whatever juicy tidbits they had heard about the woman he loved. According to the rumors, it was not only Bram who visited Grace. The other name most often linked with hers was Michael but if the stories were accurate, a quarter of the garrison, even some of the married men, visited Grace regularly.

He knew the tales were patently false. Not only was he confident in her love and fidelity, what the gossips alleged was simply impossible. She spent practically every waking moment weaving the ribbon his mother requested. He had watched her do the painstaking task, advancing less than a finger's length an hour and she worked until she had an ell or more finished every day.

He staunchly defended her against each accusation, but soon realized she had been right. His denials were greeted with expressions ranging from skepticism to pity.

He was acutely aware of the stares cast their way as he left the castle walls with her to walk on the headlands. As much as he hated to give voice to all he had heard, he believed she would want to know. When they were well away from the castle, and Kristen was occupied picking flowers, he broached the subject. "Grace, after I left this afternoon, I tried to find out the nature of the gossip about ye."

She nodded. "Was it as I feared?"

"Sadly, it was worse. Apparently I am not the only man ye are dallying with."

She paled. "What? Bram, I didn't—I've never..."

He wrapped his arms around her. "Wheest, love, I know that."

"Who do they say I...I..."

"Frankly, about a third of the garrison, but most commonly, Michael MacBain."

"I only know a handful of the men, and Michael? Michael is a friend. He was kind and helped me when I needed it. That is all."

Bram arched an eyebrow. "Why would ye ask Michael for help instead of me?"

"In most circumstances I wouldn't but ye were away at the time anyway. He was in the hall when yer mother asked me for the first ten ells. He saw that I was upset and offered to get Teasag to help me. He also found the small table I carry outside to work on and the piece of wood that I made Teasag's loom from."

"Aye, I remember ye mentioning that now."

"Bram, this is much worse than I imagined."

"I know it is, love. I have done what I can to stop the gossip."

"I'm afraid that is like telling the tide to stop."

"It will blow over, Grace."

"Until it does, ye have to stop visiting me."

"Why would I do that? It just gives ye more time for all those other men."

Grace slapped his chest. "Stop teasing, this isn't funny."

He captured her lips in a quick kiss. "I'm sorry. But, I'm

not going to stop visiting ye. Now that Innes will no longer be working late in the kitchens, we will be properly chaperoned. This will all be forgotten when we are married."

~ * ~

Although Grace had prayed Bram was right about the rumors dying away, things only got worse.

The next day, the laird had all of their belongings put on a wagon and taken to their new home. While still very modest, it was much larger than the cottage in outer bailey had been. However, it was at the farthest edge of the village—the last cottage on the north side.

While Innes was thrilled, Grace heard the message Laird Sutherland was sending loud and clear. She suspected the villagers heard it as well—I am displeased with Grace and moving her as far away from my men and my son as I can. Consequently her new neighbors, people who she had begun to think of as friends, treated her as a pariah.

On Tuesday morning, after they had moved to the new cottage, Una arrived at their door. She held Teasag's loom in her hands.

"Good morning, Una, what a surprise. Please come in," said Grace.

She stepped past Grace, completely ignoring her. "Good morning, Innes. Are ye finding the new cottage to yer liking?"

"Aye Una, I am. It is nice to have a bit of room and time to spend with my lassies."

"I'm glad to hear that. Actually, it is why I came. With ye here to care for wee Kristen, it's clear ye no longer need Teasag's help."

"I suppose that's true, but she seemed to be enjoying learning to weave. She's welcome to come any time," said Grace.

Again Una ignored her. "As I said, Innes, ye no longer need Teasag, and I fear yer granddaughter is not a good influence for an impressionable young lass."

Innes appeared confused. "Una, I don't understand…"

"Clearly much has gone on behind yer back and I don't blame ye for it, but I can't have my daughter associated with the likes of Grace." She laid the loom on the table. "Good day, Innes."

Una swept past Grace, out of the cottage.

"What is she talking about Grace?"

"Grandmother, perhaps ye should sit down and I'll tell

ye."

Grace told her about the rumors that had spread through the clan. For her part Innes believed no more of it than Bram had. "Lass, ye've been working so many hours on that ribbon, ye have barely been eating and sleeping. I know ye've spent a bit of time with Bram and there were some whispers about it, but I see no real harm in that."

"I didn't either." But that wasn't exactly true. Grace knew she shouldn't be spending a bit of time with Bram any more than she should have accepted his proposal. Laird Sutherland had other plans. Still, Grace hadn't told her grandmother about Bram's proposal yet or the laird's request that he wait for one month, and now didn't seem like the right time. The month would be up soon enough and then they could marry with the laird's blessing.

Chapter 21

Several days passed and little changed. Bram still came every evening, and Grace still faced ridicule every day. It became increasingly difficult to bear but Grace kept reminding herself that in a few weeks she would be able to marry Bram and perhaps things would get better then. She continued to work practically every waking moment on the ribbon. Having her grandmother's help with Kristen had allowed Grace to work more, but she hated that she had so little time with her daughter.

Still, the tenth day was only two days away and after the ribbon was completed, she would make it up to both Kristen and Innes. She sat at her table outside, at the end of the cottage, away from the direct view of the villagers. It was the only way to avoid their scathing comments.

She tried to focus on her work but on hearing horses approach from the direction of the forest, she looked up. Laird Sutherland and one of his guardsmen approached. She looked down again, praying they would ride on past, but the horses stopped in the lane. Laird Sutherland dismounted, handed his reins to the guardsman, and walked towards her. Ye still aren't listening to me are ye, God?

"Good afternoon, Grace."

"Good afternoon, Laird."

"'Tis a fine day."

"Aye, Laird, it is."

"Walk with me."

"Laird, I have work to do."

"That was not a request, Grace."

Grace nodded. "Aye, Laird." She put the loom and thread into her work basket and sat it inside the bedroom window.

Laird Sutherland gestured in the direction from which he had just ridden. She fell in step beside him, walking towards the forest. The guardsman remained behind.

"It's time we talked." Without further preamble, Laird

Sutherland said, "I do not want ye to marry my son."

"Ye've made that abundantly clear."

"Mind yer tongue, lass. I am yer laird and right about now, whipping ye for insolence is very enticing."

Grace bowed her head. "Forgive me, Laird. I forgot myself."

He inclined his head slightly, accepting her apology. "So we have established that I do not want ye to marry Bram and I am yer laird. As yer laird, I am here to assign ye an extremely important task. However, I know ye've led a sheltered life and have very little knowledge of the world, so I intend to educate ye a bit before giving ye yer task."

Grace had a sinking feeling in her gut. This was bad. This was very bad.

"Grace, the Highlands, in fact most of the civilized world, is divided into land areas, each of which is governed by a nobleman and his family."

Grace fought desperately not to roll her eyes or do anything else that could be considered insolent, but for the love of God, did he think her an eejit?

He continued in the same vein. "To maintain order and withstand aggression, friendly connections and strategic relationships must be developed. We send our sons to live and train with other families and select spouses for our children to help maintain those alliances. I realize that as a lass who grew up in a small fishing village, you couldn't possibly understand the importance of this. Commoners have the luxury of marrying for love. Noblemen do not." He paused for a moment. "Do ye understand me?"

Of course she understood him—much better than he could possibly know. But she simply answered, "Aye, Laird."

"Our neighbors to the north, Clan Sinclair, have been troublesome over the years. We have never had a formal relationship with them. However, of late, they have been entering into a number of alliances, with our other neighbors. If one clan does this, creating a block of allies, the united clans can invade and seize a lone clan's holding, dividing it among themselves. So we have to guard against this. When Laird Sinclair married his granddaughter to Laird MacLeod's heir I became worried. I need an alliance with Laird Sinclair to protect my clan."

Grace couldn't hold her tongue. "I thought yer youngest

son was in training with Clan MacLeod? Surely they wouldn't join with Sinclair against ye?"

His eyes narrowed for a moment. "That remark reveals yer incredible naiveté. A marriage bond is much tighter than one created by fostering. Only a firm alliance with Sinclair will ensure my clan's safety. Do ye understand?"

His condescension galled her. "Aye, Laird."

"Then ye will understand my request. Ye will tell my son that ye do not wish to marry him."

"I can't, he won't believe me."

"Ye can and ye will. Ye will tell him whatever ye need to in order to convince him his affection is misplaced."

"I won't. Banish me if ye wish. I will leave now, but I won't lie to Bram."

"Curb that insolent tongue, lass, or suffer the consequences. It is only my son's affection for ye that has stayed my hand so far. Is that perfectly clear?"

Grace nodded.

"Answer me!" he roared.

"Aye, Laird. I'm sorry."

He stared at her for a long moment, appearing to seethe with anger. "Now, listen well. This is what ye will do this evening when my son visits ye, as he always does. Ye will tell him ye don't love him and ye never did. Ye will tell him the only reason ye went along with this farce was to improve yer station in life, to become Lady Sutherland someday, but ye have fallen in love with someone else."

"Please, Laird, he won't believe that. He knows it isn't true."

"Ye will make him believe it. If he doubts ye, if he learns I am behind this, if ye leave Sutherland land before ye have done this hoping he follows, if ye do anything that results in Bram abandoning his birthright, this is what will happen. I will find ye, and I will see ye married to one of my men. If ye think Bram seeing ye live yer life married to another man will be easier for him to take then do it. But I can promise ye, the kinder choice, the only choice if ye truly love him, is to cause him a little pain now that will heal with time.

"And one last thing. If ye think the answer is to run away somewhere with him to be married in secret, like yer parents did, put that out of yer head. I will find ye both. I will kill ye before his eyes and then banish him anyway. He will lose his birthright and the woman he loves because of one selfish act that ye could have prevented. Furthermore, Kristen will lose her mother and be left to my care. Consider that."

"Aye, Laird," she whispered.

"Grace, I am not evil incarnate. The welfare of my clan, yer clan, is in jeopardy here, which makes the stakes very high. If ye do this, I will reward ye well. I will see that ye, Innes, and Kristen are always cared for. If ye wish, I will find ye a home with another clan. Ye will be comfortable for the rest of yer life and free to marry whomever ye choose, except one of my sons."

It was all Grace could do to keep a small bit of control over her temper. "Reward me, Laird? If I do this ye will reward me? No thank ye, Laird. I will accept nothing from ye—not so much as a farthing. I will do as ye have commanded, but not for any reward. Ye believe this is both in Bram's best interests and for the good of the clan. It doesn't matter whether I believe that or not, yer threats give me no choice. But please, don't insult me by offering to pay me."

"That's yer choice. As long as ye understand what is expected of ye, we're done here." He turned and walked back toward the cottage, leaving her standing in the lane.

She would not panic. She would not break down. She would not let him see her cry. She continued walking toward the forest. Once she reached the cover of trees, and was sure no one could see her from the village, she knelt and wept. There was no railing against God. This was her own fault. She had known better. She had prayed for God to protect her from love because she knew she was weak. Now this pain was the price.

When she finally regained control, she stayed in the forest until she figured out her best course. As soon as possible, she would do what was expected of her and lie to Bram about not loving him. Just thinking it rent her heart. After that she would work every waking moment to spin and weave. When Dugald and Mary returned at Michaelmas near the end of September, she would go with them to sell her work. She would take Kristen, and Innes if she wished, and they would not return to Sutherland.

It was a plan. Not one that made her happy and she worried that it took her too close to Fearchar Morrison, but it was all she had. Her reputation here was in tatters. Once she had severed her relationship with Bram, she wouldn't have the security of his protection. She needed to leave Sutherland for good.

With a heavy sigh, she rose to leave. As she brushed the dirt from her skirt, leaves crunched behind her. She unsheathed the knife she always wore strapped below her knee and spun around to face whomever it was.

"Hold, lass," said Michael, putting up his hands. "I mean ye no harm."

"Michael, ye scared me."

"I'm sorry. That wasn't my intention."

"I should really be getting back. I have work to do and Kristen will be waking from her nap. It will worry grandmother if I'm not there."

"I understand, but I need to speak to ye."

"It's been a bad day, Michael. Can it wait?"

"I suspect I'm about to make yer bad day worse, but I'm afraid it can't wait."

"Michael, ye don't understand—"

"Aye, I do. I saw the laird riding through the village, coming from this direction. I know what he was planning to do today."

"I don't know what ye're talking about."

"Grace, yer eyes are red and swollen from crying. Ye know exactly what I'm talking about. The laird ordered ye to break all ties with Bram and threatened ye with a forced marriage to someone else if ye didn't."

"How do ye know that?"

"Because I am who the laird plans to marry ye to. I'm sorry, Grace. This is not by my choice, which is why I'm here. I won't lie, I think ye are perfectly lovely. I enjoy yer company, I'm fond of yer daughter, and I would happily make ye my wife if that was yer choice. But I know it isn't."

"I don't understand."

"I'm sure ye don't but I'll explain what I know. Laird Sutherland never intended to give Bram the opportunity to marry ye. When Bram told his father he would accept banishment to be with ye, the laird grasped at any straw. He is a hard man, but he loves his sons. He also firmly believes the clan needs an alliance with Sinclair. He had hoped the love Bram professed was only infatuation, but perhaps as forbidden fruit ye were all the more attractive. He thought if he removed that allure, Bram would lose interest. He knew within days that he was wrong, but he had made the bargain. He also thought ruining yer reputation would turn Bram away from ye."

"Laird Sutherland started the rumors?"

"Aye. That's when I realized what was happening. He said things to Lady Sutherland or Guardsmen, in front of servants who would carry the tales. He said things about you and I, which eventually got back to me. I knew they were completely untrue so I assumed the other tales were as well. What the laird didn't count on was the whole scheme backfiring. Bram also refused to believe the rumors so instead of turning him against ye, it made him more protective than ever."

Grace smiled. "Aye, it did. His unswerving faith in me has made this whirlwind of gossip tolerable."

"Unfortunately it meant the laird had to find another way to separate ye. He came to me asking if I would be willing to marry ye."

"Why ye?"

Michael grinned a little sheepishly. "Shortly after ye arrived, he overheard me say that I meant to court ye. And I did, until I realized ye had given yer heart to someone else. He told me that he wanted ye married before Bram could stop it. I told him I couldn't marry a woman who loved someone else. After he finished ranting about love, he leveled a threat. If I didn't agree to marry ye, he would send me packing and find someone else who would marry ye. In fairness to him, he said he knew I would treat ye well and that might make it easier on Bram in the long run."

"So ye agreed?"

"Grace, I do not like to be manipulated by anyone. I agreed, but I had no intention of forcing ye to marry me. I planned to tell Bram when and where it was to take place so that he could interfere and marry ye himself. Then Laird Sutherland changed his plan again. He decided to order ye to sever ties with Bram first and use the threat of a forced marriage to see it done. He reckoned it would be better to cleanly break Bram's heart once and let him move on than to allow him to pine after the woman he loved forever. I came here to tell ye to leave with him now. I'll tell him what has happened while ye pack up. It would probably be best if Innes didn't go with ye immediately but I'll see she joins ye wherever ye settle."

"We can't do that, Michael. Laird Sutherland swears he will find us, kill me, and banish Bram anyway. I would do as my parents did and try to escape him if it were only me, but I have to think about Kristen."

Michael looked shocked. "God's bones. I never would have thought him capable of that. I thought simply ensuring that ye and Bram could elope was the solution."

"The only solution is for me to do as I have been ordered. For Bram's good and the good of the clan, I must look into the eyes of my beloved and lie. I must break the heart of the man who loves me and believes in me. Only then will the laird leave me be."

"That's just it, Grace. The laird has no intention of allowing ye to remain unmarried. He knows the attraction between the two of ye is too strong. He doesn't think Bram will believe ye forever, unless ye marry someone else right away. So as soon as ye have Bram convinced, the laird is going to force ye to marry anyway. He wants any hope Bram has of changing yer mind to be dashed before Annice Sinclair arrives.

She turned away from him and put her face in her hands. "I'm so sorry, Michael. Ye shouldn't have to suffer for my mistake."

"Yer mistake? What's that rot?"

"I knew better. I tried not to love him, but…"

"Oh by all that's holy, Grace, stop. Ye couldn't have prevented this. There was an instant, powerful connection between ye and Bram. Everyone saw it. Even so, I never believed he would risk his future by defying his father. I think ye're a grand lass, but I'm not sure whether I would have in his position. Still, I'm not in his position so I intended to be the one to pick up the pieces when he broke yer heart."

She gave a little laugh and turned back around. "Ah, Michael, ye're quite the romantic. Talk like that will turn a lassie's head."

He shrugged and grinned. "I aim to please." Then his expression sobered. "I don't want to see ye hurt, Grace but I fear there is no way to avoid it."

"So, what do we do now?"

"If ye don't want to lie to Bram, ye can tell him the truth. The end will be the same either way but ye won't be the one to hurt him."

"He'll be hurt anyway and absolutely no good will come of it. He may refuse to marry Annice or she'll refuse to marry him. The laird was right about one thing—the kinder choice is to cause

Bram a little pain now, from which he will quickly recover."

"I'm not sure he'll recover as quickly as the laird believes. Still, it would kill him to know ye love him but ye were forced to marry me. Besides, he might kill me…and his da. I'd rather avoid that." He gave her a mirthless smile, which told her that he might not be jesting. "So, here is the way I see it. The laird's reason for forcing ye to marry is to help convince Bram ye don't love him. If we run away together, that would do the same thing. We'll take Kristen and Innes with us. I'll escort ye to yer old home on Lewis. For that matter, I would happily stay there and court ye. Perhaps, when yer heart has healed some, there might be a bit of room in it for me."

"Michael, I can never go back to Lewis."

"Don't tell me ye're covering some dark past," he teased.

"Nay. Laird Morrison's son, Fearchar, wanted…well he wanted…me. He threatened to hurt me if I didn't submit. The men in my village knew he wouldn't relent. Ye remember Mary and Dugald?"

"The friends from Durness that visited ye a few weeks ago? Ye mentioned that ye stayed with them for a while."

"Aye, well that's why. As soon as Fearchar threatened me, my father's friends wanted me to leave the island immediately. They had no other way to protect me."

"Then I will take ye to yer mother's clan."

"I don't know who they are. Ye've heard the story. My parents feared them. My mother never told me where she came from."

"Grace, ye aren't leaving us many options."

"Well, there's Mary and Dugald. They will take me in. I worry that Durness is too close to Fearchar but I don't see any other option. Before ye found me, I had just decided I would take Kristen and go with them when they came by this way at Michaelmas."

"Aye, Durness isn't yer best option either. Grace, would marriage to me be so bad? If we were married, I could take ye to my clan."

"Nay, of course marriage to ye wouldn't be bad. Ye are a friend, a good friend. There are marriages built on less, but I think ye deserve more."

"And if I don't want more?"

"Well at the rate things are going, ye might not get it

anyway. But if ye wish to stay wherever we go, I won't tell ye nay. And maybe someday…but I'm afraid my heart won't survive this loss."

"It will, Grace." He gave her a half smile. "So, we will go to Durness."

Chapter 22

Grace and Michael decided the task of convincing Bram she didn't love him may as well start immediately. They walked from the forest together, holding hands, making sure that they were seen. When they reached the cottage door she turned to face him. Michael put one hand on the door near her head, leaned in, and brushed her cheek with his other hand. Any villagers who could see them would believe it was a lovers' tête–à–tête. "Grace, I expect Bram will visit ye later. It is probably best to tell him then. Ye need to pack and have Kristen ready to go immediately after Bram leaves. I'll come for ye as soon as I know he's gone."

Grace knew she had to do this, but it was torture to think on it. "Aye, I understand."

"I'm going to kiss ye now and then I'll leave. Will ye be all right?"

"I have to be."

"That is the indomitable lass I know." He brushed his lips against hers in a brief, chaste kiss. "Until later."

She nodded but feared crying again if she said anything. When she entered the house, her Grandmother knew instantly that something was wrong. Grace told Innes the truth, or at least a version of it. She explained about Bram's plans to marry her and the month that he had promised his father. Grace also told her grandmother what Laird Sutherland had asked her to do for the good of the clan.

"Oh, sweetling, I am so sorry. I know ye do love Bram, but the laird wouldn't have asked this of ye if it weren't absolutely necessary."

"Aye, Grandmother. I know that. The laird is also concerned that Bram may not completely believe me. He wants me to marry someone else…immediately. But, I can't."

"He's the laird, dear. Who does he want ye to marry?

"Michael."

"Well, he is a very nice man. He would make ye a good

husband.

"Aye, he's a good man, but that isn't the point. I can't marry him when I love someone else and if I stay here I will be forced to."

"Grace, I don't think the laird would force ye."

"Aye, he would and I won't let that happen."

"How can ye stop it, lass?"

"Michael has agreed to take us to Durness. I have friends there. We'll have to leave tonight. As soon as I have told Bram."

"I can't leave, Grace. Not like this. We could leave in a few days perhaps."

"Nay, Grandmother, Kristen and I have to leave tonight."

"Grace, I don't want ye to go, lass, please. Please stay here and do what the laird asks of ye. Please, lass."

The thought of leaving Innes broke Grace's heart. "Oh, Grandmother, I—I will think on it a bit." Grace knew she couldn't stay, but she wouldn't upset Innes further now. She would send for her once she was settled.

They were washing up after dinner when he knocked on the door. Grace girded herself and opened it. Mother of God, the hurt in his expression nearly undid her. Clearly he had heard about Michael.

Kristen came barreling towards him. "Sir Bwam." She threw her arms around his legs as she always did.

He knelt on one knee and wrapped her in his arms. Kristen couldn't see the raw pain on his face but Grace could. "Kristen, my sweet wee lassie, I'm going to give ye a good night kiss now. Yer mama and I need to talk for a bit, and I don't think I'll be back…to tuck ye in."

"Good night, Sir Bwam. I wuv ye." Kristen planted a wet kiss on his cheek.

"I love ye too, Kristen." His voice was thick with emotion. He gave her a tender kiss on her forehead. Then, standing, he looked at Innes. "Excuse us."

"Certainly, Sir Bram. Grace, I'll see Kristen to bed."

"Thank ye, Grandmother." Bram held the door for her and she stepped out into the evening cool.

"Shall we walk to the forest? That seems to be a popular spot." The whip Laird Sutherland had threatened her with earlier could not have stung more than the bitterness in Bram's voice.

"Whatever ye wish."

"Ye aren't even going to deny it?"

"I can't. I have never lied to ye before."

"Haven't ye? I believed ye when ye said the vicious gossip wasn't true. I defended ye. Why, Grace? Why did ye let me believe ye loved me? Why did ye let me make a fool of myself to my father? Why? What purpose did it serve if ye loved another."

His father's words echoed in her mind. Ye will tell him the only reason ye went along with this farce was to improve yer station in life, to become Lady Sutherland someday but ye have fallen in love with someone else.

"I...I..." dear God, how could she lie to him?

"Ye what, Grace?"

"I—I wanted to become Lady Sutherland someday." That wasn't completely untrue. While she didn't particularly care about a title, she had wanted to be Bram's wife and she didn't want him to lose his birthright. So that would have made her Lady Sutherland.

The shock and disgust in his expression felt like another lash of the whip. "Ye did this to me to become Lady Sutherland? Ye said ye would accept banishment to marry me. That wouldn't have made ye Lady Sutherland."

"Aye, but..." Something Michael had said came to her. He is a hard man, but he loves his sons. "Yer father is a h-hard man but he loves his sons. I had hoped he wouldn't banish ye." This was also true. She had never wanted to create a rift in his family like the one in hers.

"Then why now? If ye had maintained the act a little longer, until after the Sinclairs' visit, ye could have been my wife and the future Lady Sutherland."

"I-I'm...in love." That too was horribly, painfully true. She loved the man in front of her with every fiber of her being. She loved him so very much that she would protect him from the pain she currently felt. The pain she knew she would always feel. The pain of loving someone who she could never have.

"Ye're in love," he scoffed. "Well then, far be it from me to stand in yer way. Michael can have ye." He gave her one last scathing look. "Good night, Grace." He turned and walked away.

"Goodbye, Bram."

Chapter 23

The laird summoned Michael to his solar after the evening meal to tell him that Grace would do what was expected of her this evening. "I was going to wait a few days, but I think we need to get this over with. I'll summon Father Damian as soon as it's done."

"If ye don't want Bram to know ye were involved, perhaps ye shouldn't do that."

"Well what do ye suggest?"

"I can take her to the Dominican Abbey."

"Do ye think she will just go along with that?"

"I think I can talk her into leaving, maybe even into marrying me. Either way, I'll take care of things."

"See that ye do."

"Aye, Laird."

"By the way, I heard a rumor earlier that ye had a tumble in the woods with her and then kissed her at her door in broad daylight. I don't know how rumors like that get started, but it is damned fortuitous today."

Michael smiled. "Aye, it is."

"Michael, ye rogue, did ye start it?"

"I reckoned it would be more believable when we elope if there had been at least whispers about a romance first."

"I suppose, but in case he's heard the rumor, ye'll probably want to stay out of Bram's way. Don't be seen in the hall when he returns or he might vent his anger on ye. I wouldn't want that. I don't like this business at all."

"But this is what ye wanted isn't it, Laird?"

"I want my son to marry Annice Sinclair, aye, but he's my son. Causing him this kind of heartache is distressing, even if it is the right thing to do."

"Aye, Laird." Michael didn't believe it was the right thing to do. The distress this would cause both Bram and Grace couldn't be worth it. Surely there was another way to make allies of the

Sinclairs. Still, Michael had no power to stop it. All he could do was try to protect Grace as much as possible.

A knock sounded at the door.

"In," called Laird Sutherland.

A travel worn messenger entered the room. "Good evening, Laird. I have news for ye."

"Aye, I'm sure ye do, just a moment please. Michael, perhaps ye should leave the keep. If ye stay outside, near the kitchens, I'll send someone to ye when I'm sure it's done and ye can be on yer way."

"Aye, Laird. I'll wait for word from ye."

That had been well over an hour ago, and Michael still paced nervously outside the keep. Surely it was done. Perhaps he should just go. He had nearly made up his mind to do that when Laird Sutherland himself came out the rear door of the keep.

"Michael, God may be smiling on us. I've just received some good news. We'll hold off on that wedding for a bit. It may not be necessary after all. We still have time, if anything changes.

"Aye, Laird. Good night then."

The laird returned to the keep and Michael went straight to Innes' cottage. When he knocked softly, Grace came to the door and stepped outside. Her eyes were red and swollen. "I'm so sorry, Grace. By the looks of ye, I'd say he believed ye."

"Aye, he did. I'll just be a minute. I need to get Kristen."

"Nay, Grace, ye don't. I'm not sure what's happening. The laird summoned me and wanted me to take ye to the abbey tonight. But then he received a messenger. Now the laird says the wedding may not be necessary after all. I don't know what it means but maybe it would be better to wait and see."

"Aye, we should. If he isn't going to force a wedding on us, there is no need for ye to lose yer position here. I will go to Durness after Michaelmas. This will be so much better. Grandmother will have time to decide what she wants to do. Thank ye, Michael."

"As ever, ye're welcome, Grace.

Chapter 24

Eanraig was not surprised when Bram told him the next morning that he would marry Annice Sinclair if she would have him. Bram hadn't told Eanraig what happened but like every other bit of news in a clan, the story of Grace's tryst with Michael and Bram's subsequent reaction spread like fire through hay. By midday, Bram's temper was foul. Eanraig hated to admit it even just to himself, but after the midday meal, he hid from his son in his solar.

Bram was hurting and Eanraig felt remorse over that, but the clan came first. He would get over it and because Grace had done her duty so beautifully, Eanraig expected that it would be soon but it would certainly help if Grace were gone for good. Now it looked like that was going to happen too.

There was a knock at the door. For a moment, Eanraig considered not answering. Being cornered by his angry bear of an oldest son was not an appealing prospect. But after a moment he called, "In." Thankfully it was just a messenger.

"Good afternoon, Laird. I bear news from the Earl of Ross."

"Come in. Ye're most welcome."

"Thank ye, Laird. I fear I bring sad news. Laird Terran, the Earl of Ross, died early this morning, God rest his soul."

Eanraig made the sign of the cross. "God rest his soul. I am sorry to hear of this loss. He was an honorable man and a good friend. He'll be missed."

"The requiem Mass will be two days hence."

"Clan business will prevent me from attending, but my sons Bram and Ian will attend in my stead. Come, I'll see ye downstairs and send for refreshment."

"Thank ye Laird, but I can't tarry. I still have to reach Naomh-dùn tonight.

"Aye, that's right, I'd forgotten Laird Eoin MacKay is Terran's grandson." Terran's daughter Morven was Kentigern

MacKay's first wife.

When the messenger was on his way, Eanraig summoned his sons. Terran, I'm sorry to lose ye, friend, but yer passing has come at a particularly helpful time. He needed for his sons to be occupied for the next few days. Bram had trained under Laird Terran and would certainly wish to attend his funeral. He wanted Ian to go for an altogether different reason.

When his sons arrived, Bram looked as if he hadn't slept the previous night and again. Eanraig felt a stab of remorse. "Lads, I have sad news. Terran Ross has passed away. God rest his soul."

Both Bram and Ian made the sign of the cross, but Bram closed his eyes and bowed his head for a moment. When Bram looked up again he said, "He'll be missed."

"Aye, he will. The requiem Mass will be Monday."

"We'll leave tomorrow morning," said Bram.

"Aye lads, but I can't go with ye, there is some business I must attend to. Ye'll represent me."

"Certainly, Father," said Bram. It was a mark of how distracted his son was that he didn't ask about the business Eanraig mentioned.

"There is something else I would like for ye to do. I have been considering Saundra Ross as a possible wife for ye, Ian."

"Da, do ye really think it is appropriate to open betrothal negotiations at a funeral?" asked Ian.

"Nay I do not. What do ye take me for? However, I thought ye might take the opportunity to get to know her a bit. It might make negotiations easier later if ye are compatible." Bram shook his head in disgust but Eanraig chose to ignore it. "Ye'll go by boat tomorrow after Mass. Twill be much faster."

"Aye. Is there anything else?" asked Ian. "I heard another messenger arrived yesterday."

"Oh, nay. That was nothing important."

"Then excuse me," said Bram. He left the room without waiting for permission.

Eanraig scrubbed his face with his hands.

"Do ye have any idea what really happened with Grace, Da?"

"What do ye mean, what really happened? She was a faithless, conniving wench. She led yer brother on and broke his heart. Thankfully it happened well before the Sinclairs are due to arrive. He'll have time to get over it."

"Da, if ye think a wee bit more than a week is enough for him to recover from this, ye are daft."

"We'll do what ye can to help him, lad."

~ * ~

The next morning Bram went to Mass with his family as usual. For the last few weeks Sundays had been perfectly wonderful. He had accompanied Grace and Kristen for their walk on the hiww and ate on the gwass. Then Kristen would curl up for a nap and he and Grace talked and laughed, and more recently, he had held her in his arms and kissed her. How had she managed to fool him so completely?

He tried to put her out of his mind. He caught a glimpse of her as she left Mass. He wondered how long it would take him to stop looking for her beautiful auburn hair in a crowd. As sorry as he was that old Laird Ross had passed away, frankly he was glad to be leaving for even a few days. He had to get over her…but he didn't think he ever would.

How had she turned love off so fast? Ye eejit, she never loved ye in the first place. How could she have?

Ian, Bram, and four guardsmen left midmorning, riding to the port village. As they rode into the village, Bram wondered if this was like the little port where Grace had grown up. Damnation, he had to stop doing this. Aye, a few days away would be a start.

~ * ~

Grace had spent most of the previous day inside. It was the tenth day, and she finished the ribbon in the late afternoon. Part of her wanted to hand it to Lady Sutherland herself. She had done what was asked of her. Everything that was asked of her. But she simply couldn't walk through the village to the keep. She couldn't bear the scornful stares and whispers. Nor could she bear the thought of seeing Bram. She put all of the remaining thread in a basket with the completed ribbon and asked Innes to deliver it for her.

Michael had stopped by for a bit in the evening. They had to keep up the farce, which in turn would keep the rude comments coming. After the excruciating day, she cried herself to sleep for the second night in a row, waking with a headache in the morning.

How could she walk to Mass to the chorus of disparaging remarks only to stand in the back of the church, so close to the man she loved with her whole heart but who was beyond her reach forever? Losing Callum to death was easier than this.

"I'm not going to Mass, Grandmother."

"Of course ye are. Tis a mortal sin not to."

"God doesn't seem to pay much attention to me. I don't think he'll miss me."

"Grace! Stop that kind of talk. Ye'll be branded a witch."

"I'm already a harlot according to most of the Sutherlands."

"Sweetling, ye know those rumors aren't true. I know they aren't. The rumors will die eventually. I expect it was jealousy when the young laird was smitten with ye. Ye've done this clan a great service and someday people will know that.

"Nay, they won't. They can't ever know. If Bram ever found out, it would kill him and I can't imagine what it would do to his wife."

"But someday…"

"Nay, Grandmother, never. Do ye understand? Never."

Innes sighed. "Aye, lass. I understand. Now come with us to Mass."

Kristen, who had been unusually quiet for the last two days, heard Grace say Bram's name. "We'ww see Sir Bwam at Mass, Mama. Then he can cwimb the hiww wif us."

Grace drew in a ragged breath. When Laird Sutherland had threatened her, Grace had forgotten that Kristen too was losing another loved one, and she would never understand why. Grace needed to talk to her, to try and explain, but she couldn't find the words yet.

"We can't climb the hill today, sweetling. But we will find something fun to do. I promise."

"We have to leave for Mass now, or we'll be late," said her Grandmother.

Grace couldn't fight it. She nodded and left with them. The slurs came as she knew they would. She tried to ignore them. Perhaps if people thought they didn't bother her, they would stop. When Kristen asked, "Gwanny, what's a hawwot?" Grace nearly lost all composure

"Nothing. Don't say that word, lass," Innes scolded.

"But—"

"Wheesht, lass."

After Mass, before the people were dismissed, Laird Sutherland announced the death of the Earl of Ross and that his sons would be traveling to Ross to represent the Sutherlands at the funeral. Grace knew Bram had trained there and she worried about how he would take this loss. She wanted to offer him comfort as he had her on so many occasions. Instead, she hurried out of Mass to avoid seeing him.

Grace had to leave Sutherland and the sooner the better.

Chapter 25

The late morning sun streamed in the windows as Eanraig paced his solar. His messenger had returned three days ago. The Morrisons were to have only been a day or two behind him. What could possibly be taking them so long? The Earl of Ross' funeral would have been yesterday. Bram and Ian could return at any time and he did not want Bram present when the Morrison men arrived. He felt sure it would be a painful scene with Grace spouting more lies. He wanted to spare Bram the ordeal. As if simply thinking about the Morrisons had conjured them, a guardsman knocked at the door. "Laird, a party of men who bear the Morrison banner approach."

Thank the good Lord. Perhaps Eanraig would see this mess resolved without causing Bram further pain and perhaps even ease the loss he felt. "Aye, I've been expecting them. When they arrive, show them into the great hall, I will meet with them there."

His thoughts were interrupted a moment later by another knock as his wife joined him in the solar. "I understand a party of Morrisons approach. They are from Lewis are they not?"

"Aye, Rodina, they are."

"Is this about Grace?"

"I'm afraid it is." He told her the news the messenger brought. "It is what I feared from the start. That is why I sent a man to find out all he could about her."

"The only thing the messenger was told was that Grace was lying. About what? Why wouldn't they tell him more?"

"I don't know. Apparently Laird Morrison decided to send men to fetch her home and assured the messenger they would tell us everything."

Rodina's brow furrowed. "And yer messenger heard this directly from Laird Morrison?"

"Aye, I suppose."

"Ye suppose? Ye don't know?"

He scowled at her. "I sent a messenger to meet with all

three clan leaders on Lewis, Macauley, the Lewis MacLeod's, and Morrison. I didn't know which clan she was from."

"But ye are sure he spoke with the lairds?"

"Aye, Rodina, I'm sure." But he wasn't. He hadn't asked. Still, the messenger's instructions were to speak with the head of each clan. "Besides, clearly Laird Morrison sent men to claim her just as he told the messenger he would. This should please ye after what she did to our son. Now I must go to the great hall to meet with them."

Rodina frowned. "I know she hurt Bram. But something isn't right there. I don't know what it is. She finished that ribbon as I asked her to in ten days. She must have worked nearly around the clock. Why would she push herself so hard?"

"I don't know, Rodina. It doesn't matter. What matters is finding out the truth."

"Eanraig, ye have to be sure they are telling the truth. This will break Innes' heart…again."

"I will, Rodina. I don't want Innes hurt either."

"Then do ye not think it would be kinder to Innes if ye meet with them here, privately, instead of in the hall?"

"Mayhap, but Innes loves Grace unreservedly. She refuses to see what low morals the lass has. This needs to be witnessed so others can convince Innes that she'd be better off without Grace."

"Aye, I suppose so, but it won't be easy. We will have our hands full."

"We? Rodina, it isn't necessary for ye to be there."

"Do ye not think Innes will need support when she hears all of this?"

"Innes doesn't need to be there either."

She gave a most unladylike snort. "Eanraig, sometimes ye are a very dense man. When ye send for Grace, there isn't a single chance that Innes will let her come alone."

He scowled at her. "I could order her to wait in her cottage."

"And what would that do? She must be told the outcome in any event. It will be better if she hears it for herself."

Eanraig nodded. "I suppose ye are right. Well then, shall we go?"

"Are ye not going to send for Grace first?"

"Nay Rodina, I want to hear what the men have to say first then I'll send for her."

~*~

The day was unusually hot. By midmorning the sweat ran down Grace's back as she worked the new loom. Just past midday her Grandmother had urged her to take a break but she didn't. She couldn't bear the comments and after Kristen asked what a harlot was, Grace needed to protect her little ears too. Besides, she had to produce enough to be able to live off of the sale of her goods. She had to pay their rents and keep them fed. She had meant it when she told the laird that she wouldn't accept anything from him. Aye, he had provided her with wool and flax, but she had earned it. The value of the ribbon she made for Lady Sutherland was twenty times what those raw materials cost.

Still, she had nearly decided to go outside for a while anyway. Her grandmother played with Kristen in the shade of a tree just down the lane. It was far enough away that perhaps people would leave her alone. She could take advantage of the breeze and spin in peace. She stood, stretched, and stepped outside the cottage just as Donal approached in the lane. His expression was grim.

"Donal, what's wrong? What has happened?"

"Laird Sutherland sent me for ye. He said ye were to gather yer possessions."

Dread gripped her heart. "Gather my possessions? Why?" What was happening?

"Just do it," he snapped.

Donal had always been friendly and jovial. Even over the last couple of weeks, when the rumors started, he had been kind. His change in attitude clearly told her the dread she felt was not unwarranted.

"Aye, of course." She went back into the cottage on the edge of panic. He followed her, standing just inside the door. She had no more belongings than when she arrived. She made a bundle containing her mother's box, the ribbon loom, and her spinning tools. When she had added the few articles of clothing she owned, Donal stepped forward. "That will do. We can't keep the laird waiting."

"But I haven't packed any of Kristen's things or my father's knives."

"Ye won't need them. Let's go."

"What do ye mean I won't need them?"

"Just what I said, ye won't need them." He grabbed her elbow with one hand and the bundle in the other.

"Nay Donal, let me go. I need to tell Grandmother and fetch Kristen." But even as she said it, she saw her grandmother rushing toward her from the end of the lane. Maisie was with her and held Kristen.

"Innes will come with ye but ye don't need Kristen to speak to the laird. My mother will mind her for a bit."

Grace dug in her heels and pulled back. "Donal, please stop. Tell me what's happening."

"What's happening at this moment is ye are defying Laird Sutherland's order. Come with me quietly now or I'll throw ye over my shoulder and carry ye up to the keep. That will be a fine spectacle for the villagers to see."

Innes had reached them by then. "Grace, please, I'm sure whatever it is can be sorted out. Laird Sutherland is fair."

Grace loved her Grandmother, but she didn't understand how she could believe that after the last few days. Grace looked over her shoulder at Kristen who waved merrily at her. "Mama, I'm going to make bwead wif Maisie."

Her heart lurched. She knew something was dreadfully wrong but she didn't want to scare her daughter. "Aye, pet," she managed to choke out. "I love ye."

"I wuv ye too, Mama."

Donal gave her arm another tug and she didn't resist him.

Terrified by what was happening, Grace stumbled blindly through the village and up to the keep with Donal half dragging her.

Michael was one of the guards on the gate as they reached the castle. "What the hell is going on? Donal stop, ye're hurting her."

"Michael, ye don't know what she's done."

"I know ye don't need to be so rough with her."

"I think ye need to join us in the hall, then ye can be the judge." Donal motioned to another guard who was walking though the bailey. "Kent, take Michael's post for a while. He is needed in the great hall."

Under his breath he asked, "Grace, what's happening?"

"I don't know, Michael. I'm scared."

"Wheesht. I'll be with ye."

When they entered the hall, Laird and Lady Sutherland sat at the refectory table looking as grim as Donal had. Six men who she didn't recognize as Sutherlands stood by. One of them stepped towards her reaching for her hand. "Nina, love, it's time to come home now."

Her grandmother gasped.

Grace jerked her hand from him, stepping backwards. "What? My name's not Nina. Who are ye?"

"Nina, ye're breaking my heart. I'm yer husband, lass."

"My husband? I've never seen ye before."

"Husband? Grace?" The confusion and fear in her grandmother's voice echoed her own.

"Laird Sutherland, please, what is happening?" Michael asked.

"I'm glad ye're here Michael, ye need to hear this too. I was worried that this young woman was not what she seemed. Especially when she seemed so determined to win my son's affection and then yers. I sent a messenger to Lewis to see if he could learn more about her. I'm sorry, Innes. Tristan and his wife did indeed live there, but this lass isn't their daughter."

"That is ludicrous," said Michael. "She has friends in Durness who know who she is. I've met them."

"Michael, don't interrupt."

Grace couldn't believe her ears. "That's a lie. I am their daughter. Anyone in our village could tell ye that." She rapidly scanned the faces of the other men. Her heart sank as realization dawned. She recognized several of them as guardsmen who had been with Laird Morrison when he collected the rents. Somehow Fearchar had found her.

"Aye, Laird, I'm certain she's my granddaughter. They are lying."

"Nay Innes, they aren't. Roddy here is her husband. He has a marriage certificate with her mark on it and a letter from Laird Morrison."

A letter from Laird Morrison? Nay, this had to be Fearchar's work. He must have sent these men. Laird Morrison would have no reason to lie about her.

Innes turned to the man who claimed to be Grace's husband. "I don't care what he has, Grace is Tristan's daughter."

"I'm sorry, mistress, she is my wife Nina. She knew Tristan's family well. She and Grace were friends from childhood. An illness swept through our clan last winter. Tristan and his family were all taken by it—all but his wee granddaughter, Kristen, the real Grace's daughter."

Grace was speechless, she could only stare in horrified silence.

Roddy continued, "Sadly we lost our own daughter as well. After that Nina—well it was a terrible blow. She went a bit off. She thought our Myra was simply lost. She would wander off searching for her. I thought Nina would recover with time and tried to be patient. Then in April, just after the Feast of Saint Mark, she disappeared. She kidnapped Kristen from the family who was raising her. She must have stowed away with the child."

Michael swore. "Laird, I've never heard anything so ridiculous. Grace is Kristen's mother. I don't care what they say."

"Michael, hold yer tongue."

Grace finally found her voice. "Please, Laird, none of that is true. Not a word of it. Laird Morrison would not have written those lies about me. Laird, please, ye must believe me. I am Grace Breive, Tristan Murray's daughter and Kristen is my child. I showed ye my father's brooch and I proved it to ye with the knife."

Roddy shook his head. "I am ashamed to say she stole things from Grace's cottage—things that had been packed to send here to ye. A brooch and a knife belonging to Tristan were among the pilfered items."

"She didn't prove her identity by producing her father's knife, ye spineless eejit. She showed them the throwing skills he taught her."

"Michael, enough!" roared Laird Sutherland.

Grace saw a brief flash of surprise on Roddy's face but he recovered quickly. "As I told ye, Nina and Grace were the closest of friends from childhood. Tristan taught them both knife skills. Perhaps that is why she stole the knife."

"Laird, they're lying. I have a letter that my da wrote to grandmother."

Innes nodded. "Aye, Laird, the letter explained why Tristan went away. There was no question that he composed the contents. Grace rea—"

"Stolen too," Roddy said, cutting her off.

Her grandmother's shoulders sagged as if the weight of what was happening was simply too much to bear. Lady Sutherland rounded the table, putting her arms around Innes, comforting her. "I'm so sorry Innes."

Ashen faced, Innes turned to Grace. The doubt in her eyes rent Grace's heart.

"Nay, Grandmother, ye must believe—"

Laird Sutherland banged his fist on the table. "Don't say another word! I've had enough."

"Laird, please, at least look at Tristan's letter. There could be something in it that would help," Michael implored.

"Eanraig, what could it hurt to look at Tristan's letter? We need to be sure."

"I am sure, Rodina, don't question me again. And, Michael, I know she has twisted ye round her finger as she did Bram, but he has her marriage certificate.

"How do ye know it's real?"

"It bears her mark! Nina, what ye have done is unconscionable. Ye have stolen a child and caused immeasurable pain to one of my clanswomen, not to mention my son and poor Michael here. Ye should be horse whipped."

Michael tried again. "Dear God, nay. Laird please, listen."

Roddy said, "Nay Laird, not that. Please forgive her. She isn't in her right mind. Let me take her home." He stepped toward her again, attempting to put his arm around her.

Michael shoved him away, nearly sending him sprawling. He pulled Grace behind him.

"I am not his wife. I swear, I don't know him."

"Maybe a whipping will help her remember who she is," muttered a Sutherland servant.

"Aye, and teach her a bit of respect," said another.

"Get her out of my sight," Laird Sutherland ordered.

"Please, Laird, hear me out," begged Michael.

"Not another word, Michael."

This was happening. They didn't believe her and she was being taken back to Lewis. To Fearchar Morrison. Keep yerself together, Grace, and keep Kristen. They know the truth on Lewis. "Fine. I'll go. Just let me fetch my daughter."

"She isn't yer daughter, Nina," said Roddy.

"Nay, she isn't," said Laird Sutherland. "She was Tristan Murray's granddaughter and thus a Sutherland. She will stay here."

Leave Kristen? "Nay!" she screamed.

Michael put his arms around her. "Laird, ye can't do this! Grace is Kristen's mother, I don't care what papers they have. Ye need only see them together. Please, Laird, after what she did for ye don't do this to her."

"What's he talking about, Eanraig?"

"Silence, Rodina. Michael, I warned ye." To the other guardsmen in the room he said, "throw him in the dungeon for a few days and see if he can learn to respect his laird." Two guardsmen grabbed Michael. He fought like berserker.

In spite of the number of times she had given her mother the answer panicking never helps, panic engulfed Grace. She turned to run with one goal, get to her daughter. She had barely gone a few steps when strong arms gripped her from behind.

"Let go of her!" Michael still struggled to reach her until one of his fellow guardsmen knocked him out.

Grace screamed and fought with everything in her. She struck out, kicking at the Morrison guards who tried to subdue her. Several times her feet struck hard flesh, resulting in masculine grunts of pain. She refused to give up. She couldn't lose her beloved child. Then someone struck her hard in the face, sending her into black oblivion.

Chapter 26

When Grace awoke, her head throbbed and every bit of her ached. She lay on the ground, her hands and feet bound. Her thoughts were foggy. Where was she and why was she bound? She opened her eyes slightly, the light causing a piercing pain in her head. As much as she wanted to close them again, she had to figure out where she was, so she forced her eyes fully open. Although the summer days were long and the sun had not yet set, the heat of the day was gone. The combination of the damp earth and a cool evening breeze chilled her. As her head began to clear, images of what had happened in the Sutherlands' great hall flooded her. She groaned.

"Well lads, look who has joined us." She recognized the voice as the man called Roddy.

Grace tried to push herself to a sitting position. A hand grabbed her upper arm, roughly jerking her upright. Roddy thrust a costrel to her lips. "Drink," he ordered.

For an instant she thought to refuse, but in truth she was dreadfully thirsty. She swallowed greedily until he pulled it away from her lips. He held an oatcake out to her. She took it with her bound hands, bringing it to her mouth and taking a bite. It was dry and stale, but she was starving.

She surveyed the surroundings. It appeared that they had made camp in a small clearing. The horses had been secured for the night. The men sat around a small fire, silently staring at her as she ate. In addition to Roddy there were five others: a young man, younger than she was by the looks of him; two older men, one of whom had burn scars on his face; and two more who looked to be about the same age as Roddy, perhaps either side of a score and ten.

Now that she saw them closer, she remembered having seen them all before. She certainly recognized the scarred man. He would be hard to forget. If she had noticed him when she first entered the great hall she would have known immediately who they were.

When she had finished eating the oatcake, Roddy put the costrel to her lips again, taking it away before she had drunk her fill.

Despair washed over her. She thought the pain of losing her husband and parents had been unbearable. Then, she met Bram. Every instinct had warned her not to open her heart but she had. After glimpsing love for a second time, she had lost him too. She didn't think anything could be worse than the pain of hurting him, pushing him away, letting him go for the good of the clan.

What a fool she was. Today she had lost her whole world. She had no doubt what lay in store at Fearchar's hands. Even if she could escape, what would she do? The Sutherlands believed she was a demented stranger. She would never again be welcomed there nor would they return Kristen to her. She looked away and fought back tears. She wanted to curl up in a ball and give up.

Still, part of her refused to let them see she was beaten or let them see her cry. When she had regained her composure, she looked at Roddy. "Why?"

"Because Fearchar wanted ye, Grace. He told ye that. He told ye if ye resisted him he would make ye sorry. I'd say you look right sorry now."

Aye, surely her heart was damaged beyond repair. "But why was it necessary to take my daughter from me? Fearchar would still have gotten what he wanted."

"Now that was something he and I disagreed on. I thought we should say ye kidnapped another couple's baby and bring her along. I reckon ye'd do anything ye were asked to do if it meant keeping her safe. But Fearchar wanted rid of her. He figured it would be best to leave her among her kin. He also predicted ye'd cause an uproar when ye realized she was being left behind. I have to admit, that was quite a show. Too bad Kenneth had to knock ye out. Ye should have seen the looks on their faces. The Sutherlands are convinced ye're barking mad. Making the sign of the cross they were as we dragged ye away. And they're pretty sure ye bewitched that guardsman, Michael."

Michael. The only Sutherland who tried to help her. Nay, that wasn't true, Lady Sutherland made an attempt too, but was silenced by her husband. Lady Sutherland would certainly be alright, but what would happen to Michael? Lord, please help Michael. She was fairly sure that was wasted effort but she had to ask. After a few moments she asked Roddy, "Who is Nina?"

"She was my wife. A pretty face, but weak and useless. She died of a fever shortly after we were married a few years back. That is why Fearchar picked me."

It had always been said Fearchar was ruthless but she had no idea another human being could be this cruel. Still, in spite of the pain it caused her, she realized that Roddy had been right. If they had brought Kristen, Grace would do anything to keep her safe. She would have gone like a lamb to the slaughter if it meant Kristen would be unharmed. But with her daughter safely back with Innes, Grace could do whatever she needed to do to escape without fear. She had nothing more to lose. If she kept her wits about her, she believed she could get away. Furthermore, if she could reach Dugald and Mary in Durness they would be able to help her. They knew who she was. Perhaps they would help her convince the Sutherlands of the truth. She wasn't sure it would work but it was her only option and she had to try.

~*~

Grace had been left bound all night.

"We can't have ye tryin' to sneak away," Roddy had said. But he and a couple of the other men laughed. Clearly they believed it was unlikely she could accomplish that.

When she had asked him to remove her bonds and give her a few moments of privacy to answer nature's call that morning she expected him to refuse. But he simply removed her bonds and told her to hurry. "The sun is well up and we need to get going."

She was still sore from yesterday and laying bound all night on the ground had left her stiff. She walked into the trees a bit to relieve herself without an audience. She couldn't help think that in her current condition she moved with less agility that Innes. *Perhaps that is why he doesn't fear I'll run.* Even as she had the thought she realized this might be her only chance. She ran further into the forest as swiftly and quietly as she could. She hadn't planned to, or even thought her actions through. She simply seized the moment, which was probably her first mistake.

Her second mistake occurred when she heard the cry go up that she was missing. She hadn't gone far yet. If she had been thinking, she would have turned back then and lied. She would have told them that she had only gone a bit deeper into the wood than she intended. But instead she kept running, as fast as her feet would carry her. It had been absolutely foolhardy.

The man called Derek caught her quickly, dragging her back to the clearing.

Roddy was furious. He backhanded her. "Ye stupid wench! Ye have no chance of eluding us and only make things worse for yerself by trying." He slapped her again and she braced herself for a beating. He laughed at her when she cringed. "Nay, I won't beat ye now. Fearchar wants ye alive and generally unharmed. He wants the pleasure of breaking ye, and believe me, break ye he will. But I'll see that ye don't run away again. If ye want to travel by foot, I'll let ye. Today, ye walk."

Without warning, he kicked her legs out from under her. She hit the ground hard enough to knock the wind out of her. Before she realized what he was doing, he had removed her boots. Then he tied her wrists together again before yanking her to her feet.

"Mount up lads," he ordered, giving her a wicked sneer. He tied one end of another length of rope to the one binding her wrists, held onto the other end, and mounted his horse.

"I'll warrant ye won't be so anxious to run away after today. I'll be surprised if ye can even walk."

The youngest man asked, "Are ye sure that's a good idea Roddy? Ye said yerself, Fearchar didn't want her harmed."

"Shut yer gob, Augie. Fearchar doesn't want her to escape him again either. After a day of walking barefoot there will be no chance of that."

None of the other men seemed inclined to interfere so as Roddy had promised, he forced Grace to walk barefooted while being practically dragged by the rope attached to her hands. Her feet were bruised and scraped within an hour. By the late afternoon, she had sustained several cuts from sharp stones. The cuts oozed blood and made each step more painful than the last. She fell occasionally but each time Roddy dragged her a few steps before yanking her upright by her tether, causing the ropes binding her wrists to cut into her tender flesh. Eventually, hot, exhausted, and in pain, she fell every few minutes slowing their pace tremendously.

After one such fall he didn't yank Grace up from her knees immediately. He stopped his horse, turning to watch as she struggled to her feet. "Have ye had enough, Grace?" Roddy sneered.

"Roddy, she can barely walk," observed Augie. "We are

moving at a snail's pace. We can make up some time if ye let her ride now."

"She brought it on herself," said Roddy.

The oldest man among them, who had been riding in the lead, said, "Aye, she did. But God's bones, Roddy, it will take ages for us to get to Durness at this pace. I have children and a wife at home. No offence lad, but I'd rather share a bed with her than the cold ground with ye lot."

"Ye hear that, Grace? Gordon here is anxious to swive his wife and tender-hearted young Augie fears for the state of yer feet. They think I should let ye ride. Now that I think on it, I might be convinced to let ye ride for what is left of the day...if ye are willing to pay the price."

Grace stared at him mutely. She wouldn't ask the price. She was fairly sure she wouldn't pay it, whatever it was.

"Don't ye wish to hear what it is?"

Not wanting to give in to him at all, Grace said, "I feel sure if ye want me to know, ye'll tell me in yer own time."

"Ye might want to curb that insolent tongue, Grace. I am a tolerant man but Fearchar is not so forbearing."

"Aye," agreed Derek. "Give him that kind of lip and he'll skelp ye good."

As if any of them cared what happened to her. Grace simply stood there.

When it became obvious she wasn't going to respond, Roddy said, "As it happens, I too grow weary of this plodding pace, so I will tell ye my price. It's simple enough. Ye can ride the rest of the afternoon if ye kneel and beg me sweetly for mercy...or ye give me one kiss."

Again Augie spoke up. "Roddy, Fearchar didn't want her touched."

Conan, the older man with the scarred face, scowled. "Augie, would ye shut up? Fearchar didn't want her raped. Teaching her insolent tongue a lesson hardly counts and if it gets us on our way, I don't care. Kiss him, lass, and save yerself a bit of pain."

Grace remained silent. Frankly, she was in no hurry to get to Fearchar and she wasn't about to pay either price. Roddy could drag her by her wrists all the way to Cape Wrath and she wouldn't willingly kiss him or beg him for mercy. Part of her longed to tell him so, but the wiser part of her urged caution, lest he actually drag her to death behind his horse.

"Well, Grace? Will ye pay the price and ride for what remains of the day?" Roddy smirked. She felt sure he didn't expect her to. This was meant to humiliate her.

She glared at him. "Nay."

"Nay?" Roddy asked. "Stubbornness will bring ye naught but pain and heartache, but have it yer way." He yanked on the tether as he urged his horse back to a walk.

Even though she had turned down his offer, she had hoped Roddy would take heed of the men who had urged him to let her ride in the interest of making up some lost time. She doubted they had even covered a league over the last three hours of travel. Even so, he didn't relent and she refused to beg him for mercy.

Just as Roddy had predicted, by the time they stopped that evening she could barely walk. She would never be able to escape on foot, she thought bitterly. However, she had learned a few tidbits of useful information. Augie had said Fearchar wanted her alive and generally unharmed. Perhaps that is why, after they had stopped, Roddy unbound her hands and pointed her to a small burn where she could wash the dirt out of her destroyed feet.

She had also learned their destination. They were traveling to Durness. She had assumed they were traveling to a port as they would have to travel by ship to Lewis, but it could have been one of several along the northern or western coast. But if they were heading to Durness, she certainly had a better chance of reaching her friends if she stayed with her Morrison captors until they reached the port. Then, just maybe, she'd have another opportunity to escape.

She prayed her feet would have enough time to heal a bit before then. When she travelled with Dugald and Mary by wagon, it had taken four and a half days to reach Sutherland Castle from Durness. Men on horses could travel almost twice as fast. She wasn't sure how far they had come the previous day when she was unconscious. However, having forced her to walk barefooted, they hadn't made much progress today. It was likely they were barely a day's ride from Castle Sutherland, if that. She guessed they might have one more night on the road before reaching Durness. That was a bit less than two days to recover…and to plan.

Chapter 27

Bram stepped off the boat followed by Ian and the guardsmen who had accompanied them. A cool evening breeze blew away the heat of the day. Over the last few days Bram hadn't done anything more strenuous than lift a full tankard but he felt weary to the bone. His time away had done little to exorcise Grace from his thoughts. Of course, this was only made worse by seeing Eoin and Fiona MacKay at the funeral. They were blissfully happy and the envy he felt nearly bore a hole in him.

Ian, on the other hand, was energy personified. Oh the wonders of a happy heart. For Ian, Saundra Ross had turned out to be a light in what was otherwise a sorrowful event. Lovely, gentle and soft spoken, he had been instantly smitten with her. She too seemed equally as taken with Ian. She blushed sweetly whenever he spoke to her, which was as often as he could maneuver to her side.

They could have returned the day after the funeral but instead, Ian had convinced Bram to linger for another day. He wanted a little more time with Saundra. In truth there was nothing for Bram to race back to. Still, after the days of tedium, he pried Ian away by telling him the faster they returned home, the faster Da could open negotiations with Saundra's father, the new Earl of Ross. That was a wee stretch of the truth. He knew, out of respect, Da wouldn't raise the issue until a suitable mourning period had passed.

On their way to Clan Ross, they had stabled their horses at the small inn in the port village. Returning there now, Bram paid the inn keeper and they saddled their mounts, setting out for home immediately. It was less than an hour's ride to Sutherland castle. Ian and the other men exchanged friendly banter. Bram soon grew tired of it and fell back a bit, riding in brooding silence. Soon Ian slowed his mount to ride next to Bram.

"What has ye bothered, Bram?"

"Ye."

Ian snorted. "Well, that's good to know. I thought it might be thoughts of a certain widow."

Bram clenched his jaw, angry that Ian had read him so well.

They rode in silence for a few moments before Ian said, "Ye may not want to hear what I'm about to say."

"Any conversation that begins with those words is probably best avoided."

Ian chuckled. "Nevertheless, I will tell ye. I have given this a lot of thought over the last few days and I think ye are making a mistake."

"Do ye? That's a pretty fair guess. I've made so many recently. To which one do ye refer?"

"Ye believed Grace when she told ye she loved someone else."

"Ian this isn't any of yer concern."

His brother continued to push. "Bram, ye loved her."

Bram snorted. "I don't think it was love after all. I enjoyed her company. Nothing more. Evidently she didn't enjoy mine. Michael is more enticing these days."

It was Ian's turn to snort. "Ye enjoyed her company? Bram, ye loved her and ye still do, which is going to irritate Da beyond all understanding."

"What does Da have to do with it?"

"He wants ye married to Annice Sinclair."

"And I'll marry her, damn it all. I've agreed to that. I gave Da the month that he asked for and I'm glad I did."

"Nay, brother. I don't think this has ever really been about whether or not ye would marry Grace. Looking back on it, Da could have made sure that didn't happen in any number of ways. At the moment ye told him ye wanted to marry her, he could have thrown ye in the dungeon and taken steps to ensure that didn't happen."

"If he had done that, I would have left anyway."

"And Da had to know that. I think he bought time with his offer of a month. He was hoping to change yer mind or figure out a way to get rid of her that wouldn't push ye to leave too. Laird Sinclair added a particularly troublesome wrinkle to the problem."

"How so?"

"Perhaps Grace had yer head too muddled, but have ye forgotten? Laird Sinclair will only agree to a betrothal for Annice if she is willing. How willing do ye think she'd be if she heard whispers about ye and Grace and ye clearly loved another woman? Da is canny enough to know this. He needed to get Grace out of yer sights and for yer only focus to be on winning Annice's hand."

"Well, he got his wish. Grace doesn't love me."

"Bram, would ye put yer damn pride aside and think? Until Friday did she ever give ye that idea?"

"There were rumors."

"That ye knew were false."

"Ian, drop it."

"By all that's holy, Bram, Da started working to separate the two of ye at the first whisper that ye were attracted to her. He sent ye out for three days to review crops, in June when things are barely started. Mother had her make that blasted ribbon and then Da doubled the order. Looking back that was pure genius. Grace must have spent ten hours or more a day bent over her loom, knowing it was for the lass ye would marry. After ye told Da about Grace, it only got worse. He retired Innes, moving her from her home to the farthest edge of the village. Then the rumors started and the clan began to turn on Grace."

"Da wouldn't have done that."

Ian shook his head. "I would have thought not, but now I'm not sure. Someone had to have started the rumors and Da had the most to gain.

Bram said nothing. He had no rebuttal. Da had made it clear for weeks that he wanted Bram to stay away from Grace but Bram hadn't listened.

"Something Da said to me on Saturday makes me think he was growing desperate to end the relationship."

"What did he say?"

"Ye had been an ogre all day. I had only heard rumors and I asked if he knew what happened. He told me the rumor version but he also said, 'thankfully it happened well before the Sinclairs are due to arrive.' He thought ye'd have time to get over it."

Bram was stunned. "He thought I'd get over this in a week?"

Ian grinned. "That's what I told him. But clearly his focus was much more on ye being ready to win Annice's hand than anything else."

"This doesn't change the fact that Grace admitted to loving someone else."

"Bram, time was running out. If ye still hoped to marry Grace when the Sinclairs arrived, the chance of an alliance was over. Da knew threatening ye wouldn't work. What is the only other thing he could do?"

"He wouldn't threaten Grace? How could he? What did he have over her? If he had banished her, I would have gone with her. She knew that."

"I don't know what he threatened her with. Maybe it was something to do with Kristen or Innes. Whatever it was, I'm not even sure he would have made good on it, he's not heartless. But Grace wouldn't know that.

"Nay I can't believe he would threaten a young widow. He wouldn't."

"Desperate men do desperate things and if he thought it was for the good of the clan, he might. Ye know full well Grace wouldn't risk getting Innes or Kristen hurt. Better to set her own heart aside...and hurt someone stronger and better able to handle it...ye."

Bram stopped his horse and stared at Ian. If Ian was right and Da had threatened her, Bram had no doubt Grace would see it this way. She would do everything in her power to protect Innes and Kristen. "Do ye really believe Da might have done this? And what about Michael? She didn't deny that."

"Bram, it was obvious to everyone that Grace loves ye as much as ye love her. And Da had too much riding on this alliance with the Sinclairs. Ye needed to believe whatever Grace felt for ye was gone. I don't know what Michael's role was in all of this, but it certainly helped convince ye."

Realization flooded him. "Damnation!" Bram clicked to Goliath, preparing to urge him into a gallop.

"Wait, Bram. Where are ye going?"

Bram spun Goliath around. "I need to see Grace. I need to know if Da did threaten her."

"And completely destroy the sacrifice she made for ye and this clan?"

"God's breath, Ian. I will stay away from her if I must, but I can't bear the thought of her fearing some retribution from Da." Bram turned Goliath toward home. They weren't far now so he gave the horse his head. Ian and the guardsmen followed suit, tearing down the road after him toward Castle Sutherland.

They reached the outskirts of the village in a few minutes.

Bram stopped before he reached Innes' cottage. He dismounted, handing Goliath's reins to Ian. "See to him for me, please."

The guardsmen wouldn't question him but his brother was not as circumspect. "Bram—"

"Please, Ian. Grant me this."

Ian shook his head in frustration. "Aye, I will." He clicked his tongue at Goliath. "C'mon, lad."

Bram waited until the men were well down the lane before walking to the little cottage. It was early evening. Grace would be putting Kristen to bed. He thought back to the night they met, and so many since then, when he heard her sweet lullabies. He had longed to hear her singing to their children. He sighed heavily. It would never be. As he drew closer he didn't hear the melody he expected. Instead he was met with the sound of Innes trying to quiet Kristen's distressed cries.

Something was wrong. He ran the last few steps and knocked at the door. Innes opened it, looking as distraught as the child she held. "Dear God, Innes, what has happened? Where is Grace?"

"Gone." She trembled and began to sob too.

"What do ye mean?" But even as he asked it, he knew he needed to calm them both before he would get any answers. He took Kristen from Innes and guided the old woman to the chair. Kristen clutched at him, burying her face in his léine, continuing to sob. "Wheesht, my sweet wee lassie. Wheest now, it will be all right." He bounced her gently, rubbing her back as he had seen Grace do. "Innes, ye need to calm down and tell me what has happened."

"It was all a lie. She wasn't Tristan's daughter. She isn't Kristen's mother. Her name is Nina and she's married." Innes burst into a fresh wave of tears.

What? Where did this nonsense come from? Of course she was Kristen's mother. Bram tried again to calm them both. The wee lass finally had exhausted herself with tears. She was falling asleep in his arms, her little body still jerking occasionally with a sob.

Innes still wept, so he turned his attention to her. He rested a hand on her shoulder. "Innes, please calm down and tell me what has happened."

With great effort, Innes too managed to stop crying. She put her hand over his where it rested on her shoulder. "Thank ye for calming the babe, Bram. Put her on her pallet and then sit here with me. I'll tell ye what I know."

Bram stepped through the door into the little room where they slept. He gently laid the sleeping child on the pallet, patted her back until he knew she was asleep, and kissed her forehead before returning to Innes.

"Now, what is this about Grace not being Kristen's mother?"

"Did she ever tell ye where she came from?"

"Not specifically. I knew she was raised on the Isle of Lewis. Why?"

"Aye, she was raised on Lewis. I guess yer da was worried about me—that she might be hiding something. He sent a messenger to Lewis, to the heads of all the clans to see if he could find out more about her. The messenger learned she had lived among the Morrisons. I knew that and 'twas no secret. I would have told yer da if he'd asked."

Bram was impatient and he wanted Innes to get to the point, but he held his irritation in check. "So, Da found out she was a Morrison. What else?"

"He found out she isn't Grace Breive." Innes launched into the story, telling him everything that the Morrison men had revealed.

Bram tried to remain calm. On its surface, the story sickened him but he forced himself to listen. He needed to hear it all to understand what had happened. As he listened, he realized all of the pieces didn't add up. The Morrisons alleged that Tristan and his family, including Grace, died of an illness. But Kristen had memories of her father and grandparents dying. She had told Bram, *There was a storm. Da and Gwandda didn't come home. Gwamma was sick. She died too. Me and Mama were awone.* Surely if her real mother had died, she would remember that.

Furthermore, if "Nina" had stolen the child from another family just before leaving Lewis, Kristen wouldn't have memories of things they had done together on Lewis. *It is wike the hiww we cwimbed at home. We don't go neaw the edge...We awways ate wif Da on the gwass.* Kristen couldn't have these memories with a woman who had stolen her, even if "Nina" was supposedly a close friend of the family.

"Innes, I don't believe the Morrisons. I can't understand why Laird Morrison would have written such a damning letter, but

I don't have a single doubt that Grace is Kristen's mother. Besides, she proved herself to us. She had Tristan's brooch and she throws a knife as expertly as he did."

"That's what Michael said."

"What does Michael have to do with this?"

"Michael tried to help her when this was happening. He said she had friends in Durness who knew her and he had met them. He also said ye only had to look at Grace and Kristen together to know Grace was her mother. The laird wouldn't listen to him. Besides, the Morrisons said Nina and Grace were friends and Tristan taught them both to use knives. They also said she stole the brooch and Tristan's letter from the real Grace's cottage."

"What letter? Neither of ye ever mentioned a letter."

"It was a letter to me from Tristan. His wife wrote it for him years ago. He feared sending it to me because of her father. The seal was unbroken when Grace arrived. Michael begged the laird to look at it. Yer mother even tried, but the laird wouldn't."

"Has Michael seen it?"

"I don't know."

"Can I see it?"

Innes' eyes filled with tears. "She took it with her. It was in a little wooden box with the brooch. She also had a brooch and pendant that belonged to Tristan's wife."

"What was in the letter?"

"Tristan explained about his wife's father. It was the reason they fled to Lewis in the first place and why he couldn't contact me. He didn't hate me as I always imagined he did. He begged my forgiveness."

The existence of the letter was a complete surprise. He wondered why Grace had never mentioned it. Perhaps there was more information in the letter—something that could help her now. "Innes, did Father Francis read it to ye? Maybe ye are forgetting some important detail that he will remember. Or if Michael read it, maybe he knows something."

"Ye could ask Michael but yer da threw him in the dungeon for interfering and Father didn't read it to me. The lass herself did."

"Grace can read?" This too was a surprise.

"Aye, she can. She said her mama taught her."

"But Innes, ye said the man named Roddy had a marriage certificate that bore Nina's mark. Other than Laird Morrison's letter was this the only proof they offered?"

"Aye, well that and their testimony. She didn't even recognize her husband. They said she had lost her mind when she lost her own child. When the laird gave them leave to take her, she certainly looked like a mad woman, screaming and kicking. Of course, Michael fought too. It took four guardsmen to subdue him. One of the Morrisons knocked Grace out."

One of them struck her? It was all Bram could do to rein in his temper. "Innes, I don't believe a word of their story. Kristen knows who her mother is and ye say Grace can read. Surely if she were truly this man's wife, Nina, she would have signed the certificate—not simply marked it."

Innes' eyes grew wide. "I didn't think of that. Aye, and Kristen does know her mama. She has been distraught since they left yesterday morning, crying for her mama."

"Two days? They've had her for nearly two day? Did Michael go after her?"

"Nay, I told ye, he's in the dungeon."

His heart sank. "Innes, I must go. I will find out what my father knows and then find her."

Innes stood with tears streaming down her cheeks again. "I let them take her. I doubted her. She begged me to believe her and I didn't."

"Innes, ye couldn't have stopped this, not with my father condoning it. Ye might be in the dungeon alongside Michael if ye'd tried. But I will bring her back. I swear. Even if it is to let Michael have her."

He wasted no time getting to the keep, running the whole way. When he reached the great hall, Ian and his father looked at him from where they sat at the refectory table. Clearly their father had told the story to Ian whose eyes held only pity. His father, on the other hand, looked ready to do battle.

Fine. Bram would give him a battle. "Where did they take her?"

"Back to Lewis, where she belonged," Eanraig answered.

"Through which port?" Bram ground out.

"They were heading for Durness, and good riddance."

Bram exploded. "Ye have no idea what ye've done, Father."

"Mind yer tone with me, Son."

Bram continued. "Ye had to meddle. Ye would have done

anything to get rid of her. But it was over between us. Why couldn't ye just leave it be?"

"I did it for the good of the clan. It wasn't over as long as ye thought ye loved her, Bram. But it is a good thing I found out the truth. She is a mad woman. She's married and she stole the child. Even her story about how Tristan and his family died was false. They all died of an illness that swept the village. She stole the real Grace's belongings. I know ye don't want to believe it but she lied to us."

Bram trembled with rage. "Nay, Father, she didn't. Ye were willing to believe Laird Morrison's letter and his men, without bothering to find out the truth of it, even with a trusted guardsman telling ye they were wrong. Besides, Kristen remembers when her father died. She will tell ye, her da and grandda died in a storm."

"Michael is as blind as ye are and Kristen is a bairn."

"That doesn't matter. She remembers and she knows who her mother is."

"Bah." His father waved his hand, as if he refused to credit a child. "Besides, I didn't rely only on Laird Morrison's letter. Nina's husband had their marriage certificate bearing her mark."

"Good point, Da. But why would a woman acknowledge a document with a mark if she can read and write?"

"Clearly, Nina can't read and write."

"Aye, I'm sure Nina, whomever she is, can't. But the woman who lived among us can read. Surely, if she were truly married, her husband would know that."

For the first time, Bram saw a glimmer of doubt in his father's eyes. "She can read? How is that possible? Tristan couldn't read."

"Her mother could, but the question of who taught her doesn't matter. Ye let six men drag Innes' granddaughter away based on a letter from a clan leader with whom ye have no formal ties and a marriage certificate which might have belonged to anyone. And ye threw the one person who tried to help her in the dungeon. Did ye ever consider Laird Morrison might have had another motive?"

"Bram, be reasonable. What cause would Laird Morrison to have to lie about who she is?"

"I don't know, but that brings me to another issue. Yer messenger arrived before Ian and I left. Ian asked ye about what news he brought and ye said it was nothing important. This seems worthy of at least a mention."

"I didn't know it then," said his father.

"What do ye mean, ye didn't know it?"

"Laird Morrison told the messenger she was lying to us but didn't offer details. He said he would send men for her."

"Doesn't that seem odd to ye? Wouldn't it have been reasonable for him to say, Grace Breive died or to tell ye that the woman in our midst had lost her mind and stolen a child so ye could prevent her from harming someone else before they arrived? Did it ever occur to ye that he gave ye no details because he needed time to make a plausible story?"

More doubt flitted across his father's features even as he insisted, "I had no reason to doubt Laird Morrison."

"But ye doubted a man to whom ye trust yer life? I think the truth is ye would rather let them haul away an innocent lass to ensure she didn't interfere with yer plans for me. But ye had already taken care of that, hadn't ye? Ye threatened her and forced her to tell me she loved another."

"It was for the good of the clan Bram. Who told ye anyway?"

"Ye just did."

His father had the good grace to look contrite. "Son, I—"

"Nay, I've heard enough. I am going to find Grace and bring her home. Kristen and Innes need her. That is, if there is anything left of her." Bram stormed out of the hall, barely registering the horrified looks on the servants' faces.

Ian caught up to him when he reached the stable. "Bram, wait."

Bram had just realized Ian had said nothing in the great hall and spun to face him. "Did ye know any of this?" Bram didn't think he could bear it if Ian had kept this from him.

"Nay, Bram. Da had just finished telling me about it when ye arrived."

"Don't try to talk me out of going after her."

"I won't. In fact, I'll go with ye. But Bram, we can't go tearing off after them alone and it's getting dark. We can leave with fresh horses at dawn."

"It is at least an hour until sunset, and another hour of gloaming after that. We can ride hard for two hours, then rest the horses until first light and we'll be that much closer. If they pushed hard, they could reach Durness by midday tomorrow. I only pray the tides are in our favor. We must reach them before they board a ship."

"Aye, we do," Ian said, "but it isn't likely to take them much less than three days. They had no reason to push and I'm sure Grace didn't make it easy."

Bram glowered at him. "Fine, we'll leave tonight. Just give me enough time to gather some men and supplies."

Bram knew Ian was being prudent, but waiting even a moment seemed too long. "Thank ye, Ian. And for the love of God, get Michael out of the dungeon."

"It was Michael? He threw Michael MacBain in the dungeon?

"Aye. No one else helped her." Bram's throat tightened with emotion. "Six men, Ian."

His brother gripped his shoulder. "We'll find her."

Chapter 28

Grace gave the Morrisons no more trouble. Clearly, her injured feet were as effective as a locked cell at preventing her escape. Roddy hadn't even bothered to bind her hands again. He allowed her to ride the next day. Frankly, he had no other choice if he wanted to reach Durness in less than a sennight. Although Roddy had her ride sitting in front of him initially, he soon complained that his mount was tiring under the extra weight.

Grace suspected an entirely different problem. She had been a married woman and could certainly recognize a man's erect member when it pressed against her. If she wasn't much mistaken Roddy had ridden for several hours in an uncomfortable state of arousal before foisting her off on Kenneth, the man who was apparently his second in command.

Kenneth was as cruel as Roddy, taunting her throughout the afternoon about what awaited her at Fearchar's hands. Grace refused to react, so Kenneth kept goading her with increasingly dire predictions. With each foul suggestion, much to her revulsion, Grace realized Kenneth too became aroused.

Eventually, Conan growled, and cursed before riding up beside them. "Ye're disgusting, Kenneth, and if ye don't shut yer foul mouth, I'll shut it for ye." Before Kenneth could react, Conan had pulled Grace onto his own lap.

"Thank ye," she whispered.

"Frankly, I don't care what Fearchar does with his whores, but I was tired of hearing Kenneth yammer on about it."

She rode with Conan for much of the rest of that day. She had hoped perhaps she could befriend one of them and maybe get help in escaping but after Conan's pronouncement she didn't even try with him. Conan handed her off to Gordon for a few hours in the late afternoon.

At least Gordon was polite but he refused to be drawn into a conversation. This left her alone with her thoughts so she envisioned one escape scenario after another. Then one after another she discarded them. They all hinged on needing to move quickly and her feet were too injured for that. She couldn't hope to outrun any of them. She fantasized about obtaining six knives and making short work of all six men, but the chances of that happening were slim. Besides, she wasn't entirely sure she would be able to take a single man's life, much less six. It would be especially hard for her to hurt Augie. He didn't seem as cruel as the rest. Perhaps that was where she needed to focus her efforts.

That evening when they made camp, she overheard Roddy say he expected to reach Durness sometime after midday tomorrow. "The captain should be waiting for us. He was to be ready to sail yesterday. With a bit of luck we could reach Lewis late tomorrow night. Just think, Gordon, ye might be swiving yer wife by the wee hours."

"And Fearchar will be teaching Grace what happens to wenches who defy him," said Kenneth.

"For the love of the saints, Kenneth, find yerself a woman to spill yer seed in and stop imagining what Fearchar is doing while ye yank yer knob yerself," said Derek. The argument only escalated from there.

She stopped paying attention. With a bit of luck we could reach Lewis late tomorrow night. Although she had clung steadfastly to the hope that she could get away from them before they boarded a boat to Lewis, her hope was swiftly being supplanted by doubt. Her feet were swollen and had barely begun to heal. While Roddy had given her back her boots, she couldn't get them on, so she still hobbled barefooted. Now they were less than a day's ride away, and she still hadn't thought of a viable escape plan.

Just when she felt ready to curl up and give into tears, her sweet Kristen filled her thoughts. Nay, she wouldn't give up. She would figure out a way to escape them in Durness. She prayed fervently to the Blessed Mother to guide her. Surely one mother would understand the heart of another and maybe she would listen and bend God's ear, as Grace believed He had stopped listening to her pleas months ago.

~ * ~

When she woke the next day it was with new resolve. In the absence of a better plan, she would do her best to befriend Augie in the little time she had left. Perhaps the Blessed Mother had intervened because Roddy declared that she would ride with

Augie that day. After they had been on the road a while she began asking him questions and unlike the other men, he responded. He told her about his family. She told him about hers, particularly about Kristen. However, before long Conan growled, rode up beside them, and shut Augie up in the same way he had Kenneth, by dragging Grace onto his own horse.

Grace was angry and frustrated. She could only hope that the brief conversation they had was enough to make Augie more kindly disposed to help her when the time came.

As they drew nearer to the village of Durness, Grace paid close attention to everything around her. She hoped to see something or someone that would help her.

Focused as she was, she failed to notice that Roddy had spoken to her. She only realized it when Conan nudged her and Roddy vented his anger on her. "Ye are a widowed, penniless, peasant, Grace, and are in no position to snub anyone. What will ye do when Fearchar is done with ye? Having a friend who doesn't mind his leavings could serve ye well."

She could barely believe her ears and she couldn't hold her tongue. "Having a friend who wouldn't hand me over to him in the first place would serve me a good deal better."

Roddy laughed. "Ye'll not find that among the likes of us. Fearchar will be laird soon enough and it's the men who serve him well now that will benefit the most then."

Grace looked over her shoulder at him. "Ye are quite certain of that?"

"Aye, I am," he said confidently.

Grace suspected Fearchar's loyalty would only stretch as far as what served him at the moment and for some reason she felt compelled to point that out. "I've always heard that Fearchar is relentless in gaining what he wants."

Roddy rode up beside her. "Aye, he is. He wanted ye, didn't he?"

"Aye he did." She remained quiet for a few moments before asking, "so what if he wants something precious to ye someday? Do any of ye have women that ye care about? What if he turns his eye to yer sister or mayhap yer wife…or even yer daughter? Won't he be equally as relentless then?"

"Ye're daft, Grace. He won't reward those who serve him well that way."

There was a nervous edge to Roddy's voice, so she

pushed. "Ye said he stops at nothing to get what he wants. So what's to stop him?"

"Common sense."

"Ah," said Grace. "So ye think Fearchar is sensible?"

Conan snorted.

"Aye, I think he is," Roddy answered.

"I see. Sending six men across the Highlands, for the sole purpose of bringing him a woman he fancies, is sensible."

Now Roddy was visibly agitated. "Shut up, Grace."

"If ye ask me, he is more guided by his urges than any bit of sense. So I don't think knocking one of ye senseless to have his way with another woman he desires seems that farfetched."

"I said shut up, Grace. If ye say another word, I will bind and gag ye until I hand ye over to Fearchar."

She said no more. She had made her point.

Chapter 29

They rode through the village to the docks. Roddy had a dark scowl on his face. Grace knew she probably shouldn't have goaded him—after all, making him angry wouldn't help her escape—but it had certainly felt good.

She returned her focus to her surroundings, searching for anyone she knew. She had met a few people in the month she stayed with Dugald and Mary who might get a message to them. Now, she didn't see a single familiar face.

As they reached the docks, her hopes rose again. If Lachie or one of the other men she knew who owned larger vessels waited for them, maybe they could help her. But as they drew closer to the ship, she didn't recognize it…still, perhaps. Roddy dismounted and called a greeting to the captain. The man who disembarked to speak with Roddy was a stranger to her. Her shoulders slumped, and she felt as if the wind had been knocked out of her.

As if reading her thoughts, Conan growled in her ear, "Roddy's an eejit but even he isn't stupid enough to hire a friend of yer da's."

Grace swallowed hard but said nothing. It was better to pretend she hadn't heard him.

"Oh, and if ye were thinkin' of talkin' young Augie into helping ye, think again. It won't work, ye'll be recaptured and Fearchar would horsewhip the lad to within a hair's breadth of his life. Do ye want that?"

Dear God, was Conan right? If she could convince Augie to help her, would that be the price he'd pay? "Nay," she whispered. But without help she had no hope of escaping. An errant tear slipped down her cheek before she was able to blink it back. It landed on the back of Conan's hand. He lifted his hand and wiped it on his knee. "Ye're going to break now? I thought ye were made of sterner stuff. When the devil's on yer heels, lass, ye can't stop and cry."

Somehow, instead of bringing on more tears, his callous

action hardened her. She wouldn't ask Augie for help, but she would keep watching for an opportunity. She had Kristen to think of. She couldn't give up. Not ever.

She might still have a chance today. One look at the harbor told her the tide was going out and it was unlikely they would set sail for hours. What's more, clouds were thickening on the horizon. A summer storm was brewing. The captain might not wish to sail into it.

Even if she didn't escape them before they sailed for Lewis, she would try to escape before they reached the castle. And if not then, she would endure what lay in store for her and find a way to escape Fearchar someday. She had done it once and she could do it again. She would get her daughter back.

When Roddy had finished talking to the captain, he returned looking irritated. "We can't sail yet. He said we are an hour or so from low tide."

"When can we sail?" Kenneth asked, sounding more like a whiny child than a warrior.

"The next high tide isn't until after sunset."

"He can't sail then," Gordon said.

"He can if ye order him to, Roddy," Kenneth said.

Derek rolled his eyes, and Gordon shook his head in frustration. "Would ye look at the western sky, Kenneth? There's a storm brewing. It would be reckless and foolhardy to sail into it."

Roddy scowled. "The captain said the same thing."

"So when do we sail?" Kenneth asked.

"The captain said if the storm blows itself out in the night, we can sail on the next high tide, sometime after terce tomorrow morning."

Kenneth frowned. "What do we do with her until then?"

"Just what we've done with her for the past three days. Guard her." Roddy was clearly losing his temper with Kenneth. "I wanted to lock her in the ship's hold for the night, but the captain wouldn't hear to it."

Conan barked a laugh. "No surprise there. I'm surprised ye had the stones to ask in the first place."

"Why?" Roddy demanded. "It seemed reasonable. It would have been secure. She certainly couldn't have gotten out."

It was all Grace could do to suppress a grin. She knew exactly why the captain refused.

Gordon explained, "Having a women aboard ship is bad

luck. If one must be aboard, most captains prefer it to be for as short a time as possible."

"How was I supposed to know that?" snapped Roddy.

"Roddy, ye grew up on an island, don't ye know any captains or fishermen?" Derek asked.

"Of course I do, but the subject of women on their ships never came up."

"Well, now that ye know, it is best if we secure her elsewhere," Gordon said. He was clearly more used to being a leader than a follower. "The inn where we hired the horses is not far from here. Ye can secure a room for her and a couple more for us. We'll guard her in shifts.

"I'll take the first shift," volunteered Kenneth.

"Of course ye will, ye little shite," muttered Conan under his breath. In a louder voice he said, "Augie should take the second one. He's green enough, he might fall asleep."

Augie looked affronted. "I have served the late watch many times."

"Nevertheless, ye'll take the second watch and Derek, ye take the third," said Roddy. "Then Gordon, Conan, and me. Kenneth, ye can stand guard again in the morning until we leave for the ship."

When they arrived at the inn Roddy paid for three rooms, two on the third floor and one on the second. The innkeeper's wife cast one look in Grace's direction and said, "I'll send some water up so ye can have a bit of a wash, dear."

"Thank ye, mistress." Grace took no offense. She hadn't had a proper wash or changed clothes in three days.

Roddy showed her to the last room at the end of the hall on the second floor. "It's the only room they have with a door which locks from either side."

It didn't matter to Grace. She could only have gotten past a guard if he fell asleep and the three men least likely to do that would have the watches in the wee hours.

Grace had hoped to have a moment alone with the innkeeper's wife. The woman surely knew Dugald and maybe could get a message to him. However, Roddy didn't allow anyone in the room alone with her. He guarded her himself until the wash water had been taken away and Grace had finished her dinner. Then he locked her in and set Kenneth to guard.

At least she was clean and had eaten a decent meal. The

innkeeper's wife had also brought her a small crock of salve and clean linen strips. "Put that salve on nice and thick, then wrap yer feet with the linen. It will help those cuts heal."

There was a window in the little room that looked out onto the stable yard. Sadly, there was nothing she could use to climb down on. She'd break her legs...or her neck if she tried to jump. She refused to let despair take hold again. There was still tomorrow.

She should sleep. If the chance did present itself tomorrow, she would need to be rested. Laying on the bed, she stared at the ceiling. She was still awake but the day's light was fading when the lock rattled and the door opened several hours later.

Kenneth said, "I don't know why Roddy insisted on ye seeing her before ye start yer shift. She can't have gone anywhere, the door's been locked."

"If she goes missing on anyone's watch, he says they'll have to answer to Fearchar," answered Augie.

"Well, as ye can see, she's there. I'm going down and having a few tankards of ale. And then a good sleep in a proper bed."

Grace glanced up to see Augie looking at her, his gaze filled with pity. Conan had been right. She might have been able to talk Augie into helping her but he would pay dearly for it if she did. He closed the door and locked it.

Before long, the wind whipped up and the rain that had threatened all evening started. She sighed, rising from the bed to close the shutters against the deluge. Oddly, even as the storm raged outside a peace came over her. She loved the sound of rain when she was safe and warm inside. Safe? Well, at least safe for now. Eventually, listening to the rain, she gave into her exhaustion and fell asleep.

It seemed as if only minutes had passed before the door opened again. She woke instantly. This time Derek held a candle in the room to check on her.

"I haven't learned to fly yet," she assured them.

"I've warned ye about that sharp tongue," Derek said before locking the door again.

She would worry about her sharp tongue later. The rain still hammered the little inn, quickly lulling her to sleep again.

When next she woke, Derek was handing over the watch

to Gordon. This time, she ignored them hoping to drift back to sleep as easily as she had several hours ago, but she didn't. She lay listening to the sounds of the night. The rain, which had drowned out all other noise, had tapered off to a gentle patter. The clatter of hooves on cobbles drifted up from the stable yard. More lodgers at the inn, she supposed. Again she let the steady patter of the rain soothe her but this time she fell into a restless sleep, plagued by dreams of a monstrous Fearchar.

Grace jerked awake suddenly, shaken from her fitful sleep, when Conan opened her door at the start of his watch. Of all of the men with Roddy, Conan scared her the most. Kenneth was a disgusting, spineless bully who enjoyed exerting power over people he believed were weaker. However, these were the hallmarks of a coward who would turn tail and run from a fight with a real opponent. Conan, on the other hand, appeared to be a hardened, emotionless warrior. He was not the first person she would pick to see upon waking from a nightmare. The sooner he locked her in again, the better.

But unlike the others, he didn't shut the door and lock it immediately. He looked over his shoulder and said to Gordon, "Keep an eye out until I'm done."

Shutting her eyes she held very still. Maybe he would leave if he thought she was asleep.

"Grace, I know ye are awake. Sit up, lass. I need to talk with ye."

Of course he knew she was awake. How did he do that? And what could he possibly need to talk with her about? She sat up, pulling the blanket with her. She wasn't sure she had ever been more frightened.

"Calm yerself, I won't hurt ye, lass."

"Ye haven't seemed terribly concerned about that before now." By all the saint's, Grace, why would ye goad the man who scares ye witless?

"I know the last few days have been hard, and I didn't make them any easier, but truly I'm here to help ye, lass. Do ye know anyone in Durness who would be willing to hide ye?"

Help her? That didn't seem likely. Was he trying to find out so he could make sure she didn't get help in the morning? "Why would ye want to help me? Ye said ye didn't care what Fearchar does with his whores."

"And I don't. But ye aren't one of them. Ye are the

daughter of the man who saved my family."

Grace blinked. "What? I don't understand. How did my father save yer family?"

"It was years ago, ye were just a bairn. God made certain he was in the right place at the right time. Yer da had helped Lachie deliver some goods, which Lady Morrison had sent for from the mainland. It was a bitter, cold evening and they stopped at the village tavern for a hot meal and a tankard of ale before heading home. Apparently they hadn't intended to stay long, but there was a merry crowd in the tavern that night. I'll always be thankful they didn't rush because when they were finally on their way, they saw smoke rising and raced towards it. The thatch on the roof of my cottage was on fire. I woke to the house filling with smoke. I couldn't wake my wife, so I dragged her out and went back for our children. Just as I stepped back in the house, a beam fell, hitting me in the head and knocking me out." He pointed to the burn scars on his face. "Apparently, that's when yer da and Lachie arrived. Lachie said yer da ran straight into the burning cottage without a moment of hesitation. He carried my two children out, one under each arm, while Lachie dragged me to safety."

Grace was speechless.

"I owe yer da everything. When I overheard Fearchar boasting that he meant to have ye, it sickened me. I went to the village the next day to warn ye, hoping to find a way to hide ye, but thankfully ye were already gone. I figured Lachie brought ye here but the less anyone knew the better so I didn't ask. Then Sutherland's damn messenger showed up a little over a week ago. The laird was away and not expected back for several days. Fearchar met with the man, then sent him back to Sutherland with the message that ye had lied. In no time he had concocted the story about ye being married to Roddy, forged a letter from his da, and was choosing men to go fetch ye. He wanted them gone before Laird Morrison returned. When I caught wind of what Fearchar was doing, I made sure Gordon and I were assigned to the task."

"Why didn't ye just tell Laird Sutherland the truth?"

"Because the bastard was too willing to believe the lie. If he had shown the slightest doubt, Gordon or I would have found a way to tell him the truth privately. As it was, he might have called us out in front of the others. We couldn't risk Fearchar taking revenge on our families. We thought it better to get ye away and sort out what to do with ye later. We never would have let Fearchar get his hands on ye. Which brings me back to my first question, do ye have friends here?"

"I do. But if I go missing when either ye or Gordon are on watch, will ye not be blamed?"

Conan's face screwed into a crooked smile. "Aye, we would, but ye aren't going missing on our watches. Ye are going to go missing on Roddy's watch, or Kenneth's next one."

"How?"

"At the end of my watch, when Roddy looks in, ye need to be curled up in the bed with the blanket over ye. Make sure ye move a bit, so he can see ye're really there—maybe say something. There is a ladder to the hayloft in the stable. As soon as Roddy has settled in, Gordon and I will use it to fetch ye down through the window and then take ye to yer friends. Ye need to put yer pillows under the covers to look like yer still in bed sleeping. If it doesn't fool them when Kenneth takes over, Roddy will be blamed. But given that they are both hopeless eejits, I expect it will fool them and Kenneth will be blamed later. Can ye do this?"

"Aye, and I thank ye for keeping me away from Fearchar, but what about the lies they told the Sutherlands? How will I get Kristen back?"

"Kristen is safe with yer granny for now."

"Aye, but—"

"I know, ye need to get her back. But as long as she is safe, ye will stay here with yer friends for a little while." The tone of Conan's voice brooked no argument. "I will send someone back with evidence of who ye really are. Ye must be patient for a while and for the love of God, don't do anything as stupid as ye did the first morning. I'm sorry about yer feet, but I couldn't stop that and still see ye safe in the long run."

She looked contrite. She knew trying to run away then had been a mistake as soon as she had done it. "I'm sorry. I pa—"

"Panicked. I know that. And I hope ye learned yer lesson. It never helps to panic. Ye must keep yer wits about ye, Grace."

Grace nodded. "Aye. I will."

"And ye understand the plan?"

"I do. I'll be ready to go after Roddy checks on me at the end of yer watch."

"See that ye are." He started to leave.

"Conan?"

He turned back, looking irritated. "What?"

"Do ye have a daughter?" She couldn't help but wonder if that was how he knew what she was thinking so easily.

He snorted, as she had heard him do often over the last couple days. "Nay. I had the good sense only to have boys." With that he left.

Grace was glad she had slept for a few hours earlier because she was too tense to sleep for the rest of the night. She quietly gathered her things. The rain had stopped so she opened the shutters. She didn't want to risk making any noise later. When there was nothing left to do, she curled up under the blanket.

Although she and God hadn't been on good terms lately, she recognized a blessing when she saw it. She thanked God for ensuring that her father had been able to save Conan's family and for keeping Kristen safe until they were together again. She also thanked God for sending Conan and Gordon to help her and she prayed they would not suffer because of it. Then she prayed that the bundle of pillows would fool Roddy and Kenneth in the morning because more than anything, she wanted Kenneth blamed. She could see no redeeming qualities in the man. Not that Roddy was much better, but Kenneth had taken such pleasure in describing what Fearchar would do to her, she thought it only fair that he experience a bit of Fearchar's wrath himself.

Dawn was pinking the sky when Roddy unlocked the door to check on her at the start of his watch. She raised her head up sleepily, looked at him, groaned, and pulled the blanket over her head.

"That's right, sleep while ye can. Ye won't get much more for a while," he sneered.

She heard the lock click and she lay still for a few minutes. When all was quiet, she sat up, and waited. Before long she heard something bump softly against the back wall. She hurried to the window. Below, Conan held the ladder steady as Gordon climbed it.

She handed him her small bundle of belongings. Gordon steadied her as she tried to climb out the window without making any noise. Then, he descended the ladder behind her. The rungs of the ladder caused pain to shoot through her feet and her eyes watered, but she didn't utter a sound. When she reached the ground, Gordon immediately removed the ladder, carrying it back to the stable as Conan scooped her into his arms. She started to protest, but he scowled at her and it died on her lips. He was right, she couldn't move fast enough on her own. He ran with her, out of the stable yard, down the lane and around a corner, not stopping until they were well out of sight of the inn.

"Ok, lass, where do these friends of yers live?"

"I can walk now, ye needn't carry me."

Conan snorted. "Ye can't walk nearly fast enough and I have to get back to the inn before anyone notices I'm gone."

She directed him down several streets, to the center of the village, where the merchant's shops were. "Go around to the back. That's where the door to the kitchen is. The family quarters are above the shop, but they will hear us knocking on the kitchen door."

They had to knock several times. When the door open, Dugald appeared fully prepared to chew the face off of whatever soul was pounding on his door at this hour. When he saw Grace, in the scarred warrior's arms, he pulled them inside and called for Mary.

Conan lowered her to a chair before telling Dugald, "Grace will tell ye what has happened. I must not be caught away or her safety is in danger. Grace, I will send word soon about how we will proceed with the Sutherlands." He pinned her with a stern look. "Stay put until I do." With that he left.

She sighed. She was out of danger for the moment. Now she had to focus on getting Kristen back.

Chapter 30

Bram, Ian, and the six men who rode with them kept a relentless pace, traveling as fast as the horses could tolerate. They arrived in Durness just after midnight two days later. They had slogged through rain for the last several hours. Bram wanted to go straight to the docks but Ian talked him out of it.

"Bram, it's pouring rain and there won't be anyone to ask at this time of night anyway. Besides, if they haven't left yet, they won't be able to leave until tomorrow and if they have, ye won't be able to follow them until tomorrow. Let's find an inn."

Ian was right.

The innkeeper wasn't overly pleased to be awakened in the wee hours of the morning. "Be off with ye, lot of miscreants. My rooms are full anyway." He started to close the door on them.

Bram stopped the door with his hand and pushed it open again. Under Bram's intimidating glower, the innkeeper took a nervous step backwards.

Anxious and short tempered since learning Grace had been handed over to the Morrisons, Bram's patience now was nearly stretched to the limit. Still, after two days on the road with only short stops and then riding hard through a storm for the last few hours, they were travel worn, soaked, and mud-spattered. They must be a sorry sight indeed. He took a deep breath, reining in his temper before addressing the innkeeper in tight, measured tones. "Good sir, I'll admit in our current state we look disreputable. However, I am Bram Sutherland, Laird Sutherland's heir, and we have good coin to pay for whatever shelter ye can provide us for what remains of the night."

The innkeeper heaved a sigh of relief. "I apologize, my lord. Ye do look...well..." he shrugged in apology. "Aye, of course I can find some place out of the rain for ye. There is room in the stable for yer horses. I'm afraid all my stable hands have gone to their homes, but ye're free to use whatever ye need. As fer ye, like I said, all of the guest rooms are full tonight but ye can bed down in the hall. I'll stoke the fire and find some blankets for ye while ye tend to yer beasts."

Bram nodded. "Thank ye."

The rain had tapered off a good deal by the time they returned to the inn. In addition to the blankets, the innkeeper had set out bread, cold meat, and flagons of ale. Bram was hungrier than he realized. After they ate, most of the guardsmen who had ridden with them grabbed a blanket and as clean a spot on the floor as could be found to get some sleep. Thankfully it looked as if the rushes had been changed very recently. Otherwise the stable might have been a better smelling option.

Bram, Ian, and Donal sat on benches at a table in one corner of the room, finishing off the ale. Bram stared broodily into the fire.

Ian nudged him. "Get some rest. Ye could use it. Ye wouldn't let Michael come with us because of the condition he was in but ye don't look any better now than he did then. Ye've barely slept for two days. I'll keep watch for a bit, then wake Donal."

"I'll rest when I know she's safe."

"Bram, we may be in for a battle. For the love of God, close yer eyes for a bit."

Bram shook his head. "I know yer right…"

"Then do it."

It was true. He would not be fit for a fight if he didn't have a little rest. "Fine, I'll try." He grabbed a blanket and a spot on the floor behind Ian. He fell asleep instantly.

The next thing he knew, Donal shook him awake. The sun was up, but it was still very early, perhaps just before prime. "Get up. Something is happening," whispered Donal.

"What is it?" Bram was on his feet instantly as were the other men.

Donal shook his head. "I don't know. I just heard a commotion from upstairs."

In the next instant a man's voice rang out from the stairs. "Get the men down here, now, Kenneth! How the hell did she escape?"

Bram motioned his men down. Some reassumed sleeping positions while others appeared to be waking up as the man reached the hall. "When did ye lot get here?" he asked, clearly angry.

Donal immediately stretched out on the bench where he

had been sitting and turned his back on the man. "A few hours ago. Let a man sleep."

"Sun's up, eejit," growled the man.

Bram glanced at Donal. He was the only one of the guardsmen with them who was in the hall when the Morrisons took Grace and he was clearly hiding his face. Bram caught his eye. Donal nodded ever so slightly and held up one finger. The message was clear, this was the leader of the Morrison men who took Grace—the one named "Roddy" who claimed to be her husband. By the saints, was she somewhere in this inn? Had he slept while she was enduring God knew what?

Bram started to his feet, but Ian grabbed his leg from where he lay on the floor. He shook his head, put his fingers to his lips, then pointed at one ear. Aye, he was right, they needed to see what they could learn before acting. Bram nodded at him.

Bram stood and stretched. "Aye, lads, the sun is shining."

His men feigned waking up slowly as three other men entered the hall, one very young man and two others who were roughly the same age as Roddy.

"What's happened?" asked one of Roddy's peers, yawning.

"What do ye think happened? Grace is gone," said Roddy.

He called her Grace. Bram tried to stay calm.

"How'd ye lose her, Kenneth?" the yawning man asked.

"Ye're an arse Derek. I didn't lose her. Roddy did," said Kenneth.

"I didn't lose her either. She was there at the start of my watch," said Roddy.

"But she's not there now. I think Kenneth has the right of it, this is yer problem," said the man called Derek.

"Nay," Roddy growled, "it is our problem and we need to find her."

"Well, ye can make finding her our problem, but if we don't, ye'll be the one to answer to Fearchar, not us. She was there when I went off duty," said Derek.

"What the hell is taking Conan and Gordon so long? Augie, go tell them to get down here now."

The youngest man nodded nervously and headed for the stairs.

"Ye don't suppose he helped her, do ye?" asked Derek.

"What could he have done? He had the second watch and

was in the room with Conan and Gordon. He couldn't have slipped away on them."

"This is yer fault," said Kenneth.

"Nay Kenneth, if ye hadn't scared the wits out of her by telling her what Fearchar does to people who defy him, she might not have run," hissed Roddy.

"I didn't tell her anything that wasn't true. Ye are the one that made her walk."

"By the Almighty, ye are an eejit, Kenneth," said Roddy.

Bram had heard about enough but before he stepped in, Ian spoke up. "What's wrong, lads?"

"It's not yer concern," said Roddy.

"Suit yerself. It just sounded like ye have lost someone. There are eight of us, maybe we could help."

"Eejit," muttered Roddy. Still, he appeared to be considering what Ian said. "Ah...but now that ye mention it, maybe ye could be some help."

"None of us would mind searching for a bonny lass. She is bonny, isn't she?" Ian grinned cheekily.

"Aye, she is. Green eyes, reddish hair, maybe a bit too slender but don't get any ideas. She is a clanswoman and we are takin her home."

"What did ye say her name was?" Ian asked.

"Her name is Grace and she must be found. Aye, ye can help. There might even be a reward in it for the man who finds her."

The youngest guardsman, Augie, reappeared with two much older men, one who had a badly scarred face.

Roddy went on attack immediately, further demonstrating his poor judgement. Both men looked more than capable of crushing him. "It took ye long enough. I knew it was a mistake to bring old men. Grace is missing. It was only pillows under the covers. She must have escaped on yer watch, Conan."

Conan, the man with the scarred, face snorted in disgust. "Roddy, yer memory is shorter than yer rod. Ye talked to her at the end of my watch. If she is gone, ye are to blame."

"Damnation! It doesn't matter whose fault it is," said Roddy. But clearly it did or he wouldn't have tried to shift the blame. "What matters is that we find her. These men have offered to help us search."

Both Conan and the man Bram assumed was the one

called Gordon turned to look at them. As their eyes landed on Ian, realization dawned. The men tensed, preparing for a fight. The Sutherlands responded to their change in stance by tensing for battle also. Bram had no doubt if they could have, they would have drawn swords. As it was, none of them were armed. According to custom, they had all surrendered their weapons to the innkeeper on their arrival.

"What are ye doing?" demanded Roddy. "We need to find her before high tide and they've offered to help."

"Aye, I'll bet they did," said Gordon.

"Ye're a fool Roddy, they're Sutherlands," growled Conan.

"How do ye know that?" asked Roddy, clearly not aware of the danger he was in.

"That one is the image of the laird—probably his son," said Conan, gesturing toward Ian.

"Then they have every reason to help us. They know she's my wife. They wanted rid of Nina," said Roddy.

Bram exploded when he said that name. Roddy was on the ground before he knew what hit him. Bram pounded him mercilessly. "Ye've already called her Grace."

"I meant Nina, I meant Nina. She's my wife," squealed Roddy.

Bram continued throwing punches. He was vaguely aware that a brawl had started around him but his focus was on Roddy. "Ye lying sack of shite. She is Grace Breive and ye know full well."

"Aye…she is…Grace. Please…I beg ye…have mercy," Roddy cried between punches.

"Did ye show her any mercy?" roared Bram.

"She didn't ask for it," Roddy whined.

"She shouldn't have had to," snarled Bram, knocking Roddy unconscious with one vicious blow.

Bram stopped and stood up. Roddy was a bloody mess. Bram grabbed him by the front of his léine and threw him on a bench against the wall before looking around. The man named Kenneth lay on the floor; he too had been beaten to a stupor.

Derek appeared to be holding his own against a Sutherland guardsman until he fell backwards over a bench, hitting his head and rendering him unconscious too.

Donal had his left arm around Augie's throat and Augie's

right arm bent up between his shoulder blades.

The two older men, Gordon and Conan, looked as if they had exchanged a few solid punches, but now stood with their hands raised in surrender. They were surrounded by Bram's remaining guardsmen.

Gordon's eyes travelled to the bloody heap that was Roddy and his face split into a huge grin. "Damn, I wanted to be the one to do that."

Bram's eyebrows shot up.

"And there's no reason to break that sapling's arm," said Conan to Donal. "He won't cause ye any trouble." At the look of doubt on every Sutherland face, Conan too grinned. "I swear to ye.

Bram considered Conan for a moment. One of the other men had suspected Augie of helping Grace. If that was the case, the younger man might know where she is. Bram nodded to Donal who released Augie.

Augie stepped away, rolling his shoulders. He looked affronted.

Bram returned his attention to Conan and Gordon. "Now, I want some answers. Where is Grace and why do the two of ye look so pleased?"

Conan stared back at Bram as if sizing him up. Finally he asked, "Are ye one of Sutherland's sons?"

"What has that to do with anything?"

"Ye want to know about Grace and I want to know who I'm dealing with."

"Aye, I'm Bram Sutherland, Laird Sutherland's heir."

"And I was right about ye?" Conan said to Ian. "Ye are a son too?"

"Aye, I'm Ian Sutherland."

"Well then, ye should be able to answer my questions."

Bram was floored. "Answer yer questions?"

"Aye," answered Conan calmly. "Augie, ye didn't hear a word of this. Understand?"

"Aye, Conan."

Bram growled, "I have had enough. Where is Grace?"

"Grace is somewhere safe."

"Then tell me where so I can take her home," Bram demanded.

"I need to know she'll be safe from ye first."

"Safe? Ye are the ones who lied and took her from her

family."

"Now, I'm glad ye brought that up because yer da was only too quick to believe those lies."

Bram couldn't argue. He had accused his father of just that. "Well I don't believe them and I want the truth. Tell me why Laird Morrison sent ye with the lies in the first place."

Gordon spoke up. "Laird Morrison didn't lie to ye. His heir Fearchar did. The story Grace told ye was the truth. She is Tristan and Cat Murray's daughter. She is Callum Breive's widow and Kristen is her daughter. The detail she might not have shared is that Fearchar is a vicious, self-important bastard. He decided that he wanted Grace in his bed—a fate I wouldn't wish on any lass. I suspect the men in her village knew he would stop at nothing to get her, so they spirited her off the island."

"Ye suspect?" asked Bram. "Don't ye know?"

Conan barked a laugh. "Nay. Oh, Fearchar tried to find out. The villagers would have ye believe she was taken by the fae or perhaps stowed away on some ship. The fewer people who knew where she actually had gone, the better. We believed she was safe."

Gordon continued, "Then yer da sent the messenger asking if Grace was who she said she was. 'Twas, Fearchar he spoke to, Laird Morrison was away. Naturally, once Fearchar knew where to find her, he told the messenger she was lying and sent him on his way. Then he cooked up the story about her being married and losing her mind before sending us to fetch her."

"But ye knew it was all lies," accused Bram.

"Aye, but there are men in the clan who will do anything Fearchar asks, hoping to court his favor when he becomes laird. Those three among them," Conan said, gesturing at Roddy, Kenneth, and Derek. "He can always find spineless men to do his bidding. Others pray he never becomes laird. We reckoned the only way to keep her safe was to go with them."

"We assumed that yer father wouldn't believe Roddy's story, at least not without checking a few facts. We expected to have the chance to tell him the truth, thus ensuring Grace would be protected."

"But he did believe it," said Bram, feeling no small bit of shame.

"Not only did he believe it, he seemed relieved, almost happy," said Gordon. "We couldn't leave her under those circumstances. We went along with Roddy, knowing we would have to find a way to hide her again before we reached Lewis."

Things were beginning to make more sense, but Bram was growing impatient. "Clearly ye have done that, and I thank ye. But I will see to her safety now."

Conan shook his head. "Why should I believe ye? How do I know ye aren't just another laird's son who thinks he owns the world and everything in it? What is she to ye?"

"What is she to me? She's a Sutherland and who are ye to ask that?"

Conan pierced him with a stare. "I'm the man who knows where she is and I owe it to her father to see she is well cared for."

Bram wondered what Tristan had to do with this, but he didn't want to waste more time. "She is our clanswoman. No one will ever question that again. She is loved."

"Clearly," said Gordon, sarcasm dripping from his words. "She was so well loved that only one man came to her aid and he was beaten down. Lady Sutherland made an attempt but yer da silenced her as well. The other Sutherlands who saw Grace being dragged away—forced to leave her beloved daughter—made the sign of the cross and turned their backs."

Hearing those words caused his heart to ache. "My father, their laird, believed the lies, so his people did too. They know the truth now," said Bram. "She will be welcomed again."

Conan instantly turned angry. "That's not good enough! Yer da couldn't have been happier to get rid of her. And I don't care if he was their laird, yer people, who ye say loved her, didn't turn a hand to help. Ye need to convince me that something like this can never happen again, or the devil's fingers will freeze off before ye lays eyes on her again."

His vehemence took Bram by surprise. He looked to Ian for help.

Ian shook his head. "Ye have to handle this one, Brother. He has me believing we're the villains here."

Bram sighed, what could he say? The man was right. His father had worked to turn people against her. Deep down, he wasn't sure that it could never happen again. Unless he defied his father, broke his promise to wait a month, and married her immediately.

He looked Conan directly in the eyes and said, "I love her. With all of my heart, I love her. I can't live without her. I will marry her if she will have me. I will protect and cherish both Grace and Kristen as long as I live."

"Those are nice words, lad, but ye are Laird Sutherland's heir. Ye would have us believe he'd let ye marry a fisherman's daughter?" asked Gordon.

"I will marry her anyway. If he doesn't like it, so be it. I'll become a fisherman if I have to and leave the running of the clan to Ian. Ye're right. I fell in love with Grace and that is why my father did everything in his power to separate us. I swear to ye, I won't allow it to happen again. I believe she loves me too but if she doesn't I will see her safe and well protected no matter what."

Derek groaned and began to stir.

Gordon looked at Conan. "Should we believe him?"

"I'd rather hear it from Grace, but there's no time. Aye, I'll believe him." Turning back to Bram, Conan said, "but if I ever learn ye have failed in yer vow, I will make ye pay." Then he leaned forward and said under his breath, said, "There is a merchant named Dugald whose shop is on the main square. Ye'll find Grace there."

"Thank ye," said Bram.

"Leave this lot to us and get her away from Durness," said Gordon.

Bram glanced at Roddy. He itched to finish the job.

Conan arched an eyebrow at him. "Ye'd like to finish him off, would ye? I don't blame ye, but Fearchar will do worse than ye ever could. After all, Grace escaped on his watch."

"Aye," said Augie who had been raptly silent until then. "But how?"

Conan shrugged. "Like the villagers said, it must have been the fae."

Chapter 31

Mary and Dugald immediately began fussing over Grace and her injured feet. Mary insisted that Dugald carry Grace upstairs.

"I'll see ye're nice and comfy tucked up in bed."

"Nay Mary, really, I can walk and I don't need to lie abed." Grace suppressed a smile at Dugald's look of relief. He wasn't exactly in his prime, and the stairs to the living quarters were narrow.

Mary harrumphed but acquiesced. "But ye must let me fix ye something to break yer fast, while ye tell us what has happened."

Grace agreed and launched into her story. She started from the moment the laird had summoned her. As Grace told them the story, she could hardly believe it had barely been three days since the Morrisons had taken her, three days since she had seen Kristen. It felt like a lifetime. When she finished, Mary and Dugald were both visibly upset.

Dugald paced angrily. "How could Laird Sutherland have done that to ye? He didn't question anything?"

Grace shook her head. "Nay, but he had his reasons."

Mary looked affronted. "What possible reason could he have had? Anyone who sees ye with Kristen, even for just a few minutes, has to know she's yers. That should have been enough to know the Morrisons lied. Was he blind?"

Grace sighed. They needed to know the truth. "He didn't question anything because he wanted it to be true. He wanted me gone."

"But why?" asked Mary. "Ye would be an asset to any clan. Ye are very skilled and a hard worker. Ye weren't with us a day before I knew that."

"None of that mattered to him," said Grace.

"The devil take him then," swore Dugald. "What could matter more than that?"

"His son and the alliance he had planned. Ye see, his son Bram and I became friends. I knew better. I knew I should have steered clear of him. But he was kind, and I enjoyed the time we spent together. Kristen liked him and he was so very gentle with her. I thought we could just be friends. I didn't expect more, but…"

"Oh, lass, ye fell for him, and he broke yer heart," moaned Mary.

Grace shook her head. "'Twas really more that. We fell for each other and I broke his heart." She told them the rest of the story, including all of Laird Sutherland's attempts to keep them apart.

Dugald's ire seemed to rise with each new detail of the story. "Laird Sutherland threatened ye because he couldn't control his own son? The bastard. Ye should have come back to us then."

Grace nodded. "I thought about it and believe me, I wanted to. Michael was willing to bring me. My grandmother wouldn't agree to come and I hated that."

"Why didn't he bring ye then?" asked Dugald.

"He seemed to think the laird had changed his mind about forcing me to marry. I expect the laird knew his problem was about to be solved by the Morrisons."

"Poor lass. But it's over and ye'll stay with us now. We'll help ye get Kristen back," said Mary.

"I'm still worried about Fearchar, especially since his henchmen know I must be hiding here in Durness. And I worry about what that means for ye. It would kill me if he hurt ye to get at me, but I just don't see another choice right now."

"Never ye mind about that," said Dugald. "Ye aren't going back to Sutherlands. As soon as we have proof, we'll bring Kristen here. Ye never have to see them again. I expect when yer granny hears what the laird did, she will be happy enough to come here too."

Grace hoped so. The look of doubt from her grandmother may have hurt worse than anything else. She didn't want to lose her grandmother after having just found her, but in truth she didn't want to go back. She didn't care if she never laid eyes on a Sutherland again. But even as she told herself that, she knew it was a lie. Michael was a good man and had come to her aid. But truthfully, her heart ached knowing that she would never see Bram again.

Dugald patted her on the shoulder. "Don't worry, Grace. It will all be put to rights. I'm going to open the shop now. The sun is well up, I expect it is past prime."

~ * ~

Bram and his men collected their weapons and left the inn. He gave a curt order for them to saddle up; he wanted to leave immediately. After tearing across the Highlands for two days, he had almost found Grace and he had one goal, to take her home.

Ian wore an oddly smug expression as he adjusted his mount's tack. Bram tried to ignore it only to glance at Donal who wore the same expression.

"What?" Bram demanded.

Donal shrugged. "I didn't say anything."

"Keep it that way," said Bram. "Ye too." He glared at Ian.

Ian laughed. "Since when do I pay attention to ye? I'm just glad ye'll be back to yer normal broodiness and not the absolutely foul temper ye have had for days. But of course that wasn't because ye loved her."

"He enjoyed her company," offered Donal. "At least that's what he told me."

"Aye, that was it," said Ian.

Bram scowled. "Ye were right. Is that what ye want to hear? I couldn't bear the thought of living my life without her."

His brother grinned broadly. "That's good for a start."

"Well don't be too sure my foul temper is over. After all that has happened, it may be Michael she loves anyway."

"Nay," said Ian. "I'm fairly certain it's ye."

Bram mounted Goliath. "We still have to find her and take her home. Let's go."

They rode the short distance to the center of the village. Bram called to a small lad who was trying to pull a contrary goat through the square. "Lad, which shop is Dugald's?"

Looking in awe of the mounted warriors, the lad pointed to a large two story building.

"Thank ye," Bram said, tossing him a copper. The lad's eyes grew wide and his face split into a grin.

"Wait here," he said to his men and dismounted, handing Goliath's reins to Ian.

He entered the shop, nodding to the proprietor.

"Good morning, sir. Can I help ye?" the man asked.

"Are ye Dugald?"

"Aye." The man tensed. "Who's asking?"

"I'm Bram Sutherland and I understand one of my clanswomen has taken refuge here with ye."

"I don't know what yer talking about. There are no Sutherlands here."

"Please, I know Grace is here. I have come to take her home."

"I told ye there are no Sutherlands here. I'll ask ye to leave now."

Bram was growing frustrated. "I can't thank ye enough for taking her in, but her grandmother and her daughter need her. I need her. Let me take her home."

The man narrowed his eyes. "Bram Sutherland ye say? I know who ye are and I know what yer father did. Clearly he didn't care about her or her kin. If ye're saying ye believe that she is Grace Breive, and I assure ye, she is, then I will go with ye and bring her daughter back to her. This is her home now."

Bram never imagined he would encounter this. "Please, let me just speak with her."

A door opened from the back of the shop and a matronly woman stepped through. She cocked her head to one side. "Who is this?"

"Bram Sutherland," Dugald answered, his scorn evident.

"What do ye want here?" she asked.

"He says he's come to take Grace home."

"Has he? Well, young man, that lass doesn't need more heartache. Do ye know what yer father did to her?"

"I do and I'm sorry. That is why I came after her. Please, I have been so worried. Let me see her."

The woman pursed her lips and considered him for a moment. "Before I let ye anywhere near her, I want yer word ye won't force her to go with ye or if she chooses to go, make her stay after she has her wee lass back."

"I swear to ye. I won't force her to do anything. Just let me see her."

"Fine. Come with me."

He followed her through the rear door and down a small corridor into a bright kitchen. Grace sat at the table peeling apples. She looked up at him and gave a little gasp of shock. Then her eyes filled with such hurt that it scalded him.

"Ah, Grace, I told ye to leave that for me. This scoundrel

has asked to speak with ye, pet. Will I send him packing?"

"Nay," she whispered.

"Grace," Bram's voice broke with emotion. What had the bastard done to her? Her face had yellowing bruises on it, her wrists were abraded, and her hands scraped. He was across the kitchen and had her in his arms in three strides. She threw her arms around him, buried her face in his léine and burst into tears.

"Ah, Grace, my love, wheesht. Please don't cry." He held her close, kissing the top of her head until she regained control.

"How did ye know I was here?" she asked once she had stopped crying.

"We encountered the Morrisons at the inn this morning. Eventually, Conan told me."

He was content to hold her in his arms, but before he was ready to let her go, she released him. She took a step back, hastily wiping the tears from her face. "I'm sorry. I shouldn't have done that."

"Nay, Grace. I've longed to hold ye in my arms." He stepped towards her, cupping her her face in his hands. "I feared I'd lost ye."

She looked away, taking another step backwards. Her chin quivered and tears welled in her eyes again. "But ye have."

"Don't say that. Please, don't say that. Da was wrong. He knows that now."

She turned her back to him, stiffening. "Aye, he was wrong to believe them but I'll warrant nothing else has changed."

"But it will. Let me take ye home now."

"Nay, Bram. That isn't my home. I'll go with ye, but only if ye swear to me that I can have my daughter back and leave. I don't belong there."

"Of course ye belong there. Grace, I love ye. Ye are the heart of my heart." He reached out and tugged on one arm, until she turned to face him. The look of anguish in her eyes gutted him.

She shook her head. "Nay, Bram, ye cannot love me. Ye must not."

"Grace, I have loved ye nearly since the first moment I met ye. I have never stopped loving ye. I know my father threatened ye in some way but it was ye who lied about not loving me."

"I did not lie. I have never lied to ye."

Bram's heart fell. "Then ye only wanted to be Lady

Sutherland and ye do love Michael?"

"I did want to be Lady Sutherland. Not because I care about the title, but because I wanted with all my heart to be yer wife and I had hoped yer father wouldn't banish ye because I didn't want ye to suffer the kind of rift my family had. So yes, I wanted to be Lady Sutherland, but I never said I loved Michael. Michael is a good friend—my only friend it seems—but I don't love him."

"Ye said ye did. I said if ye had waited a little longer, ye could have been Lady Sutherland, but ye said ye fell in love."

"I did, but not with Michael. I fell in love with ye, Bram. But yer father never intended to let us marry. He asked ye for a month to give him time to convince ye not to marry me. When that didn't work he told me I had to break it off. He threatened me with a forced marriage. He said he would never allow ye to marry me and that if I truly loved ye, it would be kinder to turn ye against me so ye could marry Annice.

"Bram, I truly love ye. I love ye more than I believed possible. I never thought I would love anyone again but I think I finally understand the depth of the love my parents shared. I didn't want to push ye away. I didn't want to hurt ye."

Bram's heart soared at those words. "Oh, my love, I knew Da was behind it. I just didn't know what threat he made. But that doesn't matter anymore. I love ye with all my heart."

"Nay, it does matter, Bram. Ye are still the laird's son. We aren't allowed to love each other. We can't be together."

"Aye, we can. Grace, I want ye to be my wife."

"Bram, stop. That can never happen. Ye know that."

"Nay, Grace, I don't."

"Well, it's high time ye learned then," she said bitterly. "Just as I have to learn not to love ye." Her voice broke with a sob. "Yer da has his own plans. I can't bear the pain of losing ye. I can't see ye wed someone else, and I cannot risk what he will do if we marry against his wishes. I won't. I have lost too much."

"I know ye have, Grace." He gathered her into his arms. She rested her head against his chest. Her tears were spent but the pain still flowed off of her in waves. He wanted more than anything to take it away—for her to believe him. He would marry her, but if he insisted now, if he pushed her, he might push her away. It was enough that she was willing to come with him to get Kristen. He would convince her of his love on the way or die trying.

~ * ~

The moment Grace had looked up and saw Bram standing behind Mary, her heart leapt. He had come for her. Even though she hurt him and pushed him away, he hadn't believed the Morrisons' lies. For three days she had fought to stay in control. She refused to give in or to let anyone see how terrified she really was. But when Bram wrapped her in his arms all of the pain and fear she had reined in for days came bubbling up.

He was warm and strong and in his arms she was safe. This was where she wanted to stay forever. But the little voice inside her, the voice that had kept her strong and refused to let her give in to despair, reminded her that Bram Sutherland could never be hers. She had given in to the comfort he offered in the moment, but she could not let that happen again. She had no doubt that he wanted to marry her—just as much as she longed to be his wife. That didn't change the facts. He was destined to marry another and if she did marry him, Laird Sutherland would kill her. The more she let herself love him now, the more losing him would hurt.

Finally, she took a deep breath and stepped away from him. "Please, I have been away from my daughter too long."

"Aye, ye have. Are these yer things?" He picked up her small bundle of belongings.

She nodded, feeling suddenly shy after losing all control and sobbing on him.

"Then let's go," he said, placing a hand in the small of her back and walking her through the door into the shop.

"So yer goin' with him?" asked Dugald.

"Aye, he'll help me get Kristen. I'll come back as soon as I can."

"Ye'll always be welcome here, ye ken?" he asked.

"Aye, lass, always," said Mary.

"Thank ye, both. Ye don't know what that means to me." She gave them each a hug. When she turned back to Bram, his expression was inscrutable.

"I owe ye a great debt," said Bram. "Thank ye."

They stepped out of the shop into the bright morning sun. She glanced around at Bram's men. Some had been in the hall the day she was dragged away. Her eyes came to rest on Donal.

He bowed low to her. "My lady, I am so very sorry."

"I'm not yer lady. I'm just Grace and ye were following

yer laird's orders."

"But..." He hesitated. Out of the corner of her eye she caught Bram shake his head ever so slightly. "Ah...nevertheless, I am sorry," Donal said.

She wasn't sure what that had been about, but she suddenly felt awkward and weary. She didn't want to sort out what it meant. Her eyes landed on Ian.

He smiled. "Ye're looking well, Grace."

It was perhaps the most outrageous thing anyone had ever said to her. She knew she looked anything but well. She looked down at her bandaged feet and a smile tugged at her lips. "Ye're a liar, Ian Sutherland."

It was evidently the first Bram had noticed her feet. "What in the name of all that's holy happened to yer feet?"

She shrugged. "I tried to escape the first morning. Roddy punished me by making me walk barefooted."

Bram looked livid. "I will kill him. I will find him now and kill him."

Ian shook his head, "Nay, don't do that, brother. It would be far too quick and easy. Conan said Fearchar Morrison will make him suffer for losing Grace. Let him and let's go home. Maybe someday ye'll have the opportunity to separate Fearchar's head from his shoulders." He gave Grace a look filled with determination. "If ye don't, I pray I do."

Bram drew several breaths, appearing to calm his ire. Then he nodded. "Aye, home." Grace gasped in surprise as he scooped her into his arms, striding to where Goliath stood.

"Ye don't need to carry me, I'm able to walk."

"Able to and allowed to are two different things."

"Ye can't keep me from walking, Bram Sutherland."

"Nay? Watch me," he said as he put her on Goliath's back before mounting behind her.

She turned to scowl at him but he grinned, before kissing her furrowed brow. Then he called to his men, "We're off, lads."

He had kissed her. In front of his brother and guardsmen. What was he thinking? "Bram, ye can't do that," she whispered.

"We've already been through this and I assure ye, I intend to make certain yer feet have time to heal."

"That's not what I meant," she hissed.

"Then what else do ye think I can't do?"

"Ye can't just kiss me...in front of yer men."

"Oh. Ye mean like this?" He tipped her chin up with one hand, lightly kissing her lips.

Dear God, the feel of his lips on hers was wonderful. What would it be like to…nay she could not allow herself to imagine a life as his wife. She frowned, looking away. His arm tightened around her, pulling her closer.

~ * ~

When they stopped that evening by the shore of a small loch, to Grace's frustration, Bram was true to his word. He carried her to a plaid he had spread on the ground. If he had ordered her to stay put, she would have had no trouble ignoring him, but he did something much worse. He knelt beside her and, taking her hands in his, he kissed her palms. Then he captured her gaze with his crystal blue eyes. "Please, Grace, let me take care of ye this evening. I know ye can walk. Please don't. Let me do this."

Asked so tenderly, she couldn't deny him. All she could do was nod.

After the men had settled the horses for the night, they went for a swim in the loch, leaving Grace and Bram alone. He brought her a costrel of fresh water, oatcakes, dried beef, and a pear. He sat beside her but didn't say anything for quite a while. She ate quietly, not knowing what to say or how to break the silence.

"Grace, I need for ye to listen to me."

She arched an eyebrow at him. "I'm not going anywhere."

He smiled and looked away for a moment. "I can't tell ye how much it makes my heart ache when I think of all that's happened to ye over the last few days and weeks. Considering much of it, God's bones, all of it was because of me…I'm sorry."

"Bram—"

"Nay, Grace, let me finish. I would not have seen ye hurt for anything and yet as we rode today, I thanked God that I was simply able to hold ye in my arms all day because of it. I want to get ye back to Kristen and Innes but I dread it. This morning ye said I had already lost ye. Please Grace, I don't think I can bear that. I want the right to hold ye in my arms every day. I want to build a life with ye and Kristen."

"Bram, how is that possible?"

"It's possible if ye marry me."

"I can't marry ye."

"Why?"

"Because the alliance with the Sinclairs is important. It is for the good of the clan." Laird Sutherland's words spilled out of her mouth, feeling empty even as she said them.

Bram ran his hands through his hair in frustration. "I don't care. I love ye more than words can say. I can't imagine a life with anyone else. Please say it is the same with ye."

Tears filled her eyes. "Ye know it is. But that doesn't change the fact that yer father won't let ye marry me. Ye were born a nobleman. Ye are to be the laird. Ye have obligations to yer family and clan."

"Those sound like my father's words."

"It doesn't make them less true."

"I refuse to believe that marrying ye will cause irreparable damage to the clan. We will find another way to build an alliance with the Sinclairs. I am destined to be chief. Does that mean I cannot also have the woman I love beside me?"

"Aye, it does. Ye can't marry a poor widow from the islands. Yer father won't allow it. The clan would despise and revile me. They already do."

"I told ye, Grace, I don't care what my father wants and the clan will see the truth. I will do anything else required of me but I will follow my heart this one time."

Grace shook her head. "I cannot risk yer father's wrath."

"I have heard all of the reasons ye believe we can't marry. Putting my father, the clan, and anything else that ye think stands in our way aside, do ye wish to marry me?"

"Bram, ye know I do. I love ye from the depths of my soul. Life without ye..." Her voice broke. "Life without ye...will be empty. I don't know how I will survive." A tear slipped down her cheek.

He gathered her in his arms. "Grace, don't cry. Please don't cry. We can do this. I swear we can. There is a Dominican Abbey that isn't far out of our way. We should reach it tomorrow evening. We'll be married before we reach Castle Sutherland. There will be nothing anyone can do. The clan will accept it. My father will accept it. They will have no choice."

"Nay, Bram. Absolutely not. We can't."

"Why do ye believe so firmly that we can't?"

Grace grasped for an excuse. Anything that would prevent her telling him his father threatened her life. "Because it's wrong."

"Nay Grace, it isn't. It's what's right for us."

"Bram, ye know why my parents fled to Lewis, why Da never let Innes know where he was or even that he was alive."

"Aye, yer mother's da was against the marriage."

"But they married anyway and they hurt so many people."

"Grace, I am sorry yer parents had to make that choice, but I finally understand it. If it meant we had to run away and never see my clan or family again in order to be together, I would do it. But love, that won't happen. My father will be angry, the clan elders will be disappointed, but they will get over it."

"Ye don't understand."

"I understand something is scaring ye. Please, tell me what it is."

Grace she saw no other choice, she had to tell him. "Bram, when yer da told me I had to turn ye away, he threatened me with a forced marriage. I didn't know to whom. I didn't know how that person might treat Kristen and I couldn't bear the idea of being married to anyone but ye. But that threat was mild compared to what he said he would do if we eloped. If we did that, he said he would find us, kill me before yer eyes, banish ye, and because Kristen is a Sutherland, she would be left in his care."

"Oh for the love of God, Grace, I am so sorry but I wish ye had told me. It was an empty threat. He only meant to scare ye out of marrying me and it worked. But I swear to ye, he would never do that."

"Ye don't know that for certain. It is exactly what my mother's father threatened."

"Grace, I am certain. He is as callous and rigid a man as ye'll ever meet. He might be angry enough to banish us. If he does, we will build a life somewhere else, as yer parents did, but he would never kill ye. I swear to ye, we won't be in fear for our lives as yer parents were. But frankly, I'm no longer convinced he'll even banish us. I suspect we will simply have to weather the storm for a bit after we tell him."

"I wish I was as sure as ye are." She rested her head on his chest. She wanted this. With her whole heart she wanted to spend the rest of her life with this man, by his side, in his arms. Grace wanted to believe him. She wanted to put her happiness—their happiness—first and trust that everything would be fine, but could she? She tried to explain her hesitation. "Bram, when I read Da's letter to Grandmother I was shocked. I thought their choice was selfish, that they had pushed aside duty, loyalty, clan honor, even loved ones for their own desires. It had caused grandmother so much pain. I can't help but think my mother's family and clan experienced the same, even if her father wanted only vengeance."

"Innes mentioned yer Da's letter but neither of ye have ever said much about yer mother's family. Was she from a Highland clan?"

She had promised her mother to keep the secret, but she couldn't. She had to tell Bram. "Aye, she was. Do ye remember how shocked yer da was that my father ran away? How he didn't believe my da would hide from any man?"

"Aye, I do."

"He wasn't just any man. He was a powerful laird."

"Yer gradda is the laird of a clan? Who he is."

"I can't tell ye that."

"For the love of all that is holy, Grace, why not? This could be the answer. We could negotiate a betrothal with him. If he is a powerful laird, allying with him could be a very good thing."

"I can't tell ye, because I don't know who he is."

"What do ye mean, ye don't know?"

"My mother never told me. She refused to. In fact, she said I was never to seek out her family."

"Why not? Things have changed, Grace. Yer parents are no longer in danger."

"My mother believed that my grandfather would see me as a commodity. I understand better now what she meant. Noble marriages can feel like cold business transactions."

"But don't ye see, my beautiful lass? Ours doesn't have to be. We love each other already. If we could find out who yer grandfather was..."

Grace finished his sentence. "He might refuse the betrothal. He might even do it out of spite for what my parents did. It is possible he would thank ye for returning his property and marry me off to someone of his choosing." Bram's expression darkened. "Ye know I'm right. Ye have no claim on me. He could demand my return. Then we would be in an even worse position. If ye failed to return me to him, it could start a feud. Instead of gaining an ally, ye would have an enemy. Please, Bram, ye have to understand, ye have lived yer whole life amongst the nobility. My only experience with men who have power is...fear. I want to believe ye, I do. I know ye love yer da, and I'm certain he loves ye. Perhaps that's why I firmly believe he would kill me if he thought it was in yer best interest."

"Grace—"

"Please stop, Bram. How can I make ye understand? Parents make different decisions. I'm not certain I could kill someone to protect myself, but I would bury a knife in yer da's chest without blinking before I let him hurt my daughter. Although he thinks I'm insolent, I have tried to treat him with respect but he has only shown me cruelty. I have no reason to believe he is any different from my grandda, or Fearchar Morrison, particularly where it concerns ye."

~ * ~

Just as he had in Mary's kitchen, Bram knew once again he needed to drop the argument for the moment. He was beginning to understand a parent's love. He too would bury a knife in his father's chest to save Kristen from harm. What's more, he would do the same to save Grace. However, he firmly believed he would never have to. His father was different from the men she feared.

Bram slept that night with Grace in his arms. Nothing had ever felt so perfect. He woke just before dawn but simply continued to lay with her, holding her a bit longer while all was still. Somehow he would find a way to convince her to marry him tonight. Then she would be his forever. He rose silently, tucking the plaid around her. Ian had taken the last watch. He walked to where his brother leaned against a tree.

"Did ye persuade her?" Ian asked.

Bram hadn't said anything to the men when they returned from the loch. "Not yet."

"Ye know it isn't Michael," said Ian.

"Aye, I know that. It's Da."

"Does that surprise ye? If it weren't for Kristen, I'm certain she'd never set foot on Sutherland land again."

"I guess it shouldn't surprise me. What shocked me was the threat Da used against her."

"Michael told me he intended to force Grace into a marriage to prevent ye from marrying her."

"Aye, but that's not the worst he did. He told her if we eloped, he would kill her before my eyes, banish me, and Kristen would be left in his care."

Ian laughed. "She didn't believe him?"

"Aye, she did." Bram told him about Grace's mother.

"By the saints, that explains a few things. It wasn't that

Tristan feared a single man. He would have been up against an army. One warrior, no matter how skilled, could not defend himself or his loved ones against that."

"Aye, and her mother believed the threat was real."

"But ye know Da wouldn't kill Grace. And ye also know, even if something did happen to her, he would never harm that bairn. Mother would kill him first. Besides, he likes the little imp."

"Grace doesn't believe that. Ye know Da wields intimidation better than any man alive and he has terrified her. On top of what she believes about her grandda and what that evil bastard Morrison did, she is willing to believe the worst. But I have to change her mind, and soon. I want to marry her at the abbey tonight, before we go home."

Ian sucked in a sharp breath. "Ye're sure this is the best course, Bram? "Da will be furious. He won't kill her, but neither will he accept it lightly and she's bound to get hurt in the process."

"I don't see another option. I won't risk losing her again and the only sure way to prevent that is to marry her before we return."

"Aye, I suppose ye're right."

Bram frowned. "He may banish us, Ian."

"After all he has done to keep ye from leaving, I don't think he will."

"I'm not certain either, but if he does…"

Ian shook his head. "We're not going to talk about this. He won't."

After a few moments of quiet, Bram said, "Ye needn't be a part of this. There is no reason to make Da angry with ye as well. As long as I can convince her to, Grace and I will go to the abbey alone. Ye'll be home by midday tomorrow. We won't be too long behind."

Ian looked at him incredulously. "Ye've lost yer mind. First, I will stand with ye when ye marry. I don't care if it does anger Da. And second, there is no way I'm facing him alone with the news ye are on yer way home by way of the abbey."

Bram grinned at him. "Well then, I guess we will face the storm together."

"Aye," said Ian. "Maybe he'll banish both of us and make Boyd his heir."

"Not until he has that betrothal to Kara MacNicol signed and sealed. He won't risk this again."

Ian laughed. "I guess Boyd is doomed to suffer any lessons Da learned from us."

Bram chuckled. "Poor lad." They sat in silence for a moment before Bram said, "Ian, since ye agree that it is best for me to marry Grace before we reach Sutherland Castle, I may need a bit of help convincing her that Da isn't the monster she thinks he is."

"I'll do what I can. As far as Highland lairds go, he certainly isn't the worst."

~ * ~

Bram had set an easy pace the previous day. He knew Grace was anxious to reach Kristen, however, he and his men had pushed their mounts relentlessly to reach Durness. They would have risked injuring the beasts by continuing to push them. Although they might have been able to safely travel a little faster today, Bram still needed time to convince her. Not to mention that he wanted to keep Grace in his arms as long as possible and she seemed content to be there.

The casual pace allowed for some banter between the men and Bram decided to raise the issue of his father's threat head-on. "Gentlemen, I learned something last night that distresses me, because it terrifies Grace."

She gave him a horrified look. "Bram!"

"What is it?" asked one of the men.

"Ye are fully aware that Grace broke my heart by turning me away a little over a week ago."

"Bram, stop."

Bram put a finger to her lips. "I think it is important for us both to hear this. Maybe I am blinded by the love I have for my Da."

She huffed in frustration but nodded.

"So, where was I? Ah, yes, ye knew she broke my heart but ye also knew my father was behind it and he had threatened her in some way. Last night I learned the worst of the threats. Apparently, Da was shrewd enough to know if I knew what he had done, I would have married my precious lass immediately and left Sutherland forever. So, he told Grace if we eloped, he would find us and kill her."

"He wouldn't do that," said one of the men. At Grace's affronted look, the man added, "what I mean is, I'm absolutely certain he would make that kind of threat. But he would never follow through. He wouldn't kill ye, Grace. He might beat the shite out of his wayward son."

"He's always been a great one for intimidation," said Donal. "Have ye ever seen him stare someone down, waiting until they looked away before making a move?"

Bram had seen him do this to Grace. He caught her eye and raised an eyebrow in question. She acknowledged the unspoken comment with a slight nod.

Ian snorted, "The only one who isn't susceptible to that is mother."

Bram noticed that Cam, a slightly older guardsman, had a furrowed brow. "Cam, is there something ye wish to say?"

"Ah…well…aye, I suppose there is. Ye told Grace it was important for both of ye to hear the answers."

"I did."

"Well, I don't disagree that yer da uses intimidation extremely well and I also don't believe he would make a public threat which he wouldn't be willing to carry out. He would never be taken seriously again if he did that. However, I will admit there is a difference between an openly stated threat and one that's unwitnessed. So the question is, if he wanted to intimidate Grace, would he have threatened her privately with something he would never consider doing?"

"What do ye think?" asked Grace.

Cam seemed to contemplate it for a few moments before answering. "I think he believed two of the things he values most, his family and his clan, were in jeopardy and he would have done anything to safeguard them—even threatening a lass he had no intention of killing…but I'm not absolutely sure. However, I am absolutely sure if ye enter Sutherland territory and ye aren't married to Bram, ye will never be married to him. Laird Sutherland will force ye to marry someone else on the spot."

"God's bones, Cam, I wouldn't allow that to happen," said Bram.

"Ye are one man and he's the laird. Ye won't be able to stop it."

"Why are ye so sure of this?" Asked Ian.

"I'm one of the men he discussed his plan with and to whom he offered Grace's hand."

Grace gasped. "One of the men? I thought it was just Michael."

Cam nodded. "The laird thought Michael was the best choice and if push came to shove, that is who he would have married ye to. However, if ye did as ye were asked and things went well, he considered giving ye a choice."

"Well, wasn't that thoughtful," said Grace with disdain.

Ian laughed uproariously and even Bram couldn't hold in a chuckle.

"Ye find this humorous?" demanded Grace.

Bram tried to school his features but failed miserably. "Ah, nay, pet. Well, I guess, aye, it's funny. But only because it helps make my point. No matter how…misguided…Da saw this as a kindness. I don't think it's in him to kill ye before my eyes."

Ian managed to regain some control and in his best imitation of his father said, "Why yes, Grace, it is yer duty to break my son's heart for the good of the clan, and even when ye do, I must insist that ye marry someone else immediately. But I'm not all bad, lass, I'll let ye pick between these three." Ian doubled over in spasms of laughter again.

In all seriousness, Cam said, "Ian, she would have had her choice of six men."

That only made Ian laugh so hard Bram feared Ian was going to fall off his horse.

Grinning, Donal chimed in, "Now, Grace, lass, ignore the laughing eejit, I know forcing ye to marry was repugnant to ye and I understand that. But in fairness, if ye fouled it up at all, yer punishment would have been to marry Michael MacBain, one of the finest men I know. And if ye did well, ye'd have had yer pick. I realize it doesn't change the fact that the laird was forcing ye to marry, but I do believe he was trying to make it as tolerable as possible. This is not a man who would follow through on a threat to kill ye."

"He handed me over to the Morrisons."

"That's a fair point," said Donal. "I'll also agree the evidence was weak when examined. There is no doubt he wanted rid of ye and believing the story they told was expedient. But the point is, he did believe it. Even wanting rid of ye, I don't think he would have handed ye over if he had known what lay in store."

Bram felt the tension in her body. He kissed her head. "Sweetling, my father has behaved abominably. He thought his reasons were good, but it doesn't change what he did to ye. For that I am sorry. I also think to give the devil his due, he tried to show ye some consideration regardless of how far he missed the mark. But I also think Cam makes an excellent point. He is the laird, all Sutherland men, even those riding with us now, have sworn him fealty. If we enter the village or the castle and are not married, I won't be able to stop him from forcing ye to marry someone else any more than Michael could help ye alone when the Morrisons arrived."

"So my choices haven't changed. Marry someone else or risk death by marrying ye."

"Nay lass, they have changed. I don't believe my father will kill ye for any reason. But if ye are not convinced, I won't expect ye to marry me. Either way, we'll go to the abbey tonight. If ye fear marrying me, I will leave ye there for yer safety until I can bring Kristen to ye. Then I'll take ye back to Durness if ye wish. However, my preference, my fondest desire, my most heartfelt prayer, is that ye marry me. I won't push ye for an answer now. Think about what ye've heard. We'll talk alone, before we get to the abbey."

Chapter 32

For the next few hours, Grace's head and heart went to war. She loved Bram with everything in her. Being his wife, linking her life to his for the rest of her days, was also her fondest desire and dare she think it, her most heartfelt prayer.

Her head still told her it was wrong. She was a bit less worried about Laird Sutherland killing her over it. When she recovered from her outrage over his plan to offer her a choice of six men, she could almost see the humor in it. She also had to acknowledge that while she didn't love Michael. If she had been forced to marry him, it would not have been a fate worse than death. Perhaps Laird Sutherland was trying to protect his clan and his son, while still showing a bit of compassion for her.

The weapon her head still wielded against her heart was the pain and anguish she knew her parents' decision had caused.

They had stopped to rest the horses several times throughout the day and Bram didn't raise the issue again. However, when they stopped in the early evening, he spread a plaid on the ground for them away from his men. She knew the time had come to make a decision.

Before he said anything, Bram cupped her head in his hand and gave her a soul-stirring, toe-curling kiss. She melted under his touch, her hands wandering over his muscular chest.

He broke the kiss far too soon. Smiling at her he said, "So it is agreed, ye love me as much as I love ye."

She rested her cheek against his chest. "That was never at issue."

"Then please marry me, Grace."

Grace started to protest but he put a finger to her lips. "Before ye tell me one more time all the reasons why we can't marry, I have one question and I want ye to answer with absolute honesty. Will ye?"

She nodded. "Aye, I will."

"Good. Then I want ye to tell me, if yer parents were both

here and ye could ask them if they would make the same choice to marry, even knowing everything they do now, what would they say?"

The question stunned Grace. She had wrestled all afternoon with the terrible consequences of their choice, from the outside looking in. Would they have done it all over again? She remembered her father's words from his letter. I love her more than life itself I cannot imagine living without her. Then she remembered the last conversation with her mother. I'm sorry we caused so much pain, but God help me I would do it again. Bram had asked for absolute honesty and the answer was clear.

"They loved each other deeply. I believe that in spite of everything, they would have made the same choice to follow their hearts."

"Then do ye suppose they would advise ye to do the same?"

Grace remembered her mother's last words to her, I love ye so much. Be happy, Grace. She sighed. "Aye, they would."

"Then it is decided. Ye'll become my wife when we reach the abbey and if there are consequences, we will face them...together."

She nodded. "It is decided."

When they rejoined his men, Bram announced, "To my great relief and complete joy, Grace has agreed to become my wife."

After the men had offered their congratulations and good wishes, Bram continued, "We all know how angry my father is likely to be over this. Ye are all sworn to him, not me. If ye would rather not be a party to this, I fully understand. We can part ways now and those who wish to can travel straight to Castle Sutherland."

Ian said, "I have already told ye, I will stand with ye."

Donal grinned. "Bram, while the laird may have tried to prevent it, he has never issued an order forbidding us to see ye wed. However, it is our sworn duty to protect ye and Ian. Leaving ye to the perils that might await between here and the abbey would be a dereliction of duty." The other men laughed at the idea that any serious perils awaited them on the short ride to the abbey but they all agreed with Donal.

They arrived at the abbey a few hours later, just after sunset. The men dismounted and stood back ten paces or so with the horses while Bram approached with Grace and rang the bell at the gate.

A tall man of about two score wearing the robes of the order, with hair and beard that were whiter than brown, answered the bell. Grace was more than a little surprised by the friar's appearance. The only religious men she had ever encountered were bookish and not particularly well built. This friar was every bit as tall and broad shouldered as Bram. "Good evening, gentlemen, my lady. I'm Father Colm. What brings ye to our abbey this evening?"

"My lady and I wish to be married tonight."

He looked at Grace for a moment. His bright blue eyes caught her gaze, giving her a discerning look. "Ye will need the abbot's permission for that. We've just finished vespers. I will find him for ye. Ye can all enter and wait here in the courtyard. The well is here, and there is a trough there in front of our stable. Ye can water yer beasts while ye wait."

Father Colm left, returning before long with an elderly, short, slightly portly friar who had ruddy cheeks and a bulbous nose. He appeared a bit doddering. "Good evening and welcome to our abbey. I'm Brother Christy, the abbot here. Father Colm tells me ye wish to be married."

"Aye, Brother Christy, we do," answered Bram.

"Well, that is nice, very nice. But Father says, ye wish to be married tonight and I'm afraid that isn't possible."

"Please, Brother, there must be a way," said Bram.

Grace's heart fell. "Why do ye do this to me, God?" she muttered.

Father Colm arched an eyebrow, but Brother Christy didn't seem to have heard her and went right on talking. "Nay it isn't possible. We must post the banns for three weeks first."

"Brother, I know the banns are supposed to be posted in advance, but we must be married tonight."

"I'm sorry, ye see, there are rules to be followed. It simply isn't possible."

"Please, Brother, I understand that but the banns are to ensure that there are no impediments to marriage. I assure ye, there are none."

"Young man, everyone who wishes to be married assures me they have no impediments."

"My men, my brother here can vouch for us. It is imperative that we be married this evening."

Brother Christy's manner shifted from convivial to shrewd in a matter of moments. "It is imperative is it? Well, young man, I'd like for ye to come with me and explain more about why it is imperative that ye marry this evening."

"Certainly, Brother," Bram said, taking Grace's hand.

"Not her. Ye. Alone. Father Colm will speak to yer lady."

Bram brushed her cheek with a kiss. Her dismay must have been written on her face because he whispered, "Don't worry so. It will be fine."

Bram followed the abbot. Father Colm said, "Gentleman, the chapel is open if any of ye wish to pray." He grinned at their surprised looks. "I just thought I'd offer, but since none of ye seem so inclined, the lass and I will chat in there."

He took her elbow, leading her to the chapel. Grace knew he had heard her comment about God and figured she was in for a lecture. When they entered the chapel, Father Colm lit several candles before saying, "What's yer name lass?"

"Grace. Grace Breive."

"Ye wear a kertch. Are ye a widow?"

"Aye, Father. My husband was a fisherman and he died in a storm."

"I'm very sorry for yer loss, Grace. God rest his soul." Father Colm made the sign of the cross, offering a silent prayer before addressing her again. "Now, please sit down, and don't look so distressed. When couples come to the abbey requesting to be married immediately, Brother Christy always refuses three times. If they persist beyond his refusals, he speaks to each of them alone before he agrees. He wants to make certain all is well. It is getting late, so tonight he asked if I would speak with ye."

"Oh," said Grace. Somehow this didn't exactly quiet her nerves.

"So, is all well? Do ye wish to marry this man?"

Unable to lie, Grace answered, "Father, those are two separate questions. I wish to marry Bram with my whole heart. But all is not well."

"Tell me, why."

Grace launched into the story. She had just intended to give him the important details, but she found herself telling it all, from the night she lost her husband and father to ringing the bell at the gate. When she had finished, she felt as if a great weight had been lifted off her shoulders.

"Ye have been through quite a lot, Grace, and now I understand yer comment to our Lord earlier. I feel we need to discuss a few things, but first I want to assure ye, if the abbot is happy enough with Bram's answers, I will marry the two of ye."

She sighed with relief. "Thank ye, Father."

"I'd like to talk about yer belief that God has abandoned ye. I could give ye a lot of pious rhetoric about how we can't understand the ways of God and that He has reasons for everything including our suffering, but I don't believe that."

His words shocked Grace and it must have shown on her face.

He chuckled. "Grace, if yer wee daughter reached to touch a hot pot, what would ye do?"

"I'd tell her no, or pull her hand back."

"What if ye were too far away or she couldn't hear ye, and she burned her fingers. Then what would ye do?"

"I would put cool water on them, try to give her comfort, and just in case she hadn't learned her lesson, I'd tell her not to do that again."

"The fact is, we live in a world in which bad things happen, sometimes caused by the evil one himself, and sometimes by people who chose evil. Just like ye would wish to keep Kristen from burning her fingers, God doesn't want to see us hurt. Sometimes it happens anyway. Then He is there to comfort us, and to help us learn."

Grace harrumphed. "What I learned is God doesn't listen to me."

"Child, He listens better than ye think He does. He didn't send ye all these trials, but He did give ye the strength to get through them and the people ye needed to help ye."

"But Father, He couldn't even grant the simplest request."

Father Colm laughed. "If Kristen asked for something that was bad for her, would ye give it to her?"

"Nay, but how could protecting me from the pain that inevitably comes with love be bad for me?"

"Think of all the people ye love, the ones ye've lost as well as those ye still have. Would ye be better off if ye had never loved any of them? If ye could go back and change things, would ye choose to prevent the pain by never knowing their love?"

It was hard to imagine not loving her parents but Grace thought of Callum—her quiet, gentle, soft-spoken husband. Would it have been better never to have loved him? Tears welled in her eyes. Even knowing their time together would be short, she certainly would have chosen to love him and marry him again. She shook her head. "Nay."

"So, I don't think it was a case of God not answering yer prayer—it's just that sometimes, the answer was 'Nay.' And the truth is, we can't pretend to know God's ways, we just have to believe that He will give us what we need. In fact, I suspect ye have been completely frustrating Him. He sent ye someone He believes ye need and ye've been dragging yer feet. So shall we get that young man out of his misery?"

She chuckled and wiped the errant tear from her cheek. "Aye, Father."

Chapter 33

Bram had been thoroughly raked over the coals by the rather perceptive abbot. He found himself telling Brother Christy the whole sordid tale. When they were finished, Brother Christy once again became the genial friar he had appeared to be at first.

"Brother, do ye do that to everyone?"

"Nay, lad, not everyone. Just everyone who arrives at my gate telling me it's imperative that they be married immediately. I take a little more care with it when the one ringing the bell is traveling with seven warriors and the lass in question looks like she has just returned from a stroll through hell."

"Ah…well, I guess I understand that."

As long as it had taken Bram to gain the abbot's approval, he feared Grace would be waiting in the courtyard, pale and worried. On the contrary, somewhat to the delight of his brother, Bram had been the one who paced nervously until the priest appeared with her at the door of the chapel.

So, after weeks of longing and several days of utter despair, Bram was finally able to make Grace his wife. As they exchanged their vows, he sensed a calm in her that had been missing. She spoke her vows in a strong, clear voice that suggested she had exorcised any doubt that remained about the wisdom of marrying him.

When Father Colm said, I now pronounce ye husband and wife—ye may kiss yer bride, Bram felt elation like no other. He lifted Grace off her feet, kissing her soundly. She threw her arms around his neck and returned the kiss. Bram finally released her when Father Colm cleared his throat.

The abbot, who stood to one side, said, "Friends, the hour grows late and the time for compline approaches. Sir Bram, ye may stable yer horses in our stable. The infirmary is empty at the moment so yer men are welcome to sleep there if they wish. We also have a small cottage on the grounds for guests. Ye and yer wife are welcome to pass the night there. Will I show ye to it now?"

"Go on," said Ian. "I will tend Goliath."

"Thank ye, Ian. Aye, Brother, my wife and I would very much appreciated yer guest accommodations. Thank ye."

In a matter of minutes, they were alone in front of the tiny cottage. Bram scooped her in his arms.

"I can walk, Bram."

"It's tradition, Grace."

She rolled her eyes but chuckled. It had been too long since he had heard that. He stepped into the little cottage and kicked the door closed behind him. Several candles were lit. A small bed stood in one corner of the room, which looked as if it had just been freshly made. A small vase of fresh lavender stood on the little table in the middle of the room, along with a cloth covered platter, two goblets, and a corked jug.

"I think Brother Christy has a bit of a romantic streak. If I'm not much mistaken, he's arranged for us to have a jug of mead."

"That was thoughtful…Bram, ye can put me down now."

"Can I?"

She grinned. "Aye."

"Anywhere?" he asked.

She laughed again. "Aye, anywhere."

"Ah, well then, if I get to choose…" He lowered her to the bed and captured her mouth in a kiss. She kissed him back, running her hands over his chest. Her fingers found the brooch holding on his plaid and worked blindly to undo it. When she had accomplished the task, he broke the kiss and tossed the garment to one side.

She smiled up at him from the bed.

"Allow me to return the favor, my lady." He removed the pin holding her plaid then he tugged on the back of her kertch, drawing it from her head and freeing her auburn curls. He ran his fingers through the silk. "Ye have beautiful hair, Grace. I've longed to see it free."

"I think we have several things we need to set free." She smiled coyly and reached for his belt. "Ye won't be needing this, will ye?" she asked even as she undid the buckle and tossed it to one side.

"Oh, nay, lass, nay I won't. No more than ye will be needing this." He unbuckled her belt and threw it over his shoulder.

She smiled broadly and untied the ribbons of her léine. Rising onto her knees she pulled the garment seductively over her head, letting it drop to the floor beside the bed. She was left wearing nothing but her linen shift.

Bram leaned forward, planting kisses over her face and down her neck as he pulled at her shift, tugging it up, over her hips. He stopped kissing her for a moment. "Raise yer arms for me, lass." She did and he pulled the shift up and off. The sight of her kneeling on the bed, naked but for the glorious hair spilling around her shoulders, took his breath away. "I have never seen anything more beautiful than ye are at this moment, Grace."

She blushed under his perusal, and as if a wave of shyness passed through her, her hands fluttered up, covering her breasts. "Nay, my bonny lass, hands away." Ye are mine now. Let me savor yer beauty for a moment." She dropped her hands to her thighs and looked into his eyes. The longing he saw there nearly undid him.

Bram stripped off his remaining clothes and climbed on the bed beside her. Capturing her lips again, he kissed her passionately. When he released her lips, she panted, breathless. He kissed her neck, then nuzzled behind her ear, causing her to giggle. He gave a low, throaty chuckle and sliding her hair out of the way, planted kisses around to the back of her neck and then down her back. She shivered and gave a throaty moan. When he reached the base of her spine, he planted kisses around and over the curve of her hip. "Lay back, sweetling."

Grace shifted off of her knees and rested back onto the bed. He kissed his way across her slightly rounded belly and up to her breasts.

Again her hands came up to cover them nervously. "They aren't...they aren't..."

He took her hands in his and gently pulled them away. "They aren't what, Grace? To me they are perfect. They tell me ye are a mother, and there is nothing more beautiful. Don't hide them from me."

His hands roamed freely over her body before cupping her breasts and brushing his thumbs gently over the peaks. She too explored his body with her hands, her feather light touch inflaming him. When she trailed her hands down to his hips and over his buttocks, he groaned.

"Ah, lass, I can't bear it."

He touched her between her legs, stroking her sensitive nub, eliciting a moan.

She raised her hips toward him. "I can bear it no better than ye can."

"Nay, Grace, not yet." He continued to stroke her as she writhed under him. He teased and stroked, bringing her ever higher.

"Bram, please, I need—I need—oh, Bram...I need ye."

"My beautiful lass, I need ye more." He knelt between her legs and moved his hands under her, lifting her and joining with her in one firm stroke. She rose to meet him, seemingly lost in the primal act, which irrevocably connected their souls. Soon she was overcome with the shuddering waves of her climax. The muscles at her core contracted repeatedly around him and he too found his release, filling her with his seed. She was his forever.

He held his weight off her as he caught his breath. Then he gently withdrew from her and lay beside her on the bed, still panting. "Ye delight me, Grace."

"I'd say ye have the same effect on me." She snuggled against him, resting her head on his chest.

"I'm glad to hear it," he said, stroking her head. "We'll make it a point to delight each other regularly."

She yawned. "I'll hold ye to that."

~ * ~

Grace had been tense and tired for so long she could barely remember feeling anything else. But somehow, telling Father Colm the whole story had been cathartic and had left her feeling at peace. Then the act of making love with her husband, of coming apart in his arms, left her feeling more relaxed and complete than she had thought possible. She was vaguely aware of him stroking her head as she fell asleep on his chest.

Sometime, just before daylight, she woke. She had been sleeping so soundly it took her a moment to remember where she was. The hard body under hers was a quick reminder. She smiled and kissed his chest. She was truly married to this man. Come what may, he was hers forever. She began sprinkling kisses across his chest, reminded of the way he had trailed kisses down her back. She shivered again just thinking about the incredible sensation.

As she kissed and stroked his chiseled muscles, he woke, emitting a low rumbling growl. "What wicked creature wakes me with such enticement?"

"'Tis just yer wife, but ye needn't wake if ye don't wish to." Even as she said it, she knelt up, putting her knees on either side of his hips. "Still, ye might regret sleeping through this," she said with a cheeky grin.

He chuckled richly. "Ah, well, then lass, do yer worst."

She joined with him again. The pace this time was slower and more sensual, but the results were every bit as shattering. As she reached her climax, the world shimmered around her, and she was lost in pure sensation. She was barely aware of Bram's primal groan and the heat that filled her as she floated back to consciousness. Spent, she collapsed on his chest, barely able to breathe.

Once again, she snuggled against him and drifted into a dreamless sleep.

Chapter 34

Bram woke with Grace draped across him and sleeping soundly. Although he would have liked to stay sequestered with her longer, he knew as attractive as it would be to delay seeing his father, Grace was anxious to be reunited with Innes and Kristen. He rubbed her back until she too stirred.

"Good morning, husband," she murmured.

That greeting filled him with joy. He was indeed her husband. "Good morning, wife. Ye are looking well."

"Ye're as big a liar as yer brother."

"Nay, precious. Naked, looking drowsy and replete in my arms, ye couldn't be more beautiful."

"Well look quickly then, because I'm hungry."

He laughed. "So am I. Shall we see what Brother Christy left for us?"

"Mmmm. But stay where ye are."

She pushed herself off of him, climbed out of the bed, and brought the platter to him in bed. Together they ate their way through the bread, cheese, and fruit the old friar had prepared for them.

Bram once again contemplated luring her back to bed and staying a bit longer but she slid out of the bed and began gathering their clothes. "Will we be going soon? While I dread facing yer father, I have been away from Kristen far too long."

"Aye, my love, we'll go as soon as ye're ready."

Clearly anxious to leave, she was washed and dressed in no time. Aye, he needed to get her home. They bid farewell to Brother Christy and Father Colm and were well on their way before terce.

Sutherland Castle was only a few hours away. As they drew near, he felt her tension build. He too felt a rising trepidation and he suspected most of the men did as well.

Finally, Ian asked the question that Bram suspected everyone had been contemplating. "Bram, how are ye going to do this?"

"I would like to simply enter the hall with Grace, announce that we are married, and face the consequences."

Ian shook his head. "Ye will be putting him on the spot if ye do that. He may say or do things publically that he can never relent on. We can leave Grace at Innes' cottage."

"I'm not sure that's a good idea," said Bram. He wasn't completely comfortable being separated from her until things were settled.

"I want to see Kristen and Grandmother first anyway," said Grace.

Ian nodded. "And it will give us a chance to find Da and tell him privately."

Bram scowled. "I fear it is as if I am hiding her if I do that."

"Ye're not hiding her," said Ian. "Ye are protecting her feelings and preventing Da from doing something that he may regret forever."

In the end, Bram decided that Ian's plan was best. It was well before midday when they approached the village. "There she is," said Grace, pointing to where Kristen played under Innes' watchful eye outside the little cottage. Bram helped her off the horse and she ran to Kristen, sweeping the little girl into her arms.

Innes, tears streaming down her cheeks, followed Kristen, embracing them both.

"Mama, Mama, Mama, Mama," Kristen said over and over, holding onto Grace with all the strength a three year old lass could muster.

"Oh my precious lass, I missed ye so."

"Don't weave me again," said Kristen.

"Sweetling, I didn't want to leave ye this time."

Innes stepped back. "Grace, I'm so sorry."

"Grandmother, it wasn't yer fault."

"But I doubted ye. I should never have done that. I saw the hurt in yer eyes."

Grace touched her grandmother's cheek. "Ye have lived here yer whole life. Ye've known and trusted the laird for his whole life. Ye've only known me for a few weeks. I understand that."

Innes seemed to have just noticed Bram and the other men who waited nearby. She wiped the tears from her face with her apron. "Sir Bram, Sir Ian, thank ye for bringing Grace home to me."

"I promised I would." Bram walked up beside Grace, putting one arm around her back and resting the other on Kristen's shoulder.

"Don't ye weave eiver, Sir Bwam.

"I won't, my sweet wee lassie."

Grace said, "Bram and I were married yesterday."

Innes looked shocked. "But...oh my..." Innes covered her mouth with one hand.

"What's mawwied?"

"It's what a man and a woman do when they want to live together and have a family. Yer da and I were married."

"Wiww he wiv wif us?"

"Aye, he will live with us, but maybe not here."

Bram said, "Kristen, I am going to go talk to the laird and then we'll know where we will live."

Kristen nodded, but Innes still looked very distressed. "Grandmother, what is it?"

"Sir Bram, the Sinclairs arrived yesterday."

Ian swore, "Mother of God, could this timing be worse?"

Bram shook his head. "I completely forgot. We will have to figure out a way to talk with Da alone immediately. Grace, we need to leave ye here until we sort this out. I'll be back as soon as I can. Be prepared to leave if necessary."

She nodded.

He kissed her before remounting Goliath and riding with his men to the castle. Bram and Ian handed their horses over to a stable hands and headed for the hall. Bram paused before entering the keep. "This is going to be much worse than I imagined, isn't it?"

"With the Sinclairs here, I fear it is," agreed Ian.

"If anything happens, please get Grace and Kristen off of Sutherland land as fast as ye can."

"Aye. I will."

~ * ~

It was good to be reunited with Kristen again and for her part Kristen was happy as a lark. Innes, however, was beside herself with worry. Grace tried to distract her by telling her a mild version of what had happened over the last week. She packed Kristen's things as she talked. When she had finished, Innes asked,

"What's going to happen? The laird won't like this."

"Nay, I'm sure he won't. Bram expects that he will banish us. That's why I am gathering Kristen's things. Grandmother, if he does, I would like ye to go with us. But I understand if ye can't."

"Grace, I have always been devoted to Laird Sutherland but ye are my granddaughter. I will not stay here and serve a laird who sees fit to banish ye. Aye, I'll come with ye."

Innes too packed her things to be ready to leave. Once everything was ready to go, they waited.

And waited.

It was taking much longer than Grace had expected for Bram to return.

Innes occupied herself making bannocks. "If we have to leave, we will have them to take with us."

Kristen begged to go out and play. Grace wasn't anxious to run into any of the villagers until she knew what was happening.

"But I wanna pway," whined Kristen.

"I know ye do. Let's have our midday meal and maybe we can go later."

"We could cwimb the hiww and eat on the gwass."

"Nay, we need to wait here for Bram to come back."

"But mama, I wanna cwimb the hiww. We haven't done that for a wong time."

"Kristen, ye know we shouldn't go alone."

"Because it wowwies Sir Bwam."

"Aye, because he worries." Frankly, although she could wear her shoes again, she wasn't quite sure she was up to climbing the headlands. "I suppose we could sit under the big tree and have our meal. Would ye like that?" It was just beyond the cottage and far enough away from other cottages to afford a bit of privacy.

Kristen nodded.

"Grandmother, will ye join us?"

"Nay, lass. I'll finish making the bannocks. The two of ye enjoy yerself."

So with a fresh hot bannock, some cold chicken, and a jug of water, Grace and Kristen walked the short distance beyond the village to the big tree. They spread a plaid on the ground and ate their meal. When they were done, Grace leaned her back against the trunk. Kristen snuggled up next to her, putting her head in Grace's lap. Grace stroked Kristen's reddish-blond curls. She had missed this.

"Wiww ye sing to me, Mama?"

"Aye, precious, I'll sing." She closed her eyes and sang to her baby. It fed her soul like nothing else. Even after Kristen had drifted off, Grace kept singing. She only stopped when she heard movement in the grass nearby. Her eyes flew open.

There was an older man standing perhaps ten paces away from her, staring. "Hello." He said. "And who might ye be?"

Two more men stood a distance away on the road. Grace glanced back towards the village. If she called for help, would anyone come? She wasn't capable of running away with Kristen and she hadn't had a knife strapped to her leg since the Morrisons took her.

The fear must have shown on her face because the man said, "I'm sorry. I didn't mean to startle ye. Ye have nothing to fear, I won't hurt ye. I heard ye singing. Ye have a lovely voice."

"Thank ye," she said cautiously.

What's yer name lass? Are ye a Sutherland?"

Grace's first instinct was to say no, but she was, in fact, Grace Sutherland now. "Aye. I am. My name is Grace."

Mild surprise registered briefly on his face. "Very nice to meet ye, Grace. My name is Ranulf."

"Are ye a Sutherland?"

"Nay, lass, I'm not. I'm visiting. Do ye mind if I sit with ye for a spell?"

"Ye're visiting? Are ye a Sinclair?"

"Aye, I am."

Really, God? Didn't we just sort this out? "I should be going. My grandmother will be expecting us back."

"Please, don't go yet. Ye didn't look like someone preparing to rush home a moment ago and if ye leave now, ye'll wake the wee lass. I would enjoy the pleasure of yer company for a few minutes. Grant an old man this boon."

Grace didn't wish to be rude, and he seemed pleasant enough. "Aye. Well then, please sit."

He sat on the ground a few feet away. "Thank ye. Tell me about yerself, Grace."

"There's nothing to tell."

"Oh, I expect there is. Ye said ye were a Sutherland and ye mentioned yer grandmother. Do ye live here in the village with her?"

"Aye, I do. In that cottage." She motioned behind her.

"Have ye always lived here? Do yer parents live here too?"

"Nay, I grew up on the Isle of Lewis. I lost both my parents and my husband in the last year. I came here to my grandmother after that."

"I am sorry to hear of yer loss, Grace." A look of profound sadness crossed his face. "Losing someone ye love is never easy."

Grace had the distinct impression he too had recently lost someone. "Ye seem sad. Have ye lost someone dear to ye recently?"

"Aye, I have," he answered but he didn't elaborate further.

"I'm sorry for yer loss as well." They sat in silence for a few moments.

"So one of yer parents was a Sutherland?"

"Aye, my father was."

"And yer mother? Was she from Lewis? A MacCauley or a Morrison?"

"Nay, she wasn't."

"If she wasn't from the island, what took yer parents there?"

Grace looked away for a moment. "I suppose love did."

"Love?"

"Aye. My parents were very much in love." She smiled as images of her parents together flashed through her mind. Over the last few weeks, she had dwelt largely on the consequences of their decisions. She had almost forgotten their abiding love. "Very much in love indeed. However, my mother's father was opposed to the marriage. The only way they could be together was to leave. So they went to Lewis. My father worked as a fisherman. My husband was a fisherman too. Their boat went down in a storm last October."

"And yer mother?"

"She had been ill before Da died, but after we lost him, she never recovered. I'm not sure she wanted to go on without him. She died in February."

"So when they died, ye decided to come live with ye father's kin. Why not yer mother's?"

Grace was becoming a little uncomfortable and she didn't want to tell him the truth. "I just didn't."

"That's not a reason. Tell me why ye didn't seek out yer mother's kin?"

His tone was stern, but not unkind. She felt compelled to answer. "I...I...well the truth is...I don't know who they are."

His brow furrowed. "How is that possible?"

Grace sighed. "I grew up thinking neither of them had any family left. I only learned about my father's clan as my mother was dying. She refused to tell me anything about her own."

"Why?"

"I told ye. She was afraid of her father. Even after all these years she worried about what might happen to us or even that he might seek vengeance on the Sutherlands if he found out who my da was." Grace stroked Kristen's head.

"Surely she didn't believe her family would harm ye?"

"I don't know. I guess she didn't want to take the chance. She made me promise I would never try to find them."

He shook his head sadly. "'Tis awful when children and parents are so at odds."

"Aye, it is. When I first learned what my parents had done, I didn't completely understand it. Their choice has caused others pain. My grandmother's heart ached over the loss of her son. Surely my mother's family felt the same."

"Ye say that as if ye understand it now."

Grace nodded, but she couldn't meet his eyes.

"What changed?"

"I fell in love with a man who I had no right to love." Grace gave the man an imploring look. For some reason, she felt the need to make him understand. "I tried not to—I swear I did. But I couldn't. I love him so very much, the thought of losing him causes me more pain even than the deaths of my parents and my husband." She turned her head away for a moment.

When she looked at him again, he smiled gently. "I can see how much he means to ye. Does he feel the same way?"

She nodded. "Aye."

"And who is this lucky man who has won the heart of such a lovely young woman?"

She bit her lip and looked away. "Ye said ye were a Sinclair. I've said too much. Please excuse me." She struggled to lift Kristen from her lap."

"Stay put. Ye needn't wake the bairn. I know who ye are and who ye fell in love with."

"Ye do?"

"Aye, it's causing a bit of a stir at the moment. I

understand ye married Bram Sutherland last night.

She nodded and looked at him again, expecting to see censure.

His smile was warm. "Are ye happy?"

Her mother's voice came to her, Grace, be happy. She smiled. "Aye, I'm happy. I suspect we're in quite a bit of trouble with Laird Sutherland, but I'm very happy to be Bram's wife."

"I dare say. Perhaps if his father knew ye were a noblewoman—"

"But I'm not."

"Aye, Grace, ye are. Ye didn't say so, but the only man who could have had the power over yer parents which ye describe would be the laird of a clan, or a close member of his family. Am I right?"

She nodded. "He was the laird."

"Then we should try to find out who they are."

"But I promised my mother…"

"I understand. Still, yer mother extracted that promise from ye because she had no other way to protect ye. Now ye are married to Laird Sutherland's heir. Ye can't be forced to marry another. Frankly, I don't think any reasonable man would visit vengeance on his own granddaughter but even if he were still alive, ye are well protected and yer parents are beyond his reach now."

She frowned. "I hate to break my promise, but ever since I learned the truth and saw the pain it caused my grandmother, I have worried about my mother's family. I would like for them to know. I can't imagine losing my daughter like that. But I really know nothing about them."

"Do ye have anything belonging to yer mother?"

"Aye, I have a small box with a few personal items."

"Have ye shown them to anyone? To Bram or Laird Sutherland?"

"Nay."

"Perhaps something on them will identify her clan. If I could see them, I might be able to tell ye who they are."

Grace hesitated. "I don't know…"

"It is up to ye, lass. But if ye want to know who yer mother's people are, if ye want them to know what happened to her, her belongings could hold answers."

He was right, but he was a stranger. "Mayhap. But I

should probably show them to Bram first."

"Aye, that may be best. I should be getting back anyway."
He stood. "I'll carry the lass to yer cottage and perhaps yer
grandmother will mind her while we go to the keep."

"Ye needn't. I'm not going to the keep."

"Aye, Grace, ye are."

"Nay—but—I can't."

Despite her protests, he gently lifted Kristen from her lap,
adjusting the child so she laid against his chest. "There is
something altogether wonderful about holding a sleeping child and
I haven't done it since my own were wee ones."

She stood and brushed the bits of grass from her skirt. "I
appreciate ye carrying her to our cottage, sir, but I can't go to the
keep."

"Aye, ye can, and ye will. And what's more, ye'll bring
yer mother's belongings. Eanraig will need to see them."

Chapter 35

Grace stopped and stared at the man who had introduced himself as simply, "Ranulf." Realization flooded her. "Ye called Laird Sutherland by his given name."

"That I did."

She swallowed hard. "Ye introduced yerself as just Ranulf. I thought ye were a Sinclair guardsmen. Oh sweet mother of God, ye're Laird Sinclair. What have I done?"

"Aye, I am Ranulf Sinclair, Laird Sinclair, but calm yerself, Grace, ye've done nothing wrong."

"Please Laird, I am so sorry. Please forgive me. I'll take Kristen—"

"That's enough, lass. Let's get Kristen tucked up for the rest of her nap."

She nodded and led him into the cottage. The fresh bannocks sat cooling on the table. Her grandmother dozed in her chair by the hearth. "Grandmother, we have a visitor," Grace said, holding the door for Laird Sinclair. Her grandmother looked up, surprise registering on her face when she saw the stranger carrying Kristen. Grace opened the door to the little bedroom for him. "There is a pallet for her in here." She watched as Laird Sinclair gently laid Kristen on the pallet, covered her with a blanket, and to Grace's utter surprise, kissed her forehead before coming back into the main room.

Overwhelmed, Grace said, "Grandmother, I would like ye to meet Laird Ranulf Sinclair. Laird Sinclair, my grandmother, Innes Murray."

Her grandmother's eyes grew wide with alarm, but she stood, curtsied and said, "Welcome, Laird."

"Very nice to meet ye, Innes. Please sit down. I have spent the last little while getting to know Grace and she has completely charmed me."

Innes glanced cautiously at Grace before asking, "Is there anything I can get ye, Laird?"

"Nay, thank ye Innes. Would ye object to minding Kristen for a bit while Grace and I go up to the keep?"

Innes shot worried glances at Grace. "The keep, Laird?"

"Aye, Innes, the keep. Do ye mind?"

"Nay, Laird, of course not. Whatever ye wish," Innes said weakly.

"Grace, get yer mother's box and we'll go."

"Please, Laird. Don't ask me to do this."

"I already have asked ye to and I am not accustomed to my requests being ignored. I promise ye everything will be fine. Now, yer mother's box please."

He had gone from kindly stranger to commanding laird in a matter of moments. He was polite, but his request brooked no refusal. She retrieved the box and followed him outside. The men who she now realized were his guardsmen waited for them.

"That's the box? May I see it?"

Reluctantly, she handed it to him. He looked at it and ran a hand over the carved lid. "It's very pretty. We'll look at what's inside it when we get to the keep." He gave the box back to her. "Grace, lass, ye look terrified."

"I don't want to go to the keep. Bram said I should stay here and...I—I'm afraid of Laird Sutherland."

"Why are ye so afraid of him?"

"He doesn't like me. He's bound to be livid with me...and Bram."

"Oh he is, but he'll get over it."

"But..."

"But what, lass?"

"Laird Sutherland threatened to kill me if I married Bram."

"Did he?"

"He wanted Bram to marry Annice for the good of the clan but—"

"—but he didn't want to be the villain. He didn't want his son to hate him. He gave ye that privilege." Laird Sinclair looked furious.

"I'm so sorry, Laird."

"There is nothing to be sorry for, Grace."

"Ye're not angry?"

"Oh, I'm very angry, but not with ye or Bram. I am furious with Eanraig."

"But he tried to stop us."

"That's what annoys me. He knew Bram loved another woman and let us travel here anyway. I guess he hoped to fool us. My wife is affronted, even my mother is upset by this whole mess. Frankly, I had to leave the keep before I did something I would regret. That's why I was out walking."

"What about Annice?"

"What do ye mean?"

"Is Annice terribly upset?"

He smiled at her. "Annice will be fine. She is rather in love with the idea of being in love. She is more concerned about Bram and his new bride"—he looked pointedly at Grace—"than she is herself. Well, my sweet lass, a few problems await us at the keep but they should be easy enough to solve now." He took her by the elbow. "Ye have nothing to fear."

As they passed villagers—people who she had considered friends until Laird Sutherland had turned them against her—most of them stared at her with derision. However, she saw pity on a few faces. That was something at least. Perhaps a few minds and hearts were changing.

Laird Sinclair's scowl grew darker as they went. "Why do they show ye such contempt?"

"Laird Sutherland tried to turn Bram against me and, well, it worked on nearly everyone else."

"This will stop. Eanraig will see to it."

Grace wasn't convinced but she was already in enough trouble so she held her tongue.

When they reached the doors to the great hall, he stopped and faced her. "Things might get...tense. I know ye are Bram's wife, but Bram is likely to be at the heart of any...uh...tension. For the next few minutes at least, if I ask ye to do something, will ye do it? Without question?"

"I—I—I suppose."

"Why doesn't that instill me with much confidence?"

She shrugged and gave him a half-smile. "Because I'm not particularly good at following orders but I have trouble lying."

He chuckled, opening the door for her. "Just remember, no matter what is said, I'm on yer side."

When they entered the hall, things were indeed tense. Bram and his father were having a heated discussion. Bram's mother sat to one side, looking worried and not a little frightened. Ian also stood by silently, arms crossed and face set in a scowl. A young woman and a much older woman sat at the opposite end of the table from Lady Sutherland, watching the proceedings with concern. These were surely Annice and her grandmother. Another woman, who Grace assumed to be Lady Sinclair, had been pacing in front of the hearth and men from both clans stood by, clearly poised to act at the slightest hint of trouble.

Lady Sinclair was the first to notice them. She rushed toward her husband, her face flooding with relief. "Ranulf, ye were gone so long, I was worried."

"I'm sorry, Lara." He kissed her cheek. "I met a lovely young woman while I was walking. I'm fairly certain she has a vested interest in these proceedings. This is Grace."

Bram turned his head towards them, a pained expression on his face. "Grace, my love…"

Lady Sinclair glanced at her and gasped. The elder Lady Sinclair looked equally shocked, exclaiming, "By the angels, Ranulf…"

"Aye, we have a few things to sort out. Annice, pour yer grandmother a goblet of wine."

"Ranulf, she—"

He shook his head at her. "We'll figure it out, mother." Turning his attention to Laird Sutherland, he said, "Eanraig, I understand ye threatened to kill Grace if she married Bram. Are ye prepared to do that? Here she is."

Grace gasped. Laird Sinclair still held her elbow and tightened his grip as she tried to pull away.

Confusion reigned for several minutes, with everyone talking at once.

Both Laird Sinclair's wife and mother were outraged.

"Papa, ye can't," exclaimed Annice.

Lady Sutherland jumped to her feet, facing her husband, "Ye did what?"

As shocked as she was, Grace could barely take it in. Laird Sinclair seemed so nice and he had said he was on her side. What was he doing?

"Rodina, stay out of this," ordered Laird Sutherland.

Bram turned on his father. "Nay. Father, ye didn't mean that, I know ye didn't."

Grace tried to escape Laird Sinclair's grip but he only pulled her close and whispered, "Be still, Grace. Let this play out. I told ye, I'm on yer side."

Finally, Laird Sutherland roared, "Silence!" He glared at Laird Sinclair. "She is my son's wife and the mother of a charming wee lass. Ranulf, ye know I didn't want Bram to marry her, but nay, I will not kill her."

"Then ye'll banish them? This is a grave insult, Eanraig."

"Ye've already said that several times."

"So banish them and be done with it. Maybe that will assuage my temper."

Lady Sutherland said, "Nay, please don't ask that, Laird Sinclair. Eanraig, tell him nay."

"Wheesht, Rodina. Laird Sinclair, I love my son. I'm angry with him and I am terribly sorry this all happened. But nay, I will not banish him."

"Ye won't kill her and ye won't banish him. Ye intend to let this conniving tart become Lady Sutherland someday?"

Conniving tart? Had Grace completely misread Laird Sinclair?

"How dare ye?" demanded Lady Sutherland, furiously.

Laird Sinclair shrugged. "She's too bold by half. The whispers I heard about her as I walked through the village were shocking."

Even Laird Sutherland looked affronted. "Don't ever speak like that about my son's wife again."

That statement stunned Grace. Had Laird Sutherland just defended her?

"But the rumors—"

"Are false. All of them. I started them, or helped them along. I wanted…"

"Ye wanted an alliance with me for good reasons. So ye hoped to turn yer son against her by ruining her reputation."

"Aye. It was wrong, but I thought…I thought it was the best thing for my clan."

"What ye thought, Eanraig, is that ye didn't want yer son to hate ye if he could learn to hate her instead. Then ye would have both yer son and yer alliance and there was no reason to worry about a common lass of no consequence. So why do ye care now?" He pulled Grace close and unsheathed his dagger. "I have a knife right here. I can do it for ye. I'll cut her throat. Then we'll have our alliance."

Again, Grace struggled against Laird Sinclair's vice-like grip to no avail. Although he wasn't hurting her, she was terrified.

She tried desperately not to panic, but it was increasingly hard to believe he was on her side.

"Let her go," Bram roared, lunging towards Laird Sinclair. Ian and Eanraig held him back.

"Bram, stop! He's too close to her," said Ian, clearly convinced that Laird Sinclair would kill her if Bram attacked.

"Nay, Papa," screamed Annice. Her grandmother clamped a hand on her shoulder, preventing Annice from standing.

Struggling to hold his son back, Eanraig warned, "If ye do that, Ranulf, it will be war. Take yer hands off my good daughter."

"So ye are accepting her as a daughter?"

"Aye, of course I do. Bram loves her. She's a good lass."

Bram stopped struggling against Ian. "Da, do ye mean that? We have yer blessing?"

"Aye, Bram. Ye love her and she is a worthy bride. I won't see either of ye hurt."

A worthy bride? Grace could scarce believe her ears.

"And ye will fix her reputation in yer clan?" asked Laird Sinclair.

"Aye, put the knife down and let her go…please." Eanraig almost sounded desperate.

Laird Sinclair gave a small bow. "As ye wish." He kissed Grace on the cheek. "Grace, my love, show yer mother's box to Laird Sutherland."

Confused, Grace walked across the room. Both Bram and his father met her halfway. Bram wrapped his arms around her. "Ah, Grace, my love, are ye all right?"

"Aye, Bram, I'm fine." She gave the little box to Bram's father.

Lady Sutherland also crossed to where they stood, placing herself between Laird Sinclair and Grace in a protective stance. But perhaps to Grace's greatest surprise, Laird Sutherland, who had taken the box from her but hadn't looked at it, put a hand on her shoulder. "I'm sorry, Grace."

"Look at the box, Eanraig. It was her mother's," urged Laird Sinclair.

As Laird Sutherland examined the carved lid of the box, a looked of dawning realization crossed his face. "She's yers, Ranulf?"

Laird Sinclair smiled. "Well, I think it's fairly obvious she's yers now, but aye, I gave my sister that box years ago and

Grace is the absolute image of her."

Lady Sutherland looked at the box and gasped. "Eanraig, she's…"

Grace was stunned. "What?"

Both Annice and Bram looked equally shocked by the pronouncement. Laird Sutherland held the box so Bram could see the lid.

"I suspect she never showed ye this, Bram."

Bram looked and almost laughed. "Nay, she didn't. Grace, yer mother was a Sinclair. The rooster and gorse are Sinclair symbols."

"A Sinclair?"

Laird Sinclair's mother drew everyone's eye. With tears pouring down her cheeks she had risen from her seat and walked across the room to Grace. She cupped Grace's cheeks in her weathered hands. "My precious child, ye look just like Catriona. I knew it the instant ye walked in the room. I wasn't sure what my fool son was up to."

"My mother was a Sinclair and ye knew this?" Grace asked Laird Sinclair.

"As soon as I saw ye sitting under that tree, I knew ye had to be Catriona's daughter."

Annice's face lit up. "She is Aunt Catriona's daughter?" She ran across the room and threw her arms around Grace. "This is wonderful. Oh, Grace, we're cousins."

Grace was still having trouble grasping what was happening. She looked at Ranulf. "Ye're my uncle?"

"Aye, Grace. I'm sorry I didn't tell ye right away. I thought perhaps Eanraig needed to realize yer value solely as the woman Bram loved first. Otherwise, ye'd never see it yerself."

"Tristan Murray is the one who ran off with yer sister." Eanraig said, as if still trying to believe it. "I couldn't believe the Tristan Murray I knew would cower from anyone. It was one of the reasons I didn't want to believe Grace was his daughter. But by all that's holy, I never would have believed he'd cross Kynan Sinclair. Grace, lass, yer da was no coward. He was a reckless eejit."

Bram was affronted. "Da!"

"In fairness, Bram, my father was…well he was fractious. Few men willingly crossed him. He took offense easily and when offended, he was ruthless. It tore my heart when Grace told me how much Catriona feared our father, but as much as I hate to admit it, her fears weren't ungrounded. I was there the day Tristan asked for Catriona's hand. Da was furious. I fully expected him to kill Tristan at that moment. Oddly enough, it was probably my father's love for Catriona that stayed his hand. His anger when he eventually learned she had already gone knew no bounds."

Grace said, "I think what my parents feared most was that others would suffer because of their choice."

Laird Sinclair nodded. "And they were right to fear that. Da mounted an extended search for them. First he accused the MacNicols of harboring them."

"I have a vague memory of that now," said Lady Sutherland. "At some point didn't he get the idea that MacLeod was sheltering them?"

Ranulf agreed. "Aye, that's what started the feud with the MacLeods."

Lady Sinclair added, "And it's why Ranulf's father pushed for our Joan to marry Andrew MacLeod. He wanted to resolve the feud he started." Lady Sinclair blinked back tears.

Rodina crossed the room and put her arms around Lady Sinclair. "Lara, I am so very sorry."

"She was unhappy?" asked Grace.

Annice, who also had tears in her eyes, answered. "Nay, actually she and Andrew grew to love each other. She died in childbirth two years ago, God rest her soul."

"I'm so sorry," said Grace.

Everyone was silent for a moment before Laird Sinclair continued. "So ye see, our father's temper was terrible. As much as I missed my wee sister, I prayed he would never find them. If he had, I have no doubt he would have killed yer father and exacted revenge on whomever gave them refuge."

Laird Sutherland shook his head sadly. "Aye, that was his reputation. Grace, now that I know who yer mother was, I understand why yer parents didn't ever contact Innes. If Kynan Sinclair found out Tristan was a Sutherland, we would have had an all-out war on our hands."

The elderly Lady Sinclair took Grace's hand. "Come, sit with me child."

Grace followed her to the refectory table, and helped her into a chair, but remained standing to one side. It seemed inappropriate for Grace to sit with her.

The elderly woman patted the table beside her. As if reading Grace's thoughts she said, "Ye belong here, Grace. Ye are my granddaughter. Please sit with me."

Bram appeared at Grace's side, pulling out a chair for her. He placed the box on the table in front of her but stayed with her, his hands resting on her shoulders.

Her grandmother said, "Grace, yer grandfather was a rigid man with a short temper and a long memory. He was guided more by his pride and his need for revenge than anything else. I begged him for years to forgive yer parents—to let it be known that they would be welcomed home. He refused me. I knew she was out there, somewhere, with the man she loved. That gave me a little consolation but oh, how I missed her. I had hoped someday, after Kynan died, I would see her again. From things said earlier, I know ye came here after her death. Please tell me she was happy."

"Oh, she was. Until my da died last year she was blissfully happy."

The old woman smiled and nodded. "I'm glad to hear that. Would ye mind terribly…may I look at the things yer mama kept in the box?"

Grace smiled at her. "Of course ye may."

The elderly woman pulled the box toward her, removing the lid. She laid the letter to one side, picking up the gold brooch first. She touched the ring of leaves with its sprays of tiny flowers reverently. "This belonged to my mother. My father gave it to her when they wed. It's bog myrtle—a symbol of Clan Carr. I was a Carr."

Next she removed the coin, smiling. "Ranulf, tell her what this is."

He crossed to the table, taking it in his hands and smiling broadly. "This is a gold florin. When Sheena, Catriona, and I were little, our grandfather Carr gave us each one. He told us to keep it forever and we would never be poor. I still have mine. I expect Sheena does too."

"Sheena?" asked Grace.

"My other sister, yer aunt. She is married to Laird Gunn—another clan with whom we had had a long, bloody feud until it was ended with a wedding. Speaking of which, I will send a messenger to her later. She will want to know, and I expect she'll be here nearly before the messenger returns."

Grace's grandmother removed the silver brooch. "That

was my father's," said Grace.

The old woman nodded, laying it aside before removing the last item, the pendant. "Yer grandfather and I gave this to Catriona on the last Epiphany before she left. Kynan wanted her to have a pearl. In spite of everything, Grace, he did love her. I think the pain of losing her fueled his anger and he wanted to blame everyone else. He was never willing to see the role he played." She looked at Grace. "Yer mama could have sold these or even just used the florin. That she saved them tells me she remembered us with love too."

"I'm sure she did," said Grace.

Her grandmother returned each article to the box, picking up the letter last. "What is this, lass?"

"It's a letter from my father to his mother," Grace answered.

"May I see it?" asked Laird Sutherland.

Grace wanted to say no because it was a private letter and Innes should be the one to grant permission to read it. However, Innes wasn't present and Grace knew she would show it to Laird Sutherland if he asked. "Aye, I don't think my grandmother would mind."

Eanraig read it. Frowning he asked, "Bram did ye know about this?"

"Not until a day or so ago."

To Grace, he said, "Ye knew ye were a noblewomen?"

"I knew my mother was."

"Why didn't ye tell us?"

She glanced around the room, her eyes resting finally on her grandmother Sinclair. "I was afraid ye would try to seek them out. I promised my mother I wouldn't do that. I'm sorry, Grandmother."

"Aye, well I would have," said Laird Sutherland. He gave her a stern look. "And it would have been the right thing to do. Look at all the difficulties we would have avoided."

"Eanraig, she couldn't have known that," said Rodina. "Her mother was afraid for good reason, so Grace was too. Frankly, we would have avoided quite a few difficulties if ye hadn't behaved exactly as Grace expected a nobleman to."

Ranulf said, "Grace's choice was entirely reasonable, Eanraig. When Da died a few years ago, he left many relationships to mend. Grace had no way of knowing what she would have faced and I don't either. Da would never have hurt her, but he definitely would have used her for his advantage to restore an alliance. Grace, the fact is, I too would have sought an advantageous betrothal for ye, but as important as restoring alliances may be, I vowed never to force my children into an intolerable marriage. I never wanted to lose a child the way we lost Catriona. Eanraig, by some incredible miracle, we have our alliance as well as happy children."

Chapter 36

As Bram thought back over the last few hours, he could scarcely believe how things had turned out. When he and Ian returned to the keep, their father had been relieved to hear Grace was safe but positively furious to learn of the wedding. He insisted it could be annulled on the grounds that banns hadn't been posted. He ranted on, trying to convince Bram of the wisdom of that path using every threat in his arsenal.

When Grace entered the great hall with Laird Sinclair, Bram's heart had fallen. How had Sinclair found her? Bram had wanted to protect Grace from this ugliness and she had appeared in the middle of it.

But when Laird Sinclair goaded Da with his threat to kill Grace, Bram was certain his heart stopped altogether. Up until that moment, his father seemed to have nothing but contempt for Grace. However, when she was in danger he had practically begged Sinclair for her life. Da publically accepted her and promised to repair the damage he had done. Even his mother had looked like an angry mother badger when Laird Sinclair threatened Grace. Of course, some of her anger was very rightly directed at Da.

The next thing Bram knew, Sinclair kissed Grace's cheek, called her "my love", and let her go.

After all of that, Bram thought nothing could shock him, then he saw the lid of the box. Grace was a Sinclair. The strife of the last few weeks, the heart wrenching fear of the last few moments, all of it could have been avoided if he had only seen the box earlier. But in spite of all that, this meant one thing. Grace was his. Forever. This was the alliance his father wanted from the start and Bram was overjoyed.

Finally the story began to come together, but one thing Sinclair said to Grace continued to echo in Bram's head even now. I thought perhaps Eanraig needed to realize yer value solely as the woman Bram loved first. Otherwise, ye'd never see it yerself.

Laird Sinclair was right. Bram remembered Grace's words from weeks ago, *I am nothing to ye. I am the cook's granddaughter.* If his father had only accepted her after learning she was a Sinclair, Grace would have always felt like the cook's granddaughter in his presence.

Now, his beautiful wife, the heart of his heart, sat surrounded by her mother's family, answering their questions and looking...befuddled. She had been through so much, Bram knew she needed to rest. He wanted the joy of holding her in his arms, knowing all of her fears were gone. However, he was equally as sure it would be nigh on impossible to pry her away from the Sinclairs for a while. But there was something that would both settle her and give the Sinclairs something else on which to focus. "Grace, my love, I'll go get Kristen and Innes."

She looked up at him and nodded. "Aye, Kristen should be here."

As he started to leave the hall, his mother stopped him with Ian at her side. "Bram, let me get them."

"Mother, I—"

"Nay son, I need to start repairing some of the damage we've done. Ian will go with me. Stay here with Grace. This has been overwhelming and she needs ye."

Bram kissed her cheek. "Thank ye, Mother."

Ian said, "Besides, when the conversation turns to the events of the last few days, ye may have to stop Laird Sinclair from killing Da."

It wasn't long before they returned. Kristen came skipping into the hall holding Ian's hand, followed by his mother who had her arm around Innes. Kristen let go of Ian's hand and ran to where Grace sat. "Mama, Wady Suverwand says I can caww her Gwan now, and Sir Ian says I can call him Uncoe Ian."

As Bram predicted, her daughter was the balm Grace needed. She put her arms around Kristen, lifting the child onto her lap. "Aye, he is yer uncle now." Grace smiled at his mother. "And Lady Sutherland is yer gran."

"Can I caww Sir Bwam, Uncoe Bwam?"

"Kristen, do ye remember this morning I told ye Sir Bram and I were married?"

Kristen nodded.

"Well, since yer da is in heaven I figure he would like for ye to have a da here to take care of ye, would ye like for Sir Bram to be yer da?

Kristen's eyes grew big, her face split into a huge smile, and she nodded vigorously. She looked up him. "Wiww ye be my da?"

Bram thought his heart would burst. He lifted her into his arms. "Aye, if ye'll be my sweet, wee lassie."

She giggled. "I'm aweady yer sweet, wee wassie."

Bram grinned. "Of course ye are, how could I have forgotten?"

"Grandmother, Kristen, there are some other people I want ye to meet. This is Laird Sinclair, he my mama's brother."

Innes curtsied, "Good afternoon, laird."

"I didn't know gwamma had a brover."

Grace smiled. "Neither did I, pet."

Kristen whispered loudly, "I don't fink I can say Waiwd Sincwaiw."

Laird Sinclair laughed. "Well, ye needn't then, sweetling. Ye can call me Uncle Ranulf."

"Uncoe Wanuff."

"Grandmother, this is Laird Sinclair's wife and mother and his daughter Annice." Grace turned to the Sinclairs. "My ladies, this is my father's mother, Innes Murray."

Innes curtsied to the noblewomen. "My ladies."

"It is a pleasure to meet ye, Innes," said Lady Lara Sinclair.

To Kristen, Grace said, "This is Aunt Lara."

"Aunt Wawa," echoed Kristen.

Lady Sinclair came to where Bram stood, still holding Kristen, and touched her cheek. "Oh, my precious child. It is lovely to meet ye."

"I know," said Kristen, nodding.

Grace laughed. "Kristen, ye should either say thank ye, or it's lovely to meet ye too."

"It's wovewy to meet ye too."

Lady Sinclair smiled.

Annice came around the table and introduced herself to Kristen. "I'm Annice and ye can just call me Annice. I'm yer mama's cousin."

"Annice," said Kristen. "That name's easy."

Annice laughed. "I guess it is. Can I have a wee hug, poppet?" Kristen reached her arms to Annice who took her from

Bram. Annice gave her a squeeze and a kiss on the cheek before putting Kristen down to stand next to Grace.

Grace reached out and took the elder Lady Sinclair's hand. "Kristen, this dear lady is my grandmother."

"I fought Gwanny was yer gwammuver."

"Granny is my grandmother. She is Grandda's mama. This is Gramma's mama."

"I miss Gwamma," said Kristen somberly.

Bram was reminded poignantly of the day he found Grace and Kristen playing with kittens in the hayloft.

Tears stood in Malina Sinclair eye's as she reached out and stroked Kristen's hair. "I do too, Kristen."

Without preamble, Kristen climbed into the old woman's lap and touched a tear that spilled down her cheek. "But we aren't going to cwy anymore. Do ye wanna know why?"

"Aye, tell me, sweetling."

"Becuz, they are in heaven wiff God and the angels and heaven is a wuvwy pwace."

Bram remembered this was exactly what Grace had told Kristen in the loft.

Malina kissed Kristen's cheek. "Aye, that's a very good reason not to cry."

Kristen settled into her lap as if she had done it many times before. "My mama told me that."

"Yer mama is right. Has yer mama ever told ye what matters most?"

"Aye. Kindness matters most."

Malina smiled. "And what never helps?"

"Panicking never helps. My mama says that to me."

Malina hugged her close. "My mama said that to me too."

~ * ~

At one point in the afternoon, Michael entered the hall and approached Bram.

Bram smiled. "Michael, ye're looking much better."

"I can't say the same for ye. Rough few days?"

"Indeed."

"Bram, I—"

"I know Michael, I'm sorry for what my father did."

"Ah, well, he meant well and he was right, I would have cared for Grace. We are friends, and as she told me, marriages have been built on less. But Bram, I need ye to know, I don't love her. What I mean is, I do love her but not romantically. I would protect her with my life, but I am thrilled that ye married her, because she loves ye without reserve."

"Thank ye, Michael. Thank ye too for trying to help her when the Morrisons came."

"Like I said, I will protect her with my life. And while it seems she has a few more people on her side now, I just need ye to know my friend"—Michael gave him a huge grin—"if ye ever hurt her, I will kill ye."

Bram laughed. "Aye, I'm afraid ye might have to get in line behind her uncle, and once they meet her, her cousins, but I do love her and I swear, I will do my best to see that no one ever hurts her again."

"See that ye do, because I am serious."

Bram sobered. "I know ye are, and ye're a good man, Michael."

Michael grinned again. "The absolute finest and who knows, maybe I'll find a bonny lass among the guests for the wedding feast yer da is planning."

Michael left the hall but at his mention of a wedding feast, Bram realized his father had been absent from the hall much of the afternoon. In fact, both of his parents disappeared for a while with Innes. Bram assumed they were giving Grace some time with the Sinclairs and thought no more of it. He returned to Grace's side, unwilling to be separated from her for long.

When time came for the evening meal, much to Bram's surprise, his da escorted Innes to the refectory table, showing her to a place between his mother and Ian. He signaled for Bram to join them. To his surprise his father said, "Bram, I want Grace seated beside me tonight."

"Aye, Da, whatever ye wish."

As the hall began to fill, Kristen sat at one end of the table chatting happily with the Sinclair women. Grace stood to one side, her arms clutched at her waist. She appeared worried. Bram returned to her and put his arms around her. "What's upsetting ye, Grace?"

"I'm just…well, the last few weeks haven't been pleasant. The clan…well, I'm worried. I don't want Kristen to hear the names people have called me."

"That will end tonight, Grace. If I'm not much mistaken, news of what happened here this afternoon is already spreading.

Come to the table with me." He led her toward the place where his father sat.

She stopped short. "Nay, Bram. Please, let's sit somewhere else. Yer da won't like it."

"My da requested it. He wants ye seated beside him." The look of horror on her face nearly made him laugh. "He's trying to make amends." At her incredulity he added, "I'll be right beside ye."

"But—"

Bram put a finger to her lips. "Grace, ye argue too much."

She sighed and took the seat he held for her. She looked so nervous, Bram began to worry about the wisdom of granting his father's request.

~ * ~

When Michael arrived for the feast, he wasn't surprised to see much of the clan in the hall. As a guardsman, Michael often sat at the laird's table during meals. But with the addition of the visiting Sinclairs, and in light of all that had happened, he had intended to sit at one of the trestles, which were rapidly filling. Then Kristen caught his eye. She waved and called, "Sir Michael," from the end of the Laird's table where she sat next to one of the most beautiful women he had ever seen. Fair skin, chestnut hair, and eyes as green as Grace's.

He approached the table and bowed. "My lady, Kristen, ye look very happy tonight."

"I am happy. My mama came home. And I found out wots of new fings."

He grinned at her. "Like what?"

"Wike, this is my cousin Annice." She gestured to the breathtaking lass beside her. "I wike Annice. Annice, this is Michael. I wike him too."

"Good evening, my lady," Michael bowed low.

Lady Annice blushed and smiled. "Good evening, Sir Michael."

"And I found out, I have anover gweat gwandmover, and new uncoes and a new aunt, and Waird and Wady Suverwand are my gwandpawents too. That's because Mama mawwied Sir Bwam. Oh, and he is my da now."

Both Michael and Annice chuckled at her litany. Michael said, "It seems ye have much to be happy about then. Please excuse me. I need to find a place to sit for this fine feast."

"Sit here," said Kristen, pointing to the chair beside her."

"Nay, Kristen, I—"

"Oh, please join us," said Annice.

"If ye insist," said Michael. Only a direct order from his laird would have prevented him from denying that request.

"It has been quite a day," said Annice, "and I'm sure Kristen will like having a friend close."

Michael smiled. "Kristen is a fine wee lass, I'm certain she has adapted well."

"Aye, she has," said Annice.

"And what about ye, lass? I fear none of this is what ye were expecting. How have ye fared today?"

She laughed merrily. The sound was enchanting. "It is so very kind of ye to ask. No one else has, but I am fine. It isn't as if I was longing to marry Bram. I didn't even know him. Well, I suppose I met him a few years ago at my sister's wedding, but I was just a lass. Nay, I'm not the least bit upset. On the contrary, finding my cousin has been wonderful. The fact that she and Bram love each other..." Annice sighed. "Well, that is just the most romantic thing I've ever heard." She blushed. "I suppose that sounds silly."

"Not at all," said Michael.

"I don't fink it's siwwy eiver," said Kristen.

Just then, a hush fell over the hall as Laird Sutherland took his usual place at the table, standing to address those assembled. "Good evening."

The clan responded with a murmured, "Good evening, Laird."

"Tonight, I must do something that is very difficult. I must confess to ye all that over the last few weeks I have whispered lies, and aided in spreading malice about the lovely young woman beside me."

More murmurs passed through the crowd.

"I thought my reasons were sound. My son had fallen in love with her, and she with him. But in order to gain an alliance with the Sinclairs, something I firmly believed was for the good of the clan, I intended for him to marry Annice Sinclair."

"That's you," Kristen whispered loudly to Annice. Titters of laughter spread through the hall.

Laird Sutherland smiled indulgently at Kristen before continuing. "I had hoped vainly that Bram would set her aside if her character were called into question. To his credit, he knew better. He was confident of her love and fidelity. So that failing, I did something reprehensible. As her laird, I ordered Grace to lie to my son, to tell him she loved another and would not be his bride. I threatened her with a forced marriage to someone of my choosing. I even threatened her life. I told her it was for the good of the clan and convinced her it was better for her to break his heart than for me to order him to set her aside." He laid his hand on Grace's shoulder.

"Perhaps worst of all, I listened to blatant lies about her, told by men I had no reason to trust. I made no attempt at all to discern the truth, but let them drag her away, forcing her to leave her precious child behind." He looked at Grace. "Grace, I humbly apologize for wronging ye in so many ways."

Stunned and speechless, Grace just nodded.

Laird Sutherland continued. "Again, Bram saw through the lies and rescued her. What's more, he saw through the lies I had told her. He knew I could never take her life, so he married Grace last night before bringing her home."

There were no shocked gasps, suggesting the laird's revelation came as no surprise. Michael smiled to himself. That news had spread at lightning speed.

"Meanwhile, the Sinclairs arrived, believing in good faith that Bram wished to meet Annice. Laird Sinclair, I heartily apologize for misleading ye."

Laird Sinclair bowed his head briefly in acknowledgement. "Accepted."

"Still, in spite of everything, the Divine's hand has been at work. Ye all knew that Tristan and his bride fled in fear of her father and Grace was raised knowing nothing about her family. What we have learned today is that Grace's mother was Catriona Sinclair."

This time there were some shocked gasps. Clearly that bit of news hadn't circulated fully.

"So as humbling as this day has been, it has also brought me great joy. My son is married to a lass he adores and with whom he deserves to be happy. I have a good daughter who is not only talented, kind, and as stalwart as any warrior, she is a loving and gentle mother. I have a granddaughter who won my heart from the first moment I saw her. And whether I deserved it or not, I have a staunch ally in Laird Ranulf Sinclair. Please raise yer tankards in honor of the happy couple." He raised his own. "To Bram and Grace."

"To Bram and Grace," the people answered, banging the tables.

When the uproar settled, Laird Sutherland raised his tankard again. "And to Laird Ranulf and Clan Sinclair, long may ye prosper."

"Clan Sinclair," the crowd answered.

As the cheering died down again Laird Sutherland said, "We will begin the meal shortly and while, very technically, this is Bram and Grace's wedding supper, we will formally celebrate their union and our alliance with Clan Sinclair with a great feast on Lammas in just over a fortnight."

A roar of appreciation rose from the crowd.

"Wiww you be hewe then?" Kristen asked Annice.

"Aye, pet, we are staying here until then. We have only just found ye, we aren't ready to leave ye yet." Annice gave the wee lass a hug.

Michael was inordinately happy to learn that Annice Sinclair would be at Castle Sutherland for a while longer.

~ * ~

Grace leaned over and whispered, "Did ye know he was going to do that?"

"What? Apologize or announce a celebratory feast?"

"Both, I guess."

"I had a suspicion there would be a feast, particularly in light of our new bond with the Sinclairs. I didn't know he was going to apologize, but I'm glad he did."

Grace appeared to become less ill at ease as the meal progressed. When the sweet had been served, she glanced to the end of the table where a very sleepy Kristen sat with Annice. "I need to take Kristen home and put her to bed."

"Grace, this is yer home now. We can put her on a pallet in our chamber until we sort everything out."

"But my grandmother—"

"Will have a place here too. Don't worry."

He reached around her, tapping his father's arm. "Da, please excuse us, we need to put Kristen to bed."

"Ah, now I'm glad ye mentioned that. Yer mother has been busy all afternoon. Rodina, my love, it is time."

Grace looked a bit confused. Bram whispered, "Don't

worry so," and kissed her. "I'll get Kristen."

He lifted Kristen from her chair. "Say goodnight, my sweet wee lassie."

"Good night, but I'm not tired," she said, resting her head on his shoulder.

He smiled. "I can see that, but Gran has a surprise to show us."

They followed his parents from the room and up the stairs to the living quarters. Instead of stopping on the first level, where his chamber was, they continued to the second.

His mother explained. "I wanted ye to feel at home and I know Kristen has been in the habit of sleeping near ye. Innes and I discussed it this afternoon and decided it would be best to give ye adjoining rooms. One has been prepared for Innes and Kristen and the other for ye and Bram. Ye'll have privacy but still be close."

She showed them to the richly appointed chambers. "I had all of yer belongings brought up from the cottage. Yer loom has been moved to my solar, it gets excellent natural light. And Bram, I had yer belongings moved as well."

"Thank ye, my lady. These rooms are beautiful," Grace said.

"Ye are very welcome Grace, and ye needn't call me 'my lady'. Rodina is fine, or even Mother if ye wish."

Bram kissed his mother on the cheek. "Thank ye, Mother."

She smiled, clearly happy that they were pleased. "Now, Eanraig, we need to give them privacy. Good night, my darlings." Kristen was almost asleep in Bram's arms. His mother kissed the child's cheek, gave Innes a quick hug, and took both of Grace's hands in hers, kissing her on each cheek. Turning to her husband, she said, "Eanraig, I said we need to go."

"Aye, Rodina, whatever ye wish." He nodded to them. "Good night." He called over his shoulder as they walked away, "oh, never fear, I had Father Damian bless the bed."

Bram laid a sleeping Kristen on the bed and kissed her forehead. Grace removed the child's shoes and outer dress before tucking her in. "Grandmother, are ye sure this is all right with ye?"

"Grace, lass, of course it is. I can think of nothing better than spending the rest of my years helping to tend my great-grandchildren and being pampered a bit myself."

Grace hugged her grandmother. "Then we'll say goodnight."

Bram kissed Innes on the cheek, making her smile and blush.

When they reached the door of their chamber, he scooped Grace into his arms, capturing her lips with his.

When he released her lips, Grace looked bemused. "What are ye doing?"

"Carrying ye over the threshold."

"Ye did that last night."

"But we are home now."

Epilogue

Early March 1342, Castle Sutherland

The Sutherlands retired to the family solar after the evening meal had been cleared away. Grace sat by the fire, her husband's arm around her, watching their son Conall play with Uncle Ian on the floor. Conall was ten months old and chortled merrily every time Ian rolled a small wooden ball to him.

"If ye think this is fun Conall, wait till yer mama teaches ye to throw knives."

"Ian, don't tease him so," said his wife, Saundra, who was ready to deliver their first child any day.

"'Tis no jest, Saundra," said Bram.

"Grace doesn't throw knives," said Saundra.

"Well perhaps not on a daily basis," said Lady Sutherland, who was putting the final touches on several tiny garments, "but she's more accurate than any man I've ever seen."

"Flying neeps don't stand a chance around yer mama," said Ian.

"Mama," echoed Conall.

Saundra looked to Innes, who sat in a chair near the fire with Kristen's gray cat, Sprite, lounging in her lap. "Innes, are they all having one over on me?"

Innes chuckled. "Nay, they aren't. To quote the laird, Grace can 'Split a fly's hair at twenty paces.'"

Saundra looked at Grace in awe. "Will ye teach me?"

Ian laughed so hard tears streamed down his face.

"What are ye laughing at?" she demanded.

"I was just imagining ye throwing knives at flying neeps, my love."

"Saundra, ye don't need to start by trying to hit flying neeps. Aiming at a big laughing arse of a husband might be easier," said Bram.

"Bram, mind yer language," scolded his mother, "little

ears."

"It's all right, Grandma," said Kristen, who was almost five years old. "I've heard Da say 'arse' before."

Lady Sutherland looked pointedly at her errant son while Laird Sutherland tried desperately not to laugh at the wee light of his life who sat on his lap.

Grace scolded, "Kristen, ye needn't repeat everything Da says and Bram ye do need to mind yer tongue." Before she could tell Saundra that she would be happy to teach her to throw knives, there was a knock at the door.

"In," called Laird Sutherland.

A messenger entered. "Laird, I bring a message from Laird MacLeod."

Laird Sutherland held out his hand for the missive. Opening it, he scanned it and his eyebrows drew together.

"Nothing's happened to Davy, has it?" asked Grace, fear marring her features. Davy was her late cousin's son.

"Nay. Well, I mean, aye, he had a little accident but he is well. Apparently a MacKay lass was nearby and helped him." Laird Sutherland read on.

"Poor lass," said Ian.

"Is she in danger?" asked Grace.

Bram frowned. "The MacKays and the MacLeods have been feuding over their border for years."

"If she helped the boy, they wouldn't hurt her, would they?" asked Grace.

Laird Sutherland said, "Don't worry so, Grace. Laird MacLeod just wants me to send a messenger on his behalf to Laird MacKay so he can arrange to return her." He folded the missive and said to the messenger, "go down to the great hall and ask someone to get ye something to eat. I'll send Laird MacLeod's message on with one of my men tomorrow."

"Aye, Laird." The messenger bowed and left.

"Now, lass, where were we?" Eanraig asked Kristen.

"Ye were going to tell me the story about the selkie," answered Kristen.

"Aye, the selkie. Once upon a time…"

~ * ~

Later that night, long after both children were tucked into bed, Grace lay sated in Bram's arms.

"Grace, my love, ye delight me."

"I know," she said with a cheeky grin.

He laughed. "Now, lass, the polite thing to say is, thank ye, or ye delight me too."

"Ye delight me too, Bram."

He nuzzled her neck until she giggled. "I love that sound," he said. He kissed her lips, eliciting a soft moan. "I love that sound too. In fact, I love everything about ye."

"Do ye love the sound of me retching in the morning?"

"Aye, I do, because it means ye carry my bairn." He stroked his hand over her slightly rounded belly. "When will we share the news?"

"Not for a while yet. The baby won't come until late November. Maybe we can announce it on the Feast of St. John the Baptist."

"Whatever ye wish, my love. I asked ye to marry me on that day, almost two years ago."

"I won't easily forget that. Whispers had started about us, and grandmother didn't want me to go to the celebration for fear there would be more talk. I wanted to dance with ye again so badly. I sat in the kitchen and cried."

"Oh, Grace, I didn't know ye cried. I was so angry that night. Mother and Da were trying their best to keep us apart. Ye should have let me take ye to the abbey."

"Perhaps I should have but things turned out very well anyway."

They lay quietly for a few moments. Grace had started to drift to sleep when Bram asked, "Whatever happened to all that ribbon mother had ye weave?"

Grace laughed. "Ye really don't know? That's a man for ye—never notices anything."

"What are ye talking about?"

"Yer mother and I decided to give the first ten ells to Annice. I'm surprised ye didn't notice it on the dress she was married in. We gave the other ten ells to Saundra and it trimmed out the dress she wore to her wedding."

Bram kissed her soundly, then grinned. "I don't know why ye'd be surprised. I would think by now ye would have learned, when ye are in the room ye are the only woman I see."

She laughed and returned his kiss. "I believe ye, thousands wouldn't."

About the Author

Ceci started her career as an oncology nurse at a leading research hospital, and eventually became a successful medical writer. In 1991 she married a young Irish carpenter who she met at a friend's wedding. They raised their family in central New Jersey but now live with their dogs and birds in paradise, also known as southwest Florida. While she loves spending time writing "happily ever afters" she still works fulltime in the pharmaceutical industry.

The Duncurra series, Highland Solution, Highland Courage, and Highland Intrigue are available as e-books, audiobooks, and paperbacks. Ceci will be continuing this series in the near future.

Highland Echoes is the second book in The Fated Hearts series. The first in the series, Highland Revenge, tells the story of Fiona MacNicol, and Eoin MacKay. Highland Revenge is included in the collection Highland Winds – The Scrolls of Cridhe Volume One. The third book in the series, Highland Angels (Anna MacKay's story) will be released in the summer of 2015.

The Scrolls of Cridhe, Volume 2, Highland Flames, will be released in the fall of 2015 and Ceci is diligently working on her novella for this collection.

"Few authors touch hearts so deeply."
-Sue-Ellen Welfonder,
USA Today Bestselling Author

Highland Revenge - Excerpt

Curious about how Bram Sutherland's betrothal to Fiona MacNicol fell through?
Find out in Highland Revenge the first book in the Fated Heart series. First publishing Highland Winds, The Scrolls of Cridhe Volume 1, it is now available as a single e-book and paperback.

MacKay Territory, May 1340

Eoin MacKay hadn't gone terribly far when he caught a glimpse of white halfway up a massive oak. She was well hidden. Her plaid was dark green; he wouldn't have noticed her among the leaves if he hadn't been specifically looking for her. He strode closer to the tree, stopping once so he could look up through the branches. There, perched in the crotch of two thick limbs was a woman so perfectly beautiful she might have been part faery. He was left momentarily speechless. Her skin was fair, with a faint pink blush to her cheek. He couldn't see the color of her eyes, but they were ringed with sooty lashes. Something told him that, regardless of their hue, they would sparkle. Her rosy lips were full and soft—lips that were made to be kissed. The late afternoon breeze ruffled the mass of black curls around her shoulders. Her léine was torn, but otherwise she appeared none the worse for wear. *She is not a faery, she is a MacNicol*, he reminded himself.

She looked down at him silently with her head cocked to one side, as if she was trying to solve some puzzle. She didn't seem remotely frightened. That would have to change if he was to exact his revenge. "Have ye had a lovely day perched in yer tree, watching us search for ye?"

"I suspect my day was better than yers."

Her impertinent answer irritated him. "Well ye've had yer bit of fun, but it's over. Climb down."

She ignored him. "Who are ye?"

"Yer captor, and I ordered ye to climb down. Do it now."

"Nay, I asked ye a perfectly reasonable question, and ye aren't my captor if ye can't reach me. Until I know who ye are, I think I'd just as soon stay free, even if I am up a tree."

"Free? Nay lass, ye're as good as locked in my dungeon, and I promise ye will regret yer impertinence."

He called to one of his men. "Donald, it fair breaks my heart, but the MacNicol lass doesn't wish to join our company."

"An arrow would bring her down quick enough."

"Aye it would, but ye heard her guardsman. This is Fiona MacNicol, Bhaltair's niece. I wouldn't want to harm a hair on her wee head."

Donald snorted. "Ye have no love for the MacNicols, and neither do I. Have ye forgotten? One of my older brothers rode with ye that night."

"Ye're right, Donald. I have no love for the MacNicols, but the ransom this one will fetch will hurt Bhaltair's greedy, black heart nearly as much as a steel blade thrust into it. Mark my words, we'll have our revenge. We are leaving. Climb up, drag her down and bind her. She managed to evade us once and I won't have it happen again. We have already wasted too much time on her." He didn't spare her another glance but called over his shoulder, "By the way, lass, I am Laird Eoin MacKay, and ye're most assuredly my prisoner."

Highland Angels - Excerpt

Eoin MacKay's younger sister Anna's story continues in the third book in the Fated Heart series, Highland Angels, due for release Summer 2015

Northern Highlands, Late February 1342

Anna MacKay knelt with the child at the loch's edge, looking up at the MacLeod warriors who surrounded her. Numb with cold from the icy loch water soaking her wool chemise, she was painfully aware she had made a terrible mistake. After fighting with her brother, at the midday meal she was angry and just wanted solitude. Eoin never allowed her to ride alone but as long as she was on foot and didn't go too far, her brother assumed she was safe.

She had walked westward out of the village surrounding the MacKay stronghold, Naomh-dùn , then turned north once she reached the top of the bluff rising out of the east side of Loch Islich. She should not have walked that direction because it took her very close to the disputed MacLeod border. Her brother would be furious when he found out but she had wanted him to be as angry as she was. It would serve him right. She also wanted to be alone and no one would follow her onto the windy bluff on this bitter cold day. She didn't intend to actually enter the disputed land by the strait where Loch Islich and Loch Uarach joined together, but that was before she saw the wee lad.

Lost in her thoughts, she had walked along the bluff until it began to slope more gently toward the northern tip of Loch Islich and the strait. Aware that she had come much farther than she intended, she started to turn towards home when the bright colors of his plaid caught her eye. He seemed to be alone walking on the thick ice covering the strait. He wielded a wooden sword as he pretended to do battle with an invisible enemy. She was momentarily amused by his antics but became worried as he moved off of the thick ice covering the strait and further onto the deep loch where the ice thinned dangerously. Anna had yelled at him to go back, but he didn't seem to hear. There was nothing else to do, she lifted her skirt and ran headlong towards him, down the slope to the loch's edge, straight into the disputed territory. Trying to get his attention, she waved her free hand and continued to yell.

She was too late. As he lunged forward, thrusting his sword into his invisible prey, the ice gave way. He plunged into the loch screaming and flailing just as she reached the shore. She ran out onto the solid ice as far as she dared. Knowing she would need something dry to wrap him in, she pulled off her mantle and plaid, hurling them backwards onto the solid ice. She threw herself onto the ice on her stomach, distributing her weight over as wide an area as possible before she slid to the broken edge. While her body weight pushed the sheet of ice under the surface of the water soaking her, it didn't completely give way. She was able to stretch far enough to grab the back of his tunic just as he slipped under the surface. Staying as flat as she could, she pushed backward, dragging him with her onto the ice, the edges breaking away as she moved.

Finally reaching ice thick enough to hold their weight, she scooped him up, grabbed her dry clothes and carried him the nearest shore. They were on the eastern bank of Loch Islich, in MacKay territory. She whispered a prayer of thanks. The child was unconscious and blue with cold, but still breathing. Vaguely aware of the sound of horses approaching, she quickly pulled his wet clothes off, wrapping him in her dry plaid and mantle. She rubbed his limbs gently through the cloth trying to warm him. His eyes blinked open and his little body began to shiver violently.

She smiled at him. "You'll be all right now little one." Looking up, she saw the source of the pounding hooves, men on horseback thundered down the western side of the strait. In an instant a tall, broad shouldered warrior with golden hair, a closely trimmed beard and angry crystal blue eyes was off his horse and had crossed the strait. Several of the others were not far behind him. The angry warrior pulled the child from her arms. These were clearly MacLeods, the clan with whom the MacKays had feuded for years and this was exactly why she wasn't supposed to have walked northward. In a moment of terror-filled realization, it was abundantly clear—she stared trouble squarely in the face.

The Duncurra Series

All titles in the Duncurra Series are available as e-books, audiobooks and paperbacks.

Highland Solution

Laird Niall MacIan needs Lady Katherine Ruthven's dowry to relieve his clan's crushing debt but he has no intention of giving her his heart in the bargain.

Niall MacIan, a Highland laird, desperately needs funds to save his impoverished clan. Lady Katherine Ruthven, a lowland heiress, is rumored to be "unmarriageable" and her uncle hopes to be granted her title and lands when the king sends her to a convent.

King David II anxious to strengthen his alliances sees a solution that will give Ruthven the title he wants, and MacIan the money he needs. Laird MacIan will receive Lady Katherine's hand along with her substantial dowry and her uncle will receive her lands and title.

Lady Katherine must forfeit everything in exchange for a husband who does not want to be married and believes all women to be self-centered and deceitful. Can the lovely and gentle Katherine mend his heart and build a life with him or will he allow the treachery of others to destroy them?

Highland Courage

Her parents want a betrothal, but Mairead MacKenzie can't get married without revealing her secret and no man will wed her once he knows.

Plain in comparison to her siblings and extremely reserved, Mairead has been called "MacKenzie's Mouse" since she was a child. No one knows the reason for her timidity and she would just as soon keep it that way. When her parents arrange a betrothal to Laird Tadhg Matheson she is horrified. She only sees one way to prevent an old secret from becoming a new scandal.

Tadhg Matheson admires and respects the MacKenzies. While an alliance with them through marriage to Mairead would be in his clan's best interest, he knows Laird MacKenzie seeks a closer alliance with another clan. When Tadhg learns of her terrible shyness and her youngest brother's fears about her, Tadhg offers for her anyway.

Secrets always have a way of revealing themselves. With Tadhg's unconditional love, can Mairead find the strength and courage she needs to handle the consequences when they do?

Highland Intrigue

Lady Gillian MacLennan's clan needs a leader, but the last person on earth she wants as their laird is Fingal MacIan.

She can neither forgive nor forget that his mother killed her father, and, by doing so, created Clan MacLennan's current desperate circumstances.

King David knows a weak clan, without a laird, can change quickly from a simple annoyance to a dangerous liability, and he cannot ignore the turmoil. The MacIan's owe him a great debt, so when he makes Fingal MacIan laird of clan MacLennan and requires that he marry Lady Gillian, Fingal is in no position to refuse.

In spite of the challenge, Fingal is confident he can rebuild her clan, ease her heartache and win her affection. However, just as love awakens, the power struggle takes a deadly turn. Can he protect her from the unknown long enough to uncover the plot against them? Or will all be lost, destroying the happiness they seek in each other's arms?

.

The Guardians of Cridhe

The Legend:

Long, long ago, in the time before time, seven sisters were called from the far reaches of the realm. Each brought unique talents, but had one common gift; the ability to weave ageless tales of love and courage. An evil witch coveted their gifts and locked them in a tower, silencing their voices upon threat of death. But the Highlands are enchanted, and magic will not countenance seven pure hearts such as theirs to be lost.

With no one else to hear them, they sang their stories to each other. Fate blew a braw Highland wind to their prison, and the sweet, high timbre of the sisters' voices enthralled it. The wind gathered close their silver words as it raced past each day, and carried their love and goodness throughout the world...then across the ages.

Today, their words live on in the Guardians of Cridhe, seven sisters who have sworn to preserve those pure and musical hearts so long as they live. It is said these seven descend from those ancient female bards. Only their words can bear witness to that truth...

The first collection of novellas (~35,000 words each) by the Guardians of Cridhe, Highland Winds is available as an e-book and in paperback. Volume 2, Highland Flames will be available, Fall 2015.

The Scrolls of Cridhe

Volume 1 – Highland Winds

Suzan Tisdale - *Stealing Moirra's Heart*
"She didn't believe he was a thief when she rescued him…until he stole her heart"

Sue-Ellen Welfonder - *The Taming of Mairi Mackenzie*
"A forbidden love so powerful it could destroy them both."

Katheryn Lynn Davis - *A Tear of Memory*
"How can a seer paint 'Truth' when she's lived a life of lies. Will she allow a man who has twice deceived her to open her heart to the truth?"

Lily Baldwin - *A Jewel in the Vaults*
"Beneath the ruse is a woman aching to break free."

Ceci Giltenan - *Highland Revenge*
"Does he hate her clan enough to visit his vengeance on her? Or will he listen to her secret and his own heart's yearning?"

Kate Robbins - *Spirit Stones*
"Sheona MacLeod has a gift, Malcolm MacDonald seeks change. Together they can change destiny—if they dare."

Tarah Scott - *Lord Grayson's Bride*
"She can't allow his love for her to destroy him."

Find out more about the Guardians on their website
www.scrollsofcridhe.com.